MW01193278

Claudia Gray

The Rushworth Family Plot

Claudia Gray is the pseudonym of Amy Vincent. She is the author of the Mr. Darcy & Miss Tilney mysteries and the writer of multiple young adult novels, including the Evernight series, the Firebird trilogy, and the Constellation trilogy. In addition, she's written several *Star Wars* novels, such as *Lost Stars* and *Bloodline*. She and her husband, Paul, live in Turin, Italy, under the benevolent rule of a small dog named Peaches.

claudiagray.com

Also by Claudia Gray

The Murder of Mr. Wickham
The Late Mrs. Willoughby
The Perils of Lady Catherine de Bourgh

GRAPHIC NOVELS

House of El: The Shadow Threat
House of El: The Enemy Delusion
House of El: The Treacherous Hope

CONSTELLATION SERIES

Defy the Stars
Defy the Worlds
Defy the Fates

STAR WARS

Journey to Star Wars: The Force Awakens: Lost Stars
Bloodline
Leia: Princess of Alderaan
Master & Apprentice
Star Wars: The High Republic: Into the Dark
Star Wars: The High Republic: The Fallen Star

FIREBIRD SERIES

A Thousand Pieces of You
Ten Thousand Skies Above You
A Million Worlds with You

SPELLCASTER SERIES

Spellcaster
The First Midnight Spell
Steadfast
Sorceress

EVERNIGHT SERIES

Evernight
Stargazer
Hourglass
Afterlife
Balthazar

STAND-ALONE

Fateful
The Haunted Mansion: Storm & Shade
The X-Files: Perihelion

THE RUSHWORTH
FAMILY PLOT

The Rushworth Family Plot

A Mr. Darcy & Miss Tilney Mystery

Claudia Gray

VINTAGE BOOKS
A DIVISION OF PENGUIN RANDOM HOUSE LLC
NEW YORK

Published in the United States by Vintage Books,
a division of Penguin Random House LLC,
1745 Broadway, New York, NY 10019.

Vintage Books and colophon are registered
trademarks of Penguin Random House LLC.

Library of Congress Cataloging-in-Publication Number 2025933694

Vintage Books Trade Paperback ISBN: 978-0-593-68660-7
eBook ISBN: 978-0-593-68661-4

Book design by Nicholas Alguire

penguinrandomhouse.com | vintagebooks.com

Printed in the United States of America

10 9 8 7 6 5 4 3 2 1

The authorized representative in the EU for product safety and
compliance is Penguin Random House Ireland, Morrison Chambers,
32 Nassau Street, Dublin, D02 YH68, Ireland, https://eu-contact.penguin.ie.

For every person out there who volunteers at animal shelters—
thank you for making the world a kinder place

THE RUSHWORTH
FAMILY PLOT

Chapter One

February 1823

Mr. Fitzwilliam Darcy of Pemberley traveled but seldom to London. This distinguished him from many of his peers, who had a greater appetite than he for the social offerings of the city and a stronger desire to display their wealth and standing. Even more noteworthy was the fact that, when Mr. Darcy did make one of his trips to this great city, he invariably did so in the company of his family—namely his wife, Elizabeth, and whichever of his three sons was not then required at school. A few members at his gentlemen's club had openly wondered when and how the man expected to sample London's more forbidden pleasures; the answer, of course, was that Mr. Darcy did not so expect, for he did not consider gaming, horse racing, or boxing to be pleasures, nor the company of the dissolute of either sex. Those of low habits often console their battered consciences with the belief that such behavior is universal, that all partake of it in time, and to claim otherwise is hypocrisy. Mr. Darcy knew such was occasionally muttered about him and cared not one jot. London was for unavoidable business purposes, for giving Elizabeth the opportunity to visit the museums and assemblies she sometimes craved, and for socializing his three sons. The two youngest, Matthew and James, reveled in the city.

His eldest son, Jonathan, did not.

Jonathan Darcy, at age twenty-three, was already a man of decided habits. Even in his boyhood, he had proved particular about matters rarely of concern to the young: lining up his toys and other possessions very straight, in a specific order explicable only to himself, and becoming highly cross when this order was disturbed—requiring periods of solitude and silence, and quickly overcome amid the noise and bustle so common among children—and the like. Any one of these particularities on its own was not especially remarkable; however, all of them in concert distinguished him among his youthful peers, and not in a fashion likely to endear him to them.

None of these feelings had diminished in adulthood. The disapproval of them, however, was far less burdensome upon Jonathan than it had been in his youth. Kindly observers might note that maturity often fosters compassion and a greater tolerance for the harmless foibles of others, while more cynical persons might point out that maturity also promotes a higher degree of understanding of the prestige that comes with a large fortune—and as heir to the estate of Pemberley, Jonathan Darcy deserved not only civility but also deference. Regardless of which view of humanity is taken, Jonathan no longer faced the opprobrium he had so often been asked to endure as a child. Yet his experiences at school had been discouraging enough to forever darken his feelings toward society beyond that of his family and most intimate friends.

London, to Jonathan, represented the apogee of much that he despised. As he said to his mother, upon the planning of a winter trip for the family, "London is—loud, and strange, and they keep no habits there, none at all. Anything might happen at any moment."

His mother laughed. "That is precisely what many people like most about the city!" Her tone gentled as she added, "Yet I know such variety is not so pleasant to you as it is to most."

This greatly understated the matter. Jonathan relished the

calm, precise order that home life provided. When he had occasion to travel, his journeys usually took him from his own house to another that ran on very much the same sort of schedule; even that disruption was onerous, but he could adjust to it within a few days. His longest time from home had been at school, years he had found torturous for many reasons—but unpredictability had been among them. Yet the rowdiest schoolboy gang seemed but tame when compared to the tumult of London.

"Take heart," said Jonathan's mother that day, placing her hand on her son's arm, careful to do so slowly, so that he might pull away if he wished. She had learned, over time, that the same gestures that comforted her other two sons had to be offered to her eldest only with caution and patience. "Our trip will be cut short by the need to send Matthew and James off to school. It is but a few weeks, not even a month." Even a month seemed unbearably long, but Jonathan determined to make the best of it.

A mere three days into the family's stay in London, however, fate intervened in the form of young James larking about, falling, and breaking his arm. After the break was found to be a clean one, not dangerous to James's health, and likely to heal well, Jonathan began to feel guiltily pleased at the circumstance. They would all return to Pemberley now, to allow James to recover in the comfort of home.

Indeed, Mr. Darcy ordered the trunks packed and the carriage readied—but Jonathan was not to accompany the family back to Pemberley. Instead, he learned that his father had written acquaintances of theirs in the city, the one family they had yet had opportunity to call upon, and prevailed upon them to invite Jonathan to spend the London season with them instead.

"It is the last thing I should ever wish," Jonathan told his mother, upon learning this information. "I wish Father had spoken to me before he spoke to the Bertrams. Then I might have dissuaded him."

"Your father often endeavors to accustom you to habits beyond those you find most comforting," his mother said. "At times, I think he is right to do so—there is no place so orderly that it cannot, indeed will not, endure some upset, and this you must learn to face." Jonathan would have protested that his love of routine did not entirely unfit him to surprising circumstance, as his previous trips must have surely shown, had she not continued: "In this case, however, your father presumed much, both upon Mr. Bertram and yourself. Yet the very impertinence of the question constrains you, Jonathan. If the Bertrams say yes to your father's proposal, you must go. To do otherwise would be abominably rude."

Jonathan sighed. He knew the rules of etiquette as well as any (and better than most), but he could not see the sense of any rule that made it impolite to keep to one's own house and read one's own books. Still, such rules had to be obeyed even—especially, it seemed—when they made no sense at all.

Part of his displeasure arose from a matter that had gone almost unspoken among the Darcy family, yet one that Jonathan strongly sensed lay behind his father's action: namely, Jonathan's desire to court Miss Juliet Tilney of Gloucestershire.

He and Miss Tilney had known each other for nearly three years, encountering each other on three separate visits—at each of which they had been obliged to investigate both murderous intent and its accomplishment. This highly unusual activity, though arising from grim circumstances, was by far the most interesting occupation Jonathan had ever found for his mental energies. It also had allowed for him to engage with Miss Tilney in far more varied, intriguing, and honest conversations than were possible with any other young lady—or, in truth, with almost anyone else he had ever known. At all times, Miss Tilney had shown herself principled, clever, and courageous. Her family was not as wealthy as Darcy's own, but his parents did not wish an ambitious marriage for him, only a happy one. He was young yet to marry, but not impossibly so, and Miss Tilney had reached a highly eligible age. All considerations came to this same conclusion, all his sentiments in alignment: Miss Tilney was the very girl that he should wed. Even better, a conversation they had shared at Rosings Park had hinted very strongly that Miss Tilney was not at all averse to this proposition.

And yet, some manner of objection seemed to have arisen regarding Miss Tilney, one Jonathan did not know and could not conjecture. Father had remarked upon the "indelicacy" of investigating murders, which was on the face of it undeniably true, but Jonathan thought it most unfair to condemn Miss Tilney for actions he himself had taken by her side. Worse, his mother seemed to share in his father's disapproval; whenever Jonathan attempted to turn the conversation to the topic of Miss Tilney, Mother somehow said precisely the bright, funny remarks best chosen to change the subject entirely.

It was this refusal of this dear hope, and the refusal to even openly discuss it, that had worn so heavily upon Jonathan's spirits during the past year—for it was now more than a year since he and Miss Tilney had been brought together. He also knew that part of his father's plan for London had been for Jonathan to meet other young women—more acceptable young women, as judged by whatever unfathomable rubric was being used—and forget Miss Tilney entirely.

Mr. Darcy mistook the depth of his son's feelings. No sojourn in London would change them, as Jonathan had tried to explain. In these circumstances, however, Mother was correct. The Bertrams' polite invitation to visit in a city—normally a matter of just a few nights, for easier conversation—had been transformed by his father into an excuse to send

Jonathan there for weeks or months to come. Still, this invitation had been asked for and thus could not be refused if it came.

Jonathan consoled himself by thinking that the Bertrams might well refuse. They knew each other so little. Surely Father's request had taken them aback; surely they would find some tactful means of declining, leaving Jonathan free once more.

"The heir to Pemberley?" said Sir Thomas Bertram to his brother, Edmund. "But this is excellent. You could not have done better."

"Rest assured, I had no thought of my invitation being taken in quite this light," Edmund replied. "Never would I consider asking a guest for such a long time without first obtaining your permission—yet you do wish him to come?"

"Of course! It is a most advantageous connection for both our families. You do not wish it? You have some objection to the lad?"

"Not at all. His habits are respectable, and I believe his character to be excellent." Edmund hesitated briefly before continuing. His brother, Tom, had never much heeded his concerns even before the death of their father six months prior, and Tom's accession to the baronetcy had not taught him greater humility. Edmund trusted that this pridefulness was but temporary, and entirely understandable, but their fraternal confidence did not encourage conversations so delicate as the one he knew he must now begin. "It is only that I worry about Fanny. She may not wish a guest of such duration at present. Always she has been more comfortable solely in the company of family or very intimate friends."

"One does not travel to London to spend time only in the

company of family and friends. We are fulfilling our dear father's wish that Susan should have a proper visit to London, are we not? Fanny would not desire any less for her little sister, I am sure, and she ought to be delighted that one of the most eligible bachelors in England is coming to stay." Tom, though not a man of much imagination, was able to conjecture on this point at least. "What if this Mr. Darcy were to become fond of Susan? What a brilliant match for her! Even if he does not, well, he will have friends of similar estate."

Edmund accepted that he would have to speak upon the subject Fanny least wanted spoken of: "You know that neither my wife's health nor her spirits have recovered since . . . since November."

"Oh—yes, I suppose that does weigh upon a woman—but all the better that the house we have taken in London should be a lively one, full of company and good cheer. You know that Fanny will exert herself for others before herself, so it is just the thing, to invite a guest."

Edmund's expectations on this point were not so sanguine as his brother's. Yet Tom's assessment of Fanny's character was accurate; he knew her almost as well as Edmund, for she was their cousin and had grown up in their household almost as a sister.

When the family gathered for dinner that night, Edmund shared the news, gentling it as best he could for Fanny's sake. Indeed, his wife's pale cheeks flushed in consternation, but she merely dropped her chin and said nothing.

Her younger sister Susan—also resident with them these past few years—took a greater interest. "Is this Mr. Darcy congenial company?" she asked. "Is he fond of dancing?"

"I have had little occasion to see him dance," Edmund said. In truth he remembered Mr. Darcy skulking away from the ballroom as soon as it could be managed, but that might perhaps have been a response to the extraordinary circumstances at hand. "Certainly he is not as wild as some of the young bucks, but all the better for him and for us. He is intelligent and kindly, and he will make a good addition to our party."

Edmund and Tom's mother, Lady Bertram, blinked slowly, as if awakening; she did this whenever confronted with a new fact, as if hoping that closing her eyes would make it go away. "Oh, I do not know whether I should like someone new staying with us for so very long."

"But you love company, Mother," said Tom. This was not precisely true, but she had never objected to visitors, primarily because she never mustered the will to object to much of anything. "Besides, you need something to do here in London besides shop. You spend as though money were water!"

"Do I? I do not think I buy so many things as that."

"Indeed you do," said Tom, "for I have seen your bankbook." This bank-book was in fact a sore subject for Tom, who like most older sons had expected to inherit his father's title and property along with the responsibility to care for his mother in her remaining years. She had brought a modest amount of money as her marriage settlement, which in most such cases rendered a mother dependent upon the heir's generosity. Tom had fully intended to be generous—within reason, of course. But the late Sir Thomas had unexpectedly left his widow an ample jointure, a bequest made early in their marriage, at a time when he had been able to believe she might gain the acumen to manage the money well. Time had ultimately disillusioned him on this point, but the will had remained unaltered. The late Sir Thomas had trusted his sons to give their mother wise counsel and for her malleable will to be easily turned by them.

Indeed, already Lady Bertram was nodding. "I suppose I must spend a great deal, then, though I cannot think what I spend it on."

Susan, with great spirit, rose to the defense. "Aunt Bertram, you must have spent some of it on fine clothes, but so much the better, as we are in London. We have plays to attend, and assemblies, and even balls!"

"Of course, for there is the Drakes' ball next week, and all the season anticipates the Ramseys' ball to come. We may even hold one for you, Susan," Tom said, a knowing expression upon his face, "and perhaps another dance as well, one for Miss Frederica Allerdyce?"

Edmund had resigned himself to his brother's choice, which Miss Allerdyce appeared to be. Certainly he had no objections to the girl herself; though she was reserved, she was unfailingly polite and apparently good-humored. Her family was respectable and her dowry ample. Her youth struck him as a poor match to Tom's age, but as Fanny was some years younger than Edmund himself, there he could throw no stones. If Edmund could have but believed Tom to have true affection for this girl—to have chosen her for herself—he might have celebrated. As it was, Edmund could but say, "Certainly it will be a contest to see whether the Allerdyces can call upon us before we call upon them."

Susan, though a sensible girl in most ways, was young enough to hear of a wedding and think only of joy. "We are going to have such a merry time!"

"I am sure we will," said Mrs. Bertram. "Do not we always?"

Edmund said, "Our family will indeed have many reasons for happiness, particularly when the sale has gone through."

That roused Fanny for a moment. "Indeed. It is so good of you, Tom!"

"High time we signed the deal," said Tom unsentimentally, though he was the one member of the family who had actually visited the plantation in Antigua. Or, thought Edmund, precisely because Tom had seen it for himself—had witnessed the vile evil of slavery. Fanny, meek and mild in almost every other way, had taken up antislavery beliefs quite on her own; in retrospect, Edmund was ashamed that he had not considered the moral stain of the plantation long before. Upon adopting abolitionist convictions, he had immediately brought the matter to his father—who would not hear of selling what he himself had inherited from their grandfather—and then to Tom upon his accession as baronet. To Edmund's surprise and relief, Tom had been amenable, and the sale would be conducted during the family's stay in London.

This, at least, would gladden Fanny's heart! Yet when he glanced again at his wife, her momentary enthusiasm had vanished. There were moments when Edmund wondered whether she would ever smile again.

In the meantime, alight with thoughts of balls and shopping and all the other grand wonders around her, Susan did enough smiling for both sisters.

Surely many young women throughout the country were similarly occupied with these grand, glittering thoughts, already forming notions of what gowns would look best, what styles would be appropriate for hair, and what partners were to be had at each dance. Always will there be a class of individuals who look down upon young ladies for such giddy raptures, though curiously, these persons are very often the same ones who do not want girls to think upon anything more substantive, much less act upon such thoughts. To condemn the female of the species for frivolity while simultaneously *limiting* her to frivolity is patently unjust, and yet grievously common.

In Northanger Abbey, however, one young lady heard stories of her impending trip to London—by eavesdropping, no less, from a nearby room—with far more complicated feelings upon the matter.

"Juliet must and shall have the finest attire of the season," said General Tilney, who paced in front of the hearth of his study. Their ancestral home was not a place this young lady and her family visited often or easily; General Tilney's pride was of the sort that disdained a happy, respectable clergyman son like her father, while glorying in the exploits of a dissolute, untrustworthy soldier like her uncle, Major Tilney. "No expense is to be spared. My granddaughter must represent the family as it deserves. You must arrive in time for the Drakes' ball—I know the father—he will welcome you as he should, and place you rightly in society."

At that moment, Juliet was well hidden in the kitchen, a room her grandfather never entered, populated by servants who were fond of her and would not reveal her presence. Yet she could imagine the expression upon General Tilney's face, and her parents' response—an exchange of glances that betrayed equal parts concern and exasperation. She knew, as they did, that General Tilney was fond of exclamations that suggested he had no need to concern himself with money . . . a sentiment that rarely held true when bills arrived. If her parents spent too much, her grandfather would upbraid them for taking advantage of his "generosity." But if they did not spend enough, he would accuse them of deliberately exposing the Tilney family to ridicule.

"Now, then," said the cook, Mrs. Ford, as she poured cake batter into one of the wide wooden baking rings set upon the heavy metal sheet that would go into the oven. "Don't fret, miss. You're to go to London, aren't you? Most girls would break their hearts for the chance!"

"I *am* curious about London," replied Juliet in a low voice. (She leaned against the heavy kitchen door, the better to overhear—hardly genteel behavior, but in her opinion justified by the circumstance.) "But it is not just a visit. I am to be expected to . . . to make an impression upon society."

Mrs. Ford chuckled. "All the better, I should think!"

At one time, Juliet would have entirely agreed. Young ladies "came out" in a variety of manners, from the extravagance of a high society debut to the simple exigent of putting up one's hair. Juliet was already "out," so this was not to be a debut, nor would she have to endure the grand ritual of being presented at court. But to be taken to London for the season like this—she would be expected to shine, to represent the family brilliantly, and in so doing burnish all their reputations. This was a distinction she did not desire, nor did she trust she could earn it, for her grandfather's pride was easily rankled and rarely satisfied.

Her last long journey away from home had taken her to Rosings Park, the estate of one Lady Catherine de Bourgh. Lady Catherine had made it clear that she considered Juliet and her family beneath her own—and she was aunt to Mr. Jonathan Darcy, the young man Juliet considered as superior to all others of her acquaintance. Perhaps the elder Darcys disagreed with their aunt's disdain, but Juliet sensed their disapproval of any hint of courtship between herself and their son. Her father had told her grandfather of this—in an ill-chosen exercise of his wit, many months after the event when perhaps he had judged such aristocratic contempt too distant to sting—and in so doing, he had ignited General Tilney's fury. Who was this impudent woman, to judge his granddaughter as unworthy of any young man in the land? How dare the Darcys look down upon him, his family, his wealth and estate?

The fact that the Darcys were, in fact, far wealthier than the Tilneys, particularly Juliet's clergyman father—that

Northanger Abbey, elegant as it was, had none of the renown of Pemberley—none of these truths had the power to dampen her grandfather's rage. It could not be eased; it must be avenged. And so Juliet had to go to London, to remind society of the Tilney family's rightful place within it.

Worse still, she knew that her task for the London season would not merely be to look fetching and behave impeccably. She would be expected to find an eligible suitor—a man of fortune and family to become her husband.

And due to her family's wishes, this man could not be Jonathan Darcy.

Yet another young lady looked forward to the London season, and to the matches to be made there. Some might have found this rather curious, as the woman in question had already found a husband. Some would have said she had in essence found two, and all the complications suggested by this statement are thrown into sharper relief by the fact that neither gentleman was currently in her presence, nor planned to be in the immediate future. However, Maria Rushworth had resolved to make plans of her own and to carry them out, no matter the cost.

"Well, well, I have reserved for us a place in the coach, and made a good bargain of it, I daresay." These words were spoken by Aunt Norris, the elderly relative who had followed Maria into exile after her departure from her marital home and her expulsion from her ancestral one, Mansfield Park. "They say that the prices are set by the company, but they only mean to discourage us from getting our money's worth. I pressed and pressed the coachman until he might have sworn on the very Bible that the price he gave us is indeed as low as is to be had. I wager the other passengers will all have paid larger sums for the exact same journey. Yes, I have—"

"Very well, Aunt Norris," said Maria. She had long since ceased to listen to any of her aunt's long explanations, though in truth she had never attended closely. "Make certain that she is ready, will you? The coach leaves early. We must not be late."

Her family, she knew, was already in London. So was her former husband, Mr. Rushworth. So was the man she had left him for, Henry Crawford of Everingham. The tasks before would indeed be difficult to accomplish, but manage it, Maria would. All depended upon it. She would, at last, determine her own fate.

Chapter Two

Even those who most strongly prefer the gentle tenor of country life cannot but thrill at their first sight of London. Slowly, the rolling countryside populates more and more densely with houses; farms become fewer and smaller; the roads thicken with carriages, horses, and those obliged to travel upon the humblest equipage of all, their own feet. Buildings grow taller and grander. Moment by moment, the green land of England is replaced by a city that somehow feels as vast in itself as does the nation entire.

Juliet Tilney watched this progress with the most delighted attention. Her uncertainty about the coming season—and her role within it—could not make itself felt amid such a change. "Shall we see St. Paul's?" she asked her mother. "Or Westminster Abbey?"

Her mother patted her arm fondly. "We shall ensure that you see both while we are in London, but I do not believe our course takes us by them today. You must content yourself with only settling into a new house, and perhaps meeting some new acquaintances. And you will have to wait an entire day to attend your first ball! Do you think such scraps will suffice to entertain you?"

Laughing, Juliet said, "I will endeavor to be satisfied."

Mrs. Tilney and Juliet traveled to London with no male companion aside from their servants. At first Henry Tilney's intent was to travel with his wife and daughter, leaving the younger daughter and son in the care of the governess. However, before the journey, he had felt obliged to perform a delicate sort of mathematics unique to clergymen, namely the counting of parishioners likely to decease in the immediate future and the incipient infants who will replace them in the congregation. This number proved much higher than usual, and thus Mr. Tilney had remained to do his duty at the several baptisms and burials likely to ensue. "After all," he had said to Juliet, "we have both family and friends in London capable of assisting you if needed, and your mother will have no time for me, as there are publishers to be scolded and editors to be charmed."

"And other writers to be met," Mrs. Tilney had added. Indeed, even as Juliet gazed with wonder at the throngs lining the streets, her mother was meditating upon an invitation to luncheon in the days to come; her hostess had hinted that no less a novelist than Mrs. Edgeworth might be in attendance.

"There is so much of it!" Juliet exclaimed. "I declare that we could stay here a year and not see all there is to be seen."

"Longer than that," said Mrs. Tilney. "Those who know London best say that understanding the city is the work of a lifetime."

On the precise same road, not even half a mile ahead, a hired coach bore Jonathan Darcy toward the residence the Bertram family had taken in London. He had pulled down the blinds, so that at least he need not pain his eyes with the sea of persons and activity that surrounded him, but no such expedient could keep his ears from hearing the din, or even his nose from enduring the overpowering stench of unwashed persons and horses' leavings.

The Darcy family carriage would have sheltered Jonathan somewhat better, but at that moment it was traveling in precisely the direction he would have preferred—toward

Pemberley—bearing the rest of his family. Jonathan's pains had not made him so selfish that he forgot the great discomfort poor James must be in, and he wished them smooth roads with all his heart. Yet how he wished to be with them, to be anywhere other than London!

Edmund and Fanny Bertram are quiet, civil, reasonable persons, he told himself by way of consolation. *Their habits do not differ so greatly from my own. There, perhaps, I will be able to find some measure of peace.*

This prospect seemed fair upon his arrival at the house. Though it was not so grand a residence as his family had taken, the house was nonetheless large for London, and it contained a reasonably well-stocked library into which Jonathan could retreat. The Bertrams already known to him greeted him with politeness and calm, and those previously unknown to him showed pleasure at making his acquaintance. If young Miss Price babbled on a bit about the wonders she had beheld, and Sir Thomas made a few jokes suggesting that Jonathan had come to London fully intending to become a rakehell—neither went on at such length that Jonathan could not bear it; and by way of consolation, Lady Bertram was as placid as a living creature could be, interested in little beyond her fat black pug.

When he asked to be shown to his room, Sir Thomas at first attempted to dissuade him. "The servants are unpacking for you, and why should you wish to crowd them? Let me take you to Wyngarde's—I wager they will have several card tables at play already."

Jonathan could imagine few greater horrors. "I must beg your pardon, Sir Thomas, but I would prefer to first settle in. There has been much to-do regarding my poor brother, and readying the family's departure from London so much sooner than anticipated." None of these things related to his reason for desiring solitude, but Sir Thomas did not need to know it.

"Very well, very well," said Sir Thomas, much disappointed, as he had been anticipating livelier company in the city than his brother, Edmund. "Settle as you will, but we shall not give you leave for long. Perhaps we shall go to Wyngarde's tomorrow? Or the art exhibition? It is all the rage, I hear. Mind, in two days the Drakes' ball is to be held, and *that* we cannot allow you to miss!"

One member of the Bertram party was indeed dismayed at Jonathan's arrival, though she strove to disguise her feelings. Poor Fanny! So tenderhearted was she, so anxious to avoid giving offense, that she fluttered about him almost as assiduously as she would have her brother come home from sea. Little did she know that, when she parted from Jonathan Darcy at the door to his room, his relief was as great as hers.

Fanny had not wished to come to London at this time, and had even gone so far as to argue against it—she, who argued with so few about so little. Yet she had spoken so tentatively that her objections had made no impression, not even upon her dear Edmund. In the end she had given way to Susan's longing to see the city and her sense of obligation to the wishes of her late uncle. She told herself that she had no reason to object—not yet—probably none whatsoever—but certainly not yet. Fortunately, the roads had been in fine condition throughout their journey, and so there had been no need to worry in the first place.

As she descended the stair, she met Edmund, who had sought her out. He took her hand and spoke in a low voice. "I know you were not eager for company, Fanny, but you welcomed him with all the kindness I would expect of you. I hope it was not a trial for you to do so."

"Not in the slightest. Some persons, I think, would be

more difficult to welcome than Mr. Darcy, who is such a polite, kindly young man." Fanny particularly liked Jonathan Darcy because of a service he had done her once, though this service was not one that could be openly discussed even in the family home.

"Indeed. I said as much to Tom, when the elder Mr. Darcy proposed the longer visit." Edmund squeezed her hand. "It will do both of us good, to think upon other subjects, to have other surroundings. Both of our spirits need lifting—do not think you mourn alone."

Fanny could not say what was in her heart, for fear of weeping or, even worse, fear of exciting hope where none should be entertained. So she embraced her husband, closed her eyes, and wished with all her might that she might be able to put an end to mourning in a few weeks' time.

There are few young ladies of any persuasion who do not feel at least some anticipation at the prospect of a ball. Some may be giddy at the thought of wearing a new gown and seeing others wear theirs, which ideally would be slightly inferior. Others wish to dance with as many young men as they can, or with one young man in particular. Music lovers look forward to hearing the songs and perhaps, at certain smaller dances, offering a number or two themselves to general admiration. Above all, perhaps, keen observers of human nature look forward to an unparalleled chance to witness the many collisions of manners, motives, and merriment a ball can provide.

Juliet Tilney, herself such a keen observer, could not give herself entirely over to raptures at the prospect of the Drakes' ball, for they had been in London so short a time that she had no new dress—only the best brought from home—and yet long enough for Juliet to determine that this gown, though not deficient, did not represent the newest styles.

"We can do nothing about the color," her mother advised, stroking the pale yellow silk that once had been so fetchingly delicate but now seemed somewhat wan compared to the bolder shades and patterns all London had embraced. "But the sleeves are wider, at least—the dressmaker did not lead us astray there—and if you wear an extra petticoat or two, the skirt will appear much fuller."

Juliet gazed at her reflection in the old spotty mirror in her room. At least the newer fashions for hair suited her, with the heavier ringlets framing each side of her face. As for the dress . . . "You are right, Mamma. The petticoats will help. I am sure this gown will do." She said this with determined cheer, but also with all the dissatisfaction experienced by any young lady who has ever been obliged to be satisfied with a dress that will merely "do."

Despite this travail, Juliet was determined to make the most of the occasion. Dresses were being more richly trimmed these days, it seemed, but this deficit could be somewhat remedied with her grandmother's garnet necklace and a broad periwinkle sash tied about her waist. Her mother's luncheon had gone so very well that they could expect to build upon new acquaintance throughout the evening. And if Juliet looked not quite in the fashion—might that not, perhaps, discourage suitors from asking her to dance?

No. The dress was not so bad as all that. It occupied the forlorn middle, neither beautiful enough to excite general admiration nor ugly enough to entirely ward off unwanted men. She consoled herself with the certainty that no offer of marriage would arrive at the party.

However, the particular magic of a ball could not but work on Juliet's spirits upon their arrival at the handsome home occupied by the Drake family. To see such beautiful silks and furs, to hear musicians testing their instruments before the music was to begin, to walk into a room brilliantly lit by hundreds of candles: This was surely a kind of magic, an enchantment that rendered the everyday world and its ordinary citizens more beautiful by a hundredfold.

Across the room, meanwhile, Sir Thomas and Edmund Bertram had just done their duty to their hosts when they spotted the very people Tom had most hoped to see, namely, the ladies of the Allerdyce family. Though Mr. Allerdyce was absent, felled by a "most shocking" cold, Mrs. Allerdyce welcomed them warmly with both her daughters at their side. The younger, Miss Priscilla, was the prettier of the two, and far too aware of it; she simpered through their welcome in a manner meant to steal their attention—successfully so, if not in the precise light Miss Priscilla would have wished. Edmund could only be grateful that Tom had shown discernment enough to prefer the elder, for Frederica Allerdyce greeted them with both dignity and warmth. Her height and her strong features hinted that her quieter beauty would linger longer than her sister's; her bearing in turn suggested that she possessed greater intelligence and character.

Their mother, Mrs. Allerdyce, had bestowed her height and bearing upon her elder daughter and her need for attention upon the younger. If her eyes, settling upon Sir Thomas Bertram, saw his title and his wealth more than the man himself—this, Edmund had to acknowledge, was no more than the duty of any mother of a marriageable daughter.

For his part, Tom needed little encouragement. "Miss Allerdyce, you promised me the first two dances, you will recall, and I intend to hold you to your word."

"If Frederica will not, I will," declared Miss Priscilla, her dimpled smile so winsome as to obscure the forwardness of her words. "You must ask me for later dances at least, Sir Thomas. I am not one to play the wallflower!"

"I always keep my word, Sir Thomas," Miss Allerdyce said, with far more elegance. "Were I ever tempted to break it, it would not be for such a promise as this."

"But I shall still expect your favor later in the evening?" Miss Priscilla fixed Sir Thomas with her gaze, determined to flirt with any fellow that crossed her path, regardless of her sister's claims to affection.

Sir Thomas was not wholly susceptible to such maneuvering—Miss Allerdyce was already his firm favorite— but it is best not to trust such an important matter to chance. So Edmund interjected, "We have brought with us one who could perform this office for Miss Priscilla, a most eligible young man."

"Ah, yes?" Mrs. Allerdyce said. "Whom might this be? Another member of your family?"

"An acquaintance of ours, whom we met at a house party in Surrey nearly three years prior—Mr. Jonathan Darcy of Pemberley."

Edmund had anticipated the ladies' interest in this, but their open delight surprised him. It was Miss Allerdyce who saw this and swiftly explained, "The Darcys are very nearly family, you see—we are related by marriage."

"Mr. Jonathan Darcy in London alone," mused Mrs. Allerdyce. "Of course you are the perfect hosts, but we feel it very much our duty to help entertain him—tonight, and for the rest of his stay. Indeed, if ever your family requires some days without company, he will be more than welcome at our home! As a relation, he has always a place with us."

"Oh, yes, indeed." Miss Priscilla had taken on a rather pert demeanor, which Edmund disliked even if he could not wonder at it. To judge by the gleam in Mrs. Allerdyce's gaze, she had long considered a match between her family and the Darcys, and it was the younger daughter she thought likeliest to ensnare the prize.

Edmund could not have guessed just how long Mrs. Allerdyce had wished for such a marriage, or the different form that wish had taken in the beginning, more than two decades prior, when her name had been Miss Caroline Bingley. He knew only enough to feel vaguely guilty as he gestured to Mr. Darcy, beckoning him toward their little party, and presumably into Mrs. Allerdyce's web.

For his part, Jonathan had been attempting to steady himself against the tide of conversation and bustle that attended the beginning of any ball. He had nearly made up his mind to go to the card room—not to play (for he was good at cards, so good that he inevitably won and then earned resentment), but simply to observe. This was socially acceptable, and though card rooms could be raucous, on the whole he would encounter less noise and movement than in the ballroom itself. In the instant before Jonathan turned, however, he caught Mr. Bertram's gesture; no sooner had he done so than he recognized the Allerdyces.

Jonathan had encountered the family several times throughout his life, usually at the home of his aunt and uncle, the Bingleys, but their visits had never overlapped for such a period of time as would allow for a deeper acquaintance. Yet they seemed to be fascinated with him for reasons he did not understand, and therefore did not like. All he knew, as his heart sank, was that he would be obliged to ask both sisters to dance.

Mrs. Tilney ushered Juliet through the many introductions necessary at a ball held by relative strangers in a city where one has never traveled before. Even as she worked hard to associate name with face—Mrs. Lee? Mr. Ramsey?—one of the younger sons of the hosts had asked her to dance, and she was most obliged to him, and required to go with him to the dance floor.

The young Mr. Drake did not appear greatly more enthusiastic about her than Juliet was about him; this was a matter of courtesy, no more. Already his eyes were searching the very crowded dance floor (three dozen couples at least!) for the next duty he must perform. She consoled herself with the knowledge that at least she had already escaped the fate of the wallflower.

Then Juliet was struck for a moment by how fatuous, how foolish it was to concern oneself with petticoats and dancing. How she missed her investigations with Mr. Darcy! That had called for ingenuity, consideration, a deeper knowledge of all sorts of people and their concerns. Why could they not have gone on so forever? She was not wicked enough to wish for more murders, but as a clergyman's daughter she knew that sin would be ever with humanity—thus crime was inevitable—and should criminals exist, surely it was one's moral duty to investigate them if one could do so.

This ingenious embroidery upon religious doctrine ended when the first number was called and Juliet realized they were to perform the newest fashion: a circle dance, in which each group of dancers would perform their own steps, dictated by the lead couples—and with every couple moving down the ring, forever changing these groups' composition. She had read about this, but never danced it for herself; this would require great concentration.

And so Juliet's attention fastened entirely upon her partner as they began. Luckily, they were not one of the lead couples, and the steps being called were at least simple. As she realized that the lead dancers were attempting to help the others, rather than confuse them, she was able to relax somewhat and whirl through the steps. At least the young Mr. Drake was a reasonably good dancer.

"The new circle dances are so *daring*," said Miss Priscilla Allerdyce, as Jonathan dutifully took her through the motions. "Changing partners throughout—why, we young ladies are obliged to dance with strangers. Would not you prefer we danced only together?"

"We can stop if you prefer," Jonathan replied. "More traditional dances will surely be called later, and we could take the floor then."

Miss Priscilla giggled, as though he had said something very foolish, when in his view he had made an entirely reasonable suggestion. "Why, Mr. Darcy. Then we would rob you of the chance to ask me to dance again!"

Was he obligated to ask her again? He very much hoped not. Jonathan could now discern that Miss Priscilla, contrary to her stated objections, evidently enjoyed the daring nature of the new dances. He did not. Normally, dances were rendered palatable to him largely due to their predictability. They had known steps, known rules. Yes, Jonathan might be touched by strangers, which he disliked, but it would at least occur only at times, and in ways, he could predict. This circle dance, offering no such consolations, might have been designed to ensure he had the least pleasure possible upon a ballroom floor.

One advantage of the circle dance presented itself to him soon, however, when partners shifted for the first time. Miss Priscilla Allerdyce could now direct her attentions elsewhere. Jonathan's new partner was a stout, merry matron who

danced as nimbly as any girl; as she expected nothing from
him but the performance of steps, he found her more congenial company.

As they whirled around, he caught a glimpse of a girl who
looked familiar—so very familiar—that he charged himself
with the crime of wishful thinking. *What would be the chances,
that* she *would be here?* Jonathan thought. *How greatly my fortune would change! But it is not her.*

It cannot be.

Surely . . .

As Juliet swung through another set of changes, she caught
a glimpse of a young man in a nearby group, whirling about—
quite as tall as Mr. Jonathan Darcy. How inventive her imagination was, to place him among the dancers so shortly after
she had been lamenting his absence!

London is so populous, she decided, *I suppose I might see doubles
here of nearly every person I have ever known. I might make a game
of it. Certainly I should be challenged to find any who come closer to
the original than this one.*

Then she turned toward the center again, and this time the
young man was staring at her. It was indeed no other than the
young Mr. Darcy!

His animation upon seeing her was great, and Juliet knew
hers must be as well, but she could not have concealed her
delight and did not attempt it. What young lady could, when
the young man she most prefers in all the world is revealed
to be at the same ball as she? Very few, particularly not
when that joy is so evidently shared. Best was the realization
that the patterns of the circle dance would, in time, bring
them together. Juliet whirled through the steps, so rosy and

alight with pleasure that, for the first time, it occurred to Mr. Drake that he might have attended better to his partner.

Finally, the circle brought them around to each other, and she reached for him, felt the pressure of his gloved hand on hers.

"Miss Tilney!" Mr. Darcy said, matching it perfectly to the small bow demanded by the dance. "Such a pleasure to see you again. What brings you to London?"

"My grandfather thought I should experience the London season. What is it that brings you here, sir?"

"My father thought much the same as your grandfather, though I am staying as the guest of the Bertram family."

Juliet believed for a moment that the laughter and gaiety of the ball had confused her hearing. "You do not mean the Bertrams we met in Surrey?"

"The very same," said Mr. Darcy. "They will be pleased to see you here, I am sure."

"As am I." She was grateful to be dancing, so very grateful, for it allowed her to express her joy through the whirling steps. Otherwise her bliss might have gone beyond decorum. Not only did etiquette allow her to renew the acquaintance, it *demanded* that she do so. Her mother must be introduced as well. As for her grandfather, he would no doubt have insisted that the family of Sir Thomas Bertram, baronet, was precisely the sort of company most fit for his granddaughter.

The dance compelled Juliet to step forward toward Mr. Darcy, who did the same in turn. They raised their hands as the movements required, and for one moment, their palms pressed together. Despite the gloves they both wore, she could feel the echo of warmth. How she would have blushed!—had they not immediately been obliged to step back, to circle once more, and then to shift into new dancing groups yet again. Juliet's smile lasted the rest of the dance, attracting the admi-

ration of many of her other partners, not one of whom she
even saw.

The rest of the ball may be imagined: Mr. Edmund Bertram's
pleasure upon encountering Miss Tilney again—the apologies for Mrs. Fanny Bertram's absence due to her health—an
amiable introduction between Miss Tilney and Miss Susan
Price—and the long-waited meeting between Mrs. Catherine
Tilney and Mr. Jonathan Darcy. The latter of these wished
very much to make a good impression; the former to study
this young man for herself.

   Jonathan knew only that calls would be paid, and bonds
would be strengthened, while his parents were in another
county and quite unable to interfere. For her part, Juliet
thought, *How wonderful that we are brought together, and this
time no one is dead!* Despite her past experiences with murders,
she had not yet learned that the most inescapable force in the
world is irony.

Chapter Three

Unexpected guests come in two varieties. First are those most welcome in our homes—company with whom our thoughts find an audience, with whom our humor is best amused, or those with whom we share the truest bonds of love. In such cases, the guests are ushered inside with few second thoughts, perhaps no more than the wish to have twinned the joy of their arrival with the delights of anticipation.

Second, however, are those whose visits we would have discouraged, had we been given the opportunity. It is impossible to make a general description of such guests, as humanity is forever inventing new ways of being disagreeable. The reactions of their hosts, however, can be more neatly summarized. One must undertake the many duties of having company without few of the attendant pleasures, all while attempting to conceal some measure of the chagrin felt at having to entertain a person whose presence we would most gladly do without. One such guest was soon to arrive at the Bertrams' London home, but the task of entertaining them would first fall not to a host, but to another guest.

Jonathan Darcy awoke in better spirits than he had in months. His parents, could they have seen him, would have rejoiced to find their son in London, staying in a new house, yet assured and eager for all the adventure the day would bring. Had they known exactly why he was in such good temper—namely, the meeting with Miss Juliet Tilney—their responses would have been more complicated. However, they did *not* know, and would not for some time yet. Jonathan did not intend to be dishonest with his family and would reveal all eventually. Yet his parents had brought him to London against his will, then left him here with the Bertrams despite his protests, and thus Jonathan considered them the architects of the entire business. If they did not care for what they had wrought, they would have no one but themselves to blame.

In truth, Jonathan could not bring himself to believe that his parents would not accept Miss Tilney eventually. His father was an eminently reasonable man, if a strict one; his mother an amiable and understanding woman, though a protective one. They possessed few prejudices that could not be overcome by experience. Thus he did not consider himself to be disobedient in renewing the acquaintance with Miss Tilney; he was merely anticipating his parents' inevitable change of opinion.

He along with most of the rest of the household had stayed up late, remaining at the dance until near three—more or less when anyone would expect to leave such a gathering. In most houses, a ball was followed with quiet morning-after, breakfast a subdued affair for those few who came down to have it, more often brought up on trays at hours more traditionally suited to luncheon. This morning, however, Jonathan rose early, hoping that the Tilneys might call; he breakfasted alone on toast and coffee, reveling in both silence and anticipation.

Indeed, as the clock struck the earliest hours at which visitors could be expected, a rap came at the door. Jonathan went to the sitting room, telling a servant, "Do not trouble the Bertrams, if you think they would not wish to be roused—I am happy to entertain our caller."

This servant, however, had long been with the family and had glanced out the window. She shook her head. "They will join you soon. They will have no choice."

Jonathan wished to inquire about this, but there was no time. He took a chair in the sitting room just in time for the butler to announce the visitor: "Mrs. Maria Rushworth."

Mrs. Rushworth walked in, and she and Jonathan stared, equally dismayed at the defiance of their individual expectations. They had never been introduced, and therefore they could say but little to each other; Jonathan made what statement he could. "The Bertrams will be down directly."

"I see." Mrs. Rushworth seemed ill at ease, but she took her seat with apparent determination to wait as long as possible. "You, I suppose, are a guest of the house."

One could introduce one's self in this circumstance. "Mr. Jonathan Darcy, at your service, madam."

Though she nodded, Mrs. Rushworth made no endeavor to extend their conversation, and he lapsed into a grateful silence. She was a handsome woman, fair of coloring and feature, perhaps Jonathan's own age or only a few years his elder. Although her bearing suggested gentility, her dress was slightly out of date. (Despite not being a great scholar of ladies' clothes, Jonathan had overheard his mother's dismay at the fashion for more and more ruffles.)

The servant at the door had not left them, and Mrs. Rushworth observed this with some scorn. "Come now, Danvers. Do you fear I shall steal the silver?"

"No, ma'am," said Danvers. "Of course I should never think such a thing. But I have no instructions—"

"My father is not here to condemn me any longer," said Mrs. Rushworth, who appeared to be the sister of Sir Thomas and Reverend Edmund Bertram. Jonathan belatedly recalled his parents quietly speaking of some trouble regarding the Bertram family—a wayward daughter. They had not revealed any details, as their conversation had been wholly centered upon the wrongness of judging an entire family by the actions of any one member. But the details must have been bad indeed, if this Mrs. Rushworth could not be certain of her welcome even at her brothers' house.

In that moment, protocol was broken entirely as Mrs. Fanny Bertram stepped out, no doubt hurriedly dressed. Jonathan was taken aback at how pale she appeared—wan and tremulous, surely unwell—but she managed a smile. "Good morning, Mrs. Rushworth. I see you have met our friend Mr. Darcy."

Mrs. Rushworth seemed to have no more wish to learn about Jonathan than to speak to him. "Well, Fanny, you are quite the lady of the house now, are you not? Who would have thought it?"

"Not I," Fanny said. "Tom or Edmund will be down soon, if you wish to wait for them."

"If I wish to wait?" Mrs. Rushworth asked. "Why else would I have come but to speak with my family?"

Fanny took her place, very quiet, very small. "I am sure I would not know."

Jonathan's curiosity at this exchange was considerable. Mrs. Fanny Bertram he knew to be a gentle, timid, kindly sort of woman, unlikely to reject any person out of hand. Even more startling had been Danvers's reluctance to admit a family member, once among those the servant had been obliged to obey. So what, then, could lead to so chilly a reception?

Mrs. Bertram had managed the introduction, but did not seem to know how to proceed further. Jonathan sympathized with her confusion and wished he could absent himself, so that any difficult matters could be discussed beyond his earshot—but he could not think of any mannerly way to do so. Mrs. Bertram began, "I trust you had a pleasant journey to London, Mrs. Rushworth?"

"By post coach?" Mrs. Rushworth replied. "Perhaps you have had no experience traveling in so rude an equipage, as extravagant as my parents' charity has always been on your behalf. I assure you, Fanny, the journey is not pleasant in the slightest, in close quarters with strangers, obliged to endure dusty roads and uncertain schedules."

Jonathan had begun to comprehend that neither woman would take much note of him until they had had whatever conversation Mrs. Rushworth intended to provoke. He decided to remain quiet and pay close heed to what was and was not said, to deduce as much as he could from their words. Miss Tilney would encourage him thus—and would be so interested to hear it!

From what had already been spoken, he knew only: Mrs. Bertram had been brought up by Mrs. Rushworth's family, apparently also that of her husband—a cousin, then. From the comment about the coach, he knew that Mrs. Bertram had apparently come from parents with greatly reduced circumstances. From Mrs. Bertram's demeanor, he knew that the family had not showered "extravagance" on her at all; she was not a person who considered herself entitled to wealth or grandeur. This in turn meant that Mrs. Rushworth resented Mrs. Bertram for reasons unspoken.

Mrs. Bertram said, "You must be greatly fatigued, Mrs. Rushworth. Had you left a card, or written a letter, Edmund might have been able to visit you instead, to save you the difficulty."

Jonathan silently translated this as, *You ought to have warned us,* and *also, your problems are of your own making.*

Mrs. Rushworth seemed to comprehend Fanny's full meaning. "Had I written, Tom might have exercised the authority of Sir Thomas over me. He has had no opportunities yet, and surely he looks forward to the privilege."

Already I knew the elder brother has newly succeeded to the title, Jonathan thought, *and from this, it seems Mrs. Rushworth's father had refused to welcome her back after some form of scandal.*

She claims to think her brother will do the same, but in truth hopes for greater forgiveness.

"What brings you to London, Mrs. Rushworth?" Mrs. Bertram asked, her countenance betraying little emotion. From this Jonathan could infer no striking insight, other than the fact that while Mrs. Rushworth had tried to use their Christian names in the conversation, this informality Mrs. Bertram had refused.

"I am here to see my family. Is not that reason enough?" Mrs. Rushworth's smile was small, neat, and false.

She has some other purpose in London, thought Jonathan. *A purpose greatly important to her, and yet one she wishes to conceal.*

At this moment, Lady Bertram entered the room. As ever, her dress was elegant and her person striking despite her years; she carried her black pug and wore a baffled expression. "Maria? You surely cannot be here."

"Mamma." Mrs. Rushworth rose and embraced her mother, who did not return the gesture, either from astonishment or merely her canine burden. "How I have missed you!"

"But you cannot be here, I am sure you cannot." Lady Bertram blinked slowly. "You live far away with Aunt Norris. Is not Aunt Norris with you?"

"She is in London, at the house we have taken—many blocks from here, far enough to satisfy propriety, though you may be disappointed to learn it is not entirely unfashionable, that my exile is not complete." Mrs. Rushworth's daughterly feeling was not so great that she could set aside her spite. "You have welcomed Aunt Norris home in the past. Am I to be denied the same courtesy?"

Lady Bertram seemed hardly to grasp the situation. "Tom will know. I cannot always be thinking of things, you know, it is very wearisome." The door to the drawing room opened once more, to admit Mr. Edmund Bertram and his brother, Sir Thomas. How Lady Bertram's uncertainty melted, into a smile of the deepest relief! "See, Tom is here now. He will tell us what to do."

During Fanny's childhood—when she had, as Jonathan Darcy had surmised, been treated more as an impoverished ward than as a member of the family—she had barely been able to believe that reckless, rambunctious Tom would someday accede to the title of baronet. Her late uncle had embodied all that she had come to associate with nobility: dignity, propriety, stateliness. Even after reaching manhood, Tom had shown little sign of any of these qualities, or even of wishing to possess them. However, a serious illness seven years prior had at last tempered Tom's high spirits. He conducted business promptly and properly now; he drank less and answered letters in a timely fashion; he concerned himself with the needs of the Mansfield tenantry with even greater attention than the late Sir Thomas had shown.

Above all, Fanny rejoiced that Tom had chosen to sell the plantation in Antigua, a morally necessary act that she could not truly forgive her uncle for neglecting. Let Tom laugh as much and as loudly as he pleased, let him still take an interest in horse races and boxing matches: Once he had sold the plantation and cut all family ties to slavery, Fanny believed that Tom would be a far greater paterfamilias than his father had ever been, at least in the eyes of the Lord.

Yet she had not been able to guess how Tom would handle the difficulty presented by his sister Maria Rushworth. The two of them had been friendly as young siblings, but never genuinely close. Tom's conduct had become more proper, but he remained lax in judging the conduct of others. Could this, however, extend so far as to grant Maria forgiveness?

To Fanny's mind, Maria's first sin had been in marrying

Mr. Rushworth—a well-meaning but foolish young man, whose attractions for Maria had begun with his fortune and ended with his handsome estate, Sotherton, with nothing else between. Society had honored the match, as it always will where a woman is lovely and a man is rich, but Fanny reckoned that hardly a marriage at all. Still, this was as nothing compared to what Maria had done later: namely, abandoning her husband and home to run away with one Mr. Henry Crawford. She had been enamored of Mr. Crawford, ready to be in love with him . . . but his interest in her was born of more vanity than feeling. He had lost interest and left her. Mr. Rushworth had then divorced her. Since then, Maria had been obliged to live on the small allowance the late Sir Thomas had granted, and in the company of Aunt Norris, the one person who still believed Maria could do no wrong.

The sin of adultery blemished a woman's character greater than any other error could do; to be divorced for this reason was the deepest possible disgrace, and the late Sir Thomas had behaved accordingly. Would Tom instead welcome Maria back into the bosom of the family? No, it seemed—but he did not cast her out, either. "Maria," he said, somewhat sternly, "you should not have come to call without first being invited."

"Invited? To see my own mother?" Maria scoffed. "Mamma, have you ever heard of such?"

"I am sure I do not know," said Lady Bertram, clearly pleased to leave all potential decisions behind and instead attend to the petting of Pug. "Aunt Norris comes to see me sometimes, and she is not invited, but that may be a very different thing. Is it very different, Tom?"

Fanny had not known that Aunt Norris occasionally visited Lady Bertram; she had only been glad not to have to meet with this aunt herself, for Aunt Norris had always judged Fanny very harshly.

Fortunately, Edmund spoke next. "It is very different indeed, Mother. Aunt Norris has done no wrong. But Maria is a divorced woman, one divorced under the gravest circumstances, and she cannot be granted admittance to our houses, not without the family seeming to condone her conduct." In a gentler tone he said, "Maria, you must think of our young cousin. Susan cannot be stained by this association."

Maria had always been quick to anger, and this was beyond what little her temper could bear. "So, the new Miss Price is held to be of more account than that of the former Miss Bertram! You pay more heed to gossips than to the well-being of your own sister. Will you obey your younger brother, Tom?"

Tom did not seem to know how to answer this, but for once, Fanny felt she should speak. "Let us come to visit you, Mrs. Rushworth," she ventured. To give a person admittance to one's own house was a powerful statement of forgiveness; to visit them in their houses, far less so. Furthermore, despite Maria's assertions to the contrary, she could not be staying very near—surely she could afford only one of the lesser neighborhoods many blocks distant—which meant that the family's visits would be observed by fewer persons of note. "Why, I shall come tomorrow, if you will leave us your card."

"Of course," said Tom, obviously relieved to have been given a middle path to follow. "Fanny will call upon you. Will not that do?"

This compromise did not improve Maria's spirits, but it was the best she was likely to get, and she knew it. "Very well, then, if you will come, though I do not see why Fanny should be the person most concerned with me."

Maria had never cared much for Fanny, but their relationship had grown far more brittle in recent years . . . probably because, when Henry Crawford had actually proposed marriage, it was Fanny he had proposed to. This, however, was a subject Fanny thought upon as little as possible.

For her part, Juliet Tilney would gladly have urged her mother into paying a call upon the Bertrams that same morning—had she awakened before noon. Catherine was able to soothe her daughter's disappointment only by promising that they would go the very next day. How long a day can last, when it is all that stands between a young woman and a gentleman whose presence she finds most agreeable!

When they did set out on the morrow, Juliet in her favorite dress, anticipation had all but overcome her—but society dictates that men and women are to meet together only at certain times of day, at certain functions, and that company is more commonly to be kept within each of the sexes than between them both. Thus, though Catherine and Juliet Tilney arrived at the Bertrams' town house within calling hours, they missed all the men of the party, who had been taken off to Sir Thomas's London club. Juliet regretted the opportunity—and could guess how little Mr. Darcy wished to visit a place so boisterous as a gentlemen's club—but there was nothing for it but to converse with the ladies of the house.

This, however, presented its own difficulties. Young Susan Price was a bright and amiable girl, enthusiastic about London and eager to sample more of its diversions—she, at least, might prove to be a friend. Yet Mrs. Fanny Bertram, though all politeness, struck Juliet as more quiet and uncertain than she had been in Surrey, and even Fanny was an easier conversational partner than Lady Bertram.

"Oh! You are from Gloucestershire," Lady Bertram said as she absently stroked the pug in her lap. "I have never known anyone from Gloucestershire before. Is it very far away?"

"No, indeed. Your house is in Northamptonshire, I understand? Only Oxfordshire lies between us, and not much of that," said Catherine Tilney, all helpfulness. "I take it you have never traveled there?"

"No, no indeed—I do not travel if it can be helped—but my late husband wished this for Susan, and so we must be in London, or so Tom says. Tom is the head of the family now, you see, and he knows what is best. No, I am sure I would not leave Mansfield Park for all the world, were it not my late husband's wish."

"How dearly you love your home!" Catherine said, most courteously, so that no one who knew her less well than her daughter could detect her amazement at such a lack of curiosity. Juliet's mother possessed always a great eagerness to know new places and new persons and had little sympathy with those who did not.

Would she dislike Jonathan Darcy for this reason? But Juliet immediately persuaded herself that her mother would see that Mr. Darcy's need for familiarity and order was an entirely different matter.

When at last they were making their farewells, Catherine apologized for the brevity of their visit. "I must conduct a matter of business, you see."

"Business?" Lady Bertram blinked slowly, as if hardly able to believe what she had heard. "Oh, should not your husband take care of all such matters? I would not like to conduct business at all. My sister Norris has done so at times, but she had to learn upon becoming a widow. I am sure women with husbands or grown sons need not."

Catherine hesitated, for her accomplishments as an author were considered, by some, unseemly for a gentlewoman, and so she did not speak of them to such new acquaintance. "In this one matter, the task falls to me, for my husband remains at home."

Fanny quickly said, "Do not apologize for your departure, for I must make a visit of my own today."

"You will not go by yourself," said Lady Bertram. "Surely there can be no call for that. You can wait for Tom, can you not?"

"I do not believe that I can," Fanny replied. "It must be done, and I would have it over with."

Lady Bertram could not seem to make sense of this. "But Susan must go with you. Then you will not be alone—though I cannot know if I can do without her."

"Danvers is here for you," Susan said to her aunt. "You will not miss me, but I do not go with Fanny. The Miss Worthingtons I met at the Drakes' ball have asked me to tea, do you not recall?"

"Oh, yes, tea. One must have tea." Yet Lady Bertram's distress remained. "I am sure it is not right for Fanny to go alone, though."

Juliet saw her duty. "Mamma, as I need not attend you, might I go with Mrs. Bertram on her errand? If she wishes it, of course."

This was somewhat presumptuous, but Juliet's presumption had been correct, for Fanny's smile warmed and became genuine, at least for a few moments. "That would be a great blessing indeed, if you will consent, Mrs. Tilney."

Catherine nodded. "By all means." In truth, already she thought more of the upcoming conversation with her publishers than her daughter's acquaintance with the Bertrams. Our own concerns are ever clearer in our minds than the concerns of others; such is the vanity of man.

So, shortly after Catherine's departure, Juliet and Fanny set out together through the bustle and clamor of London, accompanied by a manservant and a maid. The maid carried a small hamper, which seemed to be laden with offerings of some sort, most likely from the kitchen. Juliet ventured to ask, "This is a family member you are visiting?"

"My cousin Maria Rushworth, Edmund and Sir Thomas's sister." Fanny ducked her head, as if embarrassed. "I beg your pardon, Miss Tilney, as I ought to have mentioned before—to your mother, who might have objected—you should know that Mrs. Rushworth is a divorced woman."

"Oh!" Juliet, though open-minded in many respects, was indeed shocked. She had heard of divorce, and further knew that most divorces in England were requested by husbands whose wives had strayed indecently from their marital vows. (She was of course aware that husbands strayed as well, but this, the law was less inclined to punish.) Never had she actually met a divorced person, least of all a divorced woman.

Fanny paused on the road. How many carriages rolled by them, how many persons of all stations, how many horses—and amid all this noise, Fanny remained quiet and still. "I should have spoken earlier, I see," she said. "Let us walk back to the house. I am sure Lady Bertram will arrange for a carriage for you."

However, Juliet had recovered herself. "There is no need. Your character is such that I cannot do wrong, if I go only where you go, and London is—it is too much, surely, to expect one to travel alone among streets such as these. You require companionship, and I am happy to give it."

"Thank you, Miss Tilney," said Fanny. "You are very good."

Juliet put on a show of great courage as they went, pointing out interesting sights hither and yon, and in London there is no shortage of such sights to behold. She assumed that a divorced woman would live in greatly reduced circumstances, and thus was surprised when not twenty minutes' walk took them to the address they sought: a small house divided into apartments, certainly not so refined as the homes either the

Bertrams or Juliet and her mother had taken in London, but nonetheless respectable, even elegant.

One flight of stairs took them to the inner door, upon which the manservant knocked. When the door opened, no servant welcomed the visitors, as would have been expected—instead, there stood only a small child who stared up at them with large dark eyes. A little girl, Juliet thought, though the child was not old enough for sex to be readily apparent in person or in dress, perhaps no more than three.

"Whatever are you doing, Ellen?" The older woman who now appeared at the door yanked the girl back by her shoulder. "We are not to be opening the door to strangers—oh!"

Fanny had drawn herself upright. "Aunt Norris?"

"Where is Tom or Edmund?" Aunt Norris peered into the hallway, finding neither of the persons she sought and one she did not. "No other family has accompanied you, but you have made free to bring a girl who is certainly not of our acquaintance."

"Miss Tilney, this is my aunt Mrs. Norris." Fanny's voice was scarce more than a whisper. "Aunt Norris, this is Miss Juliet Tilney, a particular friend." This suggested a far greater degree of familiarity between herself and Juliet than existed, but Juliet supposed that the extraordinary nature of their mutual visit to Donwell Abbey had fostered as much intimacy as many particular friendships ever achieved.

"They have sent only you to attend upon us? After all I have done for my sister—I have been of use to her since the late lord's death, as well she knows—" On and on Mrs. Norris went, garrulous and ill-tempered, not even inviting them in. Such a display of rudeness could not be excused on any account . . . yet Juliet had begun to sense that these unkind words were, in part, intended to draw their attention away from the child, Ellen. For her part, Ellen gazed up at them with wide-eyed fascination, even as Mrs. Norris subtly pushed her farther back.

Why should she wish to hide the little girl? Juliet thought. Only then did she note how very much diminished in spirit Fanny Bertram had become—how pale, how very shocked she appeared! Juliet stifled a gasp as she realized Fanny had not known of this child's existence. Mrs. Norris's age meant she could not be the mother. This in turn meant—

"Well." Maria Rushworth finally appeared in the hallway. She hardly even glanced at little Ellen, though the child affectionately clutched at her skirts. "I suppose it is time the family learned that my marriage is not so dissolved as they might have believed."

Chapter Four

Gentlemen's clubs always wished to possess a certain mystique. Each was selective in its membership; each presented itself as superior in some quality or another, with the unspoken addendum that this quality was, of course, the most important to men of true discernment. Despite such claims, Jonathan Darcy had found that the clubs all diligently conformed to the same pattern: rooms for cards, a ready supply of spirits, the thick scent of cigar smoke, and—his one salvation—a library. Such libraries tended to be richer repositories of newspapers than of novels, but a few volumes of fiction and poetry were generally on offer, along with some histories; and these were Jonathan's greatest comfort when obliged to attend such a club, as he was that day with Sir Thomas and Edmund Bertram.

Wyngarde's was not the most elite gentlemen's club in London; that title could not be claimed without the patronage of royalty, none of which it presently counted among its membership. However, many of the most influential names in the city were to be found written in the guest book kept at the door, and Sir Thomas was proud to be among them. Edmund Bertram, though less impressed by such worldly concerns, had much acquaintance there.

Jonathan Darcy would so much rather have been visiting with Miss Tilney!—but as ladies and gentlemen must, at that hour, be made separate, Wyngarde's had to be borne. After enduring introductions and overly hearty greetings, he made his way to the small library. Here he found two of his favorite works of all time: Gibbon's masterwork, *History of the Decline and Fall of the Roman Empire,* and the novel *Ivanhoe,* reputed to be the work of Sir Walter Scott.

This was a conundrum indeed. Jonathan's interests tended to be few in number, but far more passionate in their temper than most persons felt for their pastimes. The Roman Empire, and Gibbon's work in particular, had gripped Jonathan's imagination for many years; this was one of the interests his parents had encouraged, as it was—if remarkably acute—entirely respectable and had led to his receiving excellent marks in Latin. His enthusiasm for historical novels, particularly Scott's adventures, had come much later. Jonathan had first taken them up only because he knew the books were favorites of Miss Tilney's, but by now his fascination with them had eclipsed even her own.

Such was the intensity of Jonathan's devotion to both interests that he found it difficult, nearly painful, to choose between the two. Miss Tilney's recent reappearance in his life decided the matter—*Ivanhoe* it should be. He took the first volume, settled himself into a chair, and hoped to devote himself to it until escape from Wyngarde's could be effected.

His host, Sir Thomas, stared as though his guest had gone quite mad—the baronet was evidently one of those persons who thinks of solitude only as a state to be escaped—but Edmund Bertram was of more sympathetic temperament. When Mr. Bertram took up a newspaper and sat nearby, Jonathan felt himself to be safe at last.

Yet safety proved elusive in London, for amid all the general conversation and clamor, while Jonathan was hardly more than a dozen pages in, Sir Thomas suddenly said—"Dear G-d, Edmund, you will scarce believe who it is."

Mr. Bertram looked toward his brother just as Jonathan looked toward Mr. Bertram, whose countenance paled. As Jonathan knew Mr. Bertram to be a calm, steady sort of man, he could not but be curious as to who could inspire such a reaction, and so his gaze followed Bertram's to a figure standing at the far end of the room, cigar in hand. This man, large of person, was perhaps thirty years of age; his clothes were those of the country squire rather than the London dandy. He had the complacent air of a man who worried about little, though perhaps more from lack of acumen than lack of cares. This complacent air shifted, however, as he saw the Bertram men, though what it changed into was difficult to discern.

"We must speak to Rushworth," Edmund Bertram said to his brother. "Though our families have been divided, he remains our neighbor, and as he was the one wronged—"

"Dash it all," said Sir Thomas. "Very well, let us go and have done with it."

They went to speak to Mr. Rushworth, leaving Jonathan alone with his book. This was precisely as he would have wished. Although he naturally felt some measure of curiosity about this Mr. Rushworth—no doubt the former husband of the Mrs. Rushworth he had previously met—this interest had no power over *Ivanhoe*. So Jonathan returned to his story, hearing little of what passed next, which he would have cause to regret in days to come.

How Juliet Tilney would have given thanks for the opportunity to lose herself in a book, to pay no heed to the uneasy persons surrounding her! She had no such fortune, however, remaining trapped in a chair in the drawing room of Mrs. Maria Rushworth, such as it was. The elegance of the building, and the relative respectability of the neighborhood, stood in contrast to the smallness of the apartments. Juliet discerned other contradictions as well: the good quality of the family's clothing, for instance, in apartments with no servant to attend them. In the absence of a nurserymaid, Maria was obliged to see to her own child in the back rooms, while Mrs. Norris made them welcome, or what with her had to pass for it.

"Stay where you are, by all means, stay, if I must have aught to do in the kitchen, at least I shall not be *seen* to do so," called Mrs. Norris, amid the clatter of saucers and spoons. "Mind you, we have a maid of all work, little use as she is, but she is gone to the dressmaker's to fetch Maria's new pelisse."

"Yes, Aunt Norris," said Fanny, in a tone that suggested long experience with her aunt's ill temper. Juliet remained silent.

Ellen came toddling back in then, her hair brushed into some semblance of order. Maria, coming behind her, said, "Fixing one's own hair is tedious, but doing another's is even worse. You will not know what it is to live without proper servants to help you, Fanny."

Poor Fanny! Her timidity would not allow her to protest that she had not had a maid of her own until she was nearly a married woman.

Mrs. Norris must have been eavesdropping as best she could from the kitchen, as she called out, "Indeed, you have never worked as we have to work, Fanny, never once. You have never been forced to make your own tea!"

"I am the one who must do all the baking," Maria snapped. "That girl we have is little enough use in a kitchen."

"I do what I can, as anyone will say who has witnessed how I work." Mrs. Norris emerged with an awkwardly laden tea tray; saucers outnumbered cups, and dinner knives had been proffered instead of ones meant for butter. "I hope no one will claim that I do less than my share, by you and by the child and even by my more fortunate sister. Forever am I looking for ways to be of better use to all, thinking nothing of myself."

Maria visibly restrained herself from speaking, but her countenance betrayed the anger she would not voice.

What a terrible scene! Juliet thought. *How I wish I had not come!* But she had done so, and thus there was nothing for it but to accept weak tea and a rock-hard biscuit, and to pretend each was delicious.

Fanny Bertram would normally have been in agonies to witness such as this, doubly so to have subjected it upon a guest from outside the family. As it was, however—yes, she suffered agonies, ones so terrible she was immune to any lesser pain.

Maria has been given a child, she thought. *Maria, who has been selfish and thoughtless—who has even been wicked—who abandoned the husband she had sworn before God to love, honor, and obey throughout their lives—to her, God has granted a child.*

When Fanny had married Edmund nearly seven years prior, she had greatly hoped for children, as many as God might send them. She was fond of little ones and had always doted upon her siblings despite their rowdiness. Her own childhood had been a lonely one, save for Edmund; the distinction drawn between herself and the other three Bertram children had led to her being treated as much like a servant as a member of the family. Many long afternoons had Fanny been obliged to while away hours on her own, and this she had sometimes done by envisioning the home and family she would have someday. Any baby would have been a gift to her; to bear her beloved Edmund's children was her most cherished dream. Every night since consenting to marry him, she had prayed on her knees to become a mother as soon as possible, to sons and daughters who would be healthy and cherished, and brought up to their Christian duty with the greatest love.

And yet years had come, and gone, and come again, without bringing any child.

Devout as she was, Fanny had refused to be discouraged. She had stood fast, serene in her hopes, content to wait for the Lord's plan. In the month of their fourth anniversary, doubt had briefly touched her: Was she failing to pray enough? Was she guilty of some unguessed sin that had turned the Lord's favor away? But this wavering she had not acknowledged, even to herself, beyond a few additional prayers.

Then, finally, not quite a year ago, she had her first hope. The months of uncertainty passed with excruciating slowness, Fanny hardly able to bear the suspense until at long last, she had felt the quickening that proclaimed a child was to come. All her life, the memory of Edmund's eyes as she had told him the good news would bring her to tears. How they had embraced! How fervently they had prayed in thanksgiving!

This glow of joy had borne her aloft every day of the next two months. Fanny had knitted booties and bonnets, and Edmund had brought a fine cradle from Mansfield Park to their little parsonage. Sometimes she felt as though she had not stopped smiling, even to sleep, until the day came when she was jarred by an odd and ominous pain. It would not have taken this pain long to frighten her, but it was swiftly superseded by agony—by dizziness and confusion—and by blood, by so much blood, more than she had thought a human body could hold.

The next few days had passed in a feverish blur. Fanny knew she was very ill; she knew that the physician had bled her; she knew that she might die. She had not cared, because she had also known that her baby was gone as though it had never been. Only Edmund's place at her side persuaded her to make any effort for her own life, and though she knew it to be sinful, sometimes Fanny wished that effort had not succeeded. Then perhaps she would have been united with her child in paradise.

One morning early in her convalescence—while she lay in bed, damp with the sweat of a broken fever, too weak even to sit up—she had heard Edmund speaking with the midwife in low tones, both of them believing her to be asleep. "Never?" Edmund had said, his grief piercing her own. "In your opinion, there is no hope at all?"

"None whatsoever," the midwife had replied. "In such cases as these, I have never seen another woman so much as quicken with child. It is just as well that Mrs. Bertram cannot conceive again, for the childbearing would no doubt prove fatal, and like as not kill the babe with her."

Fanny had heard this in silence, unable even to give voice to her sorrow by weeping. She had healed during the five months since then—the physical pain was gone—but she could not be fully present in her own mind or body. Edmund was so good to her, so kind, but she could scarcely face him, thinking that by marrying her he had lost his chance to be a father. Sometimes it seemed to Fanny that the world was no more than the empty place where her child ought to have been.

Then, in the days before the Bertrams set out for London, hope had returned.

It is but two weeks, Fanny reminded herself, over and over. *Two weeks means nothing.* How desperately we try to protect ourselves against hope, and how powerless we are to do so!

She did not fear for her own life, despite all the midwife's warnings. If she conceived a child when it had been said she could not, then the midwife would be proved wrong, and if she were wrong in one particular of Fanny's condition, she could be wrong in others.

Still it stung, to look upon Maria and know that God had rewarded a sinner with that which he had thus far denied to

Fanny and Edmund: a child Maria could scarcely be bothered to attend.

"And here is our pudding!" Mrs. Norris bustled in with a second tray, upon which sat a wide, rather flat cake. As little as Fanny liked her aunt Norris, her tender heart could not but feel sorry for the old woman, exiled from the beauties of Mansfield Park, reduced to doling out slices of cake to persons she cared little for. The server had a cloth wrapped around the handle, no doubt due to Aunt Norris's rheumatism (long complained of, but more recently genuine). Her apron showed signs of wear. Indeed, her aunt had come down in the world, all for the love of a niece who felt little love for her in return. The cake proved crumbly and dry, but both Fanny and Miss Tilney managed to praise its flavor without unduly abusing the truth. Afterward, few other topics of conversation suggested themselves.

"You bring no message from my brother?" Maria finally asked Fanny, when the pretense of a normal family tea could be sustained no longer. "You cannot invite me to the house in return?"

How Fanny blushed! "That is for Tom to say. The invitation must be his to make."

"If you are not his messenger, then you shall be mine," Maria snapped. "I have hidden long enough. There are worse sinners than I in London, and many of them are welcome in the finest households, at all public engagements. Why should I be set apart? Is it fair, is it just that women pay for their wrongdoing forever, while men are allowed to forget?"

Fanny saw the justice in this, but to her mind, the correction would be for men to bear the burden, too. Quite unable to speak such a thing in the face of Maria's anger, she said only, "I wish you happiness, Mrs. Rushworth, and I know Edmund does as well, but—"

Maria scoffed. "But you do not forgive? You do not wish me much happiness, then."

"The divide within the family is foolish," said Mrs. Norris, "imprudent, only calling attention to that which is better forgot, and no doubt the late Sir Thomas would have seen as much in time. If Tom does not yet, mark my words, he shall. He shall see it yet."

"He hopes to marry soon," Fanny finally confessed. "A young woman from an upstanding family—to remind them of the scandal in our past—all might be lost."

"So *that* is his business in town! Well, he must hope the girl is not fainthearted, or that her parents desire his title enough to forget all else." Maria's satisfaction was such that Fanny knew she had erred, revealing too much. "I have come to London for the season, and I intend to enjoy myself, with or without the embrace of my family."

Mrs. Norris, as though insensible to the implied threat, smiled. "Would anyone like more cake?"

Miss Tilney spoke then for the first time in many minutes. "I do believe my mother will return to the Bertrams' to fetch me shortly. We must trespass upon your goodwill no longer."

The escape, however bluntly phrased, could not have been more welcome to Fanny. Niceties were spoken without sincerity, and at last, they could depart.

Yet as they prepared to make their leave, collecting their bonnets and cloaks at the door, Fanny caught sight of a walking stick propped in the corner, one of shining burl wood with a distinctive handle in the shape of a rabbit's head. She had seen such a stick before, many years ago; so much had she liked the rabbit's head that it had always lingered in her memory.

Henry Crawford had owned such a stick. It could, in fact, have been the very same one.

Had Fanny considered the matter, she would have realized that Maria and Aunt Norris must have been as glad to see her go as she had been to leave.

Maria and her aunt were united in their feeling that to have Fanny visit with a stranger was worse than no visit at all, but they were both industrious creators of strife, inventing reasons for arguments when none readily presented themselves, and on this occasion they did not fail. Maria thought it most foolish of Mrs. Norris to have served tea and cake, which revealed their tasks in the kitchen. For her part, Mrs. Norris had been very proud of this improvisation, feeling that it created the illusion of a grander home, and did not take kindly to the criticism.

Neither mentioned the true reason they were each in such ill temper: that they had each spent the entire visit worried that Fanny would not take herself away again before the owner of the walking stick returned to retrieve it.

Juliet Tilney's discomfort during that visit would never be forgotten, but her confusion, at least, could be remedied, as indeed it was upon their return to the Bertrams' residence. Susan Price had returned from her visit with the Worthingtons, and while Mrs. Fanny Bertram engaged with Lady Bertram, the opportunity came for Juliet's enlightenment.

"You see," Miss Price whispered, "during Mrs. Rushworth's engagement to Mr. Rushworth, she developed a great passion for a Mr. Henry Crawford, who led her on with much flattery—so Fanny has told me, and my sister is very truthful—but the Rushworths wed regardless. Then Mr. Crawford fell in love with Fanny herself and asked for her hand! She refused him, but everyone urged her to reconsider, even Edmund."

Juliet would not have imagined so docile and soft-spoken a creature as Fanny Bertram at the center of a romantic drama. "You mean, Mr. Bertram? Her husband?"

"Indeed—he thought it would be a fine thing for her to be married well. Mr. Crawford is a man of property, you know. Besides, at that time, Edmund was not yet in love with Fanny. He instead paid court to Mr. Crawford's sister, Mary."

"Good heavens," said Juliet, glancing about the room to make sure they were not being overheard. She need not have worried: The others present were all engaged in their own occupations—Lady Bertram wondering how on earth she could have spent ten pounds without even knowing it, Fanny nodding and murmuring without really attending, apparently much consumed by a private matter of her own.

Susan continued. "Mr. Crawford even came to Portsmouth to see Fanny—I met him then and quite liked him. He showed real kindness to us all, and behaved as a true gentleman. Even I thought Fanny ought to consider the match. But then Maria ran away from her husband with Mr. Crawford. Eloped, without a thought of what it would mean for her family! Miss Mary Crawford thought it should simply be hushed up, Mr. Crawford wed to Fanny after all, as though nothing were wrong in their actions. This, I understand, is why Edmund fell out of love with Miss Crawford. As for Maria, Mr. Rushworth divorced her, of course. And yet, from what you tell me, it seems that they remain connected . . ."

"Indeed," said Juliet. As young unmarried women, she and Miss Price could discuss no further the matter of Mrs. Rushworth's child. Yet such discussion was unnecessary. The age of little Ellen, contrasted with the time of the Rushworths' divorce, told all there was to tell. Juliet had known another young woman who had given birth out of wedlock—Miss

Elizabeth Williams of Devonshire, who had fallen prey to the seducer Willoughby—and the only escape from her ruination had been to move to Scotland with her child and change their names. That, perhaps, was worse than Mrs. Rushworth's situation; here, the parents had at least been husband and wife at one time, and in the minds of many, divorce was a legal fiction that could not truly sever a union sealed with vows before God at the altar.

Could a remarriage undo some of the shame? Could such a child be legitimized after the fact? Juliet burned to know, but to Miss Price, she could say not a word—and of course Miss Price would have no more idea than Juliet herself.

At Wyngarde's, the Bertram men came to sit near Jonathan Darcy again. As Jonathan was deeply engrossed in *Ivanhoe* at that time, his first impression was of disappointment that they had come to talk to him, which would interrupt one of his favorite scenes, the tournament where Ivanhoe competed under a secret identity and humiliated the Norman villain. When they did not interrupt, he then felt some slight surprise that Sir Thomas would be interested in reading. Nearly a full minute had passed before he realized they were murmuring quietly between themselves, using the library merely as a place of discretion amid a noisy gentlemen's club.

"—his congeniality, given the event, was striking," Edmund Bertram was saying. "So much so that I think there must be more to this than what he has said."

Sir Thomas chuckled. "Mark my words, they will remarry."

"I am not so sure of that, Tom," Mr. Bertram replied. "If that were to be, surely the event would already have taken place."

But Sir Thomas was not to be denied his anticipation. "I

have little doubt it will come to pass! Now, should we luncheon here? There is no call for us yet to return home."

Jonathan felt strong concern that this hour at Wyngarde's might yet turn into a day at Wyngarde's, and therefore a day without the company of Miss Tilney. Mr. Bertram was his savior. "I think not. I wish to hear Fanny's account of her visit to Maria—more, even, than I did before. From this I believe we will learn much."

Indeed, Fanny Bertram was eager to speak to her husband, considering it a matter of the greatest discretion and urgency. Until he returned, what she now knew must fester within her, anguish demanding release. Nor was any occupation available to her beyond listening to Lady Bertram's musings about money she had or had not spent; this, at least, required no more from her than nodding and the occasional yes or no. When she vaguely recalled Miss Tilney's presence, and her sister's, she saw them speaking to each other and felt they were occupied enough with themselves to make her conversation unnecessary.

At last entered Edmund, Tom, and Mr. Darcy, back from their club. Happy greetings were exchanged between many—sad though she was, Fanny did not miss the joy of Mr. Darcy and Miss Tilney upon meeting—but she could scarce speak. Edmund, recognizing this, took her elbow and led her inside, farther down the hall. "Whatever is the matter?" said he. "Was Maria unkind? Or Aunt Norris?"

That, Fanny had scarcely noticed. "It is much worse, Edmund, so very much worse."

She told him, then, of the child that Maria had borne and had hidden from the family—of her claim to have resumed at least one aspect of her marriage with Mr. Rushworth. Edmund, though very much struck, attempted to find some measure of optimism. "We saw Rushworth at our club, and he was congenial, very much so. Now all is explained."

"He spoke of Mrs. Rushworth openly?"

"No, no, not in public, of course. But he was warm toward us, toward our family, to an extent I would previously have deemed impossible. Tom predicted a remarriage, and I thought him foolish for doing so—but it appears he understood the matter more rightly than I did. If Rushworth cares for Maria enough for this, if the child is recognized by him, then there is hope, Fanny. That which he might not accept for Maria's sake, he might endure gladly for the sake of a daughter. Were Rushworth to take Maria back and marry her again . . . the scandal would remain but must inevitably be lessened. Not everyone would presume to take offense after Mr. Rushworth's forgiveness."

"But he should not forgive, for I have not told you the worst part," said Fanny. "I saw a walking stick in their home, one I remembered. I—I believe it was the one owned by Henry Crawford."

This dealt Edmund yet another blow, but he rallied again. "Nonsense. Even Maria could not be so reckless as that, and her affection for Crawford curdled into contempt long ago. One walking stick is very like another, you know."

Fanny knew now that she must say the worst, the very worst. "The little girl—it was clear to me from the moment I saw her—oh, Edmund. She . . ." The words would not leave her mouth. To speak such a shameful thing aloud!—she could not bear it.

Her dear Edmund understood her well enough to interpret her silence, and to help her past its boundaries. "You are not doing wrong in telling me, Fanny. You are no gossip.

Whatever this is, you judge it to be important, and I trust your judgment."

Finally, mustering her courage, Fanny managed to say, "Edmund . . . the little girl looks like the Crawfords. Like Henry Crawford, who is surely her father."

Chapter Five

It would not be correct to say that Mr. Jonathan Darcy and Miss Juliet Tilney were oblivious to the complicated family situations that laced through every room, every conversation, in the Bertrams' London residence. Such degrees of consternation, anger, sorrow, and avid interest could not be ignored, even by two young persons so taken with each other as Jonathan and Miss Tilney were. Each noted Fanny's low spirits, Edmund's displeasure, and Sir Thomas's uncharacteristic silence (which descended after a brief, quiet word from his younger brother). Only Lady Bertram and Susan appeared unaffected. This was primarily because Lady Bertram absorbed so little information, and because it would take more than a scandalous cousin to dampen the enthusiasm of a young girl visiting London for the first time.

Jonathan understood all this, but cared nothing for it. At last he had full leisure to speak with Miss Tilney again!

"How long will you stay in the city?" Miss Tilney asked. How eager she seemed, how pleased with his presence—Jonathan hoped greatly that he interpreted her manner correctly, for it was most encouraging. "We are here for six weeks, which seems quite a long time, but it seems to me one could live one's entire lifetime in London and never see all there is to be seen."

Before last night, Jonathan had been calculating just how brief a time he could stay in London without either offending the Bertrams or being disobedient to his father. Now, however, despite all the great city's attendant discomforts, he had no difficulty saying, "I shall remain as long as the Bertrams care to have me. How long that may be, only they can tell. But I believe they do not plan to return to Northamptonshire and Mansfield Park within six weeks' time."

"How very wonderful!" Miss Tilney's pleasure in his company, though delightful for Jonathan to witness, was less precious to him than what she said next, "Are you quite sure you can endure it, Mr. Darcy? I know that noise and disruption are unpleasant to you, and London has no shortage of either."

How well Miss Tilney understood him! Jonathan felt the strong urge to rock back and forth—normally a means of soothing himself, but also, sometimes, an expression of joyous energy. Had he been alone with Miss Tilney, he would have indulged this desire, trusting in her calm acceptance. As the Bertrams surrounded them, however, he managed to restrain himself. "No, Miss Tilney, London is not my favorite place to stay—but how can I leave, when there is such company to be had?"

How beautiful her smile could be! Looking upon it, Jonathan felt encouraged as never before.

Six weeks, he thought. Much could be accomplished in six weeks. He had heard of engagements that had unfolded in only six weeks' total acquaintance, though mostly when his mother clucked over the imprudence of such haste. Yet he and Miss Tilney had now known each other for almost three years. If he paid court to her in the proper sense, away from any investigations that might trouble his father . . .

I will court Miss Tilney, Jonathan decided. *I will pay open court to her, so that anyone can see. The Bertrams will help us, I am sure, and I will attempt to win Mrs. Tilney's approval. In three weeks, or a month, a letter to Pemberley will state all my wishes. My parents will give their consent, and then I may ask.*

This plan of action sounded more artless than it was.

Jonathan would of course ask his parents' permission before proposing . . . but if he did so after weeks of public pursuit, during which expectations would naturally be raised, the Darcys would find it more difficult to refuse. If Jonathan were considered to be a flirt, or inconstant, or the sort of man who toyed with a young woman's feelings and respectability—that would not do at all. It was dishonorable to raise the expectation of marriage in a young woman and then fail to propose to her. His parents would not see him so shamed in London society. (He perhaps put too much faith in this last article of belief, but the hopes of a young man in love are not easily thwarted.)

Miss Tilney's thoughts, if not so ambitious as his, must have taken a similar bent, for she said, "Tomorrow night Mamma and I are to attend a concert at the Argyll Rooms— some beautiful Italian music, I understand. You enjoy music also, Mr. Darcy, so I am sure you would wish to know."

"We shall obtain tickets for the concert at once," said Jonathan, before realizing his duty to his hosts. "That is, if the company will consent to join me, and will accept their tickets as my gifts of gratitude for welcoming me in London."

"A concert!" Miss Price nearly bounced in her seat with excitement. "Say that we can, Sir Thomas!"

Sir Thomas, still overcome with his own concerns, heard enough to say, "Of course, of course."

"Should I go to the concert?" Lady Bertram seemed to be asking her pug, which cocked its head as if attempting to determine the answer. "I do not like to go out, and yet I do like music. It is so difficult to decide."

Jonathan knew only that at least one of his hosts intended to join him, which gave him the freedom to attend the concert, to speak again with Mrs. Tilney, and to spend another hour with the girl he hoped to marry.

The aforementioned concert was to be one of the highlights of the season, sure to be attended by a great many. One of these persons proved to be Mr. Rushworth—Edmund Bertram's erstwhile brother-in-law—as Edmund discovered when he went to Mr. Rushworth's town house early that evening. He went without Tom; the need was for deeper conversation, not the easy platitudes his elder brother might have relied upon. The existence of the girl named Ellen complicated all, and called for a further reckoning and resolution of the previous wounds.

Edmund had thought raising this subject might prove awkward, only because he had failed to recall Mr. Rushworth's placid temperament.

"It is such a very difficult thing, to be divorced," Mr. Rushworth said as they sat together in his fine London home, one that fully proclaimed his family wealth. (This would have been rented at his mother's insistence rather than his own; though Rushworth had his faults, pretension was not among them.) "The law says one is free, and one wishes to be free, but whenever I see Maria, I cannot but think of her as my wife."

Edmund did not consider divorce acceptable even in the few instances the law allowed, but he saw no point in that discussion so long after the fact. "Your feelings are understandable, Mr. Rushworth, and do you much credit. But if you seek out my sister's company—"

"I do not. It is Maria who seeks me. I make up my mind that we will not see each other again"—Mr. Rushworth shrugged, as though he were helpless as an infant—"but then she arrives, and it is as though I cannot remember we were ever apart. She is very sorry for what happened, you know. She no longer has the slightest connection to that Crawford rascal. He is a very bad sort, I am sure, the kind of man who takes pleasure in turning a woman's head."

"On that point, we entirely agree," said Edmund. He had once been taken in by Henry Crawford, as had they all, and what a price had been paid! "Yet I am forced to ask you, Mr. Rushworth—if these are your feelings for Maria, why do you not remarry? The alternative is sin, and potential disgrace."

Mr. Rushworth's ruddy face went an even deeper red. "My mother will not have it. Besides, few in society would receive us then. I would be obliged to go about without Maria, just as I do now, so what would be the change?"

"Do not consider what the change would be to you, Mr. Rushworth. Consider what it would be to your daughter."

Edmund had not forgotten Fanny's conjecture as to Ellen's paternity, but as yet he put little faith in it. Surely all congress between Maria and Crawford was long ended. Mr. Rushworth believed himself the father, as became apparent when he smiled fondly. "Ellen is a fine little girl, is she not?"

"I have yet to meet her," Edmund said, "for Maria hid this from her family until now. But I do not doubt what you say is true. Why then do you condemn her to illegitimacy and its attendant social degradation? Were you to remarry . . . Ellen would not be legitimized, but the scandal would be greatly lessened, and with a proper dowry, she could still marry respectably."

Mr. Rushworth appeared quite miserable. "I have asked my mother, and she insists I shall not."

"Your mother is a formidable woman, but she must not govern you in this matter."

Edmund did not particularly like urging Rushworth in this direction. The match between him and Maria had been a poor one from the start. It could perhaps be possible that the child Maria had borne was not Rushworth's own. A remarriage under such circumstances would not be a union of true intimacy and honor. However, Edmund still judged this better than the current state of affairs, which involved sin for both parties and a more difficult path for an innocent child.

"My mother can govern almost anyone given the chance," said Mr. Rushworth. "Let me talk with her again—I will write and ask her to come to London—but in a few days' time, for tomorrow is the servants' day off, and I cannot have her arrive when they are to be gone, can I?"

"Speak it over with her," Edmund said, with no great hope. "I shall speak with Maria tomorrow. Perhaps we can both talk to Sir Thomas on the matter tonight."

Would his brother agree to some manner of financial settlement upon Maria, were she to wed Rushworth a second time? Highly uncertain, and unorthodox—but with Tom's own matrimonial hopes, he might consider it worth nearly any price to remove this blot from the Bertram family honor.

Also among those greatly anticipating the concert that evening were the Allerdyce family, in particular Mrs. Allerdyce. Naturally she was glad for the chance to bring her elder daughter Frederica together with Sir Thomas Bertram again, even though at this point she felt his proposal must be inevitable—a matter of weeks, if not days. Yet her greatest hopes were for Priscilla, her younger daughter, to be brought closer to Mr. Jonathan Darcy.

Many years ago, her elder brother, Charles, had become good friends with Mr. Fitzwilliam Darcy, the master of Pemberley. Caroline knew of Darcy's great house and of his great fortune; she found his person pleasing: What more was there to ask in a potential husband? She had set out to win him with the usual tricks, attention and flattery, confident that these—

when combined with her own ample dowry and considerable beauty—would bring him to heel in short order.

She had, however, misjudged Fitzwilliam Darcy. Caroline still could not fathom what had instead drawn him to Elizabeth Bennet, of all persons: an impertinent girl with uncouth relations and hardly any dowry to speak of. Yet drawn he had been, and Caroline was in time obliged to pay off every arrear of civility to the new Mrs. Darcy.

Galling though this defeat had been, Caroline had not been deeply wounded by it. Her interest in Darcy had been almost entirely mercenary; her heart had not been touched. As soon as the banns for the Darcy marriage were first read, she had set out to find another suitor of similar wealth and distinction. This had arrived the very next season in the person of Mr. Allerdyce. His estate, if not so renowned as Pemberley, was still sufficiently grand; his wealth was considerable; his charm was easy; his face was handsome. Best of all, he had proved easy to enchant.

Thus Caroline had chosen him for her husband and accepted his proposal without a single thought upon his character, which by pure happenstance proved to be excellent. Mr. Allerdyce was an intelligent, broad-minded sort of man who enjoyed conversation; she had found herself obliged to read the newspapers in order to keep up with him. He was an eager host, forever inviting others to their estate for balls, dinners, and picnics; and in these matters he always thought first of his guests' comfort rather than the opportunity for display—this, too, Caroline learned to consider. Over time, she acquired knowledge of current events, even well-formed opinions of her own. She also developed a taste for company that valued camaraderie and cordiality beyond gossip or fashion. Caroline's cleverness had never been turned to higher purpose before, but she found she rather enjoyed the life she led with Mr. Allerdyce, and preferred the friends they had made together to the company of her small-minded sister. Once, on a trip to London when the children were small, the Allerdyces had even invited the Darcys to dinner—a merry meal where Caroline and Mrs. Darcy had spoken so long, and with such mutual enjoyment, that both women spent a long hour that night in their respective beds, unable to sleep, wondering whether they had remembered each other wrongly.

But as Jonathan Darcy aged toward eligibility, and as Caroline's younger daughter Priscilla began to bloom into great beauty, old ambitions began to revive. If she herself was never to reign as mistress of Pemberley, why should her daughter not do so? Her former mercenary instincts returned, disguised as maternal concern. It was her duty to encourage the best possible match for Priscilla, was it not? The discovery that Jonathan Darcy was the guest of Sir Thomas Bertram— Frederica's suitor—was so advantageous that Caroline came near seeing it as fate.

So when Sir Thomas had sent the invitation to join them at the concert that evening, Caroline had hastily canceled their other dinner plans and encouraged the girls to wear more jewelry—and was standing between them, delighted that their gowns were the finest among the assembly, when the Bertrams' party entered. Sir Thomas saw Frederica immediately and hurried toward them, which was excellent . . . but Jonathan Darcy did not accompany him. Instead, he was making his way through the crowd to two women, seemingly a mother and daughter. The mutual pleasure young Darcy and this girl took in meeting was evident, even from across the room. Nor did the mother appear to discourage this acquaintance—hardly surprising. When presented with such a potential suitor for her daughter, what mother would not act?

And when presented with such competition for *her* daughter, how could Caroline Allerdyce not begin to scheme?

Meanwhile, Miss Tilney was at that moment attempting to show her mother and Jonathan Darcy how very much they had in common—a somewhat difficult task, as they were in fact very different sorts of people, but in such circumstances, ingenuity overflows. "Is it not excellent that we all prefer Italian music?" Miss Tilney said. "So many prefer the Germans, but as you have said, Mamma, it is Italy where true musical beauty is to be found, and Mr. Darcy quite agrees."

"A gentleman of taste, then," said Mrs. Tilney. Jonathan could not but be pleased, both by this civility and Miss Tilney's evident relief to hear it. They might have been less fretful had they known that nothing either could say mattered to this loving mother more than the tenderness with which Mr. Darcy gazed at her daughter.

Jonathan helped shepherd the Tilney ladies through the crowd toward the Bertram party. Candlelight blazed from hundreds of tapers; more than one fashionable woman was obliged to take care with the tall feathers in their hair. He was glad to see that Miss Tilney and her mother dressed more sensibly and were safe.

Yet safety proved elusive, for amid all the general conversation and clamor, just as they reached the Bertram party, Sir Thomas suddenly said—"Dear G-d, Edmund, you will scarce believe who it is."

Mr. Bertram looked toward his brother just as Jonathan looked toward Mr. Bertram, whose countenance paled. As Jonathan knew Mr. Bertram to be a calm, steady sort of man, he could not but be curious as to who could inspire such a reaction, and so his gaze followed Bertram's to a figure who had entered the concert hall. This unknown gentleman was perhaps Mr. Bertram's age or slightly younger, dark and not very tall, dressed in what Jonathan vaguely knew to be fash-

ionable colors—blue jacket, cream waistcoat, and the like—
and he carried a handsome burl-wood walking stick. At first
this person seemed rather plain, but then he smiled, and the
animation quite transformed his appearance for the better.

Yet the stranger's happy appearance dimmed as he recognized the Bertram party. Nonetheless this person stepped
forward to present himself to them all, putting on a show of
amiable politeness. "It is Sir Thomas now, is it not? My sym-
pathies for the loss of your father."

"Thank you," said Sir Thomas, rather stiffly.

Jonathan exchanged glances with Miss Tilney—most persons addressed in such a tone would have known to excuse
themselves immediately—but the newcomer did not. "I had
heard you were coming to London, and with your family,
I see."

Sir Thomas seemed at a loss for further words, but Mr.
Bertram was not. "Mr. Crawford. I can well imagine from
whom you heard of our coming to London, though we were
not informed of your arrival. Had we been, our visit might
well have been postponed."

"Come, Mr. Bertram." Mr. Crawford's smile might well
have looked genuine to anyone who stood too far away to
overhear the words. "There is no need for incivility. We were
nearly brothers, were we not? But instead, the girl I once
wished to marry is *your* wife"—this was accompanied by a nod
in the direction of Fanny Bertram, who either did not hear
or pretended not to—"while my sister, Mary's, broken heart
took some time to heal."

Sir Thomas had found his tongue. "Of *our* sister, you dare
not speak."

This apparently was true, for Mr. Crawford continued:
"I suppose you will be relieved, Mr. Bertram, to know that
Mary is betrothed at last; I have come with her to London

so that she can assemble her trousseau. She is to wed in six weeks' time."

Mr. Bertram pressed his lips together in a thin line, then said only, "I wish her joy. But you must appreciate that all connection between our families has come to an end."

Evidently this amused Mr. Crawford. "Not every member of your family agrees on that point, Mr. Bertram."

Jonathan saw Edmund Bertram's face pale and wondered why—until he glimpsed who had next entered the room: Mr. Rushworth, who stared at Mr. Crawford with more indignation than even the most histrionic Banquo could have shown toward Macbeth.

Mrs. Rushworth's two lovers have met, he realized, *and Mr. Rushworth has only just learned that he still has a rival.*

Juliet learned of Mr. Rushworth's identity from Mr. Darcy's whisper, but she felt she would have gathered as much within moments, for he was too outraged by Mr. Crawford's appearance to remain discreet. His voice was sufficiently raised as to be notable even amid the murmurings of the crowd. "Of all the cheek," blustered Rushworth, his face flushed red, "to present one's self in public without a thought of the shame!"

"There is no reason why I should not go where I will, nor any households where I will not be accepted as a guest, save perhaps Bertram's here," said Crawford.

"Please," Edmund Bertram interjected, "think of where you are. You can have nothing to say here that cannot be said elsewhere."

"I have no need to meet with this gentleman again," said Mr. Rushworth, "nor can any other person sufficiently acquainted with him."

Mr. Crawford's smile was crooked and illegible. "I believe we both know a lady who would not say the same."

The impudence of this remark made Juliet gasp. Mr. Rushworth's mouth gaped, too astonished for outrage. Luckily, Sir Thomas then stepped forward, swiftly coming to Rushworth's side and guiding him away, speaking of who knew what. Mr. Bertram and Mr. Crawford exchanged glances of mutual distaste before separating.

"How very astonishing," said Juliet. "To be so overcome in public! I little wonder that Mr. Bertram dislikes Mr. Crawford, for even apart from his former wrongdoing, he is so very indelicate."

They might have gone on to discuss the matter at more length, even beyond propriety, had the musicians not emerged and a scramble for seats begun. Mr. Darcy sat next to Juliet, which gave her a chance to translate for him, a delight that blotted lesser concerns from her mind.

The next day, Jonathan would have liked to spend peacefully at the town house—partly to recuperate from the strain of socializing in such a large crowd, partly for the chance to remember Miss Tilney whispering the English translations of various love songs into his ear. Yet peace was far from the Bertram household at present, and it was unlikely to return soon. At breakfast, they were visited by a Mrs. Norris—sister to Lady Bertram, and apparently sharing a household with Mrs. Rushworth and her illegitimate daughter.

"I do not mind it," said Mrs. Norris. "Indeed, of all things I should least mind is the chance to be of service, whether to my sister or my niece or to any person, but I cannot see why we must discuss family matters before strangers. That, I do not see at all."

This was directed toward Jonathan himself. He had no appetite for such family matters, but he did want his breakfast. Before he could suggest having the meal sent up to his room on a tray, Edmund Bertram interjected, "The unfortunate Mr. Darcy has already learned all our secrets whether he wished to or not, and I rather think he did not. There can be no more need for silence on that score."

Jonathan resigned himself to listening, in consolation for which he helped himself to more coffee. How he envied Sir Thomas, who had left the house too early that morning to be trapped! The others who had descended for breakfast—Edmund Bertram and his mother—would have to engage in all conversation with their aunt. He must take this as a lesson in human nature.

Mr. Bertram continued. "Never once did you or Maria allude to the child's existence. Not once, in either conversation or letter."

Lady Bertram looked up from her tea. "Am I a grandmother, then? I am sure that cannot be right. Perhaps it does not count where the child is not . . ." Her voice trailed off, though none could say whether it was from uncertainty or simply having lost her train of thought.

"I said as much to Maria! Many times I said, We must let them know at Mansfield, they will want to know of Ellen at once," Mrs. Norris insisted. "She would not have it said, but her hesitation came from the best, most decent cause. Do you know why I believe her to have held back? She wished to resolve matters with Mr. Rushworth. She wished to have him acknowledge Ellen as his own, to have arrangements properly made for the child, perhaps even for them to remarry. Then she could have come to you with all made right again."

"None of this can be made right," said Mr. Bertram, "but it can perhaps be made better. Had Maria told us, we might have been in a position to aid in this endeavor. Yet the presence of

Mr. Crawford threatens even these fragile hopes. How long has Mr. Crawford continued to visit Maria? Does he still do so?"

Mrs. Norris looked uncharacteristically uncertain. "There are times I think he will not prove so unworthy as we once thought him, for he is very fond of Maria, very fond indeed. Yet he is inconstant; and, say what I might of it, Maria does not listen to me. Better by far that she should remarry Mr. Rushworth, do not you agree? They were such a perfect match—what a shame that Mr. Crawford persuaded her to something so very wrong!"

"The perfection of the match, I will not presume to speak upon," Edmund said. "But if a remarriage is possible—yes, we must hope for it, for however wretched it might prove to be, it would remain superior to any alternative available to us. Perhaps Tom could encourage the matter. Well, first, let me talk again with Rushworth. We must ascertain what he makes of last night's meeting with Mr. Crawford before we can determine anything else."

What Edmund meant by this was clear to all and would be spoken by none: Did Mr. Rushworth now suspect that Ellen was not his child—that Mr. Crawford was her father? If so, no remarriage would be possible. They had no chance at all of convincing Crawford to marry Maria Rushworth, for if he were so inclined, the event would have taken place years ago. Maria's confidence in reaching out to the Bertrams again must have been couched in her faith of persuading Mr. Rushworth to marry her once more; if the unfortunate meeting with Mr. Crawford had undone this, she had no prospects left at all. Nor had little Ellen.

So it was that after breakfast Edmund Bertram set out for Mr. Rushworth's house, determined to establish what was believed and desired by him and, if possible, to encourage them to the best possible conclusion. When he came to this house, he found the front door ajar: a curious matter, though one he attributed to the absence of the servants. Perhaps, as they left for their one free day of the month, they had in their jubilation neglected to close the door behind them. Greatly negligent, yes—the sort of thing that would never occur at Mansfield—but not impossible with such a master as Rushworth, Edmund supposed. This conjecture endured until he entered the sitting room and found Mr. Rushworth lying on the floor, quite dead.

Chapter Six

So swiftly did the errand boy arrive with Edmund Bertram's note that Jonathan Darcy reached the late Mr. Rushworth's house only very shortly after the policemen came. A few passersby had congregated upon the walk, but Jonathan was able to sidestep them. As he moved to enter, one lone constable moved to object, but Mr. Bertram called out, "That is Mr. Darcy—I requested his presence here—let him pass."

Jonathan's first thought—partly born of unworthy motives—was a hope that Mr. Bertram had similarly summoned Miss Tilney to the investigation. However, as he stepped into the sitting room, he beheld a sight so ghastly that he would forever be grateful that Miss Tilney had not been forced to witness it: Mr. Rushworth, sprawled upon the floor in a most ungainly fashion, legs bent but torso flat on the floor, his face mottled, eyes bulging and glassy. Worst of all, his tongue protruded from his mouth in a manner Jonathan associated with slaughtered pigs.

"It is terrible, I know," said Mr. Bertram, "and I thank you for your willingness to endure such a scene as this."

"You think it to be murder?" Jonathan asked.

Mr. Bertram stared. "Already you have seen the signs?"

His host must be in shock to have asked such a question. Jonathan replied gently, "If you believed Mr. Rushworth to have died of natural causes, you would not have summoned me."

The policeman standing nearest—who appeared to be in charge—nodded as he said, "The signs are here to be seen, if you but look." He nudged Mr. Rushworth's body to one side, revealing a wide, dark-red band appearing at the front of Mr. Rushworth's throat, very nearly reaching ear to ear. "That is proof of strangulation, mark my words, but I cannot say how he was strangled."

"What do you mean?" Jonathan had not yet encountered a case of strangulation; of this, he had much to learn. (This avid curiosity might have appeared ghoulish to any observer unaware of Jonathan's history of investigating murders; though the sight of a corpse still shook him, he had acquired experience enough not to lose his composure.)

"When a person has been strangled, the means of strangulation show up differently upon the skin," said the policeman. "If the strangler used his hands, the bruises take the shape of finger marks. After a criminal is hanged, the bruise looks more like what we have here—but from a hanging, you can make out the marks of the twined rope upon the dead man's skin. This is smooth as anything. Wide, too. Never seen the like."

The commotion outside became louder. Jonathan glanced beyond the sitting room door to note that some of the curious onlookers had now entered the house, and they were no doubt growing in number. It would not be long before the scene was entirely overrun. "Can we not keep them away, Mister—?"

"I am called Frost," said the policeman, "and we cannot keep them back for long. They know now it is murder, and the murder of a gentleman at that. Soon they will begin taking souvenirs, cutting up the curtains and rugs, picking up knickknacks and the like. There is no stopping a London crowd when they hear tell of a murder."

Mr. Bertram, perhaps realizing that their time to speak in confidence was much limited, took the opportunity of explaining. "Mr. Darcy has, in the past, had occasion to look into the circumstances behind two murders—"

"And some attempted murders," Jonathan interjected.

It was important to be thorough. "All with the help of Miss Juliet Tilney, who is herself in town and would no doubt be willing to provide her assistance."

"Mr. Darcy and Miss Tilney are friends of our family, a gentleman and a lady, and capable of both discretion and insight," Mr. Bertram continued. "Our family was previously connected to Mr. Rushworth's through marriage, and their assistance in this matter would be greatly welcome to us, in particular to Sir Thomas."

Jonathan expected Mr. Frost to object, and in truth was unsure whether his objections could be overcome. In the matter of the attempted murder of his great-aunt, discretion had been called for, and no crime had yet been committed; as for the slayings of Mr. Wickham and Mrs. Willoughby, the proper local authorities had been either unavailable or over-whelmed. This could not hold true for the police in London, he felt certain, and probably they would not be eager to accept the counsel of amateurs.

Yet he had underestimated the power of the mere men-tion of a baronet like Sir Thomas Bertram. Frost surprised Jonathan by answering, "That would be for the best, sir. We have workers rioting in the East End, and our numbers are stretched thin. No one was seen running from the house; the servants are all out—though there, at least, we might speak to the last one out the door. Yet it appears nothing has been stolen, so what would motivate either servant or thief? My guess is it is a madman, no more or less than that, and deuced hard to find. If you can turn up more, we shall be glad to hear of it."

The onlookers had now begun pushing their way toward the door of the sitting room. Soon the noise would become overpowering to Jonathan, but he was determined to stand his ground for at least a few minutes more.

Frost gestured toward one of his underlings and added,

"Toss a tablecloth or something over him, will you? We shall haul him out presently."

"This is a very sad end for Mr. Rushworth," said Edmund Bertram, with real feeling, as Mr. Frost moved away to direct his men's efforts. "Despite the breach between our families, I never thought ill of his character."

Someone, it appeared, had very violently disagreed. Jonathan might have said so, had a voice not rung out amid the clamor: "Mr. Bertram? Mr. Darcy?" It was none other than Miss Tilney, already making her way through the throng toward them.

Jonathan glanced toward Mr. Bertram, who said, "I took the liberty of informing the Tilneys of this at the same time I summoned you. Was I right to do so?"

"Very much so, sir."

"This inquiry surely will touch upon matters no gentleman can discuss with a lady not of his own family," said Bertram. "We are fortunate to have a lady on hand who may pose such questions."

"Precisely so." Jonathan took note of this reasoning, the better to use it himself later, if future murders came their way. Unlikely, one would think—but he had already resolved never to rule out the chance of homicide on one of his travels again.

How little had Juliet Tilney guessed, when the visitor's bell rang, that another investigation was soon to begin! Instead of callers who had left a card, they had been visited by an errand boy summoning her. Her mother had of course come with her and was much taken aback by the frenzy. "Upon my word," said Catherine Tilney, "I have read of the crowds that assemble at the scenes of crimes in London, but never did I imagine them such a mob as this."

Juliet had never seen such a thing either, but she was determined to appear very worldly and unbothered, for surely that was the properest way for an experienced investigator to behave. "We must get in somehow—oh!" The policemen were carrying a heavy, tablecloth-wrapped burden, evidently the body of the late Mr. Rushworth, toward their wagon. Murmurs rose to a greater pitch. "I do wish I could have seen how things were at the place the crime was committed."

Before her mother could respond to this unfamiliar wish, Mr. Darcy appeared in the doorway. When their eyes met—

How extraordinary, the ability to communicate so much without any words, within an instant! They shared their joy in seeing each other, their eagerness to begin their shared work, even their measure of guilt in feeling happiness caused by a murder. Juliet swiftly straightened her bonnet as Mr. Darcy made his way toward her.

"Mrs. Tilney," he said, properly greeting her mother first. "Miss Tilney. We have been called upon yet again, and this time, even the police wish for our assistance."

Juliet found this unexpectedly gratifying. "Then by all means, let us do all that we may. I wish of course always to be of service to our dear friends the Bertrams, and it seems that our experience is especially called for at present. Tell me, Mr. Darcy, what did you see inside?"

She listened closely to his description of the room and of the pitiful state of the body. One point struck her with particular force: that Mr. Rushworth had been strangled by means unknown. Before she could ask more, her mother interjected, "This is most improper—most inappropriate for the hearing of a young woman."

Catherine Tilney had not been present during any of their earlier efforts. Her objections would have to be handled with great care. "Mamma," Juliet began, "please consider that

I have witnessed far worse than this, both in Surrey and in Devonshire. It is not nearly so difficult to hear of such a thing as it is to see it, I assure you."

Her mother did not appear to be persuaded. "It does not follow that you should then be exposed to all manner of cruelty and violence forever after."

Juliet decided against all lesser protests and instead spoke what she knew would be her strongest argument: "Do you not always say that we should take every possible opportunity to learn of the depth and variety of human nature? I submit to you that the investigation of murder is unusually rich in that regard."

Still, Catherine Tilney hesitated, but even that pause told Juliet the matter was as good as decided. She and Mr. Darcy would have one more opportunity to identify a killer.

In truth, Catherine's objections to her daughter's involvement in this business were not so mollified as Juliet believed. However, if the police themselves believed Juliet might be of use, then Catherine felt she should allow as much. She inwardly decided that, should this investigation become too gruesome altogether, permission could be rescinded. In the meantime, let her daughter provide what assistance she could.

Catherine also realized that this would give her the best possible chance of observing her daughter and Mr. Darcy together in the same context that her husband had during their visit to Rosings Park. Perhaps then she could understand the nature of his objections to the match—comprehend his reasons for believing that the young Mr. Darcy had no true feeling for their daughter. Her own observations suggested quite the opposite conclusion.

Might it be that Mr. Darcy becomes brusque during their investigations? That he orders Juliet about like some sort of servant? Catherine did not consider this very likely, as Juliet would not be drawn to such a person—but what was more likely, she could not guess. She trusted her husband's fairness and judgment deeply enough to believe that he must have a meaningful reason for believing that Mr. Darcy and their daughter would not be a good match.

But even her dear Henry could be wrong.

Juliet was unable to have her own look around Mr. Rushworth's house until the mob was done with its search for morbid souvenirs. By the time Mr. Darcy could escort her in, the curtains, rugs, and upholstery had all been cut and torn to shreds. The crowd had known better than to take anything of actual value while the police were on the scene, but they had nonetheless turned a gentleman's home into a mere battered shell of the same. What troubled Juliet the most was the potential loss of useful clues. "Oh, why do the police allow entrance to all and sundry? Do they not recognize how very disruptive this must be to any investigation?"

"To judge by the counsel of Mr. Frost," said Mr. Darcy, referring to the police officer she had briefly glimpsed as he left the scene, "the London police believe that every murder is solved by finding a witness to identify someone running away from the scene of its commission. There is no such witness at present, and I hope they shall not attempt to create one."

Juliet knew well that sometimes the need to find a person to blame for a murder resulted in the arrest of someone besides the actual murderer. "Show me where he lay?"

Mr. Darcy gestured toward a spot on the floor of the sitting room. A high-backed chair nearby stood at an awkward angle—crooked, and not very far from the wall, not a place that any genteel person would place this article of furniture.

Juliet turned to Mr. Darcy, whose observation and memory for detail was excellent. "Did the mob move this chair, or is this where it sat?"

He answered with confidence. "It has not been moved, or if so, not even an inch."

"You say that he was strangled?" she asked, stepping behind the chair. "If Mr. Rushworth had been seated here, someone could have come up behind him, and the chair would have made it more difficult for him to reach back and struggle against his attacker."

"Well spotted, Miss Tilney." Mr. Darcy inclined his head, a small nod of respect. "Mr. Rushworth was a large man, not athletic I believe, but certainly strong. The use of the chair may well have been critical to the killer's success."

Pleased with her deduction, Juliet continued. "You said also that they did not know what was used in the strangulation?"

"Indeed. Mr. Frost felt certain that Mr. Rushworth's murderer did not use bare hands, but what fashion of garrote was employed remains a mystery. It was at least two inches wide, and uncommonly smooth—unlike a rope, he said, though he did not know what it *was* like."

Once again, she looked around the room in dismay. "It might have been a drapery sash. Or some other tool or implement left in the house, now taken away by the mob. How are we ever to know?"

"That, I cannot say." Yet Mr. Darcy remained determined. "However, as we know from past experience, it matters less what tool was used in the killing. Far more important is the question of who used it."

The London papers, ever eager for gore and the resultant sales, rushed out their afternoon editions. SLAYING IN MAY-FAIR! Thus did the public discover of Mr. Rushworth's death. For those more intimately connected to the family, the information arrived in other ways.

Edmund Bertram went back to his family's town house and broke the news as gently as he could. Fanny very nearly fainted; Tom had spoken profane oaths aloud; Susan had instantly decided that London was filled with murderers and that they should return to Mansfield Park this very instant. The only person to receive the word of Mr. Rushworth's death calmly was Edmund's mother, who did not know whether or not to be dismayed unless Tom or Edmund specifically instructed her to be so. As Pug remained untroubled, so, too, did she.

His second duty had been to inform Mr. Rushworth's poor mother as swiftly and mercifully as possible. Edmund wrote to her with the most delicate version of the truth, omitting the pitiful spectacle of her son's earthly remains, and assurances that an investigation had already begun and the killer would surely be brought swiftly to justice. He also omitted the information that the two main investigators were young persons not associated with the police, as he understood Mrs. Rushworth would not be so comforted by that knowledge. Edmund would have time to inform her of that after the killer was caught.

Finally, he took himself to the lodgings Maria and Mrs. Norris had rented. Edmund had always intended to come here, to meet Ellen—the child did not deserve the same opprobrium as the parents, after all—but how little had he expected he would arrive there with such news as this!

When he shared the information, Mrs. Norris was immediately overcome, simultaneously declaring that none could imagine all the wickedness of London and yet that she had warned all and sundry that a visit to the city would do no good, that it was dangerous to every person whether high or low. Maria paled and clutched Ellen close, as though for comfort. Was this evidence that she had, in fact, cared for her former husband to a degree? Maybe even that she had sincerely intended to reunite with him? Edmund did not know whether to hope for this or not; his disgraced sister surely had enough to endure without grief added to that measure.

As for young Ellen, she wept, knowing only that there was trouble and that it had come very close to her indeed.

The next day, as early as etiquette allowed, Jonathan Darcy arrived at the London dwelling of the Tilney ladies. Although it was not so elegant a home as the one the Bertrams had taken in the city—nor comparable to the one rented by Jonathan's own family on their recent visit to London—it was genteel, in a fine part of town, and furnished in the best taste. To his dismay, Jonathan realized he was surprised by this; the invective of his great-aunt, Lady Catherine de Bourgh, had suggested that the Tilney family was not at all well-to-do, and his own judgment on the matter had proved regrettably easy to influence. Even if Miss Tilney did not come from such comfortable circumstances as his own, she clearly came from a family of distinction and property.

This makes my father's dislike of the match all the more shortsighted, Jonathan decided, though his assessment of the elder Mr. Darcy's objections was perhaps not as clear as he believed.

Both ladies received him, but Mrs. Tilney intelligently took herself to a corner of the sitting room to work at her desk while the two young investigators began their work—chaperoned, yet with some measure of privacy.

Miss Tilney had already taken from her mother a sheet of paper, an inkwell, and a quill. "I am sure you will agree there is only one way to begin, Mr. Darcy."

"By enumerating our suspects," he said, and was rewarded with her smile. When she tilted the page toward him, he saw that she had prepared it before his arrival with the following title:

Those Who Must Be Questioned in the Death of Mr. Rushworth

"First, it seems to me, must come that Mr. Crawford from the concert," Miss Tilney said. "The animosity between them was very great, and—if I have understood correctly—it was Mr. Crawford who persuaded the late Mr. Rushworth's wife to leave him."

"Yes," Jonathan replied, "and secondly, we must consider her. Mrs. Rushworth must have had some grievance against her husband to leave him, must she not?"

"Her motive for *that* may have been no more than a matter of a passion for Mr. Crawford," Miss Tilney said. "Still, the existence of some such grievance cannot be ruled out. Also . . . perhaps you know this, from your place in the Bertrams' household . . . but Mrs. Rushworth bore a child after her divorce." Her cheeks were burning bright red now, but she seemed determined to continue. "She insisted the child was Mr. Rushworth's, but—"

Her voice failed her. Jonathan supplied the rest. "You mean to say there are those who believe Mr. Crawford to be her natural father?" Miss Tilney, much relieved not to have to say as much aloud, nodded. He continued: "Yet Mrs. Rushworth evidently wished others to believe otherwise, including the late Mr. Rushworth."

"If Mr. Rushworth challenged that point, whatever measure of support he had given to the child might have ended," Miss Tilney said. "Yet surely that support ends with his death as well, and that must be considered a mark against Mrs. Rushworth's guilt. Still—she must be on this list."

A new possibility came to Jonathan then, but he hesitated before voicing it; it was not a point on which he wished to speak if there were not good reason to do so. Yet he decided that such reason existed. "I believe we also need to consider Sir Thomas Bertram himself."

"Sir Thomas? But why?"

"If Mr. Rushworth were to repudiate his paternity in some way that made the child publicly known, the disgrace Mrs. Rushworth has already brought upon the family would be greatly increased. Sir Thomas hopes to marry soon."

Miss Tilney considered this. "I see the truth of what you say, and yet, without some other reason to think of Sir Thomas, it hardly seems enough on its own. The Bertram family has not been socially excluded because of Mrs. Rushworth's actions, and I am not at all sure the revelation of the child's existence would change that."

Jonathan came out with the rest. "I speak of it because Sir Thomas was mysteriously absent for the majority of the day yesterday, and not very forthcoming about his whereabouts when he did return home. Nor did he evince much surprise when Mr. Bertram told him of the murder. This he accounted to the shoutings of the newsboys—to have heard of it before—but nonetheless, it struck me."

"We will find out where he was yesterday; and if that does not settle the matter, we will ask further questions." Miss Tilney wrote down Sir Thomas's name with an appropriately aristocratic flourish. "The same motives would apply to Mr. and Mrs. Bertram, and it was Mr. Bertram who came upon the body, but I cannot see either of them as likely candidates for such an action."

"Nor I," Jonathan agreed. "Mr. Bertram would bear any shame, I think, rather than compound it with further wrongdoing. Mrs. Bertram is of similarly fine character, and beyond that, surely she is too frail to have strangled Mr. Rushworth. Come to think of it, could even Mrs. Rushworth have managed it?"

"Possibly so. Women are not so weak as men often believe, and—I have been thinking about the placement of that chair." Miss Tilney rose, then pushed her own chair near the wall, much like the one that had been left in Mr. Rushworth's home. "Come sit here, Mr. Darcy."

Jonathan willingly did so. He wondered whether it would be improper for her hands to touch him if this were done strictly as a matter of inquiry into the murder. Probably not. Yet he could hope. His usual disquiet at being unexpectedly touched was entirely absent, a point Jonathan would not have the presence of mind to wonder at until much later in the day.

Miss Tilney did not touch him, however. Instead, she took the drapery tie loose, wrapped the gold cord around her hands, then lowered its length to his throat. (From the corner, Mrs. Tilney took note but did not interrupt.) "You see, Mr. Darcy, were I to pull this tightly against you, and then to wedge myself against the wall—between the wall and the chair, I mean, and bracing my arms against the chairback, thus using the weight of my person rather than brute strength to provide the necessary force—you would be unable to reach me or to pull forward the cord. I would not need to be stronger than the person I attacked; merely strong enough to hold this position. The victim's own weight would keep the chair in place. Do you see?"

"I believe that I do," said Jonathan, glancing down at the cord. "My objection to Mrs. Bertram as a suspect remains, but as for Mrs. Rushworth . . . indeed, she cannot be excluded."

"Three suspects, then." Miss Tilney let the cord drop and busied herself straightening the curtain once more. "If Mr. Bertram will help arrange for us to speak to them all, then our investigation can begin in earnest."

Though Jonathan Darcy and Juliet Tilney little knew it, the question of motive to kill Mr. Rushworth was at that very hour evolving rapidly. Mr. Rushworth's solicitor in London, who was already preparing himself for the messy business of probate and estate, had summoned Sir Thomas Bertram and his brother to the office.

"You must understand," said the solicitor, "that I advised Mr. Rushworth against this step, but he was quite determined. Then, yesterday morning, he sent to me a note indicating that he would perhaps alter his will again. I had intended to call upon him in the afternoon, but when I came, the mob was at work and Mr. Rushworth was no more—"

"What action do you mean?" Mr. Bertram asked. "What about his will?"

The solicitor held out the page for their perusal. "Some months prior, Mr. Rushworth had recognized Ellen Rushworth as his child and heir."

Sir Thomas frowned. "Illegitimate children cannot inherit."

"They cannot inherit *entailed property*," the solicitor corrected him. "As it happens, very little of Mr. Rushworth's estate was entailed. The child comes into a fortune of more than ten thousand a year—which, of course, until the age of majority, will be under the control of her mother."

"Maria," whispered Edmund Bertram, suspicion dark and cold within his chest.

Chapter Seven

Even amid the deepest and most sincere grief, there is often a strong curiosity about the contents of a will. Avarice can strike like a viper, even within otherwise benevolent hearts. Yet the desire for money is not always mere greed, where such money may make the difference between a sizable dowry and a nonexistent one—between remaining in one's comfortable home and being forced to rely upon the charity of friends and relations—in short, between gentility and poverty. Beyond all material considerations, there is also the natural wish to know that one we loved thought of us before taking their leave of this Earth.

And where the contents of a will are surprising, even shocking, the news of those contents will spread with remarkable speed. This Edmund Bertram knew, but he still judged it best not to leave the discovery of Mr. Rushworth's will to chance and so informed Jonathan Darcy and Miss Tilney at once.

"You can imagine our surprise," Mr. Bertram said as he sat in the small room of their London town house that had been designated as a study. Jonathan sat before him, with Miss Tilney by his side. It was but the day after Mr. Rushworth's death. "Few parents are as generous to their natural children. Yet as Mr. Rushworth had no other issue, no siblings, and a mother already well provided for by an ample jointure, I expect he felt that the little girl was the only person in need of his fortune."

Miss Tilney glanced at Jonathan; he could guess which question she wanted to ask. The clue was in her silence, for any matter less improper, she would have spoken of herself.

"Forgive my saying so, Mr. Bertram," Jonathan began, "but I must say that the contents of Mr. Rushworth's will are testimony to his sincere belief that—that he was indeed Ellen's father."

Mr. Bertram flushed, evidently displeased, but his reply was all politeness: "You allude, I suppose, to Mr. Henry Crawford. My wife has told me of her suspicions, and Fanny is the last creature on Earth to gossip maliciously. However, I cannot think so ill of Maria as that. She has paid so dear a price for her folly that it seems impossible she should compound it. Also—Maria can be a proud creature. Her current financial insecurity cannot be easy for her to bear. It was Mr. Crawford whose machinations reduced her to that state, and it has been my understanding that her anger toward Crawford was very great. Can it follow, then, that she would retain any fondness for him?"

"We can all forgive much from those with power over our hearts," said Miss Tilney, "but your argument is well made."

Jonathan, thorough as ever, stayed true to the central point. "Mr. Bertram, you also indicated that Mr. Rushworth was soon to change his will, according to his solicitor. Do you know the nature of the change he meant to enact?"

Mr. Bertram shook his head. "It may have had nothing whatsoever to do with the child. A bequest to a trusted servant, perhaps, or a life interest in a cottage near Sotherton for his mother."

"Of course," said Miss Tilney. "We cannot truly know."

After the conversation with Mr. Bertram, Miss Tilney suggested that Jonathan might see her back to her home. He felt a moment's hesitation—the London streets were so very loud, so very disorderly!—and yet, were they to order a carriage for Miss Tilney, eyebrows might be raised at their being alone together within. The opportunity for private conversation was too valuable to be missed, regardless of the discomfort.

Gratifyingly, Miss Tilney had considered his difficulties. "You are very good to endure this, Mr. Darcy," she said as they set out on the streets. So much shouting—so many whinnies and snorts—Jonathan fixed on her alone with all his determination. "As inconvenient as it is to be in different houses while conducting our investigation, at least we can be in public together without any fear of impropriety. One cannot be truly alone in London without determined effort."

"I hope I shall become accustomed to it," said Jonathan, with more ambition than assurance. Best to turn his mind to the investigation, which could absorb him beyond most distraction. "You and I are, I suspect, in agreement—the first, likeliest suspect can only be Mrs. Maria Rushworth."

Miss Tilney nodded. "She has by far the most to gain, assuming that she knew of the contents of Mr. Rushworth's will . . . and I believe her very likely to have known them, or at least suspected. Mrs. Rushworth would have urged him to provide for their child, and surely he would not have concealed from her that he intended to do so."

Jonathan had had but the most passing acquaintance with Mr. Rushworth, but he tended to agree. The dead man's character had been open and artless, almost to a fault. His generosity toward the little girl indicated a strong sense of responsibility, perhaps even fondness. No, he would not have hidden the truth from Maria Rushworth. "I agree. Mrs. Rushworth has benefited too richly from this murder for us not to speak to her first of all."

Juliet said goodbye to Mr. Darcy on her doorstep before hurrying inside, alight with the glow of fascination. (This inner illumination was mostly for the thrill of the investigation, though Jonathan Darcy would have been pleased to discover he was responsible for a considerable share.) She delivered her heavy cloak and gloves to the maid before searching for her mother, ready to share all.

However, Mrs. Tilney was at that moment working on a draft, and those who interrupt productive writers do so at their peril. "This is all quite interesting, I am sure, but—Juliet—remember that we are here on your grandfather's charity, and obliged to serve his purposes. He wishes you to take part fully in the London season, and I must see that you do it."

This could hardly be borne. "Mamma!" Juliet protested. "You do not think so much of such vanities—such trivialities—I know you do not."

"No, indeed." Resigned to a longer conversation, Mrs. Tilney set aside her quill and ink with a sigh. "Of course I am interested in your investigations, and I recognize that they serve the cause of justice. Far more entertaining to discuss them than the latest style of bonnets and gloves, to be sure! Never would I discourage you. All I am saying is that you must find a middle path, a way to do all that must be done in the matter of Mr. Rushworth's death without neglecting all that must be done for your debut, or else we will have to explain to General Tilney."

Juliet's paternal grandfather was a cold, prideful, fearsome man. Odd, she thought, that he should be the one in the family most interested in her dresses and dances—but so it was, and her mother was correct to remind her. "Very well, Mamma. What must we now do?"

"We must be seen at more of the season's events," said Mrs. Tilney. "The concert was a good beginning, but our attendance there should be but one of many such examples. We should go to assemblies, to plays—so long as they are worthy—

and to exhibitions. There is an art show that many have spoken of; apparently it is quite the thing to go."

None of this was displeasing to Juliet in the slightest, so long as these requirements could be balanced with the investigation. She also glimpsed certain highly inviting possibilities. "We would not be wrong in inviting the Bertrams' household to join us for some of these occasions, would we?"

Mrs. Tilney, though far from joining her husband's dislike of a potential match between Juliet and Mr. Jonathan Darcy, knew better than to count chickens before their hatching. "We should broaden our acquaintance as much as possible, Juliet . . . but, yes, we can invite them occasionally. In fact, I believe we should send a note requesting their company this afternoon."

"So soon?" Juliet could scarcely contain her enthusiasm. "Is it an assembly? A lecture?"

"Shopping for bonnets," said Mrs. Tilney. "I suspect only Mrs. Bertram and Miss Price will be interested. Lady Bertram no doubt likes a nice bonnet, but I do not think she would exert herself to obtain another. For that matter, I am not at all certain she would exert herself to depart the building were it aflame."

This excluded Mr. Darcy, and as such was disappointing. But Juliet knew that this next pause in their meetings served a purpose: Mr. Darcy would speak to Mr. Bertram or Sir Thomas, possibly both, about obtaining permission for the two of them to ask questions of Mrs. Maria Rushworth. Tomorrow or the next day, they would have their best opportunity to learn more about their primary suspect in the murder.

As long as the investigation was properly underway—as long as it had not been compromised by any lesser concerns—Juliet was not too high-minded to be glad of a new bonnet.

Far from any thoughts of bonnets was Fanny Bertram. She sat in the sitting room, ostensibly listening to her younger sister's merry chatter about balls and clothes—and that of her aunt Bertram, who hardly knew what to make of it all but was sure that whatever had been done before was right, and so should be replicated as closely as possible. Fanny nodded where she should nod, and agreed where it was wished that she should agree, but she scarce heard a word of it.

When her dear Edmund joined their group, she felt a small frisson of relief. He would know better than to ask more than this of her; Edmund had ever been Fanny's consoler, her protector. To him and him alone, she could speak the complete truth, and this she longed to do as almost never before.

In Edmund's wisdom, he let both Susan and Aunt Bertram say their piece before he drew Fanny aside. They had their privacy in the study, the very chance she had wished for, and yet it was difficult for her to speak.

"Come, Fanny," said Edmund. "You are much troubled—it is writ upon your face—so come out with it. Surely you will feel better once you do."

Fanny was not as certain of this, but she was at last ready to speak. "I cannot reconcile it, Edmund."

"What is it you cannot reconcile? The fate of Mr. Rushworth? Though he was not without his faults, I must confess, nothing in him seemed to merit such a poor end as this."

Poor Fanny, who felt so guilty for not thinking of Mr. Rushworth, murdered and not yet cold in his grave! "That is not what troubles me. It is that . . . that . . . that Maria has been granted a child, while you and I have not been."

She did not feel better for having spoken, for how painful it was to see Edmund's face crumple—to see his faith in the Lord shook. "That is a hard burden to bear, Fanny. But the birth of a child is not a mark of God's favor, for if it were, the happiest and most faithful families would always be the largest, and the unhappiest and least pious would ever be the smallest. It does not require a long tenure in the parish to recognize that this is not so."

Fanny understood the truth of this, and yet it did not wholly answer. Edmund had given her the reply of a clergyman—not that of a man who had learned he might never be a father.

Should she tell him of her hope? It had been nearly three weeks now—yet Fanny knew better than to speak. This must remain her secret alone, unless and until she again felt the quickening in her womb.

One other thing, she wondered whether she should tell him: that she had indeed recognized Henry Crawford's walking stick at Maria's home, for she had spied it again in Mr. Crawford's hand the night of the concert. Not only was Maria still meeting Crawford, but they had done so very recently indeed. At the present, though, such knowledge could only wound Edmund and would illuminate nothing. Let the shame and the hope both be locked deep within her— she would bear anything rather than cause her husband pain.

We often welcome that which calls us from difficult conversations, and so it was with Fanny that day, when the invitation from the Tilneys arrived. Little as she thought of fashion, she was grateful for distraction, and she was affectionate enough a sister to take pleasure in the delight Susan had in this summons.

"Should I go as well?" Aunt Bertram said, once again addressing herself more to Pug than to any person present. "I cannot but think that I have as many bonnets as I shall ever have need of again, but who is to say but that there might not be another? And how should I know ere I see it? But then I shall have to leave the house, and that seems so very burdensome. Do not you think it burdensome, Fanny?"

Drawing Aunt Bertram from the house was an endeavor not to be undertaken lightly, as Fanny well knew. "Very burdensome, Aunt. You should stay here rather than trouble yourself."

"I agree." Aunt Bertram smiled, slow and lazy as a cat. "I quite agree. You are grown so clever, Fanny, I declare I should hardly have known you."

This was not entirely flattering, but Fanny put little faith in her aunt's opinions, and she was one of the only persons who put any faith in them at all.

Within the hour, she and Susan had set off for the milliner's, where they were met by the Tilney women. The purpose of the day's quest, it seemed, was to find the best bonnets in which to be seen while driving or walking in one of London's fashionable parks. One might have expected Fanny to be made happy by the prospect of spending more time out of doors, for she loved to be surrounded by green growing things and took her best comfort pottering about in the parsonage garden or walking along the neighboring fields. To her, however, turning such a simple, wholesome pleasure into one of society's styles felt callow, almost blasphemous. Fanny comforted herself with the knowledge that no number of onlookers could take away her personal enjoyments in a park. Also it was good to see Susan so merry, chattering brightly with the Tilneys as they examined the newer styles, which frothed with lace.

Then Fanny heard a familiar voice say, "A wider brim, I think—and pleated, perhaps?" She turned to find that her memory had not deceived her, for she was now once again face-to-face with Mary Crawford.

Although Mary had reached the age of seven or eight and twenty, she still possessed all the rosy bloom she had during the time Fanny had last known her. Her dark eyes remained bright; her deep brown curls cascaded down each side of her face in the newest style. Her colorful clothes would have looked garish to Fanny, had not her brief stay in London already taught her that more vivid shades were increasingly in fashion.

Mary's eyes widened, and then, to Fanny's consternation, her face split into a broad smile. "Fanny! Dear Fanny! I had thought I should never see you again."

"Hello, Miss Crawford." Fanny could hardly think what to say. She was aware of having drawn Miss Tilney's attention— not that the girl was eavesdropping, but the shop was not large and anything spoken within it would be heard by most all others. "I hope that you are well."

"So very well. I am to be married next month to Bishop Braddock, so, you see, I will wed a clergyman after all. No prognosticator am I!"

What man of the cloth could have believed Miss Crawford to be an appropriate choice for a clergyman's wife? How could she be so lighthearted in her references to the past? Fanny could hardly imagine, and yet she was grateful for it, because the alternative must have been coldness and anger.

"And I hear that you became Edmund's wife in time." Miss Crawford folded Fanny's hands within her own, her warmth apparent despite the gloves they both wore. "Please know that I wish you both joy from the very bottom of my heart."

This was generous, and Fanny felt the old echoes of friendship that had, from time to time, become genuine between herself and Mary Crawford.

Always she had resented Miss Crawford's hold on Edmund's heart, particularly her use of wit and charm to blind him to the deficits in her character. Even to this day, after several happy years of marriage to Edmund, Fanny still wondered if he missed Mary Crawford's vivacity. But from the first, Fanny had been conscious that Miss Crawford's interest in Edmund was a reflection of the better part of her character, that her company could be amusing, and that she had been solicitous of Fanny's comfort and happiness at a time when few others cared.

Miss Crawford continued. "They say that a marriage between cousins is the curse of an unhappy family and the blessing of a happy one. Indeed I do hope that the Bertrams are all very happy and well." This betrayed a blithe indifference to Maria Rushworth's general circumstances—and to the role Mary's brother, Henry, played in them—but the good wishes appeared sincere. "To remain forever always within one's own family, to never be called upon to adapt to a strange home and strange ways—it is a comfort to many, I am sure, but particularly to you, Fanny, to whom familiarity is so dear. That it has been so for Edmund, too . . . Again, I am glad, glad with my whole heart that you both have each other and shall never again be lonely."

This was spoken in both confidence and utter sincerity, for Mary Crawford believed that Edmund, having declined to marry her for love, had married Fanny for comfort. This could not have wounded Fanny but for the fact that she sometimes thought so, too.

She managed to say, "I wish you joy as well, Miss Crawford."

"You are so very kind." Mary Crawford leaned closer, dropping her voice, though not enough for her words to go unheard. "Allow me to say that I believe the most foolish mistake my dear brother ever made was faltering in his courtship of *you*. His feelings *there* were far worthier, and he ought to have held true to them. To have thrown away a chance at your heart for such an idle fancy as—well, there is no point in speaking of it. Still I wish that fate might have made us sisters! As it is, know that I have a sister's love for you and ever shall."

These last words, pronounced with great feeling, could not but have the most powerful effect on a heart as tender as

Fanny's was. For a brief time, all Mary's shortcomings were forgotten. Fanny did not remember those shortcomings until after Miss Crawford's departure, when she realized she would need to speak to Edmund of this meeting . . . and that she did not know what he would say, less what he might feel.

The next day, Jonathan Darcy heard the report of this meeting from the lips of Miss Tilney as the two of them walked toward the less fashionable neighborhood where Maria Rushworth lived with her aunt and child. "I hope that I am not become a mere gossip," Miss Tilney said, "but given Mr. Crawford's connection with Mrs. Rushworth, it seems best that we know as much about their shared past as we can."

"You are entirely right, and you are no gossip," said Jonathan, all the while stifling some curiosity about the implied closeness between the upright clergyman Edmund Bertram and someone as lively and pert as Miss Mary Crawford sounded. Perhaps he was becoming the gossip. He reminded himself that, from Miss Tilney's description, this Miss Crawford seemed content with her situation and well disposed toward both the Bertrams, which made her utterly implausible as a suspect, and therefore must exclude this lady from further inquiry.

Miss Tilney's thoughts might have been very like his own, for she added, "I noted that Miss Crawford seemed wholly unaware of Mr. Rushworth's unpleasant fate, which may count against the guilt of her brother. Even if Mr. Crawford had not confessed to his sister, would she not have discerned his unease or unhappiness? Might they not have discussed Mr. Rushworth's death, even in the abstract?"

"Quite possibly," said Jonathan. "One wonders how anyone

could remain unaware after the stir in the papers." Newsboys had been baying the news of the murder, often described in gory detail even uglier than the truth.

"Before our stay in London, I, too, would have wondered," Miss Tilney said. "Now, however—it seems to me that in this city, one is surrounded by outrage upon outrage, crime upon crime. It is no miracle that a person might not hear of any one crime, and it would be unbearable punishment to have to hear of them all."

Jonathan felt heartened to hear her pronounce such a judgment upon London. She had seemed altogether too fond of such a loud place, one to which he could never fully accustom himself. All his focus upon the crime at hand could not make him forget that he wished to pay court to her, and thus it was good to know that asking her to regularly forgo London would not be too great a punishment.

"We are here," Miss Tilney continued, stopping short as Mrs. Rushworth's door stood before them. "Come, Mr. Darcy. Let us see if we can catch our next murderer."

Chapter Eight

We are exhorted to offer friendly hospitality to all visitors, but Mrs. Maria Rushworth and her aunt Norris cannot be blamed for their mixed feelings upon this particular call. How can one be delighted to face a person who wishes to find a murderer, and believes you a likely candidate? Even the innocent are likely to feel some dread, whereas one can only imagine the agonies the guilty must suffer upon such an occasion.

Juliet Tilney did not know which of those two possibilities was at work on that day, but she could sense the unease of their hosts. Having been to the modest town house before, she directed her attention to Mr. Darcy, watching him both adapt to the unfamiliar environment and evaluate those who greeted them. The garrulous Mrs. Norris, of course, was very nearly the only person who spoke, as she rarely paused to give anyone else the opportunity and, when such opportunities arose, disregarded them by not heeding what had been said.

"It is all very shocking, very wicked, to be sure," Mrs. Norris said as she bustled about the room, attempting to do as much as she might have done in larger and grander surroundings. Maria sat quietly, embroidery hoop and needle in her hands, in the genteel pretense that she had no more work to do. Mrs. Norris was not so skilled in this form of performance and could only suggest activity through motion. "Mr. Rushworth ought not to have been so rash regarding our dear Maria— there, he did wrong, but I blame his mother for it, as she was inclined to interfere and Mr. Rushworth was so obliging to her, as indeed he was to most. Rash as he may have been, however, he never judged Maria so harshly as did many others, and I believe that they would have been married again in time, and that would have set all aright. Indeed, it would all have been as it should have remained from the start."

Juliet suspected that Mr. Rushworth might have been outraged by Maria on his own behalf rather than his mother's, but it could not be denied that the dead man must have retained a deep fondness for his former wife. Otherwise, he could not have believed himself to be the father of Maria's daughter, Ellen, who currently occupied herself on the floor with bright wooden blocks.

Yet—to judge by the countenance of Maria Rushworth— that fondness had not been returned. No trace of grief was to be detected there, no redness of eye, no paleness, no evidence of even one shed tear. Juliet was wise enough to know that everyone mourns differently . . . and also wise enough to know that Maria did not mourn Mr. Rushworth at all.

"Thank you for agreeing to see us, Mrs. Rushworth," said Mr. Darcy. "You understand that we must ask questions of many, and that we do not single you out in this way."

"Yet already you have come to my door." But Maria controlled her temper. "You may proceed."

"If you keep a civil tongue in your head, mind, and I doubt that you will," interjected Mrs. Norris. "Of all the impudence! The police to need the help of those such as you! It makes one wonder what the nation is coming to, and though Edmund may have asked for you, he cannot have thought what it would mean, how rude it would be to his sister to subject her to such."

Juliet and Mr. Darcy exchanged concerned glances. If Mrs. Norris continued in this vein—and she seemed capable of doing so for quite some time—they would never get even one complete answer from Maria Rushworth.

Surprisingly, it was Maria herself who came to their rescue. "Aunt Norris, I believe Ellen has need of a walk outside. The city is so unwholesome for children, but at least the park is not terribly far."

Mrs. Norris took this hint with no good grace. "I do not see why I am the properest person for such an errand, with my old bones and my rheumatism, but with these visitors here I suppose there is nothing for it, and let it not be said that I do not always look for a chance to help whoever I can, in any way possible. Indeed, I believe no one does say so, and if they do, they speak with no justice." She continued in similar fashion until she and Ellen walked out the door, and for all Juliet knew, considerably beyond it, as Mrs. Norris's conversation did not appear to require another participant.

Once the door had shut, and the shrill tone of Mrs. Norris's voice had faded, Mr. Darcy begin again. "First of all, we must ask where you were on the day and at the time that Mr. Rushworth was murdered."

Maria answered without hesitation. "I had gone to attend the art show in town. It is quite the thing, you know, where one wishes to see and be seen."

Juliet noted that this interest in the art show did not seem to extend to the art. That, however, was surely not an uncommon attitude among London society. "Which were your favorite paintings, Mrs. Rushworth?"

"Oh, lots of mossy green landscapes," said Maria dismissively. "I liked those well enough. Several interesting portraits of gentlemen and ladies, including some at whose identity we are obliged to guess."

Pictures such as those, Juliet knew, would be found at any art show. "None stood out to you in particular?"

"One painting upon a mythological theme," Maria replied. "It stood out not for its quality but for the shocking nature of the scene. Of course, one recognizes that certain liberties are allowed in the portrayal of the human form, particularly as regards the mythological and ancient; but, upon my word, that picture would have shocked Venus herself! You will forgive me if I do not elaborate."

Mr. Darcy had heard rumors of this scandalous painting; it was quite the talk of London. Admittedly he could not but be curious as to the particulars, but this could not be asked of a lady, and furthermore was beside the point. Instead, he said, "Were you aware of the provisions of Mr. Rushworth's will that named your daughter, Ellen, as his primary heir?"

"Not in any detail, of course, but naturally he had assured me that he would do his very best for her, and I am pleased to know that he was true to his promise," Maria replied so blithely that Juliet immediately felt certain that Maria Rushworth had known every word of that last will and testament. Perhaps she had even dictated it.

And yet, this could not at all be said to constitute guilt. The fact that Mr. Rushworth's death had been convenient to his former wife did not mean said former wife had brought his death to pass.

Mr. Darcy next asked, "Mrs. Rushworth, if you were to guess who might have murdered your former husband, whom would you name?"

It was a very daring question, though one to which Juliet expected a humdrum answer: a burglar, a madman, perhaps one to whom Mr. Rushworth had owed a gambling debt. But Maria surprised her. "Do not think me without proper family feeling, but in honesty, I must say . . . you should speak more with Mrs. Norris."

Juliet could not conceal her wonder. "Mrs. Norris? Why should she wish Mr. Rushworth dead? Particularly when she so hoped for a renewal of your marital union."

"So she has always said, but of late it must have become clear to her that Mr. Rushworth would never again ask for my hand." Maria's shoulders slumped, the first time during their questioning that her hauteur had faded. "Mrs. Norris shares my exile with me, willingly but not gladly. Her temper is not one that happily accepts the presence of small children. She goes to visit my mother at Mansfield Park whenever she can—though doing so means avoiding both my brothers, who might well forbid it—simply to remember the grandeur that once surrounded her. If Mrs. Norris went to Mr. Rushworth to 'plead my case,' as one might say, and he told her no—Miss Tilney, Mr. Darcy, I can only say this: If you find my aunt a comical figure, if you think it absurd to imagine her doing harm, please trust me when I tell you that her anger, once excited, knows no limits. If she felt she were never to escape my household, my fate—there is, I declare, nothing she might not do to change it."

Matters of business are considered fit only for the masculine sphere. It is popularly felt that women have no head for such matters: that they cannot maintain appropriate calm in the face of trouble, that they cannot assess the risks involved, and that they would easily become confused by the many details. As for the many troubles women face steadily—the risks they remain aware of and live with every day—and the numerous details of which they keep account, these are held of no regard, as insignificant in this reckoning as the gentlemen who lose their tempers at slight provocation or who bet astronomical sums on horses or playing cards.

Edmund Bertram, though a liberal-minded man in many regards, subscribed to the common wisdom on this topic . . . and, indeed, it is difficult to see how he might have been persuaded otherwise, given that his primary examples of feminine thinking were those of his wife, Fanny—an intelligent person, but one with little interest in worldly cares—and his mother, perhaps of all beings the least fitted to the role of a businessperson. He therefore did not find it strange, when he inquired after his brother's whereabouts that day, to be informed by the butler that Sir Thomas had taken himself off to Wyngarde's club to conduct "plantation business." Edmund headed to the club as well, hoping to find the sale complete.

Upon his arrival at Wyngarde's, Edmund soon found Tom sitting with Mr. Drake—the buyer—much engaged in discussion, not upon the sale of the plantation but instead regarding the laws on "friendly societies" made up of workers in a single business or industry. "It is madness, sheer madness," Mr. Drake declared, "to allow such societies to grow unchecked. The government must take further steps to oversee them, to check their books, or else laborers will be quite taken advantage of."

"Hear, hear," said Tom, who in truth seemed more taken with his drink than with Mr. Drake's argument. "Ah, and here is my brother, Edmund. What say you to the 'friendly societies' run amok?"

"I am not so disapproving as the two of you, I think," Edmund replied, taking his seat in the nearest chair and nodding a quick refusal to the man who would have brought him a cup of wine. "We are so often severe upon the working classes—we assume them fit for no better than their fate—and yet we react with consternation when they attempt to better their conditions. I believe that if a man *can* aspire, if he has the mind and spirit for it, then he *should* aspire. If men aspire together, so much the better."

Mr. Drake stared at Edmund as though he were a Radical. "You must see that these friendly societies cause more trouble than good."

"That which troubles one man may be to the good of

another," Edmund pointed out. "I do not doubt that there have been examples of corruption and coercion—of monies misused—but such is true of virtually all human endeavor. Friendly societies are not singular in that way."

Although Mr. Drake was not wholly satisfied with this answer, he was placated enough to change the subject, finish his glass, and depart. As soon as Edmund and Tom were alone together, Tom shook his head. "You will end up being thrown out of Wyngarde's, and I may be thrown with you!"

"I doubt mine are the most controversial words ever spoken here," Edmund replied. "So? Is the sale concluded?"

Tom shook his head. "Not quite, not quite—a few matters must be clarified first, and of course Drake wishes to see the books, but I believe we will have the complete bill of sale very soon."

How galling to think of the enslavement of human beings as a subject to be studied on a ledger of debts and assets! How blithe Tom was in discussing it! Yet Edmund held his tongue. If Tom did not share his repugnance toward the vile practice of slavery, he did at least comprehend that it was his moral duty to engage with it no more. He had agreed to sell the Antigua plantation, and with this victory, Edmund would have to be content.

Mrs. Norris had been none too pleased to leave the house, but her mood spoiled further upon her return, when she learned that she, too, must answer the questions posed by Jonathan Darcy and Miss Tilney.

"I do not know at all what Edmund can be thinking," she said, pottering about the sitting room, moving objects from one place to another, as though these were useful tasks not to be postponed. In the background, Jonathan could hear the sounds of Maria Rushworth rather crossly insisting her daughter take a nap. Mrs. Norris paid this scolding no heed. "To subject all his relations to impertinent questions from strangers—it is most uncivil, most unlike him—I daresay the death of Mr. Rushworth has rattled him, for Mr. Rushworth could be a most obliging gentleman when not influenced by his mother."

Jonathan had, through his own mother's gentle but firm insistence, internalized the rule that elders deserved respect, female elders most of all—"as they are so much more often forgotten," Elizabeth Darcy had said. So he knew not how to tell Mrs. Norris to cease her work and attend to their questions. Luckily, Miss Tilney was not without resource. "The death of Mr. Rushworth is indeed a tragic event, ma'am," she said to Mrs. Norris, "and we wish only to bring clarity and peace of mind to all involved."

Mrs. Norris was not entirely placated—Jonathan suspected she rarely achieved such equilibrium—but she took her seat. "Well, then, let us have done with it."

He asked, "What was your relationship with Mr. Rushworth?"

Only in this instant did Mrs. Norris realize she was to be the center of attention for a time, and her temper immediately improved. "It was I who first conceived the notion of Mr. Rushworth marrying Maria, you know. Of course we knew of the Rushworth family, one of the first families of the parish—the very first, save for our own. He had a fine estate at Sotherton, and a fortune of twelve thousand a year."

This was even more than Jonathan's father received annually; the Rushworths had been wealthy indeed. "Did you have other reasons for supporting the match, Mrs. Norris?" he asked.

She sputtered, "But of course! To be sure! Maria had no need to wed for money, I assure you, not as the daughter of the late

Sir Thomas—he was a much grander figure, much more generous than his son, and as such her dowry was considerable. Mr. Rushworth, why, he was such an amiable gentleman, so civil, so friendly, as to be exactly the sort of husband we would all have wished for Maria. The match was of my conceiving, you see, of my doing, for I made certain to expand upon our acquaintance with his mother and to bring the younger persons together whenever an occasion arose."

"You were proud, then, of having helped to bring the marriage about," Miss Tilney said. "It must therefore have been all the more painful for you when the marriage ended."

The words spilled out of Mrs. Norris then with no more order than beans falling from a sack. "Many brides find it difficult to accustom themselves to married life, and Maria was among these. To be away from all her family—save her sister, Julia, of course—to be mistress of a great household and yet to have to share that duty with a mother-in-law who did not yet know her new place—why, Maria was not at all herself. Mr. Crawford, whom we all thought so charming, so pleasant—but one cannot blame him for being so very in love with Maria. For the rest of his behavior, no, there is no excuse, but how could he forget a girl so beautiful and delightful in every way? You know that he made noises about wishing to marry *Fanny*"—she spoke her niece's Christian name with such pointed disdain that Jonathan was taken aback—"but I never heard anything more ridiculous in my life. Not but that Fanny was obstinate and disobliging so as to refuse him, but I daresay even had she accepted him, the match would not have come off. No man who had loved a girl like Maria would ever settle for the likes of Fanny."

By Mrs. Norris's reckoning, Jonathan determined, it had been Fanny's duty both to accept Mr. Crawford's hand and then to be jilted by him afterward. He had always noted Mrs. Fanny Bertram to be a quiet, timid creature; he now understood that these qualities must have been exacerbated by growing up in a household where at least one of the adults responsible for her care had denigrated her at every opportunity. Jonathan had faced enough ridicule as a child at school to feel deeply for Mrs. Bertram in this regard.

Mrs. Norris continued talking. "So, as you see, it was a fine match between the two of them, a fine marriage, aside from Maria's one foolish mistake, and as to that, I blame Mr. Crawford entirely. If Maria had been able to speak with Mr. Rushworth after all that unpleasantness, before his mother got to him, I daresay all would have been forgiven. Her repentance would have been swift and eternal. There was no need to draw both families into shame and scandal."

This seemed as close to an answer to the question as they were likely to get. Miss Tilney asked, "So you considered a reunion between Mr. and Mrs. Rushworth possible, even probable?"

"Who knows but what the season would have brought?" Mrs. Norris's misery seemed genuine. "Both of them here in London, all the time in the world for them to be together as a family, for Mr. Rushworth was very fond of Ellen, you know."

The terms of Mr. Rushworth's will supported the truth of this. Jonathan said, "We have heard it suggested that Mr. Crawford and Mrs. Rushworth . . . remained in communication."

Mrs. Norris flushed with embarrassment, displeasure, or both. "It cannot be held against Maria that Mr. Crawford remained fond of her. Of course that is so. *That,* no one can wonder at. But she gave him no great encouragement, I assure you."

A swift glance toward Miss Tilney confirmed for Jonathan that she believed this statement no more than he did. Still, it appeared Mrs. Norris might have convinced herself, though no one else.

He asked, "Forgive the implications, Mrs. Norris, but you can appreciate that we must determine every person's whereabouts upon the morning of Mr. Rushworth's death. Will you tell us where you were at that time, and what you were doing?"

Surprisingly Mrs. Norris did not bridle at the question. "I was doing the marketing, which we are obliged to ourselves. We can afford but one maid, only one—Tom is so ungenerous, so unlike what one would like to see in a baronet—and that maid, Betty by name, she is not one to be trusted with money, indeed not. She kept Ellen while I went off to market, and some time it took me, for the merchants in London sell their wares very dear, and it requires no small amount of bargaining to feed three people on scarce enough money to feed one."

Her story was plausible, and it would take but a few words with the maid to confirm that Mrs. Norris had left their dwelling that morning. Yet it did not escape Jonathan's notice that it would be almost impossible to verify that Mrs. Norris had truly spent all her time away from home doing the marketing. Even if they could identify the shops and stands at which she had shopped, it was unlikely that they would all remember only one customer among dozens, much less precisely how long she had been at the task.

Jonathan said as much as he and Miss Tilney walked back. (Through some stroke of luck, the roads were slightly less busy at that time, and he could manage to think.) Miss Tilney nodded her agreement as she replied, "We cannot exclude her on that basis. Yet, as irritable as she was, Mrs. Norris seemed to greatly value Mr. Rushworth and the prospect—however implausible—of a remarriage between him and Mrs. Rushworth. Although Mrs. Rushworth suggested that a refusal by Mr. Rushworth could have greatly angered her aunt, to me it seems unlikely that Mrs. Norris would have believed such a refusal. Already there were many signs that such a reunion was not to be, and these, Mrs. Norris found easy to ignore."

"I must further note that both Mrs. Rushworth and Mrs. Norris make frequent references to their poverty, and indeed some of their style of life suggests financial hardship," Jonathan said, "but their neighborhood, and some of their attire, hints at greater means."

Miss Tilney considered this. "Perhaps it is no more than unwise expenditure. Neither woman had ever been obliged to practice such strict economy before." But she did not seem wholly convinced.

"Nor can I attribute to Mrs. Norris the strength necessary to strangle Mr. Rushworth," Jonathan said. "Granted, the placement of the chair you noted—a person less strong than Mrs. Rushworth could nonetheless have been able to complete the evil task—but it does not follow that *anyone* could do so, and Mrs. Norris seems to me unlikely. Though there, I suppose, we must ask again precisely what was used as a garrote."

"We will find our murder weapon yet, Mr. Darcy," she replied. A passerby overheard her and stared in such surprise that, despite the gravity of their task, both Miss Tilney and Jonathan found it difficult not to smile.

Chapter Nine

Every journey, by its very nature, must begin in upheaval. However, most often we find that after a few days in a new setting, we begin to fashion new rhythms and rituals, reestablishing some sense of order and routine. Fanny Bertram, little pleased by novelty, had much hoped that it would be so with her family's stay in London. She could be glad for Susan's sake that the days held such unprecedented events as shopping at the Bond Street Bazaar or attending the much-anticipated ball to be held by the Ramseys—and even Fanny herself had been awed by her first sight of St. Paul's Cathedral—but change was unwelcome to her. Her dearest wish was to be home, and until that could be accomplished, until her duty to her late uncle and to her younger sister was fulfilled, Fanny could but hope for steadiness and calm.

The horrid death of Mr. Rushworth had, of course, ended this hope, as had the presence of Maria and the revelation of her illegitimate child. Even as Fanny reeled from all of this, however, more upheaval arrived in the form of her cousin Julia—Edmund, Tom, and Maria's youngest sister—and her husband, Mr. Yates.

In most families, Julia Yates would have been the scandalous daughter. Only Maria's extraordinary efforts had rendered it otherwise, though it might have been argued that it was Maria's behavior that introduced Julia to scandal in the first place. When Maria Rushworth had abandoned her marital abode to run away with Mr. Crawford, Julia had been less surprised than most; she had accompanied her sister on her honeymoon, as so many girls did, and remained with her during the Rushworths' initial months as husband and wife. Thus she knew how infelicitous the union had proved to be. Furthermore, Julia's own attraction to the charming Henry Crawford had naturally sharpened her awareness of the undercurrents of feeling between him and Maria.

But this lack of surprise did not lessen how horror-struck Julia had been by the event. In fact, she had perhaps been the most troubled of all the family, for she was very much aware of how damaging Maria's fecklessness would be to her own marital prospects. Who would wish to marry the sister of one who had proved herself an unfaithful wife?

As it happened, there was at that time one man who did: her brother Tom's good friend Mr. Yates, who had been pay-ing court to Julia in a lackadaisical sort of way. He had shown himself to be an unserious, irreverent sort of man, but to his credit, the news of the Bertram family's disgrace had not driven him from Julia. Rather, he had been overcome by the romantic desire to rescue her through marriage, and as there was no time to lose, they eloped to Gretna Green, without even a thought of obtaining parental consent.

Such behavior would, at any other time, have led to Julia's being disowned. But her father, having lost one daughter to disgrace, could not bring himself to part with another. Also, unexpectedly, the match had proved a sound one. Julia and Mr. Yates had properly repented of their rashness and apolo-gized to their families' satisfaction. Yates's wealth made him more than eligible as a husband; he could not be accused of fortune hunting. The seriousness of matrimony had matured them both; and even if there had not been true love between them in the beginning, it appeared that they had worked together to cultivate it.

And yet, as they arrived at the London home of the Ber-tram family that morning, Mr. and Mrs. Yates showed all the merry disregard of their youth and upset the fragile order that Fanny had hoped to create.

"Well, Susan, you are a lucky girl," Mrs. Yates said, tossing her fashionably ringleted hair as she took her seat between Susan and Fanny. Aunt Bertram sat upon the chaise in the corner, smiling upon her daughter with pleasure, though scarcely more than she showed toward Pug. Mrs. Yates, used to her mother's ways, did not appear to notice. "To enjoy such a trip to London! It is more than my father did for us—though I am sure that was only because he spent so much of our first years 'out' overseeing the plantation in Antigua."

Fanny gave a moment's silent thanks that they were soon to be tied to that plantation no longer! "We are lucky that you are here, Julia," she said. "You know more of the fashions of the day than I undoubtedly, and you will be a better guide to Susan in that way, for such things are very important here."

This praise was welcome to Julia, as was her acquired position as the superior daughter of the family—a position Maria would never be able to regain. "What a terrible thing it is about Mr. Rushworth!" Julia exclaimed. "He corresponded with Mr. Yates from time to time, most civilly. Though Rushworth was severed from our family, he was a decent, respectable man who did not deserve such a savage end."

"Indeed not," said Fanny. "Few could be so wicked as to deserve that."

"London is full of villains, I am sure," Julia said, before speaking upon the true subject of her curiosity. "Maria must be much cast down by it. She, I know, hoped to reunite with Mr. Rushworth, though I do not believe the interest was very great on his side."

Aunt Bertram said, "Oh, Julia, I forget you did not know. There was no time to write. You do not know that Maria has had a child, a little girl."

Julia's astonishment was plain. "What? That cannot be!"

"The girl's name is Ellen," Fanny said quietly. "She is perhaps three years old."

This estimate inspired certain mathematical calculations within Julia's mind—so transparent was she that Fanny could practically see it upon her face. (This understanding was much assisted by the fact that Fanny had performed these calculations herself.)

"I should send something for the child," Aunt Bertram said, a rare display of responsibility on her part, but she shook her head even as she spoke. "But I do not know where the money goes, indeed I do not. Tom says I might as well toss it to the winds."

Julia paid this no mind, instead asking Fanny, "Is there anyone else of our acquaintance in town?"

"Mr. Jonathan Darcy is staying with us, and we have renewed our friendship with Miss Juliet Tilney and come to know her mother," Fanny replied. She knew full well that these names meant nothing to Julia, and so reluctantly she continued. "It appears that both Henry and Mary Crawford are in town."

At that, Julia startled so that one might have believed her still in love with Henry Crawford, as much as ever.

Jonathan Darcy witnessed none of this, for he had again been obliged to accompany Sir Thomas to Wyngarde's club. Mr. Edmund Bertram seemed little more amused by the club than Jonathan was himself, but as Sir Thomas was head of house, his wishes held sway.

Mr. Bertram was blessedly sympathetic toward Jonathan's antipathy for such loud places. "He will not wish for our presence so much once Mr. Yates has joined him," he murmured as they ascended the stairs, his words nearly lost in the appalling rumble of male voices surrounding them. "Mr. Yates's temperament is more congenial to such things, and Tom will always gravitate toward merrier company. It is my understanding that Yates has business to conduct in the city today, but from tonight onward, you and I will be much more the masters of our time."

Most young men would have been crestfallen to hear themselves described as not being merry company; Jonathan felt only relief that he would not be expected to substitute for the same very much longer. He also gave thanks that the Yateses were staying near the Bertrams' London residence but not in it; to have even more company in the house would have been greatly burdensome to him. He said only, "That will give Miss Tilney and me more opportunities to investigate," he said to Mr. Bertram. "Do not mistake any pause in our efforts as a lack of feeling, for we know well how urgent and important the matter is. Some of what we must learn simply takes time to be revealed."

"There is no need to trouble yourself in that regard," Mr. Bertram replied. "Our whole family puts its trust in you, Mr. Darcy, and in Miss Tilney as well. We fully understand that you can exercise due thoroughness without spending *every* moment in that pursuit."

As they made their way to the club's reading room, he again felt the tug between Gibbon and Sir Walter Scott—and once again, Scott proved triumphant. *Ivanhoe* was so incomparably delightful! "Have you read any of the new 'history novels'?" Jonathan asked Mr. Bertram as he took his place with his book. He was ever eager to share his enthusiasms, despite his parents' hints that he should not do so at great length.

"I am not much of a novel reader myself, though I think Mr. Peacock quite good," Mr. Bertram said. "I expect I should widen my horizons in this area."

This seemed opening enough, and Jonathan would then

have begun his fulsome praise of Scott's work had not Sir Thomas taken the seat nearest them and said to his brother, "Edmund, there is a matter I have wished to raise with you, but I did not wish to do so at home."

Jonathan hoped this would free him to lose himself entirely in *Ivanhoe,* but he nonetheless noted Edmund saying, "What do you mean, Tom? Is this about our mother's spending? She is extravagant, no doubt, but it is her money to do with as she pleases."

Sir Thomas scoffed. "Not that, irksome though it is. To think she will end dependent on my charity despite such a jointure! No, it is of Maria that I wish to speak."

Edmund said, "*She* is cared for now, at least. We have not that burden any longer. Maria and her child, as well as Aunt Norris, may establish themselves well in some new area of the country, one where perhaps the stain of her past indiscretions is not so well known. It is my hope that she will take to her heart this chance to start anew—to reform herself inwardly as well as outwardly."

"I doubt it," said Sir Thomas, with less sentiment and per-haps more accuracy. "In fact, my concern is that Maria will not go to any new place but will instead stay near, muddying our reputations and my prospects of marrying Miss Allerdyce."

"Why should she do that?" Edmund said. "It seems as much against her interests as our own."

Sir Thomas appeared grim. "Not if her interests still include Mr. Henry Crawford."

Just then, a new voice rang through the din: "Jonathan Darcy! As I live and breathe!"

Jonathan looked up from *Ivanhoe* in astonishment. "Follett?"

Approaching through the crowd was Mr. Laurence Fol-lett, an old schoolfellow of Jonathan's and purportedly his friend. In truth, Mr. Follett had been one of Jonathan's many tormentors at school, and greater maturity for them both had not fostered deeper accord. They had renewed their acquaintance more than two and a half years prior in Devonshire, at Allenham, the home of their former schoolmate John Willoughby. It was during this visit that Willoughby's wife had been murdered, a crime that had been solved by Jonathan and Miss Tilney working in concert.

As Mr. Follett had been half in love with Mrs. Willoughby, one might have expected him to feel warmly toward Jonathan Darcy for assisting in the course of justice. This had not occurred; but as time had passed, Follett might have acquired gratitude at least, for he smiled at Jonathan as he said, "I had not thought to find you in one of the smart clubs in London."

This might have been intended as a slight, but Jonathan could only reply, "I had not thought to find myself here either."

Mr. Follett laughed. "Fair enough, I suppose! I am come to London because I have a painting in the art exhibition." How sly he looked! But Jonathan could not wonder at Follett's pride in such an accomplishment.

"I am visiting friends." Jonathan then did his duty in introducing Mr. Follett to his hosts, who were all cordiality. He then added, "There is another in town whose acquaintance you share. Miss Tilney is visiting the city with her mother."

"Miss Tilney!" Mr. Follett seemed very much struck by this. At Allenham, he had teased Jonathan somewhat for being fond of Miss Tilney—a behavior Jonathan dreaded would now commence anew—but Follett's reaction held no hint of the same. His expression seemed thoughtful, even serious. "My goodness. I had little expected to see Miss Tilney ever again."

Was it possible—could it be that now, a decent interval after Mrs. Willoughby's death—that Mr. Follett might be turning his thoughts to courtship once more? That he might now look at Juliet Tilney in an entirely new light?

Jonathan could hardly bear the idea, nor could he reject it. Nothing ignites the instincts of a would-be lover more than the appearance of a rival.

"Mr. Follett in town?" Juliet said, when next she and Mr. Darcy met, late in the afternoon on the day following their inquiries to Mrs. Rushworth and Mrs. Norris. Fanny Bertram had invited her over, ostensibly to meet their visiting relations, Mr. and Mrs. Yates; but after the completion of such niceties, both Juliet and Mr. Darcy had seized the opportunity to speak together in a corner of the sitting room. "What an extraordinary coincidence. I suppose the art exhibition drew him hence."

"That is precisely his reason, for he has a painting among those on display," said Mr. Darcy. He rarely met anyone's eyes for very long, even Juliet's, so she could not miss that he was staring at her quite markedly this afternoon. "It appears his stay here will be of some duration. I informed him of your presence in town, so it is not impossible that he will come to call upon you."

"Thank you for informing me." Juliet was in no great hurry to renew her acquaintance with Mr. Follett, a brusque sort of man and unkind to Mr. Darcy, though in justice she must admit him to be a fine painter. Let him spend his time at the art exhibition, rather than with her! Her mind swiftly turned to more interesting topics. "I believe we may have an opportunity of speaking to Sir Thomas Bertram this afternoon. Ought we not seize it?"

Mr. Darcy blinked as though in surprise. "Oh—I believe you are correct, Miss Tilney. He is in his study, so let us try."

Indeed, Sir Thomas greeted them both and welcomed them into his study, which—like many such male sanctums—

smelled richly of cigars and leather. A thick accounts ledger lay open on his desk; apparently he had been tallying up certain figures, but he did not appear to resent the interruption. "You must speak to everyone, I know," he said, "so this is as good an opportunity as any."

"How would you describe your relationship with the late Mr. Rushworth?" Mr. Darcy began.

Sir Thomas gestured idly. "We were cordial before he was my brother, cordial during that time, somewhat less so after the divorce. I had asked him to reconsider the divorce—he and Maria might have lived separately, with less scandal—but he would not, and in truth I could not blame him. He repaid like for like by not holding Maria's crimes against me or anyone else in the family. But of course there could be no true friendship between our families after such a breach."

Juliet ventured, "Many in your family harbored hopes of a remarriage between the Rushworths. Did you share in that hope?"

This was met with a scoff from Sir Thomas. "Hardly likely. He evidently felt responsibility toward the child in the case—and Maria must have held some sway over him, as the child's very existence makes clear." Juliet noted the silent assumption that Mr. Rushworth was the father of the little girl. Sir Thomas continued: "But if Rushworth had the slightest intention of remarrying Maria, surely he would have done so upon hearing that the child was expected. To do so would have legitimized the girl, infinitely improving her prospects in life. After her birth, what point would a marriage have served? Forgive my speaking of such subjects before you, Miss Tilney, but it is my understanding that your efforts in these matters require a certain indelicacy, from time to time."

How bothersome it was that so many interesting subjects were considered indelicate! Juliet said only, "You do me honor by answering truthfully, sir."

Jonathan said, "One last thing, Sir Thomas—where were you on the morning of Mr. Rushworth's death?"

"At Wyngarde's. Rather early, I know, but Mr. Drake and I have much business to review in the matter of the sale of our Antigua plantation." Sir Thomas patted the ledger on his desk. "Managing property is a cumbersome business, Miss Tilney. Be glad you have no share in it!"

"Honestly," Catherine Tilney said later when Juliet told her of this. "To expect women to be glad that we can rarely own property in our own right, or have any say in what is to be done with it! I am fortunate in that your father is responsible and wise, but many a wife and daughter have had reason to rue an impecunious man's mismanagement of property."

Mr. Darcy had walked Juliet home and joined them both in the parlor. It was Juliet's hope that he might make some efforts toward winning her mother's favor, but his personality was both too particular and too fine to always be searching for material advantage. He still seemed to think of little beyond Sir Thomas's words. "There has been much talk of the sale of this plantation ever since I arrived in London," he explained, "to the extent that I am tempted to describe it as *too much* talk. My father has never had any holdings overseas, and perhaps such foreign transactions are more complex, but he has shown me how he has handled substantive sales and purchases. These were accomplished with far more alacrity."

"That on its own means little," Mrs. Tilney said thoughtfully, surprising Juliet. Was her mother also becoming interested in the investigation? "As I understand it, such matters can be straightforward or complex, all depending on the property in question. Of more importance, I believe, is your impression of the situation, Mr. Darcy. Is it your conviction that Sir Thomas has not been entirely candid in his conversation about the sale of this property?"

Mr. Darcy considered for a moment before replying. "Yes. What he conceals, I cannot say, nor whether it is tied to the business at hand. However, I do believe he is concealing *something*."

"Fascinating," said Juliet, "but what could this be? In full candor, I would think the mere ownership of a plantation so shameful that, if Sir Thomas openly speaks of it, I find it difficult to imagine what he would consider wicked enough to conceal."

"Indeed," said Mr. Darcy. "What can this be, if not murder?"

Much conversation and planning followed. Catherine Tilney—though every bit as interested in the goings-on as her daughter suspected—mostly contented herself with listening raptly. Her interest sprang only partly from the motives Juliet had imagined (it was scarcely possible *not* to be intrigued by the potential identification of a murderer); her primary concern in the matter was as a mother. She noted the great trust between Juliet and Mr. Jonathan Darcy, the evident liking between the two, and the respect Mr. Darcy had for her daughter's thoughts and opinions. When at last Mr. Darcy had left, and while Juliet hastily prepared herself for their dinner, Catherine returned to the letter she had been writing to her husband.

Already she had told him of Mr. Darcy's presence in town, of Mr. Rushworth's murder, and of the efforts to investigate, complete with reassurances that, this time at least, Juliet had not been subjected to any ghastly scenes and was not personally endangered by a potential killer's proximity. Far more significant, Catherine felt, was what she now sat down to add.

*Dearest Henry, the past few days have already
provided ample opportunity for me to observe Mr.
Jonathan Darcy and how he comports himself with
our daughter. You have described certain of his habits
as peculiar, but none I have witnessed are odious, only
slightly particular, and that is the worst I can find to
say of the young man. Mr. Darcy's respect for Juliet is
great, his liking of her even greater. She occupies the
central part of his attentions whenever she is present.
He takes on these investigations, not for the sake of
excitement or vain display, but from what appears to be
a genuine sense of responsibility.*

*All these traits, combined with his good family,
considerable fortune, and—most important of all—
regard for Juliet, would seem to make Mr. Darcy
an ideal suitor for her hand. Yet you returned from
Rosings Park entirely certain that he did not care for
our daughter, and that this was for the best, as he
would not do as a son-in-law. Can you explain this
discrepancy, Henry? Have you seen something in him
that I have not—or is it the other way around? Tell me
more of your thoughts on the matter, and I will share
more of my observations.*

*Write back quickly, my love. If I judge correctly,
Mr. Darcy is on a suitor's business, and I do not think
he will be long delayed.*

Catherine

Although ladies pay the majority of morning calls, and are generally the ones to receive them, the gentlemen have their share of the pleasure, too—and when two families are able to be brought together in this way, the meeting may prove very happy indeed. So it was that next morning, when the Allerdyces came to call upon the Bertrams, though the sources of that happiness were very much different for each person present.

Sir Thomas Bertram, for example, took great pleasure in meeting with Frederica Allerdyce again. Entirely settled upon his choice, he had already determined that the best time to make an offer for her hand would be shortly before his family's departure from London and until then was enjoying the romance of suspense. Frederica, on the other hand, was not yet certain of her sentiments toward Sir Thomas and did not enjoy suspense one whit, but this made her all the gladder for a chance to know both her suitor and his family better.

Fanny Bertram, already beset by more company than she wished, could not take much pleasure in admitting more persons into their home, and less still in Mrs. Caroline Allerdyce's announcement of a ball the family would host the following week. To be subjected to yet another crush of persons, another wave of introductions, another necessity to lie to her dear Edmund as to why she was not dancing! Yet, for this hour at least, the callers made enough conversation that Fanny could remain all but silent; with this small blessing, she attempted to be content.

Jonathan Darcy, who as the Bertrams' guest was also in attendance, sometimes felt somewhat pursued by the Allerdyce family, in particular Miss Priscilla, who fixed her eyes on him with the rapt attention a hawk shows a mouse. However, his spirits were lifted considerably by Mrs. Caroline Allerdyce's casual mention that two of the attendees at the ball would be acquaintances of that family, "a brother and sister by the name of Crawford, the sister soon to be married." At last, an opportunity to meet with Henry Crawford and perhaps to ask him questions!

Edmund Bertram recognized Jonathan's interest and gently suggested to the Allerdyces that they also invite the Tilney ladies, of excellent family, and their friends. He took heart in the thought that he was assisting Mr. Darcy and Miss Tilney, which also served as a distraction from the fact that he was soon to be in a room with Mary Crawford again. Priscilla Allerdyce, upon hearing this, instantly recognized that this Miss Tilney must be a rival for Mr. Darcy's hand, but she had the spirit to welcome a challenge and the pride to assume she would inevitably prove victorious.

As for Caroline Allerdyce, her feelings were more mixed. She was very happy to see Frederica on the verge of matrimony, for her elder daughter had reached the age of twenty-two—a perfectly respectable age to be unwed, but old enough to raise some maternal alarm. Caroline considered Frederica the plainer of her two daughters, as she personally prized Priscilla's curly hair, dimples, and fair complexion far more than Frederica's height, dignity, and grace; at times she wondered that Frederica should draw the attention of a nobleman, but this made her gratitude toward Sir Thomas all the greater.

More troubling was Jonathan Darcy's apparent lack of interest in Priscilla, particularly when combined with the encroachment of this Tilney family. Yet Caroline possessed a greater knowledge of tactics than she had as a headstrong girl, forever trying to push away Elizabeth Bennet. She knew now it was wiser to bring one's enemies close, the better to understand their allure and counteract it. By all means, she assured them, she would invite the Tilneys. How lovely it would be to welcome new acquaintance! It was of all things most to be wished.

Meanwhile, Lady Bertram was content to have callers, to remark upon the unremarkable weather, and to observe that Pug had rolled over to show her belly to all assembled, which was most obliging of her.

As soon as the Allerdyces departed, Fanny Bertram excused herself from receiving any further visitors, pleading a headache. In truth she wanted to write a letter to her brother William, who served on a ship which at that time was sailing in the Mediterranean. Their relationship had changed since his confession of sentiments and connections not sanctioned by the Lord or the law, but her love for him had not, and she did her duty to him as a correspondent—usually, with delight.

On this day, however, words failed her. Ink dried on the quill over and over again, for Fanny tried always to be open with her brother, to share the truth of her heart, but her current feelings could not be shared. She was consumed with hope, with what might be her last chance at motherhood, and this filled her thoughts so completely that even poor Mr. Rushworth's death could not fully occupy her. William would have to be contented with news of the murder, she decided, much underestimating the interest a young man of the navy would take in such a dramatic story of crime.

Distraction pricked at her for other reasons as well—most particularly, the news of the Allerdyces' impending ball, and the fact that both Henry and Mary Crawford would be in attendance.

After encountering Miss Crawford at the milliner's shop, Fanny no longer dreaded meeting with her again; Mary had been the soul of generosity, all her better qualities on display, all her flaws so well concealed that one might believe them left in the past. No doubt Mary Crawford would be similarly friendly if—or, as it now appeared, *when*—they came face-to-face once more.

What Fanny feared was the now-inevitable reunion of Mary and Edmund. She had not one doubt of Edmund's morality or fidelity; for that matter, Fanny would always credit Mary with intelligence in the service of self-interest, and thus she would be unlikely to risk her engagement to a bishop for the sake of a former attachment to a humbler clergyman. No, she had no concerns regarding their behavior.

It was their feelings she dreaded, the sentiment that would be plainly writ upon both their faces when they looked upon each other again. Fanny did not know whether Edmund and Mary would find ashes—or embers.

Peculiar as it would be in the countryside to find oneself invited to a ball being held by near strangers, this was not unheard of in London, as Juliet discovered when the invitation to the Allerdyces' arrived that afternoon.

"They know the Darcys and the Bertrams," Catherine Tilney said, "and we were introduced at the Drakes'. In the city, that is a sufficient connection. Such gatherings are more public than private during the season, you know."

Juliet held the thick paper in her hands, rereading the words of the invitation with enjoyment. She did not yet know of the investigative purpose the dance could serve, and solving the murder of Mr. Rushworth remained foremost among her priorities . . . but what person, when eighteen years of age and deeply enamored of another, would not delight in a ball that brought them together? Besides, the fruits of their visits to shops and dressmakers had begun to arrive, which naturally ignited a great desire to wear them. Her grandfather wished Juliet to expend great sums of money upon her wardrobe, and let it be said that she had done her duty.

Catherine Tilney, two decades wed, dressed simply but elegantly in a blue dress and matching velvet cap. Her attention was all for Juliet when she descended, fresh from her maid's attentions, wearing her new dress with thin pink stripes. "Oh, my dear—you are so very grown-up. How I wish your father could see you."

On this point, Juliet was not as confident her father would approve. Though sensible of the compliment her mother wished to pay, she was discovering the treacherous gap between recognizing the latest fashions and being entirely at ease in wearing them. "My ankles are showing so very much. Another inch, and they would reveal the *leg*!"

"They are not so scandalous as that," Catherine insisted. "How low waistlines have gone! But I do believe the silhouette becoming to your figure."

Juliet had grown up in a time of slim, elegantly trimmed dresses that tapered in but once, just beneath the bust; the newer gowns puffed far more at the sleeves, flared out more in the skirts, and had a waistline that was inching down to a point shockingly near the actual waist. Ruffles, braid, and all other ornament was in greater display than before as well. To her it felt nearly immodest, to fluff one's self out in so many directions and wear something near a bow in the middle, as though one were being presented as a gift. Yet, she had to admit, her person was not so much on display as it would have been ten years prior, for the rise in hemlines had been mirrored by a rise in necklines.

Her modesty was much soothed upon her arrival at the Allerdyces' elegant dwelling in London, where she was immediately surrounded by women and girls wearing even livelier dresses than she did herself. Then, when Juliet saw Mr. Darcy crossing the room toward her, she took very little note of anyone else present.

"Miss Tilney," he said with a quick, correct bow. "How good it is to see you."

"And you, Mr. Darcy." Juliet sensed greater ease in him than she had on the bustling London streets. "I take it that the order and etiquette that hold sway at any ball are more pleasing to you than the cacophony beyond these walls?"

He brightened, as ever he did when his instincts were rightly understood. "Indeed, Miss Tilney. Here at least one can know the events, the steps, nearly every moment that will take place in advance of their actual occurrences. Still there are too many people—but this is indeed more manageable, and one person who will be here tonight is of particular importance to us both."

Mr. Darcy nodded toward the corner, where Juliet spied Miss Mary Crawford, the woman who had greeted Fanny Bertram in the milliner's shop with such pleasure. Standing next to her was a gentleman so similar in coloring and features that she realized at once he must be her brother, Henry Crawford—whose connection to Maria Rushworth, and to the late Mr. Rushworth, might yet prove to be of significant importance. "Oh," she said, "we must find a way to question him. What a lucky chance!"

"Not luck," Mr. Darcy replied. "Mr. Edmund Bertram specifically asked the Allerdyces to invite you, I believe in order to provide us this opportunity."

"How clever of him. Perhaps he would be so kind as to speak to Mr. Crawford first?"

"I believe that to be Mr. Bertram's plan." Mr. Darcy had begun to look uneasy, and Juliet did not understand why until he dropped his voice and continued. "Forgive me, but . . . upon my arrival here, Mrs. Allerdyce made it rather clear that she wished me to ask her younger daughter for the first two dances. Miss Allerdyce is to open the ball with Sir Thomas, and Mrs. Allerdyce insisted that Miss Priscilla not be made to feel left out."

This was disappointing. However, a host's or hostess's suggestion in such matters was not to be refused absent compelling reason. "Then you must dance with her, by all means."

"The second two dances, though—there, we face no impediment. Will you save those for me, Miss Tilney?"

How hopeful he looked! How brightly his smile shone! Juliet did not realize how transparently her sentiments and expressions mirrored his own. The plan for the second two dances was made, and Mr. Crawford was in sight; already, the dance was going extraordinarily well.

One person less certain on that last point was Edmund Bertram. He liked a ball as well as the next man—were that man married, settled, and a clergyman—but he could never again be wholly at ease in the presence of the Crawfords.

His sentiments on this point were very far from Fanny's concerns, so much so that Edmund did not even recognize the fears she held. In fact, his strongest feeling in the matter was that of embarrassment. He had always considered himself the counselor of his family, the person besides his late father with the soberest judgment, the clearest vision, and the strongest sense of right. Ever had he counseled Fanny on how to look upon the world and the people within it.

Then came the Crawfords, who, in Edmund's opinion, had proven him something of a fool.

Henry Crawford he had thought a free and easy sort of man, but a worthy friend and potential relation. When Henry had asked for Fanny's hand in marriage—strange now even to recall it!—Edmund had been pleased, greatly pleased, and took it as evidence that Henry possessed a fine character and true discernment. Fanny's refusal had been attributed by Edmund as merely the reflection of her deep timidity and modesty, and he had possessed no doubts that in time Henry would succeed in his pursuit.

His pleasure in this possibility had been much increased by his own intention to soon propose to Henry's sister, Mary. Ever since her arrival in Northamptonshire, Edmund had been captivated by her charm, her quick wit, her cleverness, her dark beauty; to him she had seemed to be the quintessence of all that was feminine and lovely. At times, her humor verged on the improper, but this was easily ascribed to her difficult upbringing. More worrying had been her worldliness, her disapproval of his vocation as a clergyman; yet Miss Crawford's affection for him despite these objections seemed to suggest that her better self would win out in the end. Never did Edmund doubt that, at heart, her principles were good.

How wrong he had been about her! How much more wrong had he been about Henry, and to far more disastrous effect!

Still, as far as Mary Crawford went, Edmund felt he had no grounds for anger, and he walked up to her in hopes of a friendly welcome. This he met. "Mr. Bertram," Miss Crawford said, with some hint of the tenderness he had heard in her voice before. "How good of you to come to us. It is a pleasure to see you well."

"I share in that pleasure," Edmund replied, "and I understand I am to wish you joy."

"Indeed! As you may have heard, I am marrying into the clergy after all, Mr. Bertram, and if it be not impertinent to say so—I believe it was through my knowledge of you that I came to have a greater respect for that office and the men who fulfill it. Were every clergyman your equal, I daresay the reverence for the church would be greater throughout the land."

There was much in this speech that Edmund could have questioned; for instance, it did not escape his notice that Miss Crawford's eagerness to wed a man of the cloth had risen in proportion to the fortune of the particular clergyman she was to marry. (Rare was the bishop with a living less than four thousand a year.) Yet she had spoken in friendliness and charity, and he accepted her words in the spirit in which they were given. "It is very kind of you to say so, Miss Crawford."

Her smile seemed to proclaim both pleasure and relief. She had not been sure of her welcome, then, and Edmund noted her brother silent beside her, even as Miss Crawford went on: "I would wish you joy as well, were I not already so certain that you possess it! Fanny—Mrs. Bertram, I should say, is the dearest, gentlest creature, and I can but imagine her gratitude toward you. At last she has the family she has so long deserved."

"Your praise of her is just, but as for *gratitude* in the matter, I believe that to be entirely mine," he said. Miss Crawford's smile faltered slightly—in puzzlement, maybe—but he did not have enough curiosity on this point to consider it at any length. "Now, Miss Crawford, if you will excuse us, I have a request to make of your brother."

This conversation was indeed witnessed by Fanny Bertram, but from entirely across the room; her view was blocked by dancers and revelers hurrying that way and this, as well as by the wide-brimmed lace cap worn by Mrs. Allerdyce, who was at that time questioning her about Mansfield Park with all the avid curiosity of a future mother-in-law who may some-day be in residence. Fanny saw but hints of posture, almost nothing of their expressions. Instead of a truth that would have comforted her, she was left only in possession of terrible curiosity and doubt.

As the dancing was to begin, Juliet Tilney was obliged to sur-render Mr. Darcy to his duty toward Priscilla Allerdyce. She observed with mild dismay the happiness with which Miss Priscilla greeted him, yet no true doubt troubled her. The connection between herself and Jonathan Darcy was of such a nature that no mere dance floor encounter could be consid-ered a threat to it.

Then, much to her surprise, a gentleman stepped before her, his hand extended as an invitation to dance—but the greater astonishment was this man's identity.

"Mr. Crawford, I present to you Miss Juliet Tilney of Gloucestershire," said Edmund Bertram, who had arrived at their sides. His expression betrayed dislike, either of the task or of the man he introduced. "Miss Tilney, this is Mr. Henry Crawford."

"A pleasure, sir," she said, which was not entirely true. Would she be obliged to question him on her own?

As though he had intuited her thoughts, Mr. Crawford said, "Bertram here informs me that you and this young Mr. Darcy wish to ask me questions—is that correct? Then I am happy to oblige, but not, I beg of you, at a ball. Not when there is dancing to be enjoyed, and with so pretty a partner. If you will favor me?"

Juliet saw no way to refuse without removing all potential

to dance with Mr. Darcy or anyone else the rest of the night, and so she accepted as gracefully as she could. As she and Mr. Crawford took their places for the quadrille, she reasoned that any rapport she was able to build with this man might prove useful later on, when questions could finally be asked.

The music began. Juliet dropped her small curtsy, Mr. Crawford bowed, and then they were dancing.

"How very familiar you look," he said, as Juliet twirled through her first steps. "I feel quite as though I have seen you before, Miss Tilney."

She suspected she was neither the first nor the last young woman who would hear this comment, or some variation upon it, from him that night. "I am quite certain we were not previously acquainted, sir, unless you have spent considerable time in Gloucestershire?"

"No such adventuring for me," said Mr. Crawford, with a pretend shudder. "Yet, I do believe I know you by reputation at least, for rumors have spread of a young lady and gentleman who have proved quite skilled in their investigations into murders among the genteel."

Were she and Mr. Darcy acquiring renown for their efforts? This was almost too pleasing to be credited as truth. Juliet gave thanks that the heat of the room and the movements of the dance would provide their own explanations for the happy flush in her cheeks. Without even intending it, she gave credence to such renown by holding to the subject. "We have recently had such a murder in London, as you know. I believe you were acquainted with the deceased Mr. Rushworth."

"Acquainted." Mr. Crawford's smile could be rather wolfish, and yet she had to admit it was not unpleasing. "Yes, that is one way of putting it. I shall tell you more of the tale when it is time for these questions."

"When shall that be, sir? Mr. Darcy can write to you, or

you might send a card to him or to Mr. Bertram, letting us know of a time and place—"

"I suppose I have no chance of hearing your questions alone. One gentleman does not always welcome the presence of another when there is a young lady to be spoken with. Particularly one who turns so many heads as you do tonight, Miss Tilney."

He made her imagine that people were indeed gazing at her, murmuring about her—one of the many tempting illusions a dance could conjure. Juliet knew only that Mr. Crawford sought to turn *her* head with flattery, and she would not be so duped. "Mr. Darcy and I will speak to you together, at your earliest convenience."

"Very well, very well," Crawford replied, and this time his smile was less pleasant. "For the time being, then, let us occupy ourselves with the quadrille. I will think upon the delights to be had while watching a young lady go through her steps—and you, Miss Tilney, must take what satisfaction you can from dancing with a man whom you suspect of being a murderer."

She wished he had not put it that way, for afterward, she could not put another foot right, and his hand seemed to grasp hers much too hard.

Chapter Eleven

Of the rest of the Allerdyces' ball that evening, much could be said, but to little effect. No written account can fully recapture the dimensions and delights of a ball: the sound of the musicians at danger of being lost in laughter and gaiety and the soft thumping of feet; the slow accumulation of melted wax at the bottom of flickering candles that grow shorter by the hour; the flash of braid on military uniforms and the swish of silks and satins; and the enduring charm of a gathering of so many merry people. All agreed that the event was a great success, and some swore that even the Ramseys' much-anticipated ball might pale in comparison—all of which pleased Mrs. Allerdyce no end.

Juliet Tilney was of course aware that Mr. Darcy did not always find gatherings so charming, but he had given her his assurances that this he could endure, and gladly; to her observation, this appeared to be so. They danced a total of six dances together—three sets of two—which over the course of the evening did not seem like so very many, but they each silently conformed to the unspoken rule that limited the number of dances a couple could share of an evening were they not engaged or married. At a country dance, a smaller and more intimate gathering, two persons so attentive toward each other would have been considered quite each other's property. In the city, such attentions were in some ways *more* marked—where partners were greater in number, one individual being sought so often was a very decided choice—but so, too, were distractions.

Catherine Tilney, however, had not been distracted from this point. Although she had previously noted some of Mr. Darcy's oddities of manner, such as his apparent dislike of looking most persons in the eye, on this night she had seen him amiable and in good cheer, polite toward his hosts and their daughters without creating the slightest doubt where his affections truly lay. Catherine wondered how soon her husband would reply, and what account he would give of himself, for the longer she knew Jonathan Darcy, the more she marveled at the idea that such a courtship would *not* be the finest possible thing for their Juliet.

Granted, the point of a season in London was to widen a girl's acquaintance and increase the number of suitors. Instead, events thus far had conspired to ensure that almost all of Juliet's time would be devoted to the one young man already interested in her, the very one whose supposed snub had led to their London trip in the first place. But what did that signify when this gentleman was so well suited, so eligible? He was young yet to wed, but perhaps she might suggest a longer engagement—

Catherine caught herself. She should make no plans before Mr. Darcy declared his, nor should she discount the possibility that her dear Henry's reply might yet contain an objection of merit.

Back at the Allerdyce household, as the weary servants began the toil of cleaning up after the ball, Caroline felt absolutely no compunctions about making plans regarding Mr. Darcy. Never mind waiting for him to declare his own intentions; she wished to declare them for him.

Priscilla had looked incomparably lovely that night. Her dress had been in the latest style; her hair artfully and stylishly arrayed; her manner vivacious and winning without becoming pert. That not one word nor movement of her younger daughter had been natural or unaffected, Caroline disregarded; she did not mind artificiality, nor did she believe gentlemen cared either. (On this final point, she was sadly often correct.) Still, Jonathan Darcy's eyes were only for that Tilney girl.

Once more, a Darcy man had turned his face from a fashionable, wealthy woman of social standing toward a girl of relatively obscure birth whose manner and refinement was not at all equal to that in the first circles. As little as Caroline had ever truly cared for the elder Mr. Darcy, her failure in the matter continued to rankle her; she had failed at very little in life, and did not intend to begin making her peace with disappointment now.

No. Priscilla would set right what had previously gone so wrong. She and Jonathan Darcy would meet at the altar yet. As Caroline made her way up toward her bedchamber, where her exhausted maid awaited the chance to unlace her mistress's stays, Caroline realized that relatively few men besides Jonathan Darcy had singled out Miss Tilney.

Perhaps she would do well to consider why.

The next morning, Jonathan Darcy—innocent of any stratagems regarding his marital future, save for his own—made ready to depart the Bertrams' house relatively early. At the ball, Miss Tilney had apparently reached an understanding with Mr. Crawford that he would call upon her and her mother this morning, with Jonathan also in attendance. This would constitute their best and perhaps only chance to ask this gentleman their questions. Jonathan had spoken of their plan to Mr. Bertram the evening before, but he knew he must now formally take his leave of someone in the family. Why it should be necessary to explain again that which was already known to all was one of the vagaries of etiquette, but where a solid rule to govern behavior could be found, he was generally grateful for it.

It was Mrs. Bertram he met upon the stair. She listened to his plans attentively as she descended by his side, nodding all the while, but Jonathan noted that she remained very pale and very quiet—even more so than she had been at his arrival, and that in itself had been but a shadow of the woman he had first met in Surrey. He knew her health to be delicate. Surely if there were concerns, if a physician needed to be consulted, Mr. Bertram would have acted. Yet Jonathan could not content himself with that judgment. As they reached the lower hall, he ventured to ask, "Mrs. Bertram, forgive me if I speak out of turn, but are you quite well? Perhaps London does not agree with you, though I may only think so because it so frequently does not agree with me. The noise, the city air— certainly it is most unwholesome. I hope my question does not cause offense."

Her smile, though slight, appeared genuine. "You could never offend me through your desire that I be well, Mr. Darcy. It is exactly as you say. London does not agree with me." Mrs. Bertram briefly touched his arm. "But how kind of you to ask, how good of you to notice."

Jonathan knew he was being told a polite falsehood, but it was not his place to pry further. Besides, after a lifetime of often feeling he had failed to notice much that he should in the subtleties of behavior, he was much surprised that he had apparently seen something in Mrs. Bertram that others had missed—or, rather, that he had correctly interpreted what he had seen. It was something of a novelty to him, one that pre- occupied him so much he very nearly collided with someone on the stoop.

"Well!" Mrs. Norris stood before him, rearranging her clothes and basket as though they had in fact struck each other with violent force, though Jonathan had stopped a good foot short of doing so. "I see that near strangers to the family continue to be welcome, while one of their own daughters is not—but they will hold grievances, they will hold grudges, and sorry will they be for it."

"Excuse me, Mrs. Nor—"

"My sister welcomes me, she welcomes all the assistance I can give her, and it is a great deal indeed. I had half the running of Mansfield Park when the children were young, more than half if you wish to know the truth of it, and she at least is grateful. To see Tom turn out so cold! Edmund so severe!" Mrs. Norris busied herself with her mobcap; perhaps she imagined a collision would have knocked it clean off her head. "Well, Maria has had a change now, has she not, as Mr. Rushworth in the end knew where his duty lay. They may have some crawling to say sorry yet, oh, mark my words, they shall."

The lecture seemed to be one that Mrs. Norris was prepared to deliver at all times, at length, to any person who could not escape its hearing. Jonathan thought fast. "I am certain you would never reveal any private business of the family to a person so unrelated as myself."

"Indeed not." She drew herself upright, instantly convinced that Jonathan had meant to pry, and had been defeated only by her strong will and moral uprightness. With that, Mrs. Norris bustled to the door, and Jonathan was again free.

Juliet Tilney had descended to the sitting room of their London residence well before morning callers could be expected. "I must be settled, you see," she told her mother, who still wore a dressing gown after Juliet's toilette was complete. "Calm, composed, and prepared to ask vitally important questions."

Catherine smiled. "Indeed, you have become wise in the ways of such investigations. But you must be truthful with me, Juliet—your eagerness has everything to do with the man you wish to question, nothing whatsoever concerning the man who will ask questions alongside you?"

It is beyond the power of most young women of eighteen— or, in truth, most persons regardless of sex or age—to hear such a question without a smile, particularly the morning after sharing six dances. However, let us do justice to Juliet and confess that her resolve remained clear. "Mamma, my pleasure in seeing Mr. Darcy does not make me insensible of the gravity of our responsibility in this matter. Both the Bertram family and the London police have done us great honor in entrusting this matter to our care, and I do not intend to disappoint them."

Few would blame Catherine for the maternal pride she felt at that moment, or for her hurrying upstairs upon hearing a visitor arriving to the house. Thus it was that Juliet greeted Mr. Darcy alone, save for the omnipresent servants just beyond the open doors. "Forgive my earliness, Miss Tilney," he said, "but we must of course be prepared."

"I had just said as much to my mother."

Indeed, the wisdom of their forethought became clear in the very next instant, when the second visitor's knock of the morning sounded.

Within a few minutes, and after all necessary social niceties, Juliet sat with Mr. Darcy in the sitting room, Mr. Crawford in a chair opposite them. The door was left ajar, despite the fact that they were three to the room; the servants must have sensed that Henry Crawford was not the ideal person to serve as chaperone. He appeared all good health and cheer, more amused by their curiosity than concerned by it. However, Juliet had sufficient experience to know how little stock could be put in the mere *appearance* of ease.

Their first question, Mr. Crawford answered easily enough: "On the morning of Mr. Rushworth's demise," said he, "I had gone to Wyngarde's, where I am a member. Early in the day for it, I know, but my sister has all the household in such a flutter of preparation for her wedding that there is no peace to be had there. I wished only for coffee and amiable companionship, for some conversation that would not revolve around flowers or lace."

"Your sister will verify this?" Juliet asked. When Mr. Crawford nodded, she continued. "Whom did you speak with at the club?"

Mr. Crawford shrugged. "There were very few gentlemen about at that hour, but I suppose some of the servants might recollect my presence."

"Indeed," Mr. Darcy said, "and furthermore, there is a book kept at the door, where guests sign their names or have one of the staff do so for them. We can easily seek Mr. Crawford's name there."

"I had forgot all about that book—for I have not touched pen to paper there myself above once, if even then. But those of the staff are more meticulous than I." Mr. Crawford laughed in what seemed genuine good humor. "How right you are, Mr. Darcy. Yes, you will find my name inscribed there."

Juliet pressed her point. "There was no one there you recognized?"

"Not a soul," Mr. Crawford confirmed. "A few familiar faces, but no one to whom I have been introduced, nor whom I can presume to know me."

She changed the subject, which she hoped might jostle any remarks that had been prepared or rehearsed. "Mr. Crawford, what was your opinion of the late Mr. Rushworth?"

"I thought him a fool. Harmless, to be sure—obedient to his mother in a way no grown man should be—wealthy as Croesus, but a fool. Had Mr. Rushworth not inherited an estate such as Sotherton, Miss Maria Bertram would never have looked twice at him. More to the point, neither would Mrs. Norris have done so. The match would have been impossible."

Mr. Crawford seemed to Juliet somewhat . . . protective of Mrs. Maria Rushworth. Wishing to acquit her, perhaps, of having chosen Mr. Rushworth entirely on her own?

Mr. Darcy said, "You did not like him, then?"

This won a scoff from Mr. Crawford, though this was but a small victory—his contempt could be had for very little. "I did not. Nor did I hate him. He was the sort of person it would be difficult to have any feelings about whatsoever, which is the worst of all. If one hates a person, that person at least has merited attention, notice, thought, true? Mr. Rushworth could not excite even that in my heart or, I would wager, the hearts of any others. Yes, I confess that I cared nothing for the man. If this be evidence of murderous intent, mark my words: *That* motive will be shared by virtually every other soul who ever knew him."

Poor Mr. Rushworth, Juliet thought. He seemed to have harmed no one, but that had not been sufficient to make him valued or loved.

Mr. Darcy surprised her with what he asked next. "Forgive my bluntness, Mr. Crawford, but this is an occasion for plain speaking. Had you ever resumed your . . . entanglement with Mrs. Rushworth, since your elopement years prior?"

The answering smile Mr. Crawford gave was rueful, one that expected sympathy rather than condemnation. "Ever shall I have . . . shall we say, a 'soft spot' for Mrs. Rushworth. But let me add that there is no question of courtship or matrimony. Certainly it is not my wish, nor have I led her to believe otherwise. It would be ungentlemanly of me to suggest that Mrs. Rushworth's feelings in the matter at all exceed my own."

Juliet could not give voice to the dislike this reply awakened in her for another few minutes, after Mr. Crawford had been sent on his way. "He says he does not want to 'suggest' that Mrs. Rushworth is still in love with him, all while doing precisely that. And then says he would never be ungentlemanly! There is nothing of the gentleman in him, not in the slightest: no kindness, no decency, no discretion."

"To me his words seem very much to follow the pattern of a gentleman," Mr. Darcy replied, "and I could not quite put my finger upon what was wrong. You have determined it, Miss Tilney; it is that his words are hollow, devoid of feeling."

"Yet that does not make his words a lie, not exactly," said Juliet. "His story about leaving his house and going to his club can be verified easily enough. So it would seem that he could not have gone to Mr. Rushworth's that morning."

"He could have gone to the club only after the deed was done," Mr. Darcy began, but then he shook his head. "No. Mr. Crawford is a man of strong feeling, rather excitable. He is not at all the sort of person who could strangle a person and then blithely go about his morning business. Do not you agree?"

"I do indeed," Juliet said. "If Mr. Crawford went to his club, then he is innocent. And if he is innocent—if he was at the club—then we have learned something else as well, Mr. Darcy. Do you see it?"

Understanding dawned upon Mr. Darcy's face. "Sir Thomas also said he was at Wyngarde's on the morning of Mr. Rushworth's death. If both Mr. Crawford and Sir Thomas were at the club, however, they would have seen each other."

Juliet smiled at the effect of this revelation. So many girls were told not to display their cleverness to men; what an exhilaration it was to be with a man who treasured it! "As it is in both men's interest to be proved present at Wyngarde's on that date, at that time, neither has any reason to lie about the other's presence there. Unless . . . could they simply not have seen each other? Been in different rooms? I do not know how such clubs are arranged inside."

Her worry faded as soon as Mr. Darcy shook his head. "There is a wide central hall, and at that hour, I would imagine that anyone present would be able to hear anyone else. Although I cannot absolutely rule out such a scenario, I do believe it very unlikely."

"So you must go to Wyngarde's and ask to see their books," Juliet said. "Only one of the men will have their name written there. The other is lying, and then . . . have we found our murderer?"

Mr. Darcy's hopes were not so sanguine. "The book entries could easily be falsified. A pound or two slipped to a member of staff—or even a strong suggestion, particularly coming from a titled man such as Sir Thomas—and it would be done. But they may not have expected us to ask."

"Let us hope." Juliet could hardly contain her anticipation. "Mr. Darcy, I believe we are near success at last!"

After leaving the Tilneys' London residence, Jonathan Darcy intended to go to Wyngarde's as soon as possible. As he himself was not a member, he would need one of his hosts to accompany him—and as this errand was intended to check the alibi of Sir Thomas, it seemed impolitic to ask that gentleman for the favor. Impatiently Jonathan awaited the return of Mr. Edmund Bertram, all the while performing the principal office of any guest, namely listening to his hosts. It was his misfortune that the only person who remained in the sitting room throughout the day was Lady Bertram, who could not converse at any length on subjects beyond tea and Pug.

Upon Edmund Bertram's return, however, Jonathan learned that the entire company was obliged to dress for dinner and go out, "for the Allerdyces have invited us to dinner," Mr. Bertram announced. "The entire party, excepting none."

"Pug will not be able to go," observed Lady Bertram, a point upon which no one felt the need to expand. Jonathan was disappointed in his plans, but the club books could be checked as well on the next day. Were either Mr. Crawford or Sir Thomas inclined to falsify the books at Wyngarde's, they no doubt would have taken this step already, and thus delay could do no additional harm.

Sir Thomas certainly seemed to have no inkling of potential trouble. He, soon to be a bridegroom, had the opportunity to more fully acquaint his family with that of the woman he wished to be his wife; it was not to be expected that he would make anything less than the most of the occasion. This much, Jonathan detected on his own. It required a whisper from Mrs. Julia Yates, however, for him to realize the invitation was somewhat oddly timed.

"The day after a ball," Mrs. Yates muttered to her husband as they donned coats and capes, awaiting the carriage's arrival. "All of us up until nearly sunrise, and they invite us to dinner tonight? With not even a day's notice? We shall not get back to our own apartments until late yet again."

"Your brother has a title now," Mr. Yates replied in the same low tone. "You should not underestimate his desirability as a husband—the Allerdyces surely do not. They wish to secure him sooner rather than later."

Her sigh of resignation satisfied Jonathan that she believed her husband's words, and upon reflection, he was inclined to believe them, too. This hasty dinner invitation was intended to hurry along an engagement between Miss Frederica Allerdyce and Sir Thomas. In truth, that was a small part of Caroline Allerdyce's rationale. Never—not that night nor upon any other to come—did Jonathan dream that this invitation was primarily aimed at *him*.

Even being seated next to Mrs. Allerdyce at dinner did not excite any particular interest from Jonathan, who attempted to gamely make small talk while fixing his gaze at the bright jeweled clip upon his hostess's cap; this often passed for direct eye contact, he found, and prevented offense.

Yet Mrs. Allerdyce asked such odd questions! "Tell me, Mr. Darcy, do not your parents miss you terribly? Surely they write every day, asking for the date of your return."

"No, not at all," Jonathan said. "They wish me to make the most of the opportunity to be in London. In truth, I do not much care for the city, and I would have asked to return home already, but for—but for the matter of Mr. Rushworth." Which was true, even if his first impulse had been to say *Miss Tilney* instead.

"Yes, of course," said Mrs. Allerdyce. "It is so good of you to oblige your hosts in that manner. But you must not let such obligations interfere with your duty to your parents. The London season exists to bring together young men and young women from the best families, in order that each can make the most eligible match possible. Anything less is a betrayal of filial duty! Yet I am being foolish. You would never choose beneath you; you would never stain your family."

"Indeed not," Jonathan replied, never once imagining that Juliet Tilney might be considered a "stain" by any person of sense. He thought only that Mrs. Allerdyce was fixated upon such ideas due to the strong likelihood that Sir Thomas would soon propose to her elder daughter.

Yet her words did make him consider: He was, in truth, failing in his filial duty. He had not written to Pemberley since the departure of the rest of his family—in and of itself negligent but hardly extraordinary. (Neither Matthew nor James wrote more frequently than once a month; his parents were accustomed to such silences.) What made the omission egregious was that Jonathan had not told them of either the murder investigation or of Miss Tilney's presence in town, about both of which they would have expected to be informed.

Jonathan took heart. He would write them on the morrow, if it took hours of composition to do it. He would reveal all.

And he would ask for their permission to court Juliet Tilney.

Chapter Twelve

Filial duty is one of the Ten Commandments proclaimed in the Old Testament, and if it is not taken as seriously as once it was, it is to the detriment of our age. Jonathan Darcy, deeply fond of his parents and grateful for their understanding, never wished to be negligent in such duty. Yet let us not judge him too harshly if, upon the next day, he elected to write his letter to Pemberley only after checking the books at Wyngarde's. The letter would be written that very night and posted the next morning, Jonathan resolved, but he must put his pledge to his hosts first. Justice must be served.

Mr. Edmund Bertram had invited all the house to attend an assembly with him that afternoon, a talk to be given by the great Mr. Wilberforce. Jonathan agreed, and was pleased to know that a card of invitation had been sent to the Tilney household as well. With this settled, he was easily able to request being taken to Wyngarde's. Jonathan asked as tactfully as he could manage, for he knew he was asking Mr. Bertram to potentially unmake his brother's alibi for the murder of Mr. Rushworth.

However, Jonathan's tact was so delicate, so cautious, that Mr. Bertram did not even recognize that Sir Thomas's integrity was in question. His doubts were all for Mr. Crawford. "I do not think well of the man," Mr. Bertram said as they walked along the city streets, "nor should I ever have done so. Yet I cannot bring myself to consider him a likely murderer, and least of all can I imagine that he would do so for the sake of Maria. He has done little enough for my sister since her flight from her marital home. Why would he risk both hanging and eternal damnation to be with a woman he has not bothered to visit for years?"

Despite the overpowering assault of the city noise and bustle on his senses, Jonathan was able to absorb most of this. "Your reasoning is sound," he said, "but all the same, it is best to be certain. People often hold motives deep within themselves at which the rest of the world would never guess."

He did not add that it was entirely possible Mr. Crawford had visited Mrs. Rushworth more often, and more recently, than the Bertram family knew.

They reached Wyngarde's shortly before luncheon, and many gentlemen had already made their way to the club for food. Mr. Bertram was quickly overtaken by acquaintances, most of whom wished to know where Sir Thomas was, why he had not come with them. In a distant corner, Jonathan glimpsed his erstwhile schoolmate, Laurence Follett, whose presence in town he had nearly forgot—and who must not have called on Miss Tilney, or else she would have spoken of it. Much cheered, Jonathan took the opportunity to speak to the staff and examine the club's guest book.

It was the work of but a moment to find Mr. Henry Crawford's name written on the page devoted to the day of Mr. Rushworth's murder, very near the top, which lent force to his assertion that he had come to Wyngarde's early. However, all Jonathan's searching could not turn up the name of Sir Thomas Bertram, neither early nor late nor at any other point on the date.

This did not make Sir Thomas a killer—but it made him a liar.

Shortly afterward, Juliet Tilney and her mother Catherine set out from their London residence to meet the Bertrams' party at the Wilberforce assembly. Mere minutes before their departure, the servant had brought to them a letter from Mr. Tilney, which they elected to read in the carriage. As their equipage rattled along the noisy streets, Catherine read to her daughter an easy, entertaining message that told of weddings and christenings Mr. Tilney had performed, complete with the silly mishaps that had plagued each ceremony.

Catherine left off reading aloud, however, when she reached the last paragraph of her husband's letter. By long tradition, this was where he wrote affectionate words for her eyes alone. So Juliet thought nothing of the silence as her mother read on:

> *Your account of Mr. Jonathan Darcy in London has astonished me, first in that I did not believe him capable of showing such gentlemanly affection toward our daughter, second—and the more stunning by far—in that I appear to have been mistaken in my beliefs. Well might you wonder that your insightful husband has proved wrong! Yet somehow I suspect you have previously had an inkling that my judgment was not invariably infallible. Wives generally discover this about their husbands, I find, though I had hoped to postpone your disillusionment for another decade or two.*
>
> *But now I will cease to joke, now I will be serious. I truly believed Mr. Darcy to be devoid of any romantic feeling or intent for Juliet, and to me it seemed that she believed this as fully as I did. Her sentiments for him were more tender, and yet she seemed to wish them gone; she is a strong-willed, sensible girl, and so I thought that soon she would have laid all this behind*

her. Furthermore, his parents, the master and mistress of Pemberley, seemed to share my convictions (on the part of the elder Mr. Darcy, with rather unflattering fervor).

Instead, you inform me that both she and the younger Mr. Darcy are enamored of each other and you anticipate a courtship soon. I bow to your superior understanding of such things, and I confess that I had no objection to the gentleman in question other than my belief in his indifference. If he is not indifferent, then my objection is moot, and if he has sense enough to value our Juliet as she deserves, then so be it.

His family, I think, will have to be heard from— but I can report that I liked the mother well enough to endure the father if need be.

Catherine smiled as she folded the paper and tucked it into her reticule. To her it seemed that all obstacles had been overcome, or soon would be. Surely no one could disapprove of Juliet for long. Her daughter's prospects seemed quite assured—if only people would stop being murdered quite so often.

Of all the social events of the London season, assemblies are the most difficult to describe, for they come in all sizes, are set in all possible venues, and may touch upon the widest variety of topics. Certainly they are the only social event of the season that can potentially be considered *thoughtful* in nature. Although some assemblies are lighthearted or insubstantial, others might touch upon political movements, philosophical questions, tales of travels abroad, even the antiquities being discovered every day in Egypt. Some attendees, more taken with the frivolity of the season, looked upon such assemblies merely as opportunities to be seen in their afternoon clothes. Others, however, seized the chance to learn more profound truths about the persons they are coming to know.

Among these last were Miss Frederica Allerdyce and her father, who were surprised and pleased to encounter the Bertram and Tilney parties. Both Jonathan Darcy and Juliet Tilney found that, when away from her overbearing mother and flirtatious sister, Miss Allerdyce's personality showed to much better effect. Her speech was plain but thoughtful, her manner quiet but engaging, and she took a civil interest in the doings of others without dwelling upon herself. Miss Allerdyce was most disappointed that Sir Thomas had not come to the assembly as well, but when Mr. Bertram explained that the owner of an estate such as Mansfield Park had a great deal of business to conduct in town, she acknowledged the justice of this.

"All the same," Miss Allerdyce said, "I should think a cause such as this a priority. British trade must be severed from the evil of slavery, and it is through the influence of just such men as Sir Thomas that change can be brought about."

These words seemed to strike Mr. Bertram with especial force. He paused before saying, "Miss Allerdyce, I feel it incumbent upon me to reveal two pieces of information—two vital facts that may be of particular interest."

Miss Allerdyce and her father exchanged glances before she said, "Then I would be most obliged to you, Mr. Bertram."

"I must first confess to you that some part of the Bertram fortune was made on a plantation in Antigua, and, yes, that plantation is farmed by slaves." Miss Allerdyce, though clearly very shocked, said nothing, which allowed Mr. Bertram to continue: "But my second confession will be more welcome to you, for it is that Sir Thomas has chosen to sell the plantation. In fact, I believe it is that very business he attends to at present. He has seen the moral evil of slavery—he wishes no more to do with it—he will do what our father would not and restore our family from that sin."

"How very good of him!" Miss Allerdyce brightened. It seemed that this very fact might be what had elevated her sentiments from approval of Sir Thomas to something much more like affection. "Would that more men of fortune saw the world as he does, and had the courage to do the same!"

Comprehending that he had aided his brother's matrimonial prospects, rather than ending them, Mr. Bertram felt the greatest relief. "We have become an antislavery family, thanks be to God. In fact, I am most surprised that my wife did not come with Mr. and Mrs. Yates. She is the strongest abolitionist of us all."

Mrs. Julia Yates, who had been attending to nothing but the new styles of clothing on display upon the ladies present, began to listen again upon hearing her own name. "Fanny said she felt not well," Mrs. Yates said. "Upon my word, she has never been strong, but never have I seen her so retiring, so weak, as she has been here in London. Not once since our arrival have I seen her go about as usual; even at the ball, she would not dance. Did not that strike you as strange, Edmund?"

It struck Edmund as not at all the subject he would choose to discuss in company. He said only, "My wife is not always fond of noise and fuss. London is far from her favorite place to be."

"I quite agree with her," said Mr. Allerdyce. "I humor my wife and my daughters by coming to the city, and glad I am to be able to please them, but for my own pleasure, I should infinitely prefer my own house, my own hearth, and my own library."

Jonathan sensed a kindred spirit. "My thoughts precisely."

Then there was murmuring and shifting—the speakers entered—and the assembly had begun.

Fanny Bertram *was* the strongest abolitionist in the family. But for her, who knew how long it might have taken Edmund to condemn or even criticize their plantation holdings? He had taken it as given that anything his father did must be right. Fanny, forced by her circumstances to always listen and rarely speak, had by so doing gained a clarity on the subject that the rest of the Bertrams had only belatedly recognized. She had even harbored doubts that Tom would truly sell the plantation, though she was shamed by these doubts now that the task was finally underway.

So she would gladly have attended that particular assembly, regardless of the crowd. But Fanny did not want to jostle herself in a carriage. She did not want to be bumped or poked by other attendees. The slightest incident or accident . . . who could say what would prove deadly to all her hopes?

No, she thought, as she lay in bed, one hand resting upon her abdomen. *To my one hope. To my last hope.*

This time she would not invite bad luck. She would not imagine names and practice writing them in beautiful script. She would tell no one of it, not even after her physical form had betrayed her secrets to all, and she would retire into her confinement at the earliest possible date. Fanny imagined only leaving her bed for that which nature and cleanliness required—if that would strain the few servants she and Edmund were able to employ at the parsonage, then she would return to Mansfield Park for her confinement. Neither Tom nor Aunt Bertram would deny her that. They would make a comfortable room ready for her, perhaps even assign a maid or two to wait in attendance upon her at all times.

Such pampering was outside Fanny's experience, and never would she have had the will to ask for a tenth as much were it not for the sake of the baby. To protect her child, there was nothing she was not ready to do, even if it meant making demands. Even if it meant *raising her voice.*

I will not even knit, Fanny promised as she lay still. (Who she promised—Edmund, or the baby, or the Lord—even she did not know.) *I will not even strain myself that much. Instead, I will swaddle the child in whatever blanket can be spared and not begin my knitting until the very day of its birth.*

Oh, if only that day will come!

After the assembly, Mr. Bertram and the Allerdyces were so engaged in conversation that they elected to go to a nearby coffeehouse to continue sharing their thoughts. The Yateses excused themselves—they cared for neither coffee nor thinking—and Susan was taken home in the carriage of her new friends, the Worthingtons. However, to Juliet Tilney's delight, her mother agreed that they might come for coffee as well, and Mr. Darcy of course joined them.

The coffeehouse was in its own way as stunning a sight as any of the grander wonders Juliet had yet seen in London. So many men, and more than a few women, all of them animated in conversation at their various tables while the waiters moved smoothly between them, pouring cup after cup of coffee. *How exquisite,* she thought, *the scent of coffee mingled with pipe smoke!* To her that was the nicest scent of London yet.

The coffeehouse was a noisy place, filled with murmurings and laughter, with the rustling of dozens of newspapers and the clinking of cups upon saucers. Yet it was the kind of noise that allowed one to lean close and whisper to one's companion, which was of great service to their investigation. While her mother, Mr. Bertram, and the Allerdyces spoke of Mr. Wilberforce's talk, Mr. Darcy was able to discreetly tell Juliet what he had found at Wyngarde's that morning.

"So it is Mr. Crawford who told the truth," she said, "and Sir Thomas who lied. I must confess, I thought the opposite far more likely."

Mr. Darcy nodded. "As did I."

A notion came to her. "Is it possible that our theory of a false entry in the book is still true? Both men might have lied to us for different reasons, but only Mr. Crawford went to the trouble of covering his tracks later, perhaps because his was the greater guilt. Sir Thomas may have business that is private, but not criminal."

"I thought of that," said Mr. Darcy, "but on the whole I think it unlikely. The nature of the book at Wyngarde's—gentlemen sign one after the other. No spaces are left open. Mr. Crawford would have had to be exceedingly cautious to have preemptively arranged for a blank spot."

She breathed out in frustration. "Nor does he strike us as a cautious man. No, he is not a plotter. If that is how the book is, then, yes, he was there . . . and he cannot be Mr. Rushworth's killer. But what motive could"—Juliet dropped her voice to an even softer whisper—"Sir Thomas Bertram possibly have?"

Chapter Thirteen

That evening, after Lady Bertram heard the tales of the coffeehouse, she did something quite unexpected, something she had rarely done before: She had an idea.

"Should we not have Maria to dinner?" she asked her startled sons. "Maria and my sister both. It is time our entire family met again at leisure, is it not?"

It was Edmund who found his tongue first. "You know that we cannot countenance what Maria has done. To do so would be to share in her disgrace and be likewise ostracized by all polite society."

Tom, less severe in moral judgment, said, "If she married again, and married respectably, perhaps we could know her—in some contexts—but not here in London, never here. Were we to be seen putting Maria forth in society, I doubt the Allerdyces would ever visit us again, much less—" He caught himself with the sly smile of a would-be lover very certain of his suit. "Well, as Maria is not married, nor likely to be, the point is moot."

Lady Bertram, in highly uncommon spirit that day, actually pressed her case. "I do not say we should see her in society. No—that would not do, I am sure. Yet it is quite another thing to allow her into the house privately, with only the family at home."

Far from being overcome by any desire to see her sister again, Mrs. Yates objected. "We have a guest, Mamma. Mr. Darcy is here."

Jonathan, who had been sitting in the corner counting the

minutes until he could finally go up to his room for the evening, nearly startled but recovered himself quickly. "Yes, I am
a guest—but one undertaking an errand that involves Mrs.
Rushworth. Her knowledge of Mr. Rushworth, of those nearest to him, is valuable to me. So it would be opportune for us
to spend more time together, perhaps also with Miss Tilney
present?"

This was greatly daring, for not only was Jonathan, a mere
houseguest, effectively making dinner invitations to a house
not his own, but he also had obliquely alluded to Mrs. Rushworth as a suspect in their murder investigation. Edmund
Bertram's wary glance made it clear that he, at least, had not
missed that implication. Yet Jonathan's suggestion attracted
no open objection; and before the hour was out, even as the
Yateses returned to their own residence, invitations were
written to bring together the party at dinner in the Bertrams'
town house the next evening.

Jonathan was observant enough to see the difference
between "no objection" and "no disapproval." Mrs. Fanny
Bertram sat in the corner, very quiet and still. Her lips pressed
together in a thin line as Lady Bertram spoke about how very
pleasant it would all be, no fuss or trouble for anyone, the
servants would not think twice about preparing dinner for
twelve on short notice. Yet Jonathan sensed that Mrs. Bertram's unease was not related to the murder, and he was glad
there was therefore no need to interpret it.

Yet to be a spouse is to be an interpreter of much that is left
unsaid. Edmund Bertram noted his wife's demeanor as well,
and they retired early that night in order for him to be able to
speak with her.

"I know you do not approve about Maria," he said as he

fussed with the tie of his nightshirt. "In truth, I would rather she did not come, either."

Fanny spoke the first words she had uttered since before Lady Bertram's unexpected declaration of intent. "Then why did you not object?"

"I *did* object to a larger gathering. That, we cannot countenance, and certainly we must not endanger Tom's potential engagement to a young lady of such fine breeding and spirit as Frederica Allerdyce. But to reach some private rapprochement among the family, to set my mother's mind at ease, this must be very desirable." Fanny glanced at Edmund then, her meaning plain to see. He sighed. "I grant you, my mother's mind is rarely ill at ease. Very little troubles her. This, however, is all the more reason to grant her what she wishes, as such wishes are so seldom expressed. Also, we must remember that the invitation involves Aunt Norris, and no doubt it is she whom my mother most wishes to spend time with. Aunt Norris shares in Maria's exile, but not in her shame."

Mrs. Norris's severity upon Fanny had left the younger lady with little fond feeling for the elder. Yet how could she deny the claims of family? Fanny said, "Could not Aunt Norris have been invited on her own?"

"There, I think, we would go too far," Edmund replied. "It is one thing never to see Maria, and another to pointedly exclude her. Morality taken to such deliberate extremes too easily develops into cruelty. More significantly, perhaps—we need to pacify Maria. To settle her. She has already attempted once to force her way back into our family dwelling here; it is natural to assume that Mr. Rushworth's death will have agitated her, and the acquisition of wealth will have exacerbated her pride. If we set a pattern for right conduct now, if we establish such limited connection with her as can be justly sustained, then we may well be happy for it later on."

This was all good sense, and normally Fanny was the more

softhearted of them both. So Edmund was surprised to see how quiet and uneasy his wife appeared. They were in bed, the candle blown out, before he decided to speak and whispered, "Does it still trouble you—Maria having a child?"

Fanny shrugged and said nothing, which was as good as a yes.

Edmund continued speaking, the better to perhaps draw Fanny out. "I hope the girl to be Rushworth's rather than Crawford's, though I suppose we will never know. Somehow the former seems less disgraceful, a position I do not believe I could support with doctrine."

"That should be what most pains me, I know," Fanny continued. "But it is not. What I cannot forget is that God rewarded her sin, while punishing our faith."

Edmund had endeavored to put their dashed hopes firmly behind him. He did not know how far he had succeeded, for sometimes the overheard laughter of children or a baby's cry had the power to make his throat feel tight. He understood only that he was enduring the pain better than Fanny had been able to do so far. She had pleaded with him never to speak of it, and this plea he had obeyed; but daily he observed her struggle without knowing how to help her, if indeed he could.

In this particular matter, however, their feelings were not the same. "Fanny, you of all persons should realize that punishment and reward is assured only in the Hereafter. There, our Lord will turn away the wicked and embrace the just. In this life—virtue helps us to live happier and better lives, but it is no ward against sorrow and loss. And though sin brings much grief, it is not always without earthly benefit."

Fanny turned to him, her grave face even paler in the moonlight. "Still I cannot comprehend why the Lord should grant a child to Maria, who seems barely to take note of the little girl."

"Perhaps, in time, the blessing of motherhood will improve Maria's character. Now that she no longer need worry about her material future, or Ellen's, Maria will not be made desperate. She need not be so grasping. Her daughter might yet be the making of her."

"Might yet," Fanny whispered, as though those words meant something to her in particular. Their eyes met, and instead of sorrow, Edmund glimpsed a kind of eagerness there. Or was he imagining things? Her expression reminded him of the day when she had told him of the quickening within her—he would swear she was about to deliver him the same news, had not the midwife told them it was impossible. His hopes were not yet entirely governed, it seemed.

He said only, "Do not look at any of this as judgment upon Maria, or upon you. Or us."

She sighed. That small glimmer of excitement was gone. "I will try, Edmund. I will try."

The dinner invitation was received that morning at the Tilney home with pleasure by Juliet, and a weary acquiescence from her mother, Catherine. "Every day, there is a dance or a dinner or an assembly—and how well I remember dancing until dawn at party after party, without feeling the slightest need to stop! Those years are fled. I confess, I would welcome nothing so much this evening than to rest. But your grandfather did not send us here to sit by a fire we could as easily have sat by at home."

"I am sure the invitation is meant to assist in the murder investigation," Juliet declared. "We must go. Mamma, please?"

Catherine had never had any serious intention of turning the invitation down. Tired though she was, she knew her duty both to her daughter and to the cause of justice. "Of course we shall go. Yet I believe all your new dinner dresses have been seen already—what a wardrobe the London season requires! We have not time to get anything else made up."

Although Juliet had not been thinking upon such frippery, once turned to the subject, her quick mind seized upon potential solutions. "We have time to retrim a dress, though. Remember the broad green velvet ribbon we brought? Would it not look fine on the paler green dress?"

"It would indeed," said Catherine, already laying aside her day's writing plans. (Normally she would have given the tasks ahead to a seamstress maid, but theirs had remained behind at Gloucestershire, and it was not a duty to be foisted upon any hired girl of unknown skill.) Paper and ink were abandoned on the desk as she went for the small sewing basket at the other side of the room. "Furthermore, we shall go shopping again tomorrow for similar notions, from which your other garments may benefit. Tonight at the dinner, I shall ask for recommendations for a good seamstress."

Juliet laughed. "*That* expedition is one we can describe to my grandfather in a letter." They had already mutually decided that he should near nothing about the murder investigation until its completion.

"As we are speaking of correspondence . . ." Catherine had debated whether or not to share this with her daughter, fearful of raising hopes—but Juliet was a sensible young woman, and it was always better to be straightforward. "I wrote to your father regarding Jonathan Darcy. You are aware, I think, that he did not favor any potential match between the two of you."

This topic was not one Juliet had expected to broach so early in the day. "His reply—is that what he wrote on the last page of his letter?"

"It is. Do not look so worried, child! Your father has stated that his disapproval was always couched in his firm belief that Mr. Darcy did not value you, that you might be ready to break your heart over a man who did not care for you. Having observed Mr. Darcy for myself here in London, I recognize the signs of an attachment, a very strong attachment indeed. Your father says that if I have judged the matter rightly, then he has no further objections to Mr. Darcy. Should he press his suit, he will find success with us, and with you, too, I think."

Juliet was too astonished, too delighted, for any maidenly pretense of modesty. "I believe that he would begin by inviting us to Pemberley. He would wish both our families present for the—for any announcement." Mr. Darcy had suggested as much during their time at Rosings Park, though this she was not prepared to tell her mother just yet. That would be presumptuous.

Was she truly to be so fortunate? To marry the man she liked best in the world, one who would both satisfy the requirements of her family and the deepest wishes of her heart? How rarely are all our needs and desires met in one person! Young as she was, Juliet understood as much, and found herself almost upon the verge of tears, from both gratitude and hope.

She repeated, "We would first go to Pemberley," the fabled grandeur of the house striking her anew. Juliet was neither materialistic nor acquisitive; her interest in Mr. Jonathan Darcy was firmly rooted in appreciation of his character. But it is most unreasonable to expect a young lady *not* to be delighted by the prospect of becoming mistress of Pemberley.

Catherine looked up from her sewing basket and whispered, "I confess a certain curiosity to see it."

"And I as well!" With that, Juliet and her mother embraced, in mutual expectation and joy.

Yet Juliet's smile faded as she looked down at her mother's basket, shifting into curiosity—and then, perhaps, an

understanding of the murder of Mr. Rushworth that had
eluded her until that very moment.

It is for the best that Mr. Jonathan Darcy had no notion of
what was being discussed in his absence. This was not to preclude any objections on his part—for he had none, and shared
Mrs. Tilney's preference for straightforwardness. However,
after such encouragement, he would have been unable to
think upon any subject beyond Juliet Tilney the rest of the
day. He instead was able to spend his free hours in the library,
enjoying the later chapters of *Ivanhoe*. (It was his good fortune that this house held a copy of the volumes, and so he was
not required to go to Wyngarde's to continue his reading of
the text.)

What a fine escape such history novels were! How perfect
a release from the cares, irritations, and distractions that
normally surrounded him! When he read one of Sir Walter
Scott's books, he felt as though he had left the room or
house he was in, almost as though he had left his own person. Instead, he looked upon the moors or rode his horse
Ebony through thick verdant forests. He breathed in air that
smelled of peat, or of the sea. He wore the colorful, swash-
buckling garments of earlier and more adventurous times
that—in Jonathan's mind if not historical reality—lacked the
stiffness and discomfort of everyday garb.

It may surprise the reader familiar with Jonathan's love of
Ivanhoe that he was not without objections to the text. Upon
his first reading, he had been stunned that Ivanhoe had not
wed the virtuous Rebecca. Granted, Ivanhoe was a Christian,
and Rebecca a Jew, but to Jonathan that hardly seemed to
signify. Had they not shown each other the greatest loyalty?
Had not each of them proven their worth over and over again?

Jonathan's favorite scene came near the end, when Rebecca was put on trial by battle, where for lack of a champion she might have lost her life, only to be thrillingly rescued when Ivanhoe arrived, fought for her, and triumphed. How likely it had seemed that this would be followed by a kiss!

Instead, Ivanhoe and Rebecca parted as friends, and he went back to marry Rowena, his childhood sweetheart. Rowena was unobjectionable, Jonathan supposed, but her reappearance in the story was a rather pale denouement compared to what might have been possible had Ivanhoe pursued Rebecca instead.

It had never occurred to Jonathan that some of his strong loyalty to Rebecca arose from his tendency to imagine her as looking very like Juliet Tilney, not until that evening, when she and her mother arrived for dinner.

"How are you this evening, Mr. Darcy?" Miss Tilney asked, all blushes. This was unlike her, but he supposed the fire had overheated the room somewhat.

"Very well indeed. May I escort you to the table?" For this he was rewarded with a nod and a warm smile.

He was not so enraptured as to forget his duty, and knew Miss Tilney was not either. They needed to exchange no more than a glance to confirm that they both noted how little anyone spoke to Maria Rushworth, and how very little Mrs. Rushworth said herself. Ellen's absence from the conversation also seemed marked; of course she had been left at home with the maid, which in and of itself was not at all strange, but most parents of young children like to talk of them and their funny ways. This tendency might have been the stronger with Mrs. Rushworth, owing to the family's only just having learned of the little girl—but the few questions asked about Ellen were answered tersely, discouraging further conversation on the matter.

Curious as Jonathan and Miss Tilney were about Mrs.

Rushworth, it appeared that Mrs. Yates was even more so. "What a lovely dress you are wearing, Maria. However did you get it made up so quickly?"

"Why should you think I had it made up quickly?" Mrs. Rushworth very nearly preened in her rust-colored silk. "I have had this dress for the better part of a year, Julia. Do not think I went to any more extraordinary trouble this evening than you have done."

With every other person in our lives, we are able to mature and to change, to relate to people as the adult we have become. With our siblings, however, we often regress. All our childish peevishness, sulks, and teasing come to the fore anew. Against any other onslaught, we may find the strength to preserve our spirit, but against the needling of a sister or brother, there is little defense.

Discovering this at that very moment was Mrs. Yates, who seemed likely to actually stamp her foot from pure petulance. "I thought you must have it new, as you are only recently come into money—which, of course, belongs to another, but is in your keeping for now." The clear implication was that very little of Ellen's inheritance was likely to remain by her majority.

Mrs. Rushworth did not even attempt to deny it. "There are those who have cared for me with greater loyalty than my own family. We were not so impoverished as you wished to believe."

Mrs. Norris had remained silent up until this point, not from any sense of discretion but purely because she had set upon her dinner with great eagerness. Now, however, she interjected, "Indeed, we have been able to practice thrift and economy in our household, and I flatter myself that I have done the greatest part of it. Not but that Maria does not manage things well! For she does, she is so talented in so many ways. But I have done all that I could. I have stood in the place of a maid when needed, whether attending to little

Ellen or serving the cake at teatime. I have always endeavored to see us prosperous; and, mark my words, we will not abandon all our good habits now that we also have good fortune."

Mrs. Yates paid little heed to this. Her attention was all for Mrs. Rushworth as she said, "You must have had more assistance than we realized. Do you mean that Henry Crawford has behaved toward you as he should—for a change?"

This remark shot across the dining table like an arrow aflame. Mrs. Rushworth's cheeks reddened. "Would you have preferred it had Mr. Crawford sought *you* out, instead?"

At this, Fanny Bertram seemed half likely to faint. Jonathan wondered whether he should change the subject and, if so, how and to what. He should not have worried, for Mrs. Norris seemed to consider the question her very own to answer. "Mr. Crawford may reconsider certain decisions now that Mr. Rushworth is no longer with us. I should not be surprised, not at all, were he to come around. Do not you think it remarkable that a congenial young man of wealth should have gone so long without marrying? Some do not forget first love so swiftly! Yes, I wish upon Henry Crawford the blessing of a good memory."

"I do not have a good memory," Lady Bertram said as she idly slipped a bit of pheasant to Pug beneath the table. "But I remembered the dinner invitation, did I not, Sister? I believe I said every word you told me, but I cannot be certain, for I remembered it then and now cannot recall it at all."

Mrs. Norris, only slightly shamefaced to be caught as the true instigator of this dinner, set upon her plate with knife, fork, and vigor. Susan Price stifled a giggle. Sir Thomas shot his mother an aggrieved look. Lady Bertram, oblivious to his consternation, selected another tidbit for Pug.

As might be anticipated from that last, both Mrs. Rushworth and Mrs. Norris left almost immediately after dinner. To Juliet's relief, however, her mother accepted the invitation to stay longer for a few rounds of whist. Catherine Tilney, Sir Thomas, Mrs. Yates, and Mr. Bertram gathered at the game table at the far end of the room; Mrs. Bertram pleaded a headache, which compelled her sister Miss Price to see her upstairs and look after her; Lady Bertram attended only to Pug; and Mr. Yates took up a book before promptly falling asleep on the divan. This left Juliet and Mr. Darcy alone at the other end of the room, even partly obscured by a screen, and therefore fully at liberty to speak.

"Both Mrs. Rushworth and Mrs. Yates remain quite taken with Mr. Crawford," Juliet said. "They were once rivals for his attentions, you know."

"I did not know, but I see now that I ought to have guessed." Mr. Darcy could be too severe upon himself in such matters, but she had no time to object before he continued. "Mrs. Rushworth's enduring interest in Mr. Crawford is plain enough, but do you truly think it of Mrs. Yates? To me she seems very fond of Mr. Yates, so far as I have been able to observe."

Juliet considered for a moment. "I believe you have hit upon something, Mr. Darcy. It is perhaps not so much that Mrs. Yates still desires the attentions of Mr. Crawford—more that she still resents her sister's having won them. That seems a contest it was far better to lose! Yet defeat is always unpleasant and often galling. Mrs. Yates's resentment regarding her sister's dalliance with Mr. Crawford may have long outlived whatever affection she had for the man."

"Regardless," Mr. Darcy said, "this particular grievance between them does not seem relevant to the matter of Mr. Rushworth."

At last the opportunity had come! "Mr. Darcy, earlier

today, I believe I may have guessed at the murder weapon. May I show you?"

"Indeed! What is it?"

Juliet went to the small basket in the corner where Mrs. Bertram discreetly kept her sewing supplies. From this she triumphantly held up an embroidery hoop.

Mr. Darcy hesitated. "I would always wish to laugh at your jokes, but as you know, some elements of humor can escape me."

"This is not humor. It is a theory." Juliet sat next to him, showing him the details of the hoop. "It is smooth, like the mark on Mr. Rushworth's neck. Its shape would explain the curving nature of the mark, and its diameter is wide enough— just—to slip over a man's head. Most embroidery hoops are not so large as this, and the one used would have had to be even larger, but such exist."

Mr. Darcy took the hoop, turned it that way and this. "I cannot envision this being used in such a way."

"If I may take the liberty—" Juliet began, and he nodded. She grasped the hoop and went to stand behind his chair. Comprehending her intention, Mr. Darcy remained very still as she slipped the wooden hoop over his head. It bumped his nose on the way down. She then pulled the hoop back, just enough for the wood to press firmly against his flesh. "Do you see, Mr. Darcy?"

"But can you truly pull hard enough to prevent my breathing? In theory, I mean—*that,* I do not wish to experience."

After a few moments of consideration, Juliet bent enough to bring her hand and forearm up through the hoop from below. Her bare fingers brushed against the back of Mr. Darcy's neck, through his hair, and all the warmth of the nearby fire could not prevent her shivering at the touch.

"Ah," she said. "Um. If I have my arm like this, and if the chair were positioned near the wall as we saw at Mr. Rushworth's, I could pull with a great deal of force, and resist much effort to get free."

Mr. Darcy seemed to have difficulty finding his voice, and he had to swallow before got the words out. "Well. Yes. However, it seems to me—it seems that it would have had to be a very large embroidery hoop indeed to not only fit over Mr. Rushworth's head but also to allow anyone to put it on him without resistance. You could not avoid it touching my nose, for instance, and I was cooperating in the effort. And would an embroidery hoop have been present? His mother had not yet joined him in London, and surely no servant would have left her sewing kit in the sitting room."

These points were valid, and Juliet had just spied another one. "Now that I look at it, I see how very narrow the hoop is. The mark upon Mr. Rushworth's throat was, you said, very wide. I must consider my theory disproven."

She was tempted to remove the hoop for him, and perhaps touch his hair again, but she allowed Mr. Darcy to do it himself. Immediately she began setting Mrs. Bertram's sewing basket to rights again, as it gave her an excuse to look down; that way he would not see how flustered she had become, nor witness whether or not he was similarly affected by that brief brush between them. Probably not, she decided—he did not care for unexpected touches—but how could she not wonder?

Mr. Darcy said, "It was a good thought, nonetheless. The mark that would be left by this hoop might not be so broad as the one upon Mr. Rushworth, but otherwise would appear very much the same. This is not the weapon we seek, but that weapon will look something like this."

"Whatever can it be?" Juliet said, before her mother won the latest round of whist, and all chance for private conversation was lost.

Chapter Fourteen

Many young women in a shop, holding up silken cord, might ask whether it would look well at the edge of her cape, or if it could be put to better use trimming a bonnet. Very few would be wondering how thick such a cord would need to be for it to prove efficacious in a strangling. But so it was with Juliet Tilney the next day. While her mother busied herself among the newest fabrics, Juliet was wishing she had been able to see Mr. Rushworth's body for herself. No doubt the sight would have been terrible to behold, but she had witnessed gruesome scenes before; and had she had a chance to examine the mark upon Mr. Rushworth's neck, she would have been better able to guess the weapon had been used to kill him.

Mr. Darcy said the mark was smooth and even, with no signs of abrasion or pattern that would have suggested rope, she mused, running the cord through her fingers. *Yet rope is extremely coarse. Would a cord made of silk, like this, have made the same marks?* Juliet felt vaguely that it would have done, but wished there were some way to know for sure. If only she had been able to expand her weapons research beyond the bounds of the Northanger Abbey kitchen!

"What nice cording," said a female voice; when Juliet looked up from her musings, she realized that it came from Priscilla Allerdyce. "How very elegant. You should sew it onto your next gown."

The cording was far too thick to make attractive trimming for a gown. Juliet suspected Priscilla knew that, but responded civilly. "I see that you too have found the season calls for more dresses."

"My wardrobe is equal to the event," Priscilla said, sniffing, "but one must always be aware of the current fashions. I suppose no one had ever told you before. This is your first trip to London, is it not?"

"Indeed," said Juliet. She had self-possession enough to maintain her composure, though she found Priscilla's ill-mannered remarks more ridiculous than hurtful. No smirk would escape her! Yet, being human, Juliet could not help but glance down at her dress and wonder what part of it had betrayed any lack of sophistication.

We must pause at this juncture to do our duty to Priscilla Allerdyce. She was not a fundamentally wicked girl; she could be jolly company at a party or a picnic; she was obedient to her parents; and she had demonstrated considerable accomplishment in languages, music, and dancing. Had she been raised by her father alone—or had Caroline Allerdyce been able to dismiss her old resentments—Priscilla would no doubt have been a delightful person to know. Indeed, there was every reason to hope that, if she married wisely, the better elements of her character would ultimately triumph over the lesser.

Yet her mother had *not* set aside the resentments she had first felt as Miss Caroline Bingley. She could not simply look at her own happy position and be content; she always remembered the position she might have held as mistress of Pemberley. That she did not love Fitzwilliam Darcy had never signified. She had been the foremost of their social circle, the prettiest and most accomplished among them; and as such, it had been Caroline's *right* to ascend to that position. To have that place stolen by a country girl who let her petticoats get muddy and her face tan in summer—how it had rankled! So she had decided that, if she could not come to Pemberley as wife, she would come as mother to one of the Darcy sons' brides.

Frederica had been no help with this ambition. Born nine months to the day after the Allerdyces had wed, Frederica had been too old to make a match with any of the Darcy boys—two were her junior, and she predicted that Jonathan Darcy would follow most men of his class and not marry until near his thirtieth year, by which time Frederica would be an old maid. Caroline, understanding this from the beginning, had thus brought her elder daughter up simply and affectionately, which had resulted in a young woman of fine character and mind.

Priscilla, on the other hand—there, Caroline would have her chance. She had filled the little girl's head with high expectations from her nursery days onward, but the true poison had not worked its evils upon her mind until a few years prior, when the courtship game could be more immediately anticipated. Since that time, no expense had been spared upon her younger daughter's clothes and amusements; she had been introduced to the finest society. Priscilla had improved upon their chances by growing up very pretty indeed. All was in position; success seemed very much within reach.

Then, unfortunately, Jonathan Darcy had taken up the ghoulish hobby of investigating murder, and it appeared that he always did so with Miss Juliet Tilney at his side.

From across the shop, Caroline watched Priscilla speaking to this Miss Tilney. She could not hear what was spoken, but from the way Miss Tilney's countenance changed, it was evident that Priscilla had shaken the girl's abominable confidence and put her in her place. That was good, but Caroline suspected it would not be sufficient.

There must be some deficit in Miss Tilney's position or upbringing, Caroline thought. *For Priscilla's sake, it must be so.*

She left the shop some minutes later with her daughter, a receipt for six yards of brown silk to be delivered later that day, and the determination to discover something, anything, that would remove any threat of Juliet Tilney becoming the young Mr. Darcy's bride.

At the residence of the Bertram family, meanwhile, most in the household were enjoying a quiet morning. Sir Thomas had busied himself in his study; Jonathan Darcy had investigative intentions for the afternoon and so felt free to continue his rereading of *Ivanhoe*. Susan had been asked to visit the Worthington sisters again—who had turned out to possess a very eligible brother—and Lady Bertram had unexpectedly agreed to accompany her.

"I suspect she mostly did so," Edmund said to Fanny as they finished breakfast downstairs, "because she let slip that she allowed Aunt Norris to suggest the dinner invitation. My mother affects more idleness of mind than she actually possesses. She realizes that she upset Tom, and, out of respect for his position of head of house, she wishes to please him by proving herself useful."

Fanny suspected that her husband was overestimating his mother's general comprehension, as well as her supposed concern for Susan's welfare, but there was no need to debate the points. "We will not have to receive them again, will we, Edmund?"

"That, I cannot say. Never again can Maria be an intimate member of our family, but to abandon her entirely would be to effectively abandon her to vice. How can we expect her to behave better, if she has no good examples about her? Aunt Norris is an upright Christian woman, to be sure, but Maria has never much heeded her. If only Rushworth had not been

so cruelly killed! My aunt may well be correct. Such a generous bequest—does it not suggest that he felt warmly enough
toward his daughter that a remarriage to the mother would
not have been impossible?"

A pause followed, during which Fanny chose her words
with great caution. "You believe, then, that Ellen is indeed
Mr. Rushworth's daughter?"

"I know your thoughts upon the matter, Fanny, I know
them well—but, no. Maria has been wounded by her own past
folly. Surely she would not have exacerbated the wound by
taking up with Henry Crawford again."

"Edmund, you are wary of strangers," Fanny answered,
"and sometimes you judge them more stringently than you
ought. Yet when it comes to those you care for, you possess
the opposite fault: You are too generous, too forgiving, too
inclined to see virtue where it is not." The ghost of Mary
Crawford seemed briefly to join them in the room.

"I will confess I have done so in the past, from time to
time," Edmund said. "But I will not concede that Ellen's father
is anyone other than Mr. Rushworth. He himself believed it
to be so, and thus it is not ours to doubt."

With this admission, Fanny had to be content. Edmund
set out on his day's errands while she curled up with a book
written by "A Lady"—who, she was given to understand, was
none other than Mrs. Catherine Tilney. Thus far she found
it amusing, if sometimes bordering on improper—but the
moral lesson of the whole seemed to be excellent. Next to
her dozed Pug, in Fanny's keeping while Aunt Bertram was
away.

At first she thought her breakfast did not agree with her.
Then the sensations within became both more pronounced
and more familiar. Fanny, like most women, had experienced
them regularly enough to know what they presaged, but she
did not want to believe.

It cannot be, she told herself. *Your fear has convinced you that you feel something you do not.*

Within half an hour, though, further denial was hopeless. She was not expecting a baby.

All the sensations she had felt during the previous three weeks had been no more than her feverish imagination deluding her. The midwife must have been correct after all. Fanny would never be able to have a child of her own. Never be able to make Edmund a father. She would remain empty, hollow, a burden, a failure.

Fanny rose to lock the door of her room, took the necessary measures with underthings and specially folded cloths, then collapsed onto the bed to give free rein to her tears. As she wept, Pug—knowing of her sorrow, in the way that beasts sometimes do—curled next to her so that their bodies touched. Fanny put her hand on the little dog to feel its warmth, its heartbeat, the rise and fall of its breath, for in that instant, she felt that if she did not touch another living creature, she would be ripped away from all the world.

Shortly before Jonathan was to go out, a servant came to him with two letters. To his astonishment, both were from Pemberley: one written in his father's hand, the other in his mother's. These, then, would have to be the replies to his own missive—the one in which he had spoken of the investigation and his desire to win Miss Tilney's hand.

Bracing himself, Jonathan first opened the letter he knew would be harsher, that written by his father.

> *Dear Jonathan,*
> *We are pleased to hear that you are well, and that you are enjoying your time in London more than you had*

*anticipated. I have long said that if you will but exert
yourself to become accustomed to unfamiliar places and
to meeting new people, you will have a much easier
existence. This it appears you are finally able to do.*

Jonathan still felt as though he were bracing himself to get
through every single day in London. His father, though solicitous of his comfort, had higher expectations. He sighed as the
note continued:

*The murder of Mr. Rushworth is indeed most shocking.
That you should again be called upon in such an
extremity beggars belief, but of course you act rightly
in assisting both your hosts and the constabulary. Miss
Tilney's presence in London would indeed suggest that
she should cooperate with you in this endeavor; I could
not but be impressed by her cleverness and insight
during our stay at Rosings Park.*

Briefly hope sprang up within Jonathan, only to be swiftly
extinguished.

*However, I must raise the strongest possible objections
to your stated intention to court Miss Tilney, indeed to
ask her to be your wife in the near future. First, you are
as yet too young to marry. Gentlemen should not wed
before twenty-five, in my opinion, and the closer one
is to thirty, the better. You have not yet established a
household of your own, and we are not ready to house
another young family under Pemberley's roof.*

Jonathan could think of numerous rebuttals to all of this.
Women married before they turned twenty-five to general
approval—was the difference between male and female truly

so great in this regard? On his father's Derbyshire properties stood many fine cottages, mostly leased to genteel tenants of enough resource that they would not be unduly disrupted by a notice to leave within six months' time. Even if his father did not wish to evict anyone, Pemberley was so large, so comfortable, that Jonathan suspected several young families could move in with his parents possibly none the wiser.

But letters do not pause for rebuttals, and he was compelled to go on.

> *Second is the matter of Miss Tilney herself, and her participation in these investigations. As I expressed to you previously, it is perhaps unjust that society will judge her indelicate for her efforts in these matters—but ours is not a just world. Miss Tilney has seen much she should never have been compelled to see, asked questions that no person of refinement could ever ask. This would have a coarsening effect on even the finest character. For your part, Jonathan, I believe the effect has been to the good. You are more resilient now, and men are able to endure much more of the world's harshness than ladies can be asked to do. The fact remains, what has nourished you has stained her, and while you wish to ignore it, society will not.*
>
> *Finally, I will say only that you have never taken much interest in any young lady before. You have matured late in that regard. That is perhaps for the best. Would that more gentlemen could look back on their early years with so clean a conscience, so spotless a history! But this has left you inexperienced in such matters, and I cannot think it wise for you to attach yourself permanently to the first young woman to catch your eye, without even attempting to widen your sphere of feminine acquaintance. It was my hope that*

you would meet many young ladies in London, and
indeed, we have received a letter from Mrs. Allerdyce
expressing her joy that you have been enjoying the
company of her younger daughter. Perhaps her
judgment is in error, but if it is not—do not let city
morals render you inconstant. Suffice it to say that if
you were truly devoted to Miss Tilney, you could have
no energies remaining to devote to Miss Priscilla.

This injustice left Jonathan agape. Could Mrs. Allerdyce truly believe what she had written? Had he led Priscilla astray? He was aghast at the mere notion, not least because—having raised such expectations—he might in decency be obliged to marry her.

Before he condemned himself for such a fatal blunder, however, he skimmed through his father's conventional farewells and next turned to his mother's letter, which proved to be a very different epistle.

My dear Jonathan—
I will spare you the adventures of your brothers, save
for assuring you that James continues to heal well from
his injury. Of Pemberley and its doings, I predict the
only information you will wish to hear is that Ebony
remains beautiful as ever, and I have even ridden
her myself a morning or two, so that she will not feel
lonely. No, what I have to say to you cannot compare in
interest to what you have had to say to us!

As you know, I have never shared your father's
objections to Miss Tilney. These reservations are based
on the likely opinions of others, which I consider to be
a poor substitute for the moral guide we have within
ourselves. Let the world disapprove if we do what
we know to be right; let us take no pride in society's

*approval if it rises from that which we know to be
wrong.*

*But now I have begun pontificating. Perhaps we
have at last found the family resemblance between
myself and our cousin Mr. Collins! If so, then it
is well past time for me to speak plainly and from the
heart:*

*I like Miss Tilney. I like her spirit, her wit, her
cleverness. Above all, I like that she has the ability to
appreciate you—not merely as an eligible bachelor but
as your truest, best self. This appreciation is the firmest
foundation possible for love, and so I cannot help but
hope that she shares your sentiments.*

*A word of caution: Mr. Tilney seems to me no more
desirous of the match than your father. There may
be obstacles to overcome on both sides. And I must in
fairness say that your father is not wrong in pointing
out that you are still very young to marry. Both of you,
I mean—many girls are wed at eighteen, but my sisters
and I reached the age of twenty ere we married (save
for your unfortunate Aunt Lydia), and I believe we
all chose more wisely for it. If you are so impatient for
an engagement, be aware that both families may insist
upon its being a long one.*

*As for impatience, attempt to conquer yours for a
time longer. Give me a chance to speak upon this at
more length with your father. I know you are too good
a son to proceed without our permission, and I promise
to you, I shall endeavor to do all that I can to win your
father's approval, or at least his consent.*

*And do not concern yourself with the writings of
Mrs. Allerdyce. She often sees what she wishes to be
true, and cannot easily be persuaded otherwise. Perhaps,
when you and your future wife celebrate your tenth*

anniversary, she will finally surrender her ambitions.
Until then, I fear, we have no choice but to humor her.
For now, you need only wait, and hope.

That afternoon promised a novel experience even for two experienced investigators of murder, for never before had Juliet or Mr. Darcy been obliged to clandestinely follow one of their suspects—but this they set out to do that afternoon.

"You seem in excellent spirits, Mr. Darcy," she said, for indeed he walked briskly and wore a smile. "You do not find the city so overwhelming today, I think."

"Today, Miss Tilney, I believe I could endure all the noise in the world." Mr. Darcy caught himself then. "Though of course I hope I will not have to."

She laughed. "Not even I would be able to bear that!"

At the dinner precipitated by Mrs. Norris, that same woman had volunteered that Mrs. Maria Rushworth often went walking in Hyde Park. Not only was this a fashionable place to see and be seen, but it also happened to be the park closest to Wyngarde's. Mr. Darcy had posited that Mrs. Rushworth might possibly be hoping to "accidentally" encounter Mr. Crawford there. Entirely possible, Juliet thought—regardless, they would do well to see how Mrs. Rushworth spent this time she insisted on having alone.

Remaining clandestine would be a challenge now that Mrs. Rushworth was thoroughly acquainted with them both. Juliet had chosen a bonnet with an especially long brim, which made her unrecognizable from any angle save directly in front. Mr. Darcy had wrapped a thick scarf around his neck and lower face, which also helped with concealment. The weather had taken a chilly, windy turn, which would render his scarf unremarkable; however, it also meant fewer people would be in the park. They simply had to hope that Mrs. Rushworth would be distracted by other concerns.

Fortune smiled upon them first in presenting Mrs. Rushworth to their gaze almost as soon as they sought her. She even wore a vivid, mustard-colored coat that made it impossible to lose her amid any crowd. Juliet and Mr. Darcy fell into step several feet behind her, murmuring general nothings about the weather so that they would attract no notice through either conversation or the lack of it.

Then fortune struck again, even more impressively than before, for Mr. Crawford met Mrs. Rushworth upon the path—clearly, by previous agreement.

Juliet turned her head entirely to the side so that she could exchange a glance of wonder with Mr. Darcy. He nodded, but his attention was on the pair in front of them; Juliet turned hers likewise.

The first words she could make out were spoken by Mrs. Rushworth, plaintive, almost desperate: "—when we could be warm, and safe from observation. My aunt will take the child to the park any time I ask it."

"You do not wish me to meet this child, then," said Mr. Crawford. "That is a change from your usual desires, but a welcome one."

It took Mrs. Rushworth a few moments to reply. "You should want to know Ellen."

"No good could come of it if I did. A father claimed her and provided handsomely for her. There is nothing else for me to do in the matter."

"My husband's death has made it all very easy for you, I think," Mrs. Rushworth snapped. "Now you can wash your hands of her."

Mr. Crawford actually laughed. It was not a pleasant sound. "Maria, I never dirtied them with her."

Mrs. Rushworth replied, "Would that I could say the same of you. Whenever you are bored, whenever your latest intrigues have failed to amuse—you return to me, raise my hopes, persuade me to allow liberties. Then you become bored again and vanish. I am no more than this to you, am I?"

"What my feelings once were, I cannot say," Mr. Crawford said. He stopped along the path, obliging Mrs. Rushworth to do the same; Juliet and Mr. Darcy had to keep walking, but slowly, so that they would not overtake their quarry. "What they are now, I think, would not shame me so much as you believe. But what I feel for you, I will never feel for that child. She has nothing to do with me. Someday perhaps you will accept this, and when that day comes, who knows but that everything between us might change? For now, however, I must bid you adieu."

Juliet pretended to take an immediate and profound interest in a nearby shrub, which allowed herself and Mr. Darcy to stop and glance toward Mr. Crawford as he strolled away in the general direction of the club. Mrs. Rushworth stood alone, her hands in fists at her side.

"A great many people seem to dislike Henry Crawford," Mr. Darcy said. "Were I he—and I knew a murderer to be among my acquaintance—I would not be so bold."

Chapter Fifteen

Among the many delights of London are its theaters. Whether one wishes to see light comedy, serious drama, or even opera, the city offers countless choices, and the best actors in the realm are on display. Granted, certain indelicacies are required of the performers, both male and female—great playwrights are noted for their tendency to dwell upon that which is improper—but the opportunity to experience theater at its best is not to be missed.

That said, not all those in the city who attend the theater do so for cultural purposes. Theaters are where people go to meet with friends; sometimes the words of the actors can barely be made out above the chatter amid the audience. Others attend silently, but arrayed in their finest fashions, hoping to steal attention from that which unfolds on the stage. Still others simply know that going to the theater in London is That Which Is Done, and so feel obliged to obey this social commandment.

Into this last category fell Jonathan Darcy. The noise, the crowd of strangers: None of this appealed to him, and he found the reading of plays to be sufficient for his amusement. However, he anticipated that both his hosts and the Tilneys would wish to see a play during their time in London. If this was to occur, he would need to be in attendance. Best, then, to ensure that he would have to see only one play rather than two. Shakespeare, he judged, would be acceptable to all. Thus he bought tickets for all those in the Bertram household, as well as the Tilney ladies, to attend a highly praised production of *Much Ado About Nothing.* The pleasure with which all received this invitation assured Jonathan that he had chosen well.

He was also aware that, to some extent, his invitation to the theater would keep everyone busy—and therefore helped to disguise the delay in solving the murder of Mr. Rushworth. As much as he and Miss Tilney had learned, they could not yet clarify the case. Both Sir Thomas Bertram and Mr. Crawford had lied to them—Sir Thomas about his whereabouts on the fatal morning, Crawford about the connections between himself and Mrs. Rushworth—but it was not clear that either lie related to the killing. Mrs. Rushworth remained by far the most likely suspect, but her alibi could not be either proved or disproved. (Privately, Jonathan considered the more damning evidence against Mrs. Rushworth to be her attempt to throw blame upon Mrs. Norris, whose age and rheumatism made her a most unlikely strangler.) For all he and Miss Tilney knew, the crime actually *could* have been committed by some random madman, or by a person whose relationship to Mr. Rushworth remained unknown to them.

If only they could determine the murder weapon! Jonathan thought that might help them devise more useful conjectures, but until then, they could but continue to observe.

He took two boxes at the theater, anticipating general interest and thus the need for many seats. Lady Bertram surprised no one by electing to remain at the house with Pug; Susan Price astonished nearly all by agreeing to remain with her . . . until it was revealed that the Miss Worthingtons would be asked to spend the evening with them, and might be accompanied by their brother. All others, however, accepted his invitation, and all seemed very eager to do so, save one. Mrs. Fanny Bertram merely nodded and acquiesced. Her pallor and her listlessness made Jonathan concerned for her health, a concern that he judged was shared by Mr. Bertram.

"You have never seen a play, have you, Fanny?" Mr. Bertram asked, patting her hand. "Though you came far too close to seeing us perform one at Mansfield Park, this will be your first true theatrical experience—and Shakespeare, no less."

"I am of course very grateful to Mr. Darcy," was Mrs. Bertram's reply, and she gave Jonathan a smile, but a tremulous and weak one. Whatever it was that taxed her, it taxed her greatly. Jonathan sensed it had nothing to do with the murder, however, and thus he could in politeness inquire no further.

Sir Thomas was particularly pleased with the date Jonathan had chosen for their tickets, "for Mr. Allerdyce had previously informed me that he would be taking his family to the play that same night. I had half a mind to purchase tickets for us that evening myself."

"Why did you not?" Jonathan asked, only afterward realizing that it might sound as though he resented the expenditure.

However, it appeared that none of the Bertram household took his comment in that light. Mrs. Yates even laughed. "I believe I know—Tom was waiting to see whether he would be invited to join the Allerdyces in their box!" To judge by the general amusement this comment provoked, and the abashed smile upon the face of Sir Thomas, Mrs. Yates had hit upon the truth.

Jonathan could not share in this pleasure regarding the Allerdyces; Mrs. Allerdyce and Miss Priscilla, in particular, would never let him alone. Who knew what the mother might write in her next letter to his parents! But the Allerdyces would be in their box—and he and Miss Tilney would be in his.

Fanny did not blame the rest of the household for failing to glimpse her sorrow. She had kept her hopes secret, after all, and so equally secret must her disappointment be. Her dear Edmund would never even have expected her to leave her room, had he known the truth. Had her husband been aware of this, however, he must have shared in the wreckage of those hopes and her resultant mourning. If she must suffer alone to shield him from greater pain, this Fanny was willing to do. And if he wished to go to the theater, then she would accompany him.

At this particular time, Fanny rarely left the house and sometimes did not leave the bedroom. Still, various accommodations of cloth and ties remained ever in her keeping, and these she availed herself of on the night of the play. She directed the maid to clothe her in one of her best dresses, a dark blue satin, and put William's amber cross around her neck. Fanny owned no fashionable hats but accepted the loan of one of Susan's, and so she stepped out into the night as a very stylish woman indeed. When she saw how Edmund brightened to see her, Fanny wondered whether she should make such an effort more often.

No—that was not cause—Edmund was not a man to be swayed by frills and frippery. Her wifely instincts told her that he was pleased because he took her interest in her appearance as a sign of good cheer. Not wishing to disappoint him, she offered as many smiles as she could.

These smiles came a bit more easily when they entered the theater. Fanny had been too curious about such places for too long not to take some interest in her surroundings: the many candles that burned in brightly polished sconces, each of which reflected and thus doubled the available light— the press of the crowd and their animated anticipation—the richly ornamented walls, drapes, and balconies—all of it appealed to her senses. Deep though the despair within her might be, Fanny began to believe that she would at least be able to attend to the play. She would feel less guilty then, for kind Mr. Darcy would not have wasted his money on her ticket.

Her mood improved yet further when the Tilneys joined them. Fanny had always believed that an authoress must be a very forward, indelicate sort of woman, but Catherine Tilney had never been less than genteel and pleasant. Even better, Miss Juliet Tilney seemed to be renewing her acquaintance with Mr. Darcy to good effect; Fanny would never presume to play matchmaker, but she valued love highly enough to always be glad upon seeing it bloom. For this reason, she was also glad to see Tom greet Miss Allerdyce. Indeed, many people seemed to have chosen this night for a play—including, it seemed, the Crawfords.

Fanny stared across the theater as both Henry and Mary Crawford took their seats in their box, surrounded by smart friends, each one of them laughing and gay. Henry seemed to be flirting with one of the young women present, which was entirely unsurprising. It was Mary Crawford who drew her attention more: How beautiful her clothes were, how radiant her countenance! Either Mary had fallen very deeply in love with Bishop Braddock—which Fanny had to consider at least *possible*—or she was aglow with the anticipation of wealth and preeminence. Then Fanny felt guilty once more. Mary had greeted her with such kindness, such warmth; *she,* it appeared, had the greater Christian charity of the two of them, and Fanny was much ashamed.

Even worse did she feel when Mary clearly caught sight of Edmund, who saw her in return. They acknowledged each other simply—bows of the head, no more than politeness—but it was enough to return Fanny to sorrow.

"Oh, my," Miss Tilney whispered. "Look who has come."

"I see them," Fanny replied in the same tone.

But Miss Tilney looked puzzled. "Them?"

Mr. Darcy, who had taken the seat on the other side of

Miss Tilney, pointed as discreetly as he could. Fanny followed this guide to see Maria Rushworth far beneath them, in the less luxurious seats, and Maria's gaze was fixed upward, not toward her family but toward Henry Crawford.

Juliet had seen plays before, but never anything so much fun as *Much Ado About Nothing*. The crux of the plot swirled around a young couple called Claudio and Hero, whose wedding was very nearly undone by evil plotting, but she preferred the characters of Beatrice and Benedick. Their merry arguing transformed into love—love and true understanding—and Juliet liked the fierce, intelligent Beatrice far more than Hero, who seemed to be a mere prize rather than to possess any distinction of her own.

When Beatrice and Benedick were not in the forefront, Juliet's attention moved from the stage to the audience. In particular, she studied Mrs. Rushworth and Mr. Crawford. The former seemed hardly to notice the actors at all, for her head was almost ever craned upward to gaze at the Crawfords' box; the latter only rarely returned the looks and then, it seemed, solely to see whether she still stared. Most of the time, his attentions were reserved for the fashionable young woman at his side.

The play ended with each couple united in joy, though Juliet could not take equal satisfaction in both. "Claudio ought not to have condemned Hero so quickly," she said to Mr. Darcy, as they joined the throng departing the theater. "He should at least have spoken to her, should he not? To determine the truth or falsity of the claim? Were I her, I would not have forgiven him so readily."

"He seemed intemperate to me as well," Mr. Darcy replied. His gaze, however, had drifted toward others across the way.

In a lower voice, he said, "I believe we are soon to see another drama enacted."

Juliet nearly gasped upon seeing Mrs. Rushworth standing immediately in front of Mr. Crawford. Her dismay was shared by the rest of the family, all of whom had been halted by astonishment. An altercation was indeed about to unfold.

Their voices rose through the clamor: "That you were indisposed, and yet here you are, the very picture of health," said Mrs. Rushworth. "It is enough to make one question the veracity of anything you might say."

Mr. Crawford showed no shame whatsoever at having lied. "I never claimed to have no engagements beyond any I might have with you, nor am I obliged to report my doings to anyone so wholly unconnected."

"Unconnected? I?" Mrs. Rushworth's voice had risen to a shout. "You dare to claim as much when you know—when you are fully aware—"

Sir Thomas, no doubt horrified to have such a scene unfolding in front of his potential bride and her family, rushed to intercede. "Maria," he whispered. "You forget yourself."

"It is Mr. Crawford who has forgotten himself," she replied. "He has forgotten me, and he has forgotten—"

"Do not speak her name!" Sir Thomas insisted.

At last, the fuss compelled Mary Crawford to likewise intercede, and she turned to her brother. "Henry, we must go—the Hallers are waiting." She smiled and attempted to add some measure of wit. "We are already to have a late dinner—would you have it turn into an early breakfast?"

"I would delay no pleasure of yours," he replied, "particularly not on this lady's account."

Sir Thomas wheeled toward Mr. Crawford, his anger surprising to see. "You may pretend whatever you like to strangers, Crawford, but do not presume to do so before us. Your callous disregard for this entire family has already been on extravagant public display, so with us at least, you might attempt some honesty—it would make a most welcome change."

Unexpectedly, Mr. Bertram added, "Miss Crawford, do take your brother away. His statements do none of us any credit, and his shamelessness brings shame upon us all."

"The wife of a clergyman cannot be too careful." Miss Crawford's glare at her brother hinted that she shared in the general ire directed toward him. Mrs. Rushworth appeared much surprised by her family's support, and grateful as well.

Undaunted by the hatred of so many, Mr. Crawford lent his sister his arm and strolled toward the door, taking care to slow his steps as he passed by Mrs. Yates. "No shame has been brought upon *you*, surely," he said to her. "Maria can cast no shadow there." Mrs. Yates flushed, either in anger or humiliation, but she said nothing, only turned her face toward her startled husband.

Juliet felt greatly relieved once Mr. Crawford had gone. She would have expected Mrs. Rushworth to take advantage of this unexpected rapprochement with her family—to express some measure of gratitude—but apparently none of this mattered to her as much as Mr. Crawford's behavior. "He lies to me now for amusement, I think," Mrs. Rushworth cried. "It is his pleasure to make me believe, then to see me mistaken."

Mrs. Bertram reached out one hand toward her sister-in-law as Mr. Bertram said, "You will be happier, Maria, if you think upon Mr. Crawford no more."

His reply from Mrs. Rushworth was a look of the utmost contempt, almost as though he had suggested she solve her difficulties by learning to fly. She pulled her cape around her and stormed out into the night.

By this time, mercifully, the theater lobby had all but emptied. The Allerdyces were pretending to be much taken with the cherubim painted upon the ceiling, which gave the Bertram and Tilney parties a moment to converse and consider. Sir Thomas said, "Maria's behavior since Mr. Rushworth's death—I cannot reconcile it. The very event that has given her wealth has made her more desperate, not less."

"An excellent observation," said Mr. Darcy. "This is not how your sister behaved before?"

Mr. Bertram admitted, "Our sister has unfortunately always had a tendency toward, shall we say . . . erring on the side of action, rather than discretion."

"That is very true," said Mrs. Yates, conscious of the contrast to her wayward sister she must create.

Sir Thomas's concern was all for the Allerdyces. In a lower voice, he said, "She will cast shame upon us all, and then who can say where it will end?"

To Juliet's surprise, her mother spoke next. "Sometimes, in cases of family strife, it is helpful for a person *outside* the family to offer counsel. Forgive me—I know it is not my place—but if you would wish it, I will happily speak with Mrs. Rushworth tomorrow. If I can put it to her that she wounds her family through her behavior, that she does herself no service either, perhaps she will be more inclined to govern her actions. She may believe from an acquaintance what she would doubt from those far closer. Odd though this seems, I find it very often proves true." This suggestion was gratefully received by the Bertram party, and so it was decided that Catherine Tilney would call upon Mrs. Rushworth at her earliest convenience.

This proved to be the following morning. Juliet accompanied her mother on the walk to Mrs. Rushworth's London dwelling; they would have taken a hired carriage, because the cloudy skies threatened rain, but for this same reason no carriages were to be had. Juliet said, "Mamma, I do not understand at all why Mrs. Rushworth is behaving in this manner. For many days, perhaps many years, she has been content to conceal whatever doings she has had with Mr. Crawford. Now, when all is public, when all is observed, she can no longer even feign discretion. Why should she lose her self-possession only now? How can she not see that she does her interests more harm than good through this behavior?"

Catherine Tilney's face had taken on the expression that suggested a lesson was coming. "You ask the question rhetorically, Juliet. I suggest that you ask it of yourself, and this time, demand an answer."

Juliet did so. Once considered in this light, Mrs. Rushworth's actions did seem to take a more rational shape. "Before her husband's death, Mrs. Rushworth had a ready explanation as to why Mr. Crawford had not chosen to remain with her. She could believe, or pretend to believe, that Mr. Crawford kept his distance to avoid causing more conflict with a wealthy and potentially influential man. After Mr. Rushworth claimed Ellen as his own, Mrs. Rushworth might have believed that Mr. Crawford wished to prevent any confusion on that point, for both her benefit and that of her daughter. Now, however, Mr. Rushworth is gone, his last will and testament beyond further amendment. Ellen's prosperity is assured. So nothing remains between Mrs. Rushworth and Mr. Crawford . . . save, it seems, for Mr. Crawford's indifference."

"Very good," said Catherine. "We cannot know her thoughts for certain, unless she confirms them for us; but I believe you have hit upon at least part of the truth, and a vital part indeed. Always have I wished for you to be a good student of human nature, and this you have become."

How lovely to bask in her mother's pride! "Murder investigations are most instructive in this way," she said. "Not that I am glad to have undertaken so many, as each is built upon a tragedy, but at least they have been put to good use."

"You do seem to have been present at the site of many

murders, far more than one would anticipate. Ill luck you have had!"

Juliet had wondered about this herself, but not so much in her current circumstance. "This time, however, we are in London, where murders occur every single day. Surely it is no great coincidence to encounter such a crime here in the city."

Mrs. Tilney nodded, acknowledging the point, but she had become distracted by observing their surroundings. "I should not have thought Mrs. Rushworth able to afford lodgings in this neighborhood, at least not in her financial circumstances at the time of her arrival in London—unless I have misunderstood her situation, which I may well have done."

"Mrs. Rushworth's situation is a contradictory one, as Mr. Darcy and I have observed," Juliet replied. "She and Mrs. Norris show evidence of poverty in some areas, yet also seem to have benefited from occasional largess, perhaps from the late Mr. Rushworth."

"Now that she will manage near twelve thousand pounds a year for her daughter," Mrs. Tilney pointed out, "I expect Mrs. Rushworth's next neighborhood will be even finer than this one." In this, Juliet concurred entirely.

They arrived at Mrs. Rushworth's at almost the same moment as Betty, the bedraggled maid of all work, who held Ellen's tiny hand. "We have been at the park, ma'am, haven't we, dearie?" said Betty, giving Ellen a smile, and the child responded by ducking timidly behind the servant's skirts. Juliet wished the little girl were not so unfairly burdened by her parents' sin; she seemed sweet natured, and any child deserved a better start in life than the one Ellen had been given. Betty continued. "Let me go up ahead and announce you."

This they did, though the Tilneys were but a few paces behind. Although the maid called out for her mistresses, neither Mrs. Rushworth nor Mrs. Norris replied.

"Mrs. Norris was on her way out to do the marketing when we left for the park," Betty said, "and no doubt she is still at the task. But Mrs. Rushworth said nothing about going out. Came home last night and . . ." Her voice trailed away as she caught herself.

Juliet knew this was the time to press. "What happened last night?"

"She was in high dudgeon about that Mr. Crawford, if you want to know the truth. I believe she wanted to have a word with him." The maid hoisted Ellen upon her hip. "If you ladies are inclined to wait, please have a seat. As for you, little girl, let us get your coat off and see if your ma left us a note, eh?"

As the maid went down the hallway, presumably toward the bedrooms, Juliet and her mother walked into the sitting room. Mrs. Tilney was most taken by what they had heard. "After the scene last night, she still demands Mr. Crawford's attention? What else could she hope to accomplish in the face of such contempt?"

Juliet did not answer. She had glanced from the sitting room toward the doorway she knew led into the kitchen, where she saw some undetermined shape lying upon the floor. Without a word, she stepped closer, until she could peer into the kitchen—where Maria Rushworth lay, stained with blood, and very much dead.

Chapter Sixteen

The horror of the next hour can scarcely be imagined. To Juliet Tilney, experienced in such matters, fell the tasks of informing all others in the apartment, calming their panic, dispatching Mrs. Tilney to inform the police, and ensuring that the maid kept Ellen from seeing what had become of her mamma. The scene was terrible enough to haunt even a grown person had they beheld a stranger in such a state; the effect of a small child seeing their only parent this way was to be prevented at any cost.

Said cost was Juliet's presence in the doorway of the kitchen, remaining with the body until the police could arrive. How bitterly she had regretted not seeing the dead Mr. Rushworth, and even more bitterly did she now repent of that feeling, for Mrs. Rushworth made a pitiful sight, lying there on her back. The lace cap she had worn had been knocked from her head in her last fatal fall, and much of her hair had loosened from her bun. Her eyes stared open, as if in surprise. She wore a pale blue day dress, the bodice of which was stained red by the fatal wound.

With great determination, clutching her handkerchief to her nose and mouth, Juliet bent down to study this wound as best she could. It appeared to be the result of a stabbing, but a stabbing with an extraordinarily broad blade. All Juliet's kitchen experiments had not acquainted her with a knife so wide as *that*. Had the killer, in homicidal savagery, jerked the blade from side to side in order to worsen the damage and ensure Maria Rushworth's death? Or had the murderer yet again chosen an unexpected weapon, the better to confuse subsequent investigation?

Juliet noted that Mrs. Rushworth bore no signs of disarray beyond her hair and cap. Other than the fatal wound, no other signs of injury could be discerned. This appeared to indicate that Mrs. Rushworth had not struggled with her attacker, had not anticipated harm—which in turn suggested that Mrs. Rushworth had not been killed by a stranger, but instead by a person known to her, one she did not fear until too late.

Oddest of all were a few tiny white flakes upon Mrs. Rushworth's bodice. Juliet spotted a couple more such small flakes at the very mouth of the wound, though those were tinted pink by the blood. What on earth could they be? Had this substance come from the weapon used, or been shed by the murderer?

It was then Juliet saw, to her disgust, that ants had already begun to congregate near the body. So quickly does dust to dust return!

Then she heard: "Well! The door left wide open, inviting any villain to come in and help himself to all our possessions—one cannot trust servants these days, indeed, they are impudent in their manners and greedy in their demands, and for this they do less work than their masters—"

"Mrs. Norris?" Juliet stepped from the kitchen only just before Mrs. Norris entered it. The old woman held her marketing basket. "Please, do not come in!"

But it was too late. Mrs. Norris had seen too much. Crying out, staggering backward, she cried, "Oh! Maria—what has become of Maria? Fetch the doctor! Fetch him right away!"

"It is too late for the doctor," Juliet said softly. "Mrs. Rushworth is no more. We await the police."

As little as Juliet had come to care for Mrs. Norris, she could not but pity her as the woman keened her horrible grief.

The basket fell from her arms as she slumped into the nearest chair, scattering three radishes upon the floor. "How could it have happened?" she wailed. "How?"

A small cry from the bedrooms revealed that Ellen had heard Mrs. Norris's wailing and was further upset by it. Juliet would have gone to console either or both of them, but it was not her place. They must help each other. "Go to the child, Mrs. Norris," she suggested as gently as possible. "You are all she has left, now." But so great was Mrs. Norris's agony that she did not even seem able to walk. She slumped in the chair, overcome.

Shortly thereafter, Catherine Tilney returned with the police. Swift upon their heels was Mr. Frost, the detective who had personally examined the murder scene of Mr. Rushworth. "You are the young lady who assists in such inquiries?" Frost said, studying her with neither respect nor contempt, only avid curiosity. "Misters Darcy and Bertram spoke of you, when the husband was slain."

Juliet was pleased to have been mentioned, but her attention remained on the crime currently presented to her gaze. "I help where I can. In this case, I wish we could have arrived even half an hour earlier. The maid, Betty, informed us that she and Mrs. Norris each left the dwelling about an hour before, and each swears that Mrs. Rushworth was alive, well, and essentially untroubled at that time."

"A second murder," Mr. Frost said. "Ugly business, this. Though I suppose they might be unrelated—always some villain about, ready to do a woman harm."

"I do not think she was killed by a stranger," Juliet said. After she had explained her reasoning, Mr. Frost nodded, apparently much impressed.

"That is good thinking, Miss Tilney, very good indeed. But it leaves us with a killer to catch—one we must now be certain is known to all the family and its closest associates. One who has struck twice, and could potentially strike again."

Jonathan had been finishing a late breakfast when the grievous news was delivered to the Bertrams. Of their grief, much can be imagined, very little described with any hope of truly portraying the anguish felt by Edmund and Fanny Bertram, and by Lady Bertram. Mr. Bertram had immediately dropped to his knees to pray for his sister's immortal soul; Mrs. Bertram, forgetting all the petty, childish cruelties Maria had inflicted throughout their childhood, began to weep most piteously. Even Lady Bertram, so often numbed to any events of consequence that took place in a room she did not at that moment occupy, sobbed for the loss of her daughter. Had it not been only weeks, or mere days, since Maria had been a babe in her arms? What she would have given, for the chance to hold that baby once more! Susan Price, who had only come to Mansfield Park after Maria had quitted it, felt little personal grief in the matter but devoted herself to comforting both her aunt and her sister to the extent she could.

Three members of the family were not present when the news came, as they had all left the house early that morning. Sir Thomas arrived first, and was struck dumb when Edmund told him of their sister's murder. He went silently into his office and sat there a very long time, apparently unable to speak a single word.

Nearly an hour had passed before Mr. and Mrs. Yates came to call. What business they might have had that morning, they did not say, though Jonathan could not but wonder. Unquestionably Mrs. Yates was much shaken, for she was overtaken by such tremblings as rendered her almost unable to walk. Mr. Yates helped guide her up the stairs to the privacy of Susan's bedchamber, pressed into service as their refuge, from which they did not soon emerge.

Jonathan waited as long as he felt he could before he went to Mr. Bertram. "Forgive me, sir—I ought to pose this to your brother, but he seems too overcome—"

"Of course." Edmund Bertram's voice was hoarse, betraying the struggle to keep his tears unshed. "What is it that you require?"

"I should go to Mrs. Rushworth's London dwelling," Jonathan said, resisting the urge to refer to her as the *late* Mrs. Rushworth; true though it would have been, surely this phrase would be too hurtful to Mr. Bertram at this time. Accuracy could wait. "Miss Tilney will be speaking with the police, and I should join her in that endeavor as soon as possible. If it would be helpful to you, I could escort Mrs. Norris and the child back here—but forgive me. I am being presumptuous. I merely thought—"

"You thought that a small child should not remain in a house where her mother has been slain," said Mr. Bertram, "and in that you are correct. In this matter, I will presume to speak for my brother's wishes. I will send a servant with you, who can bring Aunt Norris and Ellen here. You may come with them, or continue your efforts with Miss Tilney, whichever you judge more fitting."

Jonathan dreaded speaking the next, but felt he must: "I must also beg your forgiveness. Had we been swifter in our investigations and deductions—if we had identified the killer before, then this could never have taken place."

To his surprise, not to mention relief, Mr. Bertram displayed neither anger nor blame. "The killer you seek has proved themselves more wicked and more devious than we could have imagined, Mr. Darcy. It is no great wonder that this person has eluded justice thus far. We have faith they will not do so forever. You will find an answer. You must, for all our sakes."

"We shall do all in our power," Jonathan swore, with no doubt that Miss Tilney's conviction would be as great as his own.

He arrived at the late Mrs. Rushworth's dwelling just as the crowds had begun to mass, thrilled by yet another bloody crime in their midst. By the time Jonathan entered, the body had been covered, awaiting the wagon that would bear her to the morgue.

"Oh, Mr. Darcy," Miss Tilney said as he entered. "Be glad you did not see it." It struck him that she had as great a concern for his delicacy as he had for hers.

Mrs. Catherine Tilney, quite pale with shock, chaperoned them silently from the corner of the room as Miss Tilney described precisely what she had seen. Jonathan was much impressed with the level of detail she had observed and made a point to recall, and he agreed with her conclusions. "No," he said, "you are quite right—had a stranger come upon Mrs. Rushworth, she would have made some attempt to protect her person. At the very least, she would have been very likely to scream, which would have attracted the attention of others nearby." The constant murmuring of the crowd outside made it clear that sounds traveled easily both into, and out of, this structure. "We must consider, also, that the likeliest reason for an unknown criminal to enter would have been an attempt at burglary, but I see no obvious sign that anything has been stolen." All appeared to be tidy and in order.

"There is another, darker intent that might have incited an intruder," Miss Tilney said, her cheeks pinking slightly. "Namely, the same cruelty that led Mr. Wickham to importune Mrs. Brandon at Donwell Abbey. Of this we need speak no further, however, for I saw no sign of—of—that this might have been the case."

Jonathan was relieved both that Miss Tilney had been the one to raise this subject and that they were both free to dismiss it again, forever. "So the killer is not a stranger. It is a person known to Mrs. Rushworth. Given that she was not a longtime resident of London, we may safely conclude that this person was someone to whom she had been connected in the past, thus someone in her family, or another person so intimately tied to her."

"By which you mean Mr. Crawford, for one," Miss Tilney said correctly. "We must speak to him as soon as possible."

"We can call on him after we leave." Jonathan had already begun planning this. "We can do so under the pretext that we wish to inform him of Mrs. Rushworth's fate. If he betrays no surprise, we will have our answer."

Miss Tilney did not seem equally convinced. "Surprise can be feigned, Mr. Darcy."

From the gory scene in the kitchen came Mr. Frost, his expression grave. "You are both back at your efforts, I see."

"Indeed, sir," said Jonathan. "What are your strongest impressions upon the matter?"

"Only that I cannot imagine what manner of knife might make such a cut as that." Mr. Frost's curiosity seemed to be directed less at the murder, more at its investigators. "Well, far be it for me to question my betters, but I cannot but observe that you have failed to find this killer to date, and now we have two victims instead of one. Do not think I blame you. Who knows better than a policeman how difficult it is to catch a criminal? And our own inquiries in the matter have borne no fruit either—but I must insist that you redouble your efforts. As overburdened as we are, as much other work as we are obliged to perform, soon we will have to assign more officers and take over this search entirely, unless you find an answer soon."

To Juliet's enduring gratitude, her mother declined to come with them to the Crawfords'. "I believe I have had quite enough astonishment for one day," Catherine said. "For a lifetime, I should think. Regardless, you do not require my presence, and I wish to accompany Mrs. Norris and the little girl to the Bertrams'. I do not believe Mrs. Norris is in any state to manage things herself." Indeed, Mrs. Norris had hardly stopped wailing since being told of the murder. If it had ever occurred to the old woman that she should attempt to master her feelings for Ellen's sake, she must have found herself unable to do so.

"Thank you, Mamma," Juliet said. "I do not think we will be very long. Most likely, we will learn less from what Mr. Crawford says than we will from what he does not."

They were able to obtain the Crawfords' address from Henry's card, left conspicuously upon Mrs. Rushworth's mantel. Fortunately, this did not require an especially long walk. "I wonder," Mr. Darcy said as they made their way through the crowds, "whether this proximity to the Crawfords' abode was what led Mrs. Rushworth to choose a dwelling here."

"If she knew of his location before she took her rooms, then I should not be at all surprised should that prove to be the case." Juliet wondered at Mrs. Rushworth's shamelessness, at her desperation. She did not wish to speak ill of the dead, but she could not deny the sense that Maria Rushworth had rushed headlong toward her own destruction—assuming, of course, that Mr. Crawford was the killer they sought.

As it was now afternoon, still calling hours, they had no guarantee that either of the Crawford siblings would be at home instead of making calls of their own, but both were. Juliet and Mr. Darcy were shown into a well-appointed sitting room, where both brother and sister awaited them. Miss Mary Crawford, as ever, could have stepped straight from a fashion plate; if she had, like most women in similar circumstance, hurriedly laid aside mending or some other household task, she betrayed not the slightest sign. Mr. Henry Crawford's attire and attitude were equally elegant, and Juliet could observe that he either did not know the reason for their coming, or he concealed that knowledge very well.

"Mr. Darcy," Mr. Crawford said, nodding to each in turn. "Miss Tilney. To what do we owe this unexpected honor?"

"We come with ill tidings, sir," said Mr. Darcy. "I fear we must inform you of the death of Mrs. Rushworth."

Miss Crawford gasped. Mr. Crawford paled, but otherwise showed no strong outward sign of emotion. It was the sister who asked, "Maria was no more than my age. What could have happened? Did her carriage overturn?"

How naive of Miss Crawford, Juliet thought, *to believe that an unmarried woman with a child could easily afford a carriage.* Aloud, she said only, "Mrs. Rushworth fell to the same fate as her husband. This morning, she was murdered."

The effect on Miss Crawford was dramatic—she very nearly swooned in her chair. Mr. Crawford finally abandoned his pretense of disinterestedness as he swore. "Dear G-d! What is this world coming to?"

Mr. Darcy courageously spoke next: "Forgive us, sir, but you will comprehend immediately that we must know of your whereabouts this morning."

Mr. Crawford's face reddened, but it was Miss Crawford who immediately replied, "Hyde Park. Henry took me to Hyde Park this morning. We have gone there often in the past. It is one of our favorite places to walk in the city."

Juliet stole a glance at the window, and beyond it, the overcast gloom of the sky. An odd day, surely, to undertake an excursion to the park—but the possibility could not be rejected outright. "Did you see anyone you knew there?"

"No one of our acquaintance," Miss Crawford said. "To think, we were taking the air while Maria breathed her last—oh, I cannot bear the very idea."

Equally dismayed was Juliet, for very different reasons. Once again, she and Mr. Darcy had been given an alibi that could not be easily disproved, as any person would encounter dozens or even hundreds of strangers on their way to and from Hyde Park, none of whom could be found again, none of whom would be especially likely to remember the Crawfords in any case.

"Is that all?" Mr. Crawford demanded. "For if it is, it would be more gracious to allow us solitude, and the chance to speak privately together."

"You are quite right, sir," Juliet admitted, and before five minutes had passed, she and Mr. Darcy had begun their long walk toward the Tilney dwelling.

Mr. Darcy said, "He was not unaffected by the news of Mrs. Rushworth's death, but I cannot say that his response either incriminates or exculpates him. If there is one among our acquaintance capable of a performance equal to that of the Shakespearean actors we recently saw, Mr. Crawford seems the likeliest candidate."

"I agree—from *that* display, we can tell nothing." Juliet knew the importance of not rushing to assumptions, so she took them back to the place where they should have begun. "Due to the scenes in the park and at the theater, we both first thought of Mr. Crawford as the likeliest suspect. This, I believe, he must still be. But there are other possibilities to be considered."

"So far as Mrs. Rushworth's family is concerned, both Mr. and Mrs. Bertram were at home throughout this morning, as were Lady Bertram and Miss Price," Mr. Darcy said.

"Not that any of them would have been likely candidates for murder—but in this matter, they can be absolutely excluded from our consideration. I cannot say the same for Sir Thomas or Mr. and Mrs. Yates, all of whom had left the residence early, none of whom seems to have explained why."

"It seems Mrs. Norris can also be excluded, for the maid reported that she had left to do the marketing at the same time Ellen was to be taken to the park. We shall have to clarify precisely what the maid saw and when, but it appears that all three left the house more or less simultaneously, and that Mrs. Rushworth was alive when they did so."

"That would still leave us with four suspects," said Mr. Darcy. "Mr. Crawford has an alibi, of course, but from his sister, who might be willing to lie on his behalf."

Juliet found she agreed with this assessment of Miss Crawford's character, though the willingness to lie for a beloved brother was far from the darkest possible moral blemish. "So we must learn the whereabouts of Mr. Crawford, Sir Thomas, and the Yateses. We must confirm that Mrs. Norris left at the precise same time as the maid. And—though I am not certain it will prove illuminating—I would very much like it if we could determine what kind of a knife was used in this attack, and the nature of the peculiar white flakes it left behind."

Mr. Darcy's expression was grave. "There is one other question we must consider as well, Miss Tilney. It is this: Do we seek one killer, or two?"

Chapter Seventeen

The day following Maria's death, Edmund Bertram determined that he must call upon the Crawfords as soon as possible. Mary, he would as soon not have met with again; all between them thus far had been cordial and correct, and there he would have preferred to leave the matter. Nor did he wish to leave the house so soon after such a blow as the loss of a sister, particularly so gruesome a death as this. Maria might have been estranged from the family for years, might never have been particularly close to Edmund in either confidence or character, and yet she remained his younger sister, the companion of numberless childhood memories. The mere recollection of her favorite doll, or of her high childish voice begging him to push her swing—these brought him near tears, and he suspected they would retain that power for many years to come, if not forever. However, that morning, as he saw one of the maids take up some bread and milk on a tray for young Ellen's breakfast, Edmund knew that he must speak to Henry Crawford at least, and right away.

His mother and Aunt Norris kept to their respective rooms, the Yateses showed no signs of calling that day, and Tom had departed the house yet again on plantation business. This left only Fanny to be informed of his departure.

"I wish you would not go," she said, holding his hand in hers. "Your mother or Julia may need you, and I am sure I am not equal to comforting them."

Fanny seemed to need as much comforting as anyone. This was all the more remarkable given that Maria's attitude toward Fanny had been indifference at best, but Edmund knew his wife's tender heart was incapable of remembering anything but the best about Maria at such a time as this. "Aunt Norris, I think, is the most devastated among us—but I do not believe any of them will leave their rooms for a long while yet, not at any time today."

Though Fanny seemed unconvinced, she argued the point no further, and Edmund set out on his way.

How strange it is to leave the enclosing solitude of one's grief and walk back into a world which seems to know no grief at all! Edmund's limbs felt heavy and numb with shock, his eyes remained red, his mind hardly able to comprehend anything beyond Maria and her death—and yet carriages continued to jostle along the roads, public houses still dispensed ale and gin, and young ragamuffin girls still cried out that they had flowers to sell. He found his way through this discordant, unbothered world as though blindfolded, stumbling into passersby more than once, vaguely aware that he must make a poor sight and yet not caring whether he did or no.

Upon reaching the Crawfords' house—late of their uncle in the admiralty—Edmund was ushered in immediately and met at the door of the sitting room by Mary. "Dear Edmund!" she cried, swiftly embracing him. "Forgive me, I know I am forward—I should be cold, call you Mr. Bertram, do naught but that which is correct—but I cannot. Knowing how stricken you must be, I cannot contain my sympathy for your plight, and for that of your family. You will forgive me the liberty, will you not?"

Distracted and dejected though Edmund was, it did not escape his notice that Mary thought more of herself, and what was expected of her, than she did of him. Still, he felt her sympathy must be genuine so far as it went. "You are forgiven, Miss Crawford. However, it is Mr. Crawford for whom I have come."

Mr. Crawford sat with them in the room, but thus far, he had held himself aloof. He spoke at last, and sharply: "If you have come to remonstrate with me, to say that Mrs. Rushworth would not have come to London were it not for me, know that I did not invite her hither. Her presence was unwelcome to me, and, had I had my way, she would never have set one foot in this city."

"I have not come to remonstrate with you regarding Maria," Edmund said. This was a lecture he could easily, and gladly, have given at length, but it was not the day's business. "I have come to talk about Ellen."

Miss and Mr. Crawford exchanged a swift glance. "Ellen?" Mr. Crawford said, as though he had never heard of such a name before. "You mean Mrs. Rushworth's child? I have never had anything to do with her."

"The time has come for that to change," Edmund said. How appalling it was to have to speak the rest, to acknowledge that which should have remained forever hidden. "Mr. Crawford, I will be frank. If you have ever laid eyes upon Ellen—and I believe that you have, at least in passing—you cannot have mistaken her for the child of Mr. Rushworth. Her coloring, her features, the texture of her hair: In every observable particular, Ellen resembles no one so much as yourself." This truth was one that Edmund had attempted to deny even to himself, but in the wake of Maria's murder, he was no longer capable of such self-deception. "The connection between yourself and my poor sister did not end when it should have done. Better of course that it would never have begun! But begin it did, and continue it did, and this, I believe, led to Ellen's birth. She is your natural daughter. No witness could mistake the matter. You are a sensible man, so I do not believe you mistake it either. As Ellen has lost her mother, she needs her father to do what is right."

Miss Crawford, though she blushed, proved herself equal

to the topic. "What would you consider to be right in this occasion, Mr. Bertram?" It was a relief to be Edmund to her no more.

Edmund had thought the matter through thoroughly before knocking on their door. "It is too much to ask, perhaps, that you should accept your natural daughter into your household. In most such circumstances, I believe, the child is sent to live with a respectable country family—farmers or the like—to be raised in wholesomeness, away from scandal. You could visit her from time to time, should you so choose. Once Ellen is a few years older, she can be enrolled in a school, given some measure of an education. From the late Mr. Rushworth, she has inherited a handsome sum, one that cannot entirely remove the stain of illegitimacy but will significantly improve her prospects. Despite the unfortunate circumstance of her birth, she could lead a respectable life."

Mr. Crawford unexpectedly, unforgivably, laughed. "You suggest that I take on fifteen years' responsibility for the sake of a child who I do not believe to be mine. Speak all you like of her hair or her coloring, but I am hardly the only man in England with curls and brown eyes!"

Between astonishment and anger, Edmund was briefly robbed of the capacity for speech. He had been disabused of his notion that Crawford was a good man, forcefully so, but still, he had scarcely expected such impudence as this. At last he managed to say, "You deny it, then. You deny that you are Ellen's father."

"I deny it entirely," Mr. Crawford replied, "and there is none who can prove different. As such, I have no part in the girl's future welfare, and I shall entertain no further suggestions in the matter."

Mary Crawford's head drooped, and she could do no more than stare at the rug. Give her as much as her due: In that hour, she had the decency to be ashamed of her brother.

Word of the murder of Mrs. Rushworth had spread, and the newspapers were swift to seize upon the violent death of a woman who had formerly created such scandal through her elopement and divorce. Households across London read of the gruesome scene, of her sinful past, and clucked their tongues. One family, in particular, was forced to consider how much they were already connected to the Bertrams, and how much they were willing to be connected in the future.

"Mrs. Rushworth's history—of that we were already informed," said Mr. Allerdyce to his family over luncheon. "Unfortunate though it was, some years had passed, and the family had taken the appropriate stance upon the matter. Now, however, that history is again in the public mouth, as though the events had occurred but yesterday."

"That is unfair, Papa," said Frederica. "Mrs. Rushworth is dead. She died most cruelly, at the hands of some villain. Regardless of her wrongdoing, she remained their sister, and they must feel the tragedy keenly. Are we to compound their grief by shunning them?"

Caroline said, "Frederica is entirely right." So seldom did she support her elder daughter that the novelty of it drew the attention of all the others. "The Bertrams are a fine family, and Sir Thomas has made plain his partiality for Frederica. Are we to discourage the suit of such a man because an estranged relative became the victim of crime? This could happen to any of us at any time." She tried to imagine her brother, Charles, somehow getting himself into trouble. Kind natured and trusting as he was, it would be just like Charles to let some stranger in the house and wind up murdered for his pains.

"I think it is not that the sister has died," said Priscilla, only now grasping the obvious. "It is what she did *before* that counts against her. As we knew that already, it would be very false of us to turn from them now." Certainly she did not intend to be kept apart from Jonathan Darcy any longer than necessary; and as far as Priscilla could see, shunning the Bertrams would accomplish little else.

Mr. Allerdyce admitted defeat. "You are all right, of course. I should not even have said such a thing. Forgive me, Frederica. I wished only to safeguard your reputation, and there is nothing I would not do to protect you."

Frederica took her father's hand across the table. "Dearest Papa! Do not fear. No one will think the less of me for knowing Sir Thomas, and I do not think anyone of decency will think the less of him for his sister's tragic end."

Caroline's feelings on the matter were rather more complex than she had let on. Regarding Sir Thomas's pursuit of Frederica—yes, it would proceed as it should; and should her husband falter in his approval again, she would argue once more in favor of the match. However, this second murder suggested another complication.

After the girls were upstairs, she said to Mr. Allerdyce, "I suppose young Mr. Darcy will be at his investigations again."

"Indeed. It speaks well of the young man that the police trust him in such an endeavor, do not you think?"

"Oh yes! Of course! Jonathan Darcy is truly exemplary among gentlemen. That is why I have so hoped to promote a match between him and our Priscilla."

Mr. Allerdyce did not seem to recognize the importance of this statement. "They are both rather young for matchmaking, my dear."

"That does not make Jonathan Darcy any less the sort of young man upon which scheming young girls might prey. That Miss Tilney—they say, you know, that her mother is a *writer*, how vulgar—well, that Miss Tilney seems to insert herself into his investigations. This murder will give her another opportunity to catch him."

"Maybe you should be the author of fiction, rather than Mrs. Tilney." Mr. Allerdyce, much amused, gave his wife's shoulder a comforting pat on his way from the breakfast room. "If Miss Tilney 'catches' Mr. Darcy, no doubt it will be because the young man wishes to be caught. Should it come to pass, what of it? There are other matches we can make for Priscilla when her time comes, matches equally fine if not better."

This did not answer for Caroline at all. She wanted to see Priscilla at Pemberley—to see *herself* there—but she could not think how to explain to her husband in a way that would not pain him to hear, and so she remained silent.

That afternoon, Juliet Tilney was in fact by Mr. Darcy's side, though she would have taken umbrage at the idea that these were "his" investigations rather than "theirs" and that her efforts constituted her "inserting herself" in another's affairs. She had come to the Bertrams', first to pay her respects and then to join him in speaking with Mrs. Norris.

Mrs. Norris made an unlikely murder suspect. She was not exceedingly elderly, and she appeared very spry for her age— but it was impossible to imagine her successfully strangling so hale a young man as the late Mr. Rushworth. A stabbing she could probably have accomplished, but Mrs. Norris had been seen leaving the dwelling before the murder had occurred; besides that, the old woman had scarcely stopped weeping.

"I gave up everything for Maria, you know," Mrs. Norris told them. "When all others had abandoned her, I followed her into exile, I stayed with her. She had no housekeeping to speak of—or, rather, she had been taught how to manage a large household, not a small one; and, mind you, small households are more difficult, for there, one must look after every penny, must find servants capable of performing more than one task with some skill. That, I knew how to do. My late husband was not so wealthy that I had no need to consider expense. But for me, what would Maria have done?"

It seemed to Juliet that Mrs. Norris's voluble grief was, at least in part, meant to underline her great importance in her late niece's life. Still, who could begrudge the woman such a transparent plea for consolation? Gently Juliet asked, "You got on very well with your niece, then, I imagine."

Mrs. Norris seemed to catch herself mid-sob. "Oh! Well! I do not say there is a single house in the kingdom where there is not a cross word spoken from time to time. Certainly little children, when they come, do not make matters more orderly. But never did I stray from my duty to Maria. No, I will not condemn my sister Bertram—nor the late Sir Thomas, for he was a most upstanding man, even if it made him most strict in the end—but I stayed with Maria when all others had gone."

Mr. Darcy said, "You often did the marketing yourself, rather than send Betty?"

"Oh, la, the maid serves us better by looking after Ellen, for I cannot bear noise and clamor, and I have a superior eye for a bargain. If one knows how to press one's point, the merchants will come down on their prices. It takes time, but I can get a farmer down to half price for eggs. Half! Name me the servant who can do so well. Certainly it is not our Betty. I suppose she is run off to seek another position by now."

Juliet winced. She had not considered how difficult it might be to find Betty again; she would have to hope that Mr. Frost had collected some means of reaching her. "Mrs. Norris, did your niece say anything that day about expecting a visitor, a caller, something of that nature? Did she allude to business to be accomplished?"

"No such thing. The only person she mentioned . . . she spoke briefly of Mr. Rushworth," Mrs. Norris said, and now her gravity seemed more genuine. "Little knew either of us how soon they would be reunited."

"What of you, Mrs. Norris?" Mr. Darcy asked. "Will you return to that household? Where will you take Ellen?"

Mrs. Norris's eyebrows rose so high they nearly disappeared beneath the frill of her mobcap. "I? I, take Ellen? There can be no question of my doing so. To be the sole care-taker of a small child, at my time of life, and at the age when children are the most exhausting and vexatious? No, no, the late Mr. Norris and I were not blessed with issue, and I must be obedient to the path the Lord has laid for me. I am not at all the proper person to look after Ellen. Anyone would agree, I am certain they would."

Anyone would realize that you are the only person the little girl still knows, Juliet thought, but it was not her place to say.

As it happened, another person outside the sitting room over-heard this part of their conversation: Edmund Bertram, who had that day already listened to another person deny respon-sibility for Ellen. After Mrs. Norris also washed her hands of the child, an idea that had been taking shape within his mind solidified and gained urgency. There seemed no time to waste and no reason to delay.

So it was that, as Fanny joined her husband in bed, just before she would have blown out the candle, Edmund said to her, "My dear, we should talk about Ellen."

"What do you mean?" Fanny said. In truth, she guessed what he intended to say—she could hardly not guess—but she hoped to be wrong.

"Henry Crawford will neither take her in nor lift one finger to assist her. Mrs. Norris does not wish to take on the maternal role. Thus the little girl has no home." Gently, Edmund continued: "Why should we not give her one?"

Fanny could not find her tongue. She stared at Edmund, wishing his words unspoken.

He mistook her dismay for surprise. "I know you do not wish us to talk of it, but . . . we are not to be blessed with children of our own. So why should we not adopt Ellen? She is our relation by blood, and I do not think that she would long be less dear to us than any child of our bodies could have been. The matter would be easily arranged, and she could grow up in the parsonage, near Mansfield Park, able to know her grandmother, her aunts and uncles, and all her cousins throughout her life."

Fanny drew her knees up to her chest, hugging them to herself as though she were still a little girl hiding on the stair, afraid of being scolded. "We cannot."

"But of course we can." Edmund, who had anticipated eager agreement, could not fathom why his wife hesitated. "We are not wealthy, no, but the money Mr. Rushworth left for Ellen's care is more than adequate to her needs and will provide for a fine dowry in time, one that may allow her to marry far better than most girls in such circumstances. We are in good health—you are easily wearied, I know, but we shall be able to hire a nursemaid to help, and later on a governess, so you will not be overtaxed."

"That is not what I mean!" Fanny struggled for the words, feeling as though she would more gladly choke than speak. "She is Henry Crawford's child. My most wretched memories are of his attempt to marry me—to think that I would become mother to his daughter after all! How can it be borne?" She had hardly been able to endure the horror of realizing she had inadvertently accepted Mr. Crawford's gift of a gold chain; how much more galling it would be to accept his child!

Edmund thought this objection unworthy of his wife's character and very nearly said so. Wisdom stayed him, though, and he was able to ask more gently, "I do not think that is all that concerns you. I doubt it is even foremost among your objections. Will you not tell me what truly makes you unwilling to adopt Ellen?"

"You have no faith in my words," Fanny said. "You do not believe me, you do not trust me, so say nothing more to me at all!"

He knew that this, too, was but an effort to conceal her true difficulty, but it sufficed to quiet Edmund. She blew out the candle and pretended to sleep for hours, doing her best to weep silently, and refusing to hear when the little girl cried out once in the night.

Chapter Eighteen

When inquiring into a case of murder, often an additional victim meets its end: delicacy. No question can be too rude, too far beyond the realm of propriety, to be asked, providing that the answer may help reveal the wrongdoer responsible. However, this does not entirely excuse investigators from the need to exercise discretion and good manners.

In the matter of the Rushworth slayings, for example, Jonathan Darcy had been given full permission to investigate by his hosts, who had also wisely allowed Miss Juliet Tilney to take part. However, in the course of their inquiries, they often found it helpful to speak together at length about the various questions raised, and the various answers thus far gained— and it was not possible to do so within the Bertram residence. Given the intimacy of much that must be discussed, and the inescapable fact that the murderer might well be among their number, both Jonathan and Miss Tilney thought it advisable that they should meet at the Tilney residence instead. Mrs. Tilney, a prudent yet liberal chaperone, busied herself at her writing desk at the far end of the sitting room, which allowed Jonathan and Miss Tilney to sit by the windows and speak freely.

Given her mother's need for pen and ink, Miss Tilney had turned up an old school slate and a scrap of chalk, which she used to jot down abbreviated notes regarding the main points of the case:

1)   *1 or 2?*
2)   *Motive, or if 2, motives*
3)   *Alibis*
4)   *Weapons*

The first question, Jonathan agreed, was where they had to begin. "I am inclined to think one killer responsible for both crimes," he said. "It beggars credence that two persons, so intimately connected, would each fall prey to entirely separate cases of murder within two weeks of each other."

Miss Tilney replied, "Yet it does not necessarily follow that the murders *are* separate, even if committed by two persons. Mr. Rushworth's demise may have instigated the killing of Mrs. Rushworth. If, for instance, Mrs. Rushworth did murder her former husband—or if she was believed to have done so—"

"Then that could have been the motive for the crime against her." Jonathan saw the truth of it, though he also knew this complicated every question they must ask. "If they had been killed in the same manner—if the same mysterious weapon had been used in both cases—that, I believe, would indicate a single murderer, almost beyond any doubt. Yet instead, we have two very different weapons, and two different causes of death. I would feel much more assured of our progress if we had managed to identify even one of the weapons, but we remain in the dark as to both."

Miss Tilney looked cross, rather as though, if given the opportunity, she would have scolded the killer or killers for making their task so difficult. "Mrs. Rushworth must have been killed with a knife, just an unusually wide one. No such blade was found among their possessions, suggesting that the killer brought the weapon with him—or her—and left with it. By now, no doubt, it has been abandoned in the Thames, and even if the mudlarks were to dredge it up, we would never be able to identify whether it was the one used."

"And Mr. Rushworth was strangled with some item very like an embroidery hoop—but not an embroidery hoop itself, which would be rather small for the task and not nearly strong enough to restrain a large man." Jonathan had listened to Miss Tilney's former theories about silken cord, and considered them at length. "I do not think a cord, even one most smooth and made of fine materials, could have left so even, so uniform a mark as the one I saw upon Mr. Rushworth. A solid item was used, but I can scarcely even conjecture what it would be."

Miss Tilney rubbed at her temples with one hand. Jonathan briefly remembered the touch of her fingertips along the back of his neck, and then it was difficult for him to attend as she said, "For my part, I feel that if I could identify the white flakes upon Mrs. Rushworth's corpse, I would know what sort of instrument shed them, and that weapon at least would be revealed to us. I thought of paint or plaster— a trowel could have done such damage, I suppose—but who among our company would have undertaken such a task themselves, or even been present at a place where such rough work was being done?"

The plaster thought was, Jonathan decided, an excellent one, yet her objection was well made. So far as they had been able to observe, no such repairs were being carried out in or near any of the residences of their suspects. "Nor would any random workman simply set out to enact a crime during a short respite from his labors."

"As to motives," Miss Tilney said, "it seems likeliest that Mr. Rushworth's murder was tied to his increasing doubts regarding Ellen's paternity. He may have meant to change his will; if that was the case, no doubt he would soon have been sending less money to Mrs. Rushworth. That money she was very much dependent upon."

"He must have been a generous benefactor, at least from time to time," Jonathan agreed. The household of Mrs. Rushworth and Mrs. Norris had shown signs of economy, but not true monetary distress. "Thus both of the ladies of that house had very strong reasons to wish him dead before he could cut them off entirely."

"Mr. Crawford, also," said Miss Tilney. "For he wishes to deny all responsibility for Ellen, but had Mr. Rushworth cut Mrs. Rushworth off without a cent, she would certainly have turned to him for money next."

"She wanted more than this, did she not? She wished for Mr. Crawford to return to her, perhaps clandestinely, but ideally as her husband. He had not the slightest desire to do so." Jonathan caught himself rocking back and forth, as he did when he was deep in thought. He stopped immediately, for although Miss Tilney was accustomed to this singular habit and did not mind it, the same could not be said of Mrs. Tilney; and, despite his attention to their investigation, he remained conscious of the need to make a good impression. He continued: "It seems to have been Mr. Rushworth's death that spurred Mrs. Rushworth to pursue Mr. Crawford more openly—nearly desperately. Had Mr. Crawford anticipated as much, he would have been the last person to wish Mr. Rushworth dead."

"He may not have anticipated her response," Miss Tilney pointed out. "He does not strike me as a man who is thoughtful about others, or especially insightful regarding character and temperament. Having seen Mrs. Rushworth's upset, however—after he knew that she was ready to pursue him in public, to remind all of his scandalous past—Mr. Crawford might well have resorted to murder to ensure that Mrs. Rushworth would never again importune him."

The details whirled in Jonathan's head, seeking a structure; he valued order, and was good at determining patterns where others saw only chaos. But chaotic this case remained. "All have an alibi for the times of the crimes, and yet very few of those alibis admit themselves to proof or disproof."

"It is one of the disadvantages of investigating within a city rather than a village or town. How strange and yet true—one is never more anonymous, more assured of evading notice, than when surrounded by crowds of people."

Mrs. Tilney, having crossed out several offending phrases, checked the small watch pinned to her sash. "Juliet, my dear—Mr. Darcy—it will not be long before we must prepare for the Ramseys' ball. The day has come at last!" Not even their investigation could remove their obligation to attend the event of the season.

Jonathan did not intend to again be waylaid by the wily Mrs. Allerdyce. "Let me take the opportunity, Miss Tilney, to ask for the first two dances?"

How she smiled! How warm the room suddenly became, as though a servant had stoked the fire high. "I am not otherwise engaged, Mr. Darcy. I will most happily dance with you."

In the midst of a whirl of parties, despite the dozens of social obligations and opportunities throughout London during its season, there is always one event that stands as the most significant, one that becomes *the* party upon which future prominence will depend. This is not, as commonly believed, the presentation of aristocratic young women at court, at least not for any but the upper echelons of society. This class of persons, however respected, constitutes only a small fraction of those engaged in the hubbub of the London season, and for the most part, those within that class are already assured of their position by both wealth and breeding.

For many others, however, ascent is possible. Appearing in society remains vitally important. Young ladies may be able to seize a glittering future through a match made during the season, or they may see that future slip away entirely. This year, the party that was to rule over all other gatherings was the Ramseys' ball, being held in one of the most stately homes in all London.

(Who the Ramseys were, and how they were connected to the Bertrams, the Tilneys, and the Allerdyces are beyond the scope of this narrative. Imagine them as people of fashion, people of property, capable of hosting a ball that could rival those attended by royalty: This will be sufficient attention for the Ramsey family.)

Juliet Tilney's match, it seemed, was already all but complete. So she might have looked upon the Ramseys' ball with more equanimity than the average young lady. Instead, however, her assurance only increased her anticipation. Almost free from worry upon matters matrimonial, unable to further the cause of their investigation at the party itself, she was able to enter into preparations with no concern, no anxiety, only the anticipation of splendor and fun.

The most extravagant of the dresses Juliet and her mother had ordered for her time in London had arrived just in time— shimmery silk in a soft lilac, with wide sleeves, ample lace, and a skirt in which she was determined to show her ankles boldly. Luckily they had acquired slippers that matched perfectly, for they would be so much on display. Catherine Tilney put one hand to her cheek as she saw it. "I have caught up to the fashions in most ways, but I do not think I shall ever be done with the shock of seeing skirts so short as that."

"Stop, Mamma," Juliet pleaded—though she was smiling, for both she and her mother were near laughter. Their stay in London had inured them to any shock from the length of a mere skirt. "You will make me think too much upon my ankles, and then I will end hiding behind chairs and draperies for the entire ball."

"Your costume is not yet complete." Catherine went to a small box, which she had purchased early in their visit, under strict instructions from General Tilney. "Here—a gift from your grandfather."

Juliet had little expected further generosity from the general, who enjoyed withholding his riches and affection far more than demonstrating them. Her surprise became true astonishment as she opened the box to reveal a stunning necklace of opals, amethysts, and even, as the pendant, what appeared to be a small diamond. "Oh! He cannot have meant for me to have anything so fine as this!"

"We both underestimated your grandfather, it seems. How lovely when our relations can surprise us for the better." Catherine motioned for her daughter to turn, the better to help her put the necklace on. She had guided her daughter toward this shade of silk for the Ramseys' ball knowing how well it would look with the necklace, and indeed, she made a lovely sight.

"I am so proud to wear it, and yet I almost feel as if I should not." Juliet put one hand to her throat, accustoming herself to the new weight around it. "Will I not appear forward? As though I am seeking attention too strenuously?"

Catherine shook her head. "Indeed not, for when you arrive, we will see dozens of girls and precisely twice as many ankles, as well as diamonds enough to astonish a maharajah. Neither of us will think anything of making a display any longer."

This prediction held true, though not for the reasons Catherine had suggested. When they entered the Ramseys' palatial home, Juliet was too awestruck by their surroundings to worry much over the extravagance of her necklace or the exposure of her feet. Brightly gilded ceilings arched far overhead; the rich inlay of the floors created a dazzling pattern beneath; and the candlelight seemed to be coming from everyplace at once, as though the Ramseys had managed to capture the stars and compel them to shine upon the gathering. Juliet knew herself to be dressed well for the occasion, but most remarkable was the glow she seemed to have about her—the glow of happiness, confidence, and comfort. When Mr. Darcy arrived and took her arm, all her cares seemed to have fled.

So the ball began well. It continued well enough, but something felt . . . wrong.

Juliet could not begin to guess what it was, for Mr. Darcy looked upon her with as much pleasure as she could wish. She knew her clothing and hairstyle to be correct, that her necklace was among the finest jewels on display and yet not gaudy, and that she danced well. The occasional venomous glance from Miss Priscilla Allerdyce caused no consternation; Juliet knew this to be no more than proof that she looked very pretty indeed.

No, it was the glances from others that occasionally unnerved her. Some of the men and women present appeared to *know* her—though she did not recognize them in the slightest—and to disapprove of what they saw. One gentleman outright shook his head at his son, who had begun to walk toward Juliet to ask for a dance; several ladies, after spying her, held up their fans to confer behind them in whispers.

I suppose they have heard about my taking part in the murder investigations, Juliet thought. *They think me indelicate because of it. This is not the first time a young woman's part in such an endeavor has drawn comment, and as disapproval has never stopped me before, it will not do so now.*

But how I wish people would not stare!

Still, this small blight on the evening could not steal

its luster. Mr. Darcy danced with her several times—and though she could, on occasion, detect the effort it required him to endure such a crowd, he remained resolutely by her side. How could Juliet not be charmed by such exertion, such loyalty? Each valued their ability to speak openly with the other, without artifice, but amid the sounds of the musicians and the crowd, Juliet and Mr. Darcy could barely speak three words. Yet this, too, became a boon to them, because all young lovers should, for a time, allow their gazes to communicate that which cannot ever be wholly said aloud.

At such a juncture, the reader will gladly allow both Juliet Tilney and Jonathan Darcy their privacy. Suffice it to say the ball was all they could have hoped and more. How fondly they would look back upon it, in days to come—upon their joy, and their innocence.

The Allerdyces left the ball early. Frederica had already danced with Sir Thomas as much as was proper; Caroline was becoming rather impatient waiting for his proposal, but did not doubt it was forthcoming, so there was no point in tiring Frederica out further. Priscilla had managed only two dances with Jonathan Darcy, and afterward had reported sullenly that he had spoken of nothing but the Roman Empire, and had not once so much as looked into her eyes. Meanwhile, the Tilney girl looked as well as Caroline had ever seen her, and the affection between her and young Mr. Darcy was evident to all. Why, people had been staring at them both! Even a woman as determined as Caroline Allerdyce could not witness this without discouragement.

The next morning, both the girls wished to make an expedition to the famed Vauxhall Gardens; the weather was unusually pleasant for that time of year, and Mr. Allerdyce had offered to take them in an open carriage. Normally Caroline would have accompanied them on such an outing, but this day, she wanted both solitude and occupation. She decided at last to go see the art exhibition that had attracted such attention in town. Some rumors suggested that at least one of the paintings on display was, perhaps, less than delicate. If the artwork was decent, fit for young women to look upon, Caroline would bring her daughters back in order to cultivate their conversation.

Or so she told herself. In point of fact, Caroline rather liked art, and could while away long minutes or even an hour studying a particularly fine landscape or historical work. She knew not how to say so, however, without sounding like a bluestocking, and so she found it easier to pretend her interest was purely a matter of maternal caution.

The show had been open for weeks yet still drew crowds—little wonder, as the great Turner and Constable each had a new work on display. These, it was said, were the show's masterpieces. Other paintings were of interest, too, either for their subject (Waterloo upon a broad canvas, quite as though one had been there!), their technique (some younger painters had taken Turner as an excuse to slap color around most wildly), or their infamy (multiple nudes, one upon a mythological theme considered to be quite scandalous).

It was at the exhibition that Caroline stopped fast and came to a reckoning. So shocked was she by this revelation that it took her several moments to believe it, several more to understand its utility to her purposes. She knew now how to prevent Juliet Tilney from wedding Jonathan Darcy. She knew how to part them soon, totally, and forever. It could be accomplished tomorrow, with almost no trouble at all.

"And so it shall be done," she whispered to herself, smiling up at the paintings. Some of them seemed to smile back.

Meanwhile, at the Bertram residence, the entire family had managed to come down for breakfast at once, along with Jonathan Darcy. This made the meal a cheerful affair for most. Jonathan would much rather have been alone, particularly the day after having endured such a crowd at the Ramseys' for so long, but he determined that he would at least make the most of the chance to observe the sentiments and behavior in the room.

Most remarkably, Mrs. Norris seemed already to have made herself quite at home. "Sister, the servants have made a mess of this marmalade. You must supervise them when they are putting up, supervise them closely!"

"Oh, should I?" Lady Bertram never looked up from Pug, who was begging for a sausage of her own. "But I know nothing of marmalades and jams. I should not be aware what they did wrong, or be able to explain what they did right."

Her sister's ignorance evidently pleased Mrs. Norris. "Well, then, that is another burden I shall be able to take from you. Rely upon me, Sister, you may rely upon me."

"I always do," Lady Bertram replied. "Why, I am sure I would not be able to do without you."

This pleased Mrs. Norris no end, but Jonathan could easily discern that, aside from the placid Lady Bertram, the rest of the family was not so happy about the implication that Mrs. Norris would now live with them. He assumed that this cohabitation would take place both here, in London, and at their estate, Mansfield Park, in perpetuity. Mrs. Bertram and her sister Susan exchanged a look of open dismay, as did Mr. and Mrs. Yates. Mr. Edmund Bertram glanced upward, as though pleading for the aid of the Almighty.

Most afflicted of all was Sir Thomas, and he was not a man to long suffer in silence. "Mrs. Norris—it can be arranged that you should administer all the funds inherited by young Ellen, should you consent to raise her. Such sums would provide more than amply for you both to live in comfort, wherever you wished."

"There can be no thought of my raising the child," Mrs. Norris said. "Not that there is anything I would not wish to do for this family! Anyone who has known me these many years knows how eager I always am to help, but as to raising the child, no, there is no question of that. At my years, it would be a travail, for her as well as for me. Though I am, of course, perfectly willing to manage the girl's trust, to lift that burden from you, Tom."

Edmund and Fanny Bertram looked toward each other then, as though stricken. Jonathan might have attempted to discern why, had Lady Bertram not then spoken: "And you are so clever, Sister, managing my jointure! I am sure you would do just as well with the little girl's money. Tom, do you not agree?"

"I beg your pardon?" Sir Thomas tossed down his napkin. "Mother—you mean to tell me that your jointure has been handled by Aunt Norris all this while?"

"Yes, of course," said Lady Bertram. Belatedly she recognized that her sons were angry, and that Mrs. Norris had gone both red and uncharacteristically quiet. "Why should she not? Someone must help me, why not she?"

"Because *someone*," Sir Thomas said, "has been managing your jointure very poorly. Someone has in fact been laying out vast sums of money for no appreciable gain. Over and over you have said, Mamma, that you do not understand why your account balances are low, that you do not buy yourself so many things. Indeed you do not! You have instead been paying for Maria, and the child and, above all, Aunt Norris!"

"Why should she not?" Aunt Norris cried. She was caught out now, the knowledge of which made her slow and unequal to her own defense. "Who was Maria but my sister's own daughter? Who is Ellen, if not her grandchild? Why should the Bertram family begrudge us a living, a few comforts? Why must Maria's shame be punishment to us all?"

"The points you raise are not unjust, Aunt," Edmund Bertram said gravely. "However, your behavior was grossly dishonest."

Lady Bertram had finally comprehended at least the rudiments of what had been revealed. "Oh! Is this why sister Norris wanted my checkbook? You told me I wrote too many checks, Tom, but I knew I wrote none. It was my sister who wrote them?"

"Indeed," said Sir Thomas, "and it is the last of this family's money she will ever see!"

But Mr. Bertram turned toward his elder brother. "We cannot deny them the house, not until we have determined what is to become of Ellen."

"I know only one element of that child's future," said Sir Thomas, "and it is that her monies will be managed by absolutely anyone on this earth who is not Aunt Norris!"

"You would not throw out an old woman?" Mrs. Norris cried. "Me with my rheumatism, barely able to hold a basket in my hands, you would not cast me out. You are not such a villain as that!"

Sir Thomas's laugh was unpleasant. "There is but one villain at the table, madam, and you are she!"

Jonathan would much rather not have witnessed such a family row, but such was sometimes the fate of the houseguest. At least he had learned something from the experience. Namely, he knew not only that Aunt Norris was a thief, and that this—rather than any extraordinary generosity from Mr. Rushworth or Mr. Crawford—was likely the cause of Maria Rushworth's unexpected prosperity, the touches that revealed their household was not wholly impoverished.

He knew also that Sir Thomas Bertram could not endure the thought of lost money. How this might affect the proposed sale of the plantation in Antigua, Jonathan could not say, but it struck him that this was not a man who would give away profitable property easily.

Silently he resolved to tell Miss Tilney of this at the next opportunity. He would ask her whether Sir Thomas was delaying the plantation's sale for pecuniary reasons. Or could there be another, more secret purpose yet to be revealed?

Chapter Nineteen

Juliet insisted that her mother come with her to call on the Bertram household that very next day. "My dear child," Catherine Tilney said, "have you not heard that it is very much not the done thing to rise early on the morning after a ball?"

"No—I mean, I know that most do not, but is it a rule, truly?"

"Indeed not, nor need anybody make it one, for who on earth would wish to rise at daybreak after dancing until nigh three?" Catherine, still in her dressing gown, would have laughed had she not needed to yawn. "You are young and lively, I know, but still. In courtesy, we should not call very early, for some if not all of the Bertrams may remain abed."

Juliet wished very much to get as soon a start as possible upon the investigation; if they were ever to make progress, if they were to unsnarl the tangle of alibis and motives, they must rededicate themselves to this effort. She wished this primarily for the promotion of justice and the safety of those connected to the Bertram family, but the stares from some of those at the Ramseys' ball the night before had also had their effect. Although Juliet was willing to brave public disapproval, she also, quite naturally, hoped to dispel such disapproval swiftly. "We can go at the very end of calling hours, and then, if they are still abed, the servants will simply tell us they are out. We will not importune them."

Mrs. Tilney groaned, but rang the bell so she could ask the cook to make an extra pot of coffee.

When they did at last arrive at the Bertrams', they found

the household not only awake, but also noticeably agitated. Mrs. Tilney went to visit with the ladies of the house in the sitting room, thinking that they would all have much to discuss regarding the ball, while Juliet and Mr. Darcy resumed their endeavors. Instead, she found herself alone save for Miss Price, but between the two of them, they had observations and enthusiasm enough for a very pleasant visit.

With great interest did Juliet hear Mr. Darcy's report of the morning revelations. (They sat in the study, chaperoned by a footman at the door, one so sleepy he would scarcely have noticed had they made off with the family china.) She said, "So it is possible that neither of Mrs. Rushworth's—ah, *suitors*—had been generous with her. They must have assumed her cared for by her family, which I suppose in a sense she was. Her family simply did not understand they were doing so."

"Do you think she claimed poverty so as to excite their sympathy?" Mr. Darcy said. "In the case of Mr. Rushworth, she evidently succeeded."

Juliet thought on this. "Perhaps, in part. More than anything, though, Mrs. Rushworth would have wished to conceal her aunt's handiwork. She would not have much minded wearing a shabby cloak once in a while, going about to be seen in it, if that were but the price of otherwise being comfortably housed and well attired. Do you think that is the explanation for Mrs. Norris's vagaries? That her tales of 'going to market' instead concealed her efforts to obtain and cash her sister's checks?"

"I do not think we can prove that," replied Mr. Darcy, "but we must consider it as a very definite possibility. Certainly this revelation does not deepen any suspicion of Mrs. Norris's guilt; whether it has leavened it instead, we have yet to determine. The person whom I *did* become more suspicious of this morning was in fact Sir Thomas."

When he told her of Sir Thomas's wrath that morning, Juliet was at first not convinced. Anger was a natural enough sentiment upon discovering such deceit. Yet the fact remained that something about the sale of the Antigua plantation was being concealed—some complication, perhaps—and Sir Thomas's own secrecy about matters financial required scrutiny. "Shall we ask if he will speak with us on this subject?"

"I will ask Mr. Bertram," promised Mr. Darcy, and with this he left the study.

As Juliet was wondering whether she should seek out paper and ink—financial information might need to be written to be recalled—Mrs. Norris saw herself into the study. "Well, and I suppose all and sundry have told you tales of me?"

Juliet could not bring herself to be severe; the old woman looked so bent and low. "I have heard of your handling of Lady Bertram's jointure, yes."

"I put my sister's wealth to good use," Mrs. Norris insisted. "I supported her daughter and her granddaughter, when the rest of the family would not have done so. What need has my sister of a fortune, living in Mansfield Park for the rest of her days, surrounded by servants, scarcely ever obliged to take on any exertion more strenuous than lifting a cup?"

"It is a fair point, Mrs. Norris, but it would be fairer still had you acted with your sister's knowledge and consent."

Mrs. Norris did not appear even to hear this. "All my life, I have worked for the benefit of this family. I have sacrificed many a day, many a year, to providing them advice and succor, and now they may be ready to turn me out! I, who dedicated myself to Maria—I, who came here with nothing left of my former life save my silver—will they make me destitute? A rheumatic old woman such as myself?"

Juliet felt much discomfited. "Forgive me, Mrs. Norris, but you pose questions I cannot answer. Your actions are not mine to judge."

This was as kind as anyone had been to Mrs. Norris all morning, but she was not sufficiently satisfied with Juliet's answer as to feel any gratitude. Instead, she took herself away to scold the parlormaids, who could still safely be said to be even more lowly than she.

Jonathan's request prompted Mr. Bertram to bring his brother, Sir Thomas, to the study where Miss Tilney sat, waiting. Sir Thomas laughed in a manner that sounded carefree, but was not. "Well, what is this? What is it about the buying and selling of plantations that excites your curiosity, or might have aught to do with the fate of my poor sister?"

"It is only this, sir," said Miss Tilney, as Jonathan took the chair next to her. "Conducting the business seems to have taken up a great deal of your time, more than such a transaction would require."

Sir Thomas chuckled, though there was very little humor in it. "You know a great deal about property transactions, do you, Miss Tilney? A girl of your years?"

Here, Jonathan could intercede. "Regardless of what Miss Tilney may or may not know, *I* have had some experience in selling property, for my father has divested himself of certain agricultural holdings during the past few years. As you insist that you and Mr. Drake had already come to a tentative agreement before you even came to London—yes, the business does seem to be taking an unusually long time."

"More significantly," Miss Tilney added, "on at least one occasion, you lied to us about conducting plantation business at your club, Wyngarde's. Mr. Crawford was at Wyngarde's upon the morning in question—the morning of Mr. Rushworth's demise—and he did not see you there."

"Nor was I able to find your name in Wyngarde's guest

book, though I searched all pages signed on that day." Jonathan took some satisfaction in seeing just how pale Sir Thomas had become.

Mr. Bertram, unsurprisingly, was disturbed by this. "Tom, what does this mean?"

"I have never murdered anyone," Sir Thomas said, which Jonathan noted was not quite an answer to the question posed. "Is that not all that matters?"

At that very moment, Mrs. Norris came through the door, a smirk upon her face. "If you wish to know where Tom was, what business he is about, *I* can tell you."

Sir Thomas cried, "Aunt Norris, have you not disgraced yourself enough this morning?"

But Mr. Bertram at least wished to hear, and he would have a better chance of compelling honesty from his brother and aunt. Jonathan and Miss Tilney needed only to listen.

"I had to go through many papers to locate my sister's checks at Mansfield Park," Aunt Norris said, "which I did only to provide for Maria and Ellen, only for their good, but it was hard work, let me tell you, for Tom has never kept anything in order, not from his childhood playroom to this day. I was obliged to go through nearly every paper in his study to locate that which was needed. Yes, he has told us the truth as far as it goes—the Antigua plantation is sold and gone already—but Tom is purchasing another plantation to replace it, this one in Barbados."

"*What?*" Mr. Bertram had gone white. "Tell me this is a lie, Tom. Tell me you have not done anything so wicked."

Sir Thomas had raised his chin, like a small defiant boy. "You are not the elder brother, Edmund. It is I who determine how the family will manage its fortune."

Mr. Bertram appeared as though he might soon be ill. Jonathan took the opportunity to ask Sir Thomas, "If we were to ask the seller whether you were meeting with him regarding the Barbados plantation on those mornings, would he be able to answer in the affirmative?"

"Indeed he would," Sir Thomas said stiffly. "If you like, I will give you Mr. Sinclair's address, and a note you may bring to him, which will instruct him to receive you and answer honestly."

"If you would, sir," said Miss Tilney. Though Sir Thomas showed much consternation in having to answer to a young girl in this manner, he did as he promised. Aunt Norris swept out of the room with satisfaction, for now someone else was in as much trouble as she.

As soon as the young investigators had left Tom's study, Edmund shut the door, so that they would not further scandalize the nearby footman—or the rest of the household—with what next had to be said. "Tom, I beg of you to reconsider this."

"You have plagued me and plagued me to sell the Antigua plantation," Tom said, sitting in his chair as though it were a throne from which he could issue orders. "This I have done. You never told me not to purchase another."

"I never said as much because I never believed it required saying! Does not the Barbados plantation also employ slaves?"

"Yes, of course."

How could his elder brother be so unbothered about matters of such gravity? "But it is illegal to buy and sell slaves!"

"Certain parties in Antigua and Barbados purchased slaves before the abolition—our father shrewdly sold ours to these parties years ago—and they are hired out by their legal owners. Thus the law is obeyed without either plantation losing so much as a single hand. Surely even you can appreciate the legal dexterity required."

Edmund's stomach turned. "Do you not hear your own words? To participate in commerce involving your fellow human beings—it is sin, Tom, the most wretched sin imaginable! To be responsible for such degradation, such suffering! To value mere material gain over the basic humanity of those you 'own,' over any sense of decency?"

"Even *selling* the Antigua plantation involves us in that commerce, Edmund. Or did you think the slaves would all be freed the moment we sold it? That the next owner would require no labor?"

"That is precisely what I thought," Edmund had to admit. How naive he had been to put such faith in his brother—how careless, not to have dedicated himself to every question regarding those persons' welfare! "I believed we would set them free. I believed the law of England required as much, as the law of Heaven always has."

"Set them free to what end, I ask you? Where else are they to work? What else are they to do? They own nothing, and as we are selling the plantation, we will be in a position to give them nothing. They would be much worse off then than they are now, I tell you."

"That is not true. If it were you, Tom—if you had the choice between humble captivity and humbler freedom—would not you choose freedom? I would, as I believe any person would. As I believe the enslaved in Antigua or Barbados would."

Tom had become agitated, gripping at the arms of his chair as though it held him back from rash action. "Do not you realize that if we leave the sugar business, the family's fortune in the next generation will be only a half of what we now possess?"

"What is that to us? We are more than prosperous enough to endure such a loss."

"Yes, by selling off even more of our lands. That could lead to the loss of the living you now enjoy; I might no longer be in a position to guarantee it to you. You are so willing, then, to live in poverty?"

"I should rather live in poverty than in sin!" Edmund insisted.

"You have lived in sin throughout your life, you hypocrite," said Tom, "as have we all. Mansfield Park was *built* with money from the Antigua plantation. Every stitch of clothing we wore as children, every meal we ate, our mother's fat pug dog—all if it flows from that one source, and by your reckoning is therefore eternally tainted. Will you give back the horse Fanny rides? The education you had at Eton and Oxford? The books in our library? Of course you will not, because you cannot. The slavery you affect to despise has given us almost everything we have, Edmund. Nothing can change that fact, neither the sale of the Antigua plantation nor the purchase of the one in Barbados. You are still steeped in it up to your neck. Cease your pretense of virtue and accept who you are, what you have profited from!"

The moral emptiness of every word Tom spoke galled Edmund, but not so much as the realization that—in fact, if not in philosophy—Tom was correct.

Edmund could only reply, "Whatever wrongs have been done in the past cannot justify the continuance of those wrongs in the future. If you purchase the Barbados plantation or any other—we will be brothers no longer."

With that, Edmund left humbled, wretched, sick to his stomach, and unable to imagine ever feeling better again.

Juliet found that, while exact words from the study could not be overheard in the Bertrams' sitting room, enough sound could be determined to understand that the men of the family were having an extremely vituperative disagreement. Mr.

Darcy gave her a look of great concern, but no action could they take.

She wondered whether they ought to try to use the occasion to question Mrs. Yates, whose anger toward her sister seemed to potentially point to a motive for that killing. However, Mrs. Yates had apparently not even been in London when Mr. Rushworth died, so if they sought but one murderer, Mrs. Yates was not she.

Regardless, no further questions would be asked that day, for the women of the family, along with Mr. Yates, had congregated anew in the sitting room. The various upsets the Bertrams had endured that morning were thinly disguised by small, tight smiles. Juliet judged that it would be difficult to win any openness and honesty from these persons in their current temper.

As though their need for aid had been spread throughout the land, at that moment, an invitation arrived. Mrs. Fanny Bertram opened the envelope and informed the company. "It is from Mrs. Allerdyce. She invites us to join her and her daughters at the art exhibition this afternoon."

"Oh, yes, please," said Miss Susan Price, perhaps less from an interest in fine art than from a desire to escape the ill feeling in the house. "Everyone in the city has been speaking of it."

Fanny glanced toward the study. "I do not think either Tom or Edmund will be in a position to join us—but should we go nonetheless? He will wish us to better know Miss Allerdyce, after all."

Juliet's mother seemed to spy an opportunity for escape. "It is time for the two of us to go, I am sure."

"But you are invited as well," replied Fanny. "Or, rather, Mrs. Allerdyce says she has also sent a note to your lodgings, to ask you to accompany us. It would be a favor to me if you did, for I do not feel equal to it, but I would not send my sister alone."

Why should they be invited? Juliet had caught a few of Mrs. Allerdyce's icy glares in the past, and had noted both mother and younger daughter's pointed attentions to Mr. Darcy. Yet now they included her family in their social engagements. *Perhaps,* she thought, *perhaps after observing me with Mr. Darcy at the Ramseys' ball, the Allerdyces understand that we have formed . . . an attachment.* How daring even to think the word *attachment,* but was that not the truth of it?

The voices in the study grew louder. Lady Bertram, uncertain as ever, said, "I do not know whether I would like to go look at works of art. Would I, Fanny?"

Fanny glanced with worry toward the study. "Today, Aunt, I believe you would like to, very much indeed."

"Oh, would I? How peculiar of me." But Lady Bertram had already risen, ready to set out, and so it appeared all the party shared one destination.

The art show was held in the most fashionable auction house in London, one which had moved to King Street only the year before. Despite the size of the gallery, to Juliet the space seemed to be nearly as full as the Ramseys' ballroom had been the night before, though here people strolled instead of danced, murmured instead of laughed. Mrs. Allerdyce and her daughters waited for them near the entrance, and together their party set out through the long maze of paintings and drawings, all jumbled together, sometimes with as many as two dozen richly framed artworks to each red damask wall. Mirrors carefully placed near the few windows reflected light enough to see by, and so much there was to see!

Most of the artworks were on a classical theme, including nearly all the statues. Juliet paused a moment to admire a bust of a young child, which had somehow captured the full soft cheeks of youth in marble. Mr. Darcy remained by her side; for a moment, she thought he might offer her his arm.

"The last time we studied a bust together," she said to him, "it portrayed Lord Nelson, and it had been put to dark purposes indeed."

"Even that weapon was more easily identified than the ones that we search for now," Mr. Darcy said. Then they both became aware that a bystander was giving them an odd look; it was best, perhaps, not to discuss their murder investigations in so public a setting.

The paintings reflected a broader range of styles than the statues did. Turner's phantasmagoric colors—his resplendent skies in a dozen shades—they captured more truth than any exact representation could ever have done. Juliet marveled at the turbulent beauty of the work; already she could hardly wait to attempt a description of it for her father.

"I had nearly forgotten," Mr. Darcy said, "that Mr. Follett is in town, and that a work of his is on display here."

"Is it indeed? I found him an ill-mannered young man, and I cannot at all condone his behavior toward you—but I must confess that he was an exceedingly talented painter."

Mr. Darcy nodded. "He was much wounded by the death of Mrs. Willoughby. It is my hope that the experience may have improved his character, that it may have taught him something of pity."

"I cannot be so sanguine," Juliet said, "for it seems to me that people are remarkably good at not learning such lessons—but for his sake, we will wish it so, and I declare that I shall appraise his work justly, with no prejudice born of dislike."

They walked past an enormous painting depicting a shipwreck, into one of the next chambers of the show. There, a small group had huddled around one work in particular; through the thicket of hats, Juliet could only just glimpse the painting under scrutiny, though this was sufficient to inform her that the female subject of said painting was unclothed, and in a most curious position.

"The catalog says this is Follett's," Mr. Darcy said as they fell into step behind Mrs. Allerdyce, who was headed straight for the painting. "To judge by the number of observers, I believe it may also be the 'scandalous' image so many have spoken of when describing the show."

Juliet covered her mouth with her gloved hand, so no one might see her smile. They made their way through the gathered viewers until the painting was revealed to them, and—the problem was not that the woman portrayed was unclothed. It was not that she was Pasiphaë, the woman in myth who had been struck by Poseidon with passion for a bull. It was not even that this romancing was rather more graphically displayed than one expected in fine art, or for that matter any drawing less vulgar than the cartoons sold on the street.

The problem was that the woman's face was Juliet's own.

My portrait, she thought as her face went hot and her limbs went cold. *The portrait he painted of me while I was staying with the Brandons—he painted over everything but my face and made me the subject of this . . . this obscene . . .*

They were all staring at her now. Every person in the room had realized that the subject of this painting had entered the room, that it was she and no other. Did they believe that she had posed for this? That she had displayed her entire unclothed person to the artist, and done so in such a vulgar posture?

Now, too late, she realized that they did, and that they were not the only ones. The stares she had occasionally drawn throughout her stay in London, the curiosity directed at her the night before at the Ramseys—all had come from persons who had first seen this painting, and recognized her. How could they not? It was an excellent likeness of her face.

"Miss Tilney?" Mr. Darcy caught Juliet's elbow in the moment before she would have fainted. Murmuring spread through the room as Juliet's mother hurried to her other side and began steering them all toward the nearest exit.

"Oh," Juliet said, "oh, Mamma, it was the portrait I told you about, but Mr. Follett—he falsified it, he made the rest up—"

"I realize that, my darling," said Catherine Tilney. Her voice was tight with fury, so much so that Juliet hardly recognized it. That fury was all for Laurence Follett, who was probably having an excellent laugh at her expense that very moment.

As they hurried along, more and more people turned to stare. Every single one seemed to reflect recognition. And now that Juliet had been present, someone would make the connection; soon, her name would be attached to the painting through whispers and rumor.

My reputation is lost forever, Juliet thought. *I am ruined.*

Chapter Twenty

The day may eventually arrive when a person in need may effortlessly summon a carriage in an instant, but for the present and no doubt for a very long time to come, the truism holds: The greater one's haste, the fewer cabs are to be had. Catherine Tilney had rarely felt so helpless, so overwhelmed, as she did that day, attempting to support her swooning daughter with one arm while gesticulating for assistance with the other. In the distance she saw the Bertram coachman idling with his fellows—the man who had driven them here—but it was unthinkable to return to their companions even to ask for assistance back to the Tilneys' London home. Nor would any woman of decency allow it, after such a spectacle.

"I promise I did nothing wrong, Mamma," Juliet said, her voice wavering. Already her eyes were red, filling with tears. "I swear to you, I sat for a portrait, a very correct portrait—we were in the Brandons' home all the while, and they were most attentive chaperones—"

"Hush, child. Of course you did only what was right. I would never think anything less of you." Catherine did not add what they both knew to be true: Many others would think Juliet capable of anything, after seeing such an infamous picture, one that depicted her face so accurately and her person so obscenely.

Artists employed models, of course, even for works depicting nudes, but it was understood that such women were of low birth and probably of low morals. More than one of them removed their clothing for pay in the services of purposes beyond mere modeling. Women of society, on the other hand, were only ever portrayed in correct poses for conventional portraits; even then, some families declined to have such portraits displayed outside their own homes from a sense that public exposure was indelicate.

This Mr. Follett, who played at being a gentleman portraitist, had betrayed every convention of society painting. He had abused the trust of a young woman, and for this he must pay. Catherine was uncertain how, precisely, to exact such punishment—was such a case as this grounds for a lawsuit?—but whatever Follett thought, Juliet Tilney was not without a family of standing, nor without friends, as he was soon to discover!

(Though Catherine did not fully recognize this in such a moment of travail, her thinking was for once identical to what her tyrannical father-in-law's would have been, what it *would* be, when he learned of it.)

Whatever justice was to come, Catherine determined it must be public. If Mr. Follett did not offer his apologies and clarify Juliet's innocence in the matter . . .

If he does not, she is utterly ruined, she realized. *If he does—she may well be ruined regardless.*

To be "ruined" was the worst fate that could befall a young woman save for death, and there were women who had chosen death rather than endure it. Such ruination came when a woman's purity was lost, or believed to have been lost. No gentleman would consent to marry such a woman; no family would accept her. The stain of it bled from the ruined woman to the rest of her family as well; Catherine realized that this might not only destroy Juliet's marital prospects—and not only with Jonathan Darcy—but also that of her younger daughter, Theodosia. Unjustly but undeniably, the blight did not affect males of the family so terribly, but even her son,

Albion, would find it more difficult to find a bride when the time came, after this.

At last a carriage was hailed; at last Catherine was able to bundle her daughter into its temporary safety. On the steps of the gallery, a few people had congregated; Juliet had been recognized, and the connection had been made. There could be no escape from infamy now.

Once the door was shut and the carriage set out, Catherine folded her daughter into her arms more tenderly than she had since Juliet's infancy. Juliet—her bright, brash, courageous girl—began to sob, utterly broken. In that instant, Catherine thought she could have slain Laurence Follett, given but a knife and opportunity.

But she had neither. They had no defense, no resource, no constructive action they could take besides retreating to their London home to hide from all the world.

Jonathan Darcy attempted to follow Miss Tilney and her mother from the gallery, but Mrs. Allerdyce caught him by the arm. "Let them go," she counseled. "You cannot help their situation, and in attempting to do so, you will only harm yourself."

"Miss Tilney must be greatly upset," he said, still attempting to extricate himself. "This is a foul trick of Follett's, one that will have embarrassed her deeply."

"It has done worse than embarrass her." This came from Miss Priscilla Allerdyce, who had used this opportunity to take his other arm. Between mother and daughter, he was very nearly trapped. "It has ruined her. She will have no place in polite society now."

"Ruined?" It was rude to pull away from a woman holding one's arm, but Jonathan cared nothing for rudeness at that moment. Tugging away from the Allerdyces, he asked, "Why should Miss Tilney be ruined because of the misconduct of another?"

"It is unjust, perhaps," Mrs. Allerdyce said. "But it is so. Your parents will agree, when they hear of this—and hear of it, they will."

Jonathan had become more sharply aware of the commotion that surrounded them, the mutterings and even laughter of those who had connected Miss Tilney to the image that wore her face. Always ill at ease in an unstructured crowd, he now felt overwhelmed, even dizzy.

As for the others in their party, Miss Price still stared at the image agape; no doubt she had never seen a mythological theme so literally portrayed before. Lady Bertram blinked slowly and said, "I do not think that could be accomplished with a bull. No, I do not think so at all."

"Excuse me," Jonathan said to them. "You must excuse me." With that, he hurried from the room, from the art show entirely. He made it to the front steps just in time to see Mrs. Tilney push her daughter into a hackney and tug the interior curtains shut. Although Jonathan attempted to hurry toward them, the carriage had pulled away before he reached the bottom of the steps.

The din of the London streets, which he had struggled with so manfully throughout his visit, now swelled all around him to the point of rendering him incapable. Jonathan wanted nothing so much as to crouch down upon the ground, cover his ears, and close his eyes. He felt the need to rock back and forth until some measure of the frenzy within him had been soothed, until he could think again. From this action he was only prevented by the understanding that, if he did so, he would remain surrounded by the full bedlam of London.

I must find shelter, Jonathan thought. *I must find some measure of privacy, immediately.* Then he hit upon the solution: his own hackney carriage.

He had swifter luck than the Tilney women, for almost as soon as he thrust out his hand, a carriage claimed him. Jonathan lurched into it, his legs wobbly, aware that bystanders might think him drunk. Let them think it, then.

"Where to, sir?" called the driver.

Jonathan could not imagine where to go or what to do. He felt as if he could barely even see. "Please, just—just drive. I will give you a destination later. For now, only take me far from this accursed place!" The driver, too wise to argue with a passenger in such straits, clicked his tongue at the horse, and they began to roll away.

The carriage curtain, Jonathan tugged shut; he then set aside his hat and slumped to the very floor of the carriage, covering his ears with his gloved hands. Although noise still surrounded him, the carriage muted it slightly, which in time might prove sufficient for him to regain some sense of calm. This he endeavored to bring about more swiftly by rocking back and forth—but this habit, so often a great comfort to him, was not equal to the extreme provocation.

Certain strictures of society that went largely unspoken remained ever murky for Jonathan. When he did not understand the justification behind a rule, that rule could be very difficult for him to intuit. The question of a woman's reputation—and its ruination—was not among these. *There,* society's rules were clear. Miss Tilney had become an artist's model for a painting that was not portraiture. This painting depicted her unclothed; ergo, the clear implication was that Miss Tilney was, or had been, engaged in prostitution. No matter that this statement was utterly false, for the presumption was all but irrefutable.

He found himself remembering the days after his aunt Lydia's death, when his tearful mother had told him more of

the scandals of Lydia's youth. Her elopement with Mr. Wickham had not only put her own future at risk but also that of
his mother and his aunts. Had Wickham not been pressed
into marrying Aunt Lydia—pressed by Jonathan's father, who
had wealth and authority—all the Bennet sisters' ruination
would have been complete.

This situation, he thought, was even worse. He did not
speak ill of the dead in acknowledging that Aunt Lydia had in
fact been guilty of the actions for which she was condemned,
and in her case, the remedy of marriage had been obvious
and—to her, if to no one else—entirely welcome. Miss Tilney
was utterly innocent, however, and no remedy readily suggested itself. Jonathan did not think that a marriage between
Miss Tilney and Follett would answer, and even if it would
have done, such an idea could not be countenanced.

What is to be done? Jonathan thought. He leaned back
against the carriage seat, his eyes still shut, taking the slowest
and deepest breaths he could, desperately seeking calm and
clarity. *Is there anything that can be done? Or is it a hopeless case?*

Having declined to attend the art show, and not yet privy
to the particulars of the argument her husband and Tom
were having in the study, Fanny Bertram knew nothing
of the resulting travails. She was very nearly as disquieted
as all the others, but for reasons of her own. That morning
she intended to resolve her difficulties if she could. So it was
that, only minutes after the carriage had rolled away with the
ladies attending the art show, Fanny had set out on foot with
an accompanying manservant to visit the London residence
of the Crawfords.

Even a few days prior, Fanny would never have been able to
imagine willingly calling upon this family; seeing Miss Craw-

ford in the milliner's shop had been difficult enough. To now be within their residence, to defer to them as hosts—but it had to be done, and Fanny knew she would have few chances to do it unobserved by any of her family. She felt ashamed of her plan, considered it likely that Edmund might even be angry when he heard of it, but to her it seemed she had no other choice.

She was received at the Crawfords' by Mary, who welcomed her with the same humbling pleasure as before. "Mrs. Bertram! How good of you to call. Your brothers have been very difficult with us of late—but we must not speak of it—you, at least, show proper feeling. With you, friendship endures beyond all else."

Such a reception made it very hard for Fanny to say what she must. "Miss Crawford, we must speak. You, me, and your brother, as well."

Even Henry Crawford, a man supremely certain of his welcome everywhere he went—even when such certainty would have been reckoned unlikely by most—had not anticipated being called for by the former Miss Fanny Price. Yet he had his coat on to join the ladies in the sitting room within a minute, and he smiled at Fanny just as he had in the days he had courted her. "Mrs. Bertram, such a pleasure. Rare is the woman lovelier in her maturity than in her girlhood, but it is very true of you."

Mild a creature as Fanny was, she could not help but be glad to see his smug countenance fade as she replied, "Mr. Crawford, we must speak of Ellen Rushworth."

Mary Crawford folded her hands in her lap and spoke more primly than was her wont: "Henry, you know she is correct. You must consider this matter more thoroughly."

"There is nothing to consider," Mr. Crawford said. "A woman formerly of my acquaintance—one whose acquaintance I very publicly attempted to end, mind—had a child.

Her former husband claimed that child as his own. They are both dead, which I grant is a tragic circumstance, but their daughter is no concern of mine."

As much as Fanny had dreaded this conversation, she had failed to fully comprehend how mortifying it would be. How could she utter the words that suggested a man and woman had been together absent the covenant of marriage?

Mary Crawford, never so delicate, was Fanny's unexpected advocate. "You have several tenant farmers at Evering-ham who would take in a child," said Miss Crawford to her brother. "At very little expense to you, she could be sheltered, educated, given a stable home. Her illegitimacy would not preclude her finding a husband from that class."

"Are my tenants the only farmers in England?" was Henry's reply. "Mansfield Park has tenants of its own. Let Maria's fam-ily contend with Maria's issue. I will have nothing to do with it, least of all now, for reasons you well know, Mary. Nor shall I be lectured by Mrs. Bertram, who is too prim, too hard, too unforgiving to look upon the world as it is without calling it sin." When Fanny gaped at him in astonishment, he contin-ued: "There was a time, you may recall, when my intentions were as blameless as any man's could ever be—when I wished for your good esteem, when I declared my willingness to prove myself worthy of your love—and what was my reward? Coldness and rejection. Do not blame me, Mrs. Bertram, when it was within your power to see me the most respect-able and loyal of all men!"

This impudence was almost unanswerable, but Fanny did her best: "I do not believe that to have been in any woman's power, Mr. Crawford."

"There! That serves you right, Henry," Miss Crawford said, but she was rising to her feet, and Fanny knew she was to be shown the door. Though Mary Crawford might wish her brother to do better by his daughter than he was prepared to, her loyalty would still be to him rather than to any good principle, much less the niece she had never met.

On the way back, Fanny mournfully considered her predicament. If Ellen remained in the keeping of the Bertram family, as it appeared she must, Edmund would not be the only one who would wish for Fanny to take the role of guardian, caretaker, even of mother. Yet this was impossible. Fanny feared this prospect, less for herself than for Ellen.

Her rebuke to Edmund shamed her, for it had been false—but she found it difficult to put words to her true objection, even within her own mind.

Fanny had been sent away by her family to live at Mansfield Park with her aunt and uncle when she was just a child. She herself had lost one home and been taken in to another, a home where she had largely been excluded and humbled. Of course the Bertrams had been generous to give her a room, but the room had no fire until Fanny was an adult and had already spent her childhood winters shivering so at night that she sometimes could not sleep. Of course the Bertrams had been good to feed and clothe her, even if Mrs. Norris had begrudged her every bite and her attire had been made up almost solely of fabric or dresses Maria and Julia had outgrown or simply rejected. And of course they had allowed her to take part in all family life, yet they had by and large treated her more like a hired companion—sent to fetch and carry—than a cousin or a sibling. Edmund had ever been generous and good to her, but everyone else had made it clear to Fanny at all times that she was not their equal, that she must always take a lower place. Fanny had spent her entire life attempting to find the boundary between humility and humiliation.

She was too tenderhearted to resent the Bertram family for this. She could even pity Aunt Norris, who had always been the sharpest and meanest among them. Nor could it be denied that the Bertrams had eventually opened their home to her younger sister Susan as well, and Susan had been treated as true family from the very beginning. But Ellen was unlikely to receive a similar welcome, given the circumstances of her birth, and Fanny could not countenance the idea of another child growing up in such a way. What would Ellen's existence be, forever made to feel lesser and unwelcome? Had the Bertrams learned from their mistakes? Fanny often doubted this. Mrs. Norris, it appeared, would soon be resident at Mansfield Park, which meant she would ever be around to criticize the little girl, a child for whom she showed none of the fondness that ought to have been natural between them.

Worst of all, however, was Fanny's fear that she, too, would push the child away. No, she had none of the pride or selfishness that had led to her own ill treatment—but she could only see Ellen as a poor replacement for the baby she and Edmund ought to have had together. Even if she never spoke a word aloud suggesting as much, Fanny felt sure Ellen would know. Children did know. She had known.

What had been done to her, Fanny refused to do to anyone else.

But what was to become of the girl?

It was the better part of an hour before Jonathan Darcy had regained his bearing. London's noise, though still a deluge, could again be sorted and made sense of; the relative darkness within the carriage had allowed him to rest his eyes. His heart still hammered in his chest, but less from the overwhelming sensations that had overtaken him before—more, from anger, and from an even greater understanding of the harm than he had been able to gather during the worst of his upheaval.

The damage to Juliet Tilney had been done. Her character had been besmirched, her reputation harmed if not ruined.

Laurence Follett had acted wrongly, and the more Jonathan considered his actions, the angrier he became. For it seemed clear to him that Follett's malice had not truly been directed at Miss Tilney herself, but at Jonathan. Follett had known of Jonathan's interest in her, had teased him about it during their time at Allenham. His contempt for Jonathan personally was of longer standing, going back to Jonathan's first days at boarding school. No doubt Laurence Follett had thought it a fine joke, painting the face of the girl Jonathan cared for, then placing it in an obscene tableau for all the world to see.

He has been laughing at her, at me, at us, Jonathan thought. *I will put an end to his laughter.*

A thump on the carriage roof got the driver's attention. "Yes, sir? You got a destination in mind?"

"Take me to Wyngarde's," Jonathan replied. Almost immediately the carriage turned. If he was reckoning their location correctly, it would not be a long drive.

His parents would have to be written, he knew. They would almost certainly counsel him to shun Miss Tilney's company henceforth; his mother would do so with sympathy, at least, but both she and his father would be unyielding on this point. Jonathan, however, could not help thinking of *Much Ado About Nothing,* in which faithless young Claudio had believed the calumnies against Hero and publicly abandoned her. No, he would not be a Claudio. He much preferred the valiant Ivanhoe. When Rebecca had been shamed, when she had required defense, Ivanhoe had ridden night and day to reach her and had staked his very life to uphold her honor. *That* was courage! *That* was virtue!

Upon reaching Wyngarde's, Jonathan tossed a coin to the driver, a larger one than the man could reasonably have expected. "Wait here for me, if you will—I shall not be long."

For such payment as Jonathan had just made, the driver would have been willing to wait near a month. "Sir! Yes, sir!"

Jonathan was not a member in his own right at Wyngarde's, and he expected to have to speak to the staff about his business; instead, they immediately showed him to the place in the bar where Sir Thomas sat. He seemed startlingly deep in his cups for a relatively early hour, but he attempted to smile. "Mr. Darcy. Good man. I have need of a sympathetic ear."

"I am here on business, sir," Jonathan replied, for he now knew he would not be required to ask after Mr. Follett, to track down his lodgings or his business—for Follett stood with some chaps near the window, making ridiculous bets regarding their observations. It was Follett who said, "Ten pounds—ten whole pounds, mind—says that a woman with a red hat will walk before us within the next—"

"Laurence Follett," Jonathan said, loudly enough that the entire room of the club hushed. Follett turned toward him still too surprised to surmise what this might be about. Jonathan informed him. "You have besmirched the reputation of a lady, a young woman who has never done you harm, whose reputation you have falsely sullied through your indecent work."

It took a moment for Follett to laugh, and he did so uneasily. "I admit—you know, I did not think I should ever see her again—what were the odds that she would come to London—?"

"You have assaulted the honor of Miss Tilney," Jonathan interjected, even louder than before, "and I demand satisfaction, sir."

Finally, Follett understood. "You cannot mean—Darcy, are you challenging me to a *duel?*"

Jonathan replied, "We meet tomorrow at dawn."

Chapter Twenty-One

Sometimes it is only in the gloom of our defeat that we acknowledge how high our hopes truly were. A rational creature, Fanny Bertram had understood from the beginning that she had very little chance of persuading Henry Crawford to responsibility in any situation. Even less must she have in a case such as Ellen's, which would have asked much of Mr. Crawford's decency and reputation, not to mention his bank-book. Yet it was in utter dejection that she returned to her family's London residence with no surer sense of what was to be done about little Ellen.

I will not do to another what was done to me, Fanny silently swore. Most observers would have assured her how very unlikely this would be; she was neither cruel nor proud, and she was deeply aware of how tender a child's feelings were. But most observers did not know of the wretched ache in Fanny's heart, the depth of her misery that she should never have a baby of her own. Fanny understood that, all too often, our most corrosive poisons seep from our most painful wounds.

Only upon reentering the house did she remember that, upon quitting it, she had overheard Edmund having some ferocious manner of disagreement with Tom. Consider the desolation necessary to make doting Fanny forget, even for a moment, to worry about Edmund's welfare! At least the shouting had ended; she could hope that they had already healed whatever breach had occurred.

A quick word with Danvers revealed that Sir Thomas had left some time ago, but that Edmund had secreted himself in the small library. Without even removing her cloak, Fanny went to find him thither. Her husband sat in one of the chairs, staring out the window, a volume of sermons still closed in his hands.

Edmund turned at sound of her footstep. "Ah, Fanny. How glad I am that you are here."

His attempt at a welcoming smile was so sad, so strained, that Fanny became afraid. "Edmund? Whatever is the matter?"

He told her. Fanny heard the news about the Barbados plantation first in consternation, then pain, then anger—a rare sentiment for her, but this subject was one she considered worthy of it. "Tom swore to you that the family would leave the sugar trade! We have both spoken with him about slavery—he has seen it himself in Antigua, and even he could not describe it as anything but cruelty—to imagine that it would matter which island the plantation were to stand on!"

"Tom flatters himself that he is protecting the family wealth," Edmund said, his tone flat. "Of course there are countless endeavors here in Britain worthy of investment—which would honestly employ free persons—but he will not take the time to seek and evaluate. He wishes to remain with what he knows, never mind that this is tyranny and sin. No, above all, Tom seeks to be *comfortable*."

"I am ashamed of him. Surely we can make him see the folly of his choice, can we not?"

"If we have not managed to do so by now, I do not know what else there is to be said." He shook his head and reached for Fanny's hand. "I must confess to you, my dear, that I have worried less about Tom's soul in the past hour than I have about my own."

"You, Edmund? You were eager for the sale, you promoted it at every opportunity."

"Once I had come to recognize the great moral wrong of

slavery, which only occurred after I had reached adulthood. This seems to me now to be an unfathomable lack of understanding. How could I not have rebelled against it from my childhood?"

Fanny had wondered about this, too, that Edmund should have taken so long to reach what was such a very obvious realization. "You were raised with the understanding that this was your family's business, a matter attended to by your father, whom you greatly respected. Your filial duty and love, I believe, kept you from questioning the plantation until you had established a household and independence of your own."

"Poor excuse indeed! And it is no consolation, for it reminds me that my father—whom I always considered the most decent and honorable of men—had no qualms whatsoever about the Antigua plantation, though he traveled there repeatedly and saw its evils for himself. This is a man who felt we had fallen short of our moral duty when we were to put on a theatrical at our house. To object to such as that, while excusing slavery, is both outrageous and absurd. I think that perhaps I never truly knew him at all."

Fanny shared Edmund's feelings to a great degree, for she owed so very much to her uncle the late Sir Thomas; there had been many years where a single word of praise or affection from him had been a source of shining pride. Her own awareness of slavery had come in her youth, perhaps because she attended to the newspapers far more than anyone else in the family—and yet, even she had never fully reckoned with the fact that her late uncle had been one of the perpetrators of such a wrong. She said only, "We are all sinners, Edmund. That is as true of your father as of any other soul on this earth."

"Which brings us back to Tom's words," said Edmund. "He pointed out that Mansfield Park, the house in which you and I grew up, was built with the wealth from the plantation. The living I have as a clergyman also comes from property purchased by our family, with that money. Every meal we eat, every garment we own, all of it bears the same indelible stain; and now that I have seen it, it shall never be invisible to me again."

"This is true not only of Mansfield Park," Fanny began. "When one considers the reach of the British Empire—the many plantations, all over the world—but oh, oh, that makes matters worse, and not better." She sat heavily in the chair next to her husband's, suddenly dizzied by the recognition of so much that she had unwittingly accepted, all while congratulating herself on her moral stances.

"Much worse indeed, Fanny," Edmund said. "We wish to rid ourselves of the spoils of slavery, and we cannot. It is practically the mortar of buildings throughout London, the sails of British ships at sea. How can we ever be clean of it? We cannot unmake England."

In mutual silent sorrow, they sat for several minutes, until they heard a commotion at the door. Sharing a glance, Fanny and Edmund both rose and went to see who had come home, or what visitor they might have. Lady Bertram and Susan Price greeted them; Susan was quite wild-eyed, and even Lady Bertram had not yet stooped to pet Pug. "Oh, Fanny!" Susan cried, "you will not believe what has happened! You will not believe what there was to be seen at the art exhibition!"

"For my part, I do not think such a thing possible with a bull," Lady Bertram added. "Though of course I know nothing of farming and livestock, nothing at all of agricultural matters."

"Yes, Aunt," Susan said, with some measure of exasperation. "So you have told me many times since we first beheld the painting."

It was left to Susan to explain which painting they had seen, though she may be forgiven for not describing the specific act portrayed in any detail. Fanny, who could be overcome with embarrassment upon receiving the least attention, could hardly comprehend the horror poor Juliet Tilney must have felt. "For shame," Fanny whispered, "for shame, to abuse a young woman in such a way."

"A wretched business, indeed," said Edmund, and no doubt he would have continued in this vein had not Tom arrived home, visibly drunk and agitated, with Mr. Jonathan Darcy by his side. Mr. Darcy was as pale as Tom was florid, as rigid as Tom was limp.

"Well, well!" Tom announced, clapping Mr. Darcy on his shoulder. "You will never guess what is to happen—I am sure you will not guess!"

Juliet Tilney would have taken to her bed immediately upon reaching their London dwelling, had she felt she had the fortitude to ascend the stairs. Instead, she sank onto the divan in their sitting room, not even removing her bonnet. So shocked was she that her mind had nearly emptied; her body felt the affliction instead, sapping her limbs of strength.

How often, during their time in London, had she seen people staring at her a few moments too long, or whispering about her behind their cups or fans? Every time, Juliet had told herself that she was imagining the attention, or that it related to someone else in her proximity rather than she herself. How terribly wrong she had been!

Her mother, Catherine, though also deeply troubled, could not permit herself to be overcome, for there was too much to do. "I shall have to write your father," she said, ostensibly speaking to Juliet but aware that her daughter could little heed her, and that this was her way of ordering her own thoughts. "Perhaps he will be able to tell General Tilney before we arrive home, so that the first fury of his anger will be spent. Or first—first, I think, I must send a note to our landlord, to say that we will not be remaining in London. And, oh, all the dressmakers and milliners, the glove shop, I must cancel every order, but at least some of the cloth and leather will be cut, we shall still be obliged to pay—"

None of these concerns could rival in their importance the disastrous events of that morning. But, to the extent she was able to attend to her mother, Juliet understood why Catherine concerned herself with trifles. For trifles could be mended, where a young woman's reputation could not.

They would return home to Gloucestershire in disgrace. It would take time for the shame to make its way from London to the other counties of England, but scandalous news travels swiftly, heedless of rain or snow. First it would arrive in the form of whispers, but after today's public scene, it did not seem impossible to Juliet that her disgrace might be written up in one of the newspapers that prided itself on gossip. Oh, she would only be referred to tacitly, perhaps thusly: *A Miss T, of G—shire, from a family known for its military honors, has earned great dishonor in the eyes of all London—*

Juliet tried to picture Laurence Follett's face and found that she could scarcely do so; she had known him for a few weeks, but had thought of him so little in the many months since that nothing remained of these impressions save for a sense that he was tall, with dark hair. It was on that occasion that she and Mr. Darcy had identified the killer of Mrs. Willoughby, to whom Follett had been greatly devoted since well before her marriage; given that Juliet had helped to bring about justice for his lost love, she would have thought he would remember her with gratitude. Instead, he had done *this*.

"I should have bought the painting," she whispered. "In Devonshire, I should have offered Mr. Follett money—all the money I had—or told Papa or Grandfather to send word that they would purchase it—then none of this could have happened."

Catherine Tilney, though mid-letter to the landlord, had heard every word. "You could not have known what was to come, Juliet. You could never have guessed this. It is not your fault."

"And yet, the punishment is mine to endure," Juliet replied, and to this, her poor mother could say nothing, for it was true.

When young persons travel, from time to time their hosts must step into the paternal role, to provide guidance and even restraint where necessary. Jonathan Darcy was of maturity, but it did not stop Mr. Edmund Bertram from attempting to play the part that day.

"I expressly forbid it," said Mr. Bertram. "I will not have you be fatally shot, nor fatally shoot another, while you are a guest in this house. How came you to make such a rash decision, Darcy? You cannot have thought it through, for the day of duels is all but passed."

Jonathan could be stubborn, where he chose. "That day will *not* have passed until tomorrow at the earliest, for Laurence Follett will face me and answer for this outrage upon the honor of Miss Tilney."

"Will you not consider?" Mr. Bertram's consternation was great. "If you are killed, or maimed for life, how will it help Miss Tilney's situation?"

"When a gentleman defends a woman's honor, she is thought better of, is she not?"

Mr. Bertram paused there, for Jonathan had a point, but the argument was not won. "Have you reckoned with what will happen if you prove triumphant and kill Mr. Follett?

The law will wish to hang you—or transport you to Australia, which sounds quite as bad if not worse. You will be obliged to flee England forever, to live out your life as a vagrant on the Continent!"

This gave Jonathan pause—not because he feared to live elsewhere, or even from a terror of the gallows. He did not like the thought of killing another person, even one who had wronged Miss Tilney so grievously. Jonathan did not even enjoy hunting birds. This reminded him that he was, as a result, much less proficient with firearms than the average man of his class. If he remembered correctly, Laurence Follett hunted often.

At least I do not have to worry about killing Mr. Follett, Jonathan thought, but it was poor consolation indeed! Still, he remained resolute. "I will not allow such an insult to Miss Tilney to go unanswered. To do so would be to condemn her to enduring shame and ostracism. This is the only means of helping her available to me, and in this matter, I will not be gainsaid."

Sir Thomas had begun the slow return to sobriety, enough to consider events more thoroughly than he had before. "Edmund—Mr. Darcy—you both overexert yourselves. Many gentlemen meet on the field of honor without risking either mortality or injury. These days, like as not, both men throw away their shot, firing instead into the ground or the air. Then the grievance is settled, honor is satisfied, and everyone is home in time for breakfast."

This sounded rather anticlimactic to Jonathan, but he had to admit that, if Miss Tilney's honor could be repaired with such a sequence of events, this was the best possible outcome. Livid though he was at Mr. Follett's careless effrontery, it would be better not to kill him. Jonathan would not so much have minded living as an exile in Italy or Portugal, but no doubt this would pain his parents and brothers, and what chance then had he of asking for Miss Tilney's hand?

Mr. Bertram was not so easily consoled. "You have no guarantee that Mr. Follett will fire into the air. Given how abominably he has behaved toward Miss Tilney, we cannot assume he will act decently now."

"All that matters," Jonathan said, with greater confidence than he felt, "is that Follett meets me at the appointed place and time."

"I cannot countenance this," Mr. Bertram said. "I lack any way to prevent you from going, Mr. Darcy, but I beg of you to reconsider."

Sir Thomas interjected, "I think it is splendid of him. Courageous, indeed. If you do not have a second, Mr. Darcy, I would be honored to fulfill that role."

Jonathan was uncertain of the role of a second at a duel, besides potentially taking charge of any resultant dead bodies. Still, one was needed, and no other candidates presented themselves to his mind. "Thank you, Sir Thomas. It is a kind offer. I accept."

Hours had passed before Juliet had the strength even to remove her bonnet and coat. The maids brought tea and biscuits, and although Juliet felt eating would make her immediately and severely unwell, tea could not but be welcome. Her mother took a cup also, but went with it to her writing desk, as all the notes to merchants required composition as soon as possible. Thus Juliet expected to take her tea in blessed solitude, only to have a visitor arrive and duly be announced: "Miss Mary Crawford."

"My dear!" Miss Crawford swept in, so beautifully dressed

that it was tempting to think that her gown's display was the true purpose of her visit, rather than sympathy. "Forgive my intrusion at such a time, but the word spreads, and it is useless to pretend otherwise. You may be sure that I have argued in your defense, for you are an upstanding sort of girl, not at all the kind who models for pictures such as *that* one."

"Thank you," Juliet managed to say. No other words came to her. She knew Miss Crawford's commentary had probably been much more colorful when the story had first been heard, but her sympathy at least seemed to be more honest than not, and Juliet was badly in need of it.

"At luncheon, I saw Miss Haller—the young woman my brother is courting, the one he has gone to visit every morning this week, for she has a dowry of eight thousand pounds—well, Miss Haller had previously gone with Henry to the art exhibition, and she recollected the painting in question. Most vulgar, she said. She felt it should not have been included in the show, even had it not wickedly portrayed you instead of some model from the street."

Ragged as Juliet felt, she did not miss the crucial fact. "Wait," she said, pulling herself together. "You tell me that your brother, Henry, spent nearly every morning this week at this Miss Haller's house? When we came to inquire about the circumstances surrounding the death of Maria Rushworth, you told me the two of you were in the park on *that* morning."

"Oh." Miss Crawford dimpled, caught in what she obviously considered a little white lie. "Well, you know, until all is arranged between Henry and Miss Haller, it is so important to be discreet. There are others hunting for Miss Haller's dowry, you may be sure!"

"We were attempting to identify a murderer," Juliet said. "How can you not see that this was of greater importance? That it was vitally significant that you should tell us the full and complete truth?"

A flicker of annoyance briefly marred Miss Crawford's lovely countenance. "I knew that Henry had *not* spent that morning harming Maria Rushworth, and so long as that was true, I did not see why giving one excuse was not as acceptable as another."

Lacking the wherewithal to argue further, Juliet dedicated herself to a second cup of tea. At least she felt that now, finally, Miss Crawford *had* told the truth . . . which meant Henry Crawford was probably not Maria Rushworth's killer. It appeared that he had gratified his vanity by visiting her when he found it amusing, but his interest in her went no deeper. Did this not also make it very unlikely that Mr. Crawford would have killed Mr. Rushworth? If he were not compelled to do so by any interest in Mrs. Rushworth, what other motive might he have had? Juliet could not imagine one. That did not mean one could not exist—Henry Crawford was not so well known to Juliet for any such certainty—but she doubted his guilt more than she ever had previously.

She was grateful when Miss Crawford departed, but only minutes later, once again someone arrived at the door; again, the butler announced a guest. "Miss Susan Price."

"Miss Price," Juliet said as the girl hurried in. "It was good of you to come, but I must insist you do not stay. Your reputation may be sullied by this visit."

"Oh, you do not know," Miss Price said. "I thought Mr. Darcy might have sent word to you of what he has done— I came to comfort you—but you do not yet know."

Once again, Juliet was in danger of swooning. "Mr. Darcy?" she began, her voice atremble. "What has happened?"

Indeed, word had begun to spread throughout London society. A duel—one fought between two gentlemen's sons, one of whom was heir to perhaps the finest private estate in the realm—one fought over a young woman's honor—with that honor having been so publicly and colorfully brought into question: This was gossip of the highest caliber, and therefore the swiftest to travel. Throughout the afternoon and into the evening, club after club, household after household, learned of the duel involving the Darcy heir. Some were given the knowledge in a more formal manner; before midafternoon, an express messenger had set out with a hastily written letter from Edmund Bertram addressed to Pemberley. Most, however, received the information in whispers and asides, the vehicles in which gossip most enthralls.

Darkness had just fallen when the news reached the London residence of the Allerdyce family. Mrs. Caroline Allerdyce had been thoroughly enjoying her day until the moment when she learned where her actions had led. "A duel? It cannot be so! No, surely it is a lie."

"I fear not," said Mr. Allerdyce, who had been told the news at the coffeehouse. "Mr. Darcy intends to defend the girl's honor, and it is all over town that the picture in the exhibition was once a very ordinary portrait, villainously altered by this Mr. Follett. Shameful act! Though I shall never approve of dueling, I do not blame young Mr. Darcy for wishing to defend Miss Tilney."

"We should not have taken them to the art exhibition today," said Frederica, who had been fretful ever since the terrible scene. "Had we not done so, perhaps Miss Tilney would never have been made aware, and Mr. Darcy would remain none the wiser."

Mr. Allerdyce frowned. "Today? Caroline, I thought you had gone to the exhibition yesterday."

Caroline did not know what to say, and by the time she could have begun to craft an explanation, it was too late. Her husband stepped back from her, obviously aware of exactly what she had done. That he was appalled—disgusted—was written stark upon his features. Never in all their years of marriage had Mr. Allerdyce looked at Caroline in this way, and she found she could scarcely bear it.

"For shame," he said in a low voice. "For shame. In your efforts to ensnare Mr. Darcy for Priscilla, you have lowered your character—and it seems that all you have accomplished is to endanger Mr. Darcy's life."

Chapter Twenty-Two

As the sun set on the day before the duel, Jonathan Darcy remained steadfast in his intentions, and yet the folly of his action became clearer to him, taking dimension in his mind as though shifting from a mere sketch into bas-relief. Had he remained calmer, had he waited even a few hours before confronting Laurence Follett, he would have seen that there were many potential paths of defending Miss Tilney's honor—he could have publicly called upon Follett to remove the painting from the show and clarify the circumstances of its creation, for instance—paths that would not have required him to risk both his life and Follett's.

Also troubling was his lack of experience with guns. Even though Mr. Follett was not a man of the army, he did go hunting, which meant he was reasonably familiar with firearms. Jonathan knew that hunters used rifles, and the duel would involve pistols, but he did not trust that this difference would be sufficient to put them on an equal footing. He *understood* much about guns—it was difficult to live in his society and not learn facts about their operation—but in this matter, it was practice that counted, and it was practice that he did not possess.

Most of all, however, Jonathan had realized that, if he were to perish, he would only have made a bad situation far worse for Miss Tilney, and for others. His death would turn the event into a scandal of the highest order, one that would be written of in countless newspapers. The obscene painting that depicted Miss Tilney so brazenly was already the talk of

London, but its association with a duel would make it known throughout the nation—the last thing she would wish. And Jonathan, though not a prideful man, understood that his passing would be exceedingly painful for his entire family, and probably for Miss Tilney, too.

Nor have we solved the murders, he thought as he sat in his bedchamber, watching the thin visible sliver of sky darken, quite possibly the closest thing to a sunset he would ever see again. *I ought to at least have done my duty toward my hosts before hazarding myself so rashly.*

When the last light left the sky, Jonathan took up his portable writing desk, readied ink and paper, and began the most difficult letter of his life:

> *Dearest Mother and Father, Matthew, and James—*
> *If you are reading this, then I have fallen in the duel*
> *between myself and Mr. Laurence Follett. Please*
> *forgive me for taking such a risk, for I know that no*
> *man's life is his alone; it belongs also to his family, to his*
> *dearest friends. I have betrayed that knowledge—I have*
> *betrayed you—and yet, I go into this still feeling myself*
> *strongly obliged to defend Miss Tilney's honor.*
>
> *It seems safe to assume that, if I have died, Sir*
> *Thomas and the other members of the Bertram family*
> *will have fully acquainted you with the circumstances*
> *that led to this duel. Let me then add only what they*
> *may not comprehend: Miss Tilney only met Mr. Follett*
> *through my acquaintance with the man. The portrait*
> *she posed for seemed wholly proper at that time, and she*
> *only agreed to do so in order to further our investigation*
> *of Mrs. Willoughby's murder. We cooperated in that*
> *investigation; she did what I could not have done; for*
> *this good deed, must she pay the price of her honor? No,*
> *this cannot be tolerated.*

*Do not blame Miss Tilney, as only Follett's actions
and my own have led to such an ill end. To all possible
extent, exculpate her from any wrongdoing in the
matter; otherwise, my choice to fight for her will have
been in vain.*

*Please know that I esteem, honor, and love you all,
and that I die still and eternally—*

*Your faithful,
Jonathan*

As Jonathan Darcy's uncertainty grew, Juliet Tilney's began
to wane. It was not that she had recovered from the blow—
that, she could never claim—but she had regained feeling
and strength in her limbs, and her thoughts, if fevered, had
become far more rational.

This was partly due to her determination not to allow the
news of the duel to entirely distract her from what she had
learned regarding the investigation. Miss Crawford's lie had
unnecessarily confused matters, but on the balance, Juliet
found she believed this second story regarding Miss Haller
very likely to be true. Had Miss Crawford been acting to
deceive, she would certainly have continued to assert her
original lie rather than come up with another, unprompted.
No, hers had not been a deliberate, wicked falsehood, merely
a blithe lack of candor and misaligned priorities.

It helped, also, to think more upon the investigation, for
when Juliet's thoughts instead went to the duel, and the likelihood that Jonathan Darcy might be harmed—oh, the horror!
She could scarcely bear it. Better by far to turn her thoughts,
so much as possible, to the work she and Mr. Darcy had
undertaken together.

"Henry Crawford is probably not our killer," she said to her mother, who had finally finished all the various necessary letters and was busily sealing them with candle and wax. "Not for either Mr. or Mrs. Rushworth, I would say, but certainly not for both."

"That is progress, I suppose." Catherine Tilney was merely humoring her daughter, as she took it as a given that the investigation, however incomplete, must perforce now be ended.

Juliet felt strongly that it must *not* end; her obligation to see the matter through was heightened, even made sacred, were Mr. Darcy to fall while defending her. More to the point, however, as long as the investigation continued, she and Mr. Darcy had much to discuss. "Mamma, we must call upon the Bertrams. I must speak to Mr. Darcy of this, and—and of more, besides."

Catherine Tilney had been waiting for these words for hours. She had already argued thoroughly with herself over whether it would be wise to acquiesce to such a request. Only shortly before had she come to the conclusion that quite possibly it would not be wise to agree, but that it would be cruel to refuse. "Have the maid dress you appropriately for evening, and we shall go."

"Oh, Mamma, thank you!" Juliet hugged her mother tightly, and allowed herself to shed a few tears. Better to weep now, she thought, than at the Bertrams'; if she were to cry in front of Mr. Darcy, he might feel obligated to comfort her— and given the fearsome prospect before him, he should be the recipient of solace, not the giver. She would not tax him so during what would quite possibly be their last meeting.

The Bertram household, beyond the threshold of Jonathan Darcy's door, was in an uproar. As they were by nature a calm, ordered family, their distress on this occasion was all the more marked. Fanny could hardly cease her weeping; Tom had taken it upon himself to personally check and double-check the pistols. Edmund could not cease thinking of the letter he had earlier sent to the Darcys at Pemberley—though he had apologized profusely, he doubted he had found words sufficiently repentant to describe his failure as host. Mrs. Norris expressed her conviction that the young man would surely die, that the young lady could not be worth such a sacrifice, and that had she been consulted, somehow none of this upset would have come to pass. Yet in this time of trial, her assistance to all was freely given, in the form of scolding the servants while the family was too distracted to do so themselves. Lady Bertram occasionally evidenced actual concern.

Susan Price, perhaps unexpectedly, had proved the most clear-sighted among them. It was she who had suggested that Tom send for a physician to attend the duel, the better to tend to any wounds inflicted, for swift treatment would make those wounds less likely to prove mortal. She insisted that Jonathan Darcy should wear two waistcoats, or perhaps three if they could each be fastened; this might be poor protection against a bullet, but poor protection is superior to no protection at all. Finally she had asked one of the housemaids for any linens that were damaged and awaiting repair, then set herself up in front of the fire in the sitting room, ripping sheets into bandages and neatly rolling them for easy transport to the scene of the duel. (Thirty years hence, in Crimea, her courage and steadiness would serve similar purposes, but on a far greater scale . . . but here, we divert too far from our narrative.)

Only upheaval so great could have distracted Edmund and Fanny from the appalling news of Tom's plans for a new sugarcane plantation in Barbados, and even Jonathan Darcy's endangerment could not wholly banish their horror. Fanny, who found it difficult to openly oppose anyone, kept rehearsing the plea she *must* make to her brother-in-law. Distressing though the prospect was, she could not fail in this; and she hoped the truism held, that those who speak least often are those whose words are most clearly heard.

Edmund's moral outrage was as strong as Fanny's, but as Tom's brother—as a gentleman raised with the expectations of wealth and influence—he did not imagine making a plea. He instead made a plan. If Tom could not be made to see the evils of his choice as it stood, then the choice must be made more evil yet.

The announcement of visitors that evening shook everyone. They briefly hoped that the caller might be Mr. Follett, come to make amends and avert the duel. Yet none could pretend astonishment when the visitors proved to be the Tilney ladies, nor that Miss Tilney wished to speak to Mr. Darcy. Tom volunteered his study for this purpose.

Etiquette would have required someone to either join the two young persons in the room, or at least to be near the open door; indeed, as a mark of service to the family, Mrs. Norris volunteered for this great responsibility. As it was, however, the study door was simply left open, and everyone else gathered at the other end of the house. There are exigencies in which decency has nothing to do with good manners, and where one cannot have both, decency must prevail.

Despite the roaring blaze in the study fireplace, Juliet Tilney remained cold, seemingly to the bone. Although she wore proper evening dress, she had instructed the maid to choose a gown in such a dark gray that it would have been appropriate for half mourning. *Pray God,* she thought, *that we need no full mourning tomorrow!*

She felt as though she had waited by the fire a very long time before Mr. Darcy entered. How pale he looked, how stricken he seemed! All the mortal fear that must have haunted him pierced Juliet through, and she could not have despaired of her own life as wretchedly as she despaired of his.

"Miss Tilney," he said, his voice calmer than his countenance. "I must beg your forgiveness."

"Forgiveness? Whatever can you mean, sir?"

Mr. Darcy lowered his head. "Calling for the duel was an impulsive act—rash and thoughtless. Though I meant only to act in your defense, I see now that I have made matters worse, that I have turned a smaller scandal into a greater one."

"I care little for scandal, at the moment." Hope blossomed within Juliet. "Do you mean that you will call off the duel?"

That hope died with Mr. Darcy's next words: "No, for to do so would suggest that I no longer felt sure of your virtue. This is wholly unacceptable. Were Mr. Follett to ask to be released—if he were to make recompense—but were he so inclined, he would have done so by now. Let us say that I have regrets, but no second thoughts. My path is chosen and I shall see it through."

"Oh, Mr. Darcy." Juliet's eyes welled with tears. She wanted to tell him that it was too late to save her reputation, that it had been too late since the day Follett's horrid painting had first been hung upon a wall. However, doing so would only belittle his choice, one he could not in honor take back. "Whatever put this notion into your head?"

He stepped closer, so that the firelight fully revealed his pallor as he said, "*Ivanhoe,* I believe. Also the play we went to see, where Claudio condemned Hero rather than defending her. I prefer to be an Ivanhoe." The immense gravity of their conversation could not prevent him from smiling slightly at her bewilderment. "Fiction should not dictate our actions, should it? Perhaps I made an error. I often do put more weight in stories than I ought."

"Do not blame stories," she replied, "or yourself. No less a gentleman than Colonel Brandon has been led to challenge another. Where emotions are high, decisions may be hasty, and in this you are no different than other men."

"Sir Thomas tells me there is some reason to hope," Mr. Darcy said. "Many duelers fire harmlessly clear of their opponents. Upon reflection, I suspect that this must be my choice, and Follett may well follow suit. He dislikes me, I know, but it does not follow that he would be willing to go into exile as a murderer on my account."

"Let it be so! I shall pray for it."

Mr. Darcy's smile returned fleetingly. "Then your honor will be restored, and we may return to our investigation."

How Juliet wished this could be the end of all, but she was too wise to believe such a wishful notion. "After this, I fear, your family will not countenance any further connection between us. The gossip regarding the painting will diminish, but any hope we have of future respectability lies in our parting ways. Forever after, any association we have with each other will be tainted by the memory of the duel and the scandal that inspired it."

"No. Surely this must not be so. I should never have challenged Follett, were it to put an end to our connection without rescuing you from ruination."

Juliet stepped toward Mr. Darcy, then. They stood so close now that, had this been a happier occasion, they could have begun dancing. "You will see the truth of it in time. Were we to be . . . connected, in the future, the incident regarding the painting would be our mutual humiliation. You would be censured, despised, by all the world."

After a long moment, Mr. Darcy replied in a low voice, "Hang the world."

Juliet had to turn away, for her tears could no longer be checked. "Mr. Darcy, please—do not say what will only make this worse—"

"Then I will be silent," he replied, "and say only that, should I survive tomorrow, I promise you, beyond any doubt, we will meet again."

She knew she should hope his words to be false, but she could not.

Sleep often eludes us when we are worried about the morn, and it can well be imagined that Jonathan Darcy did not find it easy to rest the night before the duel. He was not entirely certain whether he had slept at all, only that he lay abed for many hours before a servant came to tell him it was time to rise.

The valet dressed him as though for any other day, albeit with extra waistcoats, and when Jonathan came downstairs, he found Sir Thomas, also ready, in the breakfast room with coffee. "Good morning, Mr. Darcy. Will you dine? Might want your strength about you today."

Jonathan felt certain that, if he attempted to eat anything, he would promptly spend the rest of the morning being violently sick. "Afterward," he said in the best imitation of bravado he could manage. "I shall dine after all this business is done."

"Brave man," said Sir Thomas, who seemed rather over-eager for an event that had some possibility of ending Jonathan's life. "Let us go."

The appointed place for the duel, as determined by Sir Thomas and Follett's second, lay at the southern reaches of London, a place called Battersea Fields. Here, farms grew row upon row of asparagus, melons, and lavender, though in February all remained brown and gray, appropriate for the setting where two young men might die. Battersea was favored for duels, for it lay near enough the city for convenience and yet distant enough to avoid interruptions and to facilitate escape afterward, if necessary.

Jonathan's heart beat wildly in his chest as he caught sight of Follett and his second, already standing upon the meadow. They apparently had come on horseback rather than by carriage; he wondered whether that was a sign of confidence, proof that Follett did not expect to have to be carried away from the field. Despite the pale, predawn light, he could discern that Mr. Follett was as well-dressed as he and seemingly much calmer. Maybe Follett had come to the same realizations about their relative experience handling firearms.

"Here," said Sir Thomas, opening a small box to show Jonathan the flintlock pistol he had brought. "Get used to the heft of that in your hand, will you? I shall talk to Follett's second, and perhaps the two of us may be able to forge an honorable end to this conflict without the need for the duel itself." Jonathan felt briefly hopeful until Sir Thomas revealed how little faith he put in such negotiations by continuing: "Afterward, we shall load the guns."

The pistol was heavy, though not so much as Jonathan had feared it might be. At least he would be able to hold it correctly and make a decent show of himself in that way; of what would follow, it was best not to imagine.

He could not help watching Follett closely throughout. The way his old schoolmate paced between two trees betrayed more animation than his countenance, but that might come from anger or even anticipation, rather than fear. The chill in the air remained sufficient for their breaths to cloud the air. Before long, their hands would go numb—but the duel would take place very soon, which meant incapacity would be no source of rescue.

The physician stood by with his bag, patently disapproving of events but apparently determined to preserve life as best he could. If it came to it, at least they could offer him the bandages Miss Price had prepared the day prior.

Jonathan had come to stand on the ground where he might die; his gaze was fixed upon his likely killer. Only at this moment could he determine what he truly intended to do in the duel.

I will not attempt to kill Laurence Follett, Jonathan decided. *I will throw away my shot. My actions have already done all the good for Miss Tilney that they can. Murdering Mr. Follett would harm her, not help her further. Beyond that—I have had occasion to hunt many murderers, and I do not wish to join their number. Least of all do I wish to attach such a crime to Miss Tilney in any way. That would cast a far greater shame than Follett's painting has the power to do.*

Sir Thomas began walking back toward Jonathan, still in almost rudely high spirits. Follett had half turned away from his own second, his face hidden from view, and only the set of his body betraying the coiled energy within. Was that energy hatred? Fear? Jonathan almost did not hear Sir Thomas saying, "It is all settled. Come, the other second and I will both load your pistols now."

Once they were both armed, the tension thickened like fog, seeming to seal them all in from the rest of the world. Sir Thomas brought them back to back—how strange, to stand so close to a man who might very soon kill you—and then told them to count twenty paces.

This Jonathan did. He could hear the crunch of his boots, and Follett's, against the frost-crisp grass. Jonathan's breaths came more quickly, shallower; anyone observing him would know of his fear.

It is natural to be afraid, Jonathan told himself. *You will do what you know to be right. That is all that matters.*

At the twentieth pace, he stopped—they turned—Sir Thomas stood in place, holding out his white handkerchief, the fall of which would mark the signal to fire—the first flutter of white as Sir Thomas dropped it—

Jonathan pointed his pistol at the ground and fired into the dirt. In the very next fraction of an instant, pain lanced through his side. He lost his balance and tumbled to the ground. In a daze, he looked down at the injury to see blood soaking through his waistcoats, steaming slightly in the cold air.

He had thrown away his shot. Follett had not.

Chapter Twenty-Three

Susan Price had done more good than she knew with her advice, for although the three thick waistcoats had failed to stop the bullet from piercing Jonathan Darcy's skin, they had blunted its force just enough that the bullet had merely broke a rib, then lodged there, rather than smashing through it to any vital organs. The physician who had attended the duel was able to extract the bullet easily, on the site, without any need for further openings into Jonathan's skin.

This was far from the most grievous gunshot wound Jonathan could have suffered, but none present were so foolish as to believe that the danger had passed. Any wound could lead to infection, and any infection could lead to gangrene, sepsis, and death.

Laurence Follett paced the ground not far from where Jonathan lay as the doctor ministered to him. "Darcy, forgive me—may God forgive me—I thought that certainly you should shoot at me, and that I must in that case return fire— had I stayed my hand but a moment—"

"This duel was of my choosing," Jonathan said faintly. He did not know whether he was dizzy from loss of blood or from the enormity of the events that had just transpired; he knew only that he could not stand. "I accepted this possibility when I challenged you. Your actions were only those consistent with a duel, and thus I have nothing of which to complain."

"You have my disgraceful behavior toward Miss Tilney." Follett ceased his pacing then, and even through the haze of discomfort surrounding and suffusing Jonathan, it was clear that the man was utterly miserable. "It was an abominable thing to do. The girl was from the country—I fancied that neither she nor any of her people would ever see it, and thus no harm could come of it. So it amused me to create this little joke, thinking only how it would spite you. Instead, I have injured her and brought this down upon us."

Jonathan remained sensible enough to press his advantage. "You must withdraw the painting immediately. You must do so today. Go speak to the papers and tell them the full truth of the event, that Miss Tilney is utterly blameless in the matter."

"All shall be done today, at the soonest possible moment," Follett swore, "and I shall put the canvas in the fire so that it may burn to nothing."

"Yes, that, too." Jonathan winced as the doctor sewed the final stitch into his skin.

Sir Thomas seemed greatly shaken, so much so that one wondered whether he had even properly understood what a duel would mean. "Should we not take him home? That he may be nursed, looked after?"

"Indeed," said the doctor. "Fetch the carriage and get him to a place where he can rest. Close all the windows, so that no noxious fumes will further endanger his health. Be sure to dose him with both brandy and laudanum. If he becomes feverish, send for me, and I will arrive to bleed him posthaste."

Jonathan felt as though surely the blood that had soaked his clothing constituted enough exsanguination for the time being, but he was no physician, and his opinion was not asked. He only lay on the ground, listening to the carriage drawing close, and giving thanks that Follett was finally remorseful. Only that remorse had the power to save Miss Tilney.

If the Bertram household had been in an uproar on the day prior, this was as nothing compared to the resultant upheaval when word came that Mr. Darcy had been wounded. Before Sir Thomas returned with the patient, much had to be accomplished.

"We will settle him on the divan in the study," said Edmund Bertram to the servants as they scurried about, "for the bedroom where he has stayed is far too drafty to safeguard his health, and he may not be able to manage the staircase for some time to come. Bring down the mattress and several blankets—we shall require a water jug and cup—"

Susan Price, for her part, had in her nervousness continued to prepare bandages all night, fashioning more than Sir Thomas had been able to take to the duel. Now she was glad of the excess and fetched them to have at the ready. Mrs. Norris explained at length that, while she was always of service in any way she could be, she could not fulfill the office of a nurse, that she was quite overcome in matters of illness or injury; no one listened, save Lady Bertram, who assumed this excuse for inaction must apply to herself as well.

This frenzy of action reached an even greater pitch when Sir Thomas and the doctor returned home, supporting the wounded and dazed Jonathan Darcy. The sight of blood quite incapacitated Lady Bertram, even beyond her normal incapacity, and made the gravity of the situation even clearer to all. Though they gladly heard of Follett's repentance and his plans for the rehabilitation of Miss Tilney's reputation, this could but little compensate for the pain of seeing the shocking state of young Mr. Darcy.

Edmund, having given orders and seen to such immediate comfort for Jonathan Darcy as was in his power, had already taken on the office of writing again to Pemberley to inform Mr. and Mrs. Darcy of what had befallen their son, to be dispatched by express at the soonest possible moment. From him Fanny stole a scrap of paper and a dip into his inkwell in order to write a note, which was sent via a servant to the London residence of the Tilneys.

Juliet Tilney had lain awake all night, pacing the floor, crying until her head ached, praying whenever she could gather herself sufficiently to do so. When someone came to the door so shortly after dawn, she cried out in dismay. Though she donned her dressing gown in an instant, she emerged into the hallway to see her mother, already fully dressed, hurrying down the steps. Catherine said, "Wait here—I will tell you all."

This left Juliet to cling to the banister, suspended between hope and dread, during the brief interval before she heard her mother's feet upon the stair once more. When Catherine's face again became visible, she looked so pale and grave that Juliet nearly fell.

"No, no, my dear, Mr. Darcy still lives!" Catherine hurried to her daughter's side. "I fear he is wounded, but there is hope that the injury is not very serious in itself. The next few days will tell."

Wounded! Was there no wickedness of which Laurence Follett was not capable? "Can we not help the Bertrams to nurse Mr. Darcy? We should go there at once."

Her mother briefly caressed Juliet's cheek. "My good girl. Your concern is all for Mr. Darcy, none for yourself. You should know that Mr. Follett is withdrawing his wretched picture from the exhibition and that he is circulating the truth behind its creation as widely as possible, beginning as we speak. This does not wholly remediate the effects upon your reputation, but it gives me some hope that, in time, your prospects shall not be damaged beyond all repair."

Only the day before, Juliet would have been astonished how little she cared for her reputation in this instant. Yet nothing could concern her so deeply as her fear for Mr. Darcy's life.

Catherine felt another day was necessary to tie up all concerns before she could take her daughter back to Gloucestershire; so long as this was true, she had not the heart to deny Juliet the opportunity of witnessing Mr. Darcy's survival for herself. As unlikely as it was that they would be allowed to meet again in the future, her daughter's feelings would not soon vanish. Therefore, Juliet would know no peace until she could at least satisfy herself that he was well cared for. To the Bertrams they went.

The Tilneys arrived there before morning calling hours had even begun, yet all persons present had been awake for hours, and to them it seemed to be the middle of an exceedingly long day. Amid such extraordinary events, the finer forms of behavior broke down, allowing for much that would otherwise have been out of the question. Most of the family gathered in the sitting room, where Sir Thomas told the tale of the duel for perhaps the fourth time so far, this rendition intended for the benefit of Catherine Tilney, though the morbid fascination of the others showed no sign of abating. It fell to Fanny Bertram to take Juliet's hand and lead her through the hallways to the study, and to remain at the door as Juliet went to the divan where Mr. Darcy lay.

The study fire illuminated the bloody bandages around Mr. Darcy's exposed person, a gorier sight than Juliet had been prepared for. Worse yet was that he was insensible, with only the rise and fall of his chest to distinguish him from the dead.

"It is the laudanum," Fanny murmured. "They have dosed him so that he will sleep and feel nothing. Rest is ever the best cure, and they cannot allow pain to steal his slumber."

Juliet silently resolved not to leave this home until she had at least been able to speak with Mr. Darcy once more, to thank him for such salvation as her reputation could achieve.

When Fanny exited the room, a clear invitation for her

guest to follow, Juliet hesitated for one moment, just long enough that she would briefly be unobserved. This opportunity she used to bend low over the sleeping Mr. Darcy and press her lips against his forehead—a kiss as light as the brush of a feather. Then she followed Fanny Bertram, praying for the patient all the while.

Still, she knew, they must be parted soon and forever. But at least perhaps they would not be parted by death!

Once the Tilneys were settled into the sitting room with all the family, quite as though they lived here as well, Fanny allowed herself a period of solitude. She, too, had feared for Mr. Darcy's life; she, too, had lain awake and now felt a headache threatening, a sensation in her skull not unlike the gathering of dark storm clouds. So it was with the deepest relief that she sank back upon her bed and lay still for some time, drifting in the peculiar realm of consciousness that is neither wakefulness nor sleep.

The bedroom door creaked, and Fanny stirred, expecting to see one of the maids come to her with a question, or perhaps Edmund to ask after her. Instead, she saw Ellen Rushworth peering timidly around the door, her head with its jumble of curls not even so high as the knob.

Little as Fanny had wished to see Ellen, she knew how it felt to be a frightened child in a new place. "Hello, Ellen. There has been a great deal of noise today, hasn't there?"

Ellen nodded. "Maid said she would play with me."

"I am very sure she meant to," said Fanny, "but our guest is sick, and the whole house is spending the day helping him."

It seemed as if nothing remained for Fanny to do but escort the child back to the small room where she was staying, one that would normally have housed a servant had they brought more staff. But then what? Mrs. Norris had retrieved only her own items from the rooms they had stayed in with Maria; servants had fetched the little girl's clothing, but if she had any dolls or toys, they remained there still. Fanny took note and determined to get them herself at the next opportunity. Until such time as that, or until a maid could be spared to perform the office of a nanny, Ellen must be seen to.

"Now, let me see." Fanny saw that while the child had been dressed for the day, her hair had not been touched. "Would you like to have your hair up? Like grown young ladies do?" Ellen nodded.

Throughout childhood, while Maria and Julia had been attended by maids who styled their hair just so, Fanny had been left to her own devices with an old hairbrush and a rather spotty mirror. Difficult as this had been when she was small, she had ultimately learned how to perform a maid's office very well. She brought those skills to bear as she styled Ellen's wispy hair in the most grown-up way possible. Her reward was Ellen's smile when she saw herself in the bedroom mirror. That had filled a few minutes, but what were they to do the rest of the day?

"I have an idea," Fanny said. "If you wait here for only a very short while, I will bring you a surprise. Would you like that?" Ellen brightened with anticipation, and Fanny settled her upon the bed before hurrying toward the kitchen. There she retrieved a scrap of bacon from the cook, after which it was short work to tempt Pug to her side and carry the little dog upstairs. When Ellen saw Pug, she clapped her hands together in delight.

Fanny sat down on the bed with both dog and child, neither of which required any instruction to know how to play with each other. As she observed this, Fanny could not help but smile.

The resentment she had expected to feel toward Ellen was utterly absent. The strong resemblance to Henry Crawford had begun fading in Fanny's mind; already Ellen's face was no longer her father's, only her own. The other resemblance Fanny had quailed from—the ungenerous, unloving criticism of Mrs. Norris, the rejection of a child born to others—this found no echo within Fanny's soul.

Later, she would wonder at her reluctance to welcome Ellen into her home and heart, would tell herself that only the extreme upset surrounding Maria's death had kept her from seeing clearly. However, there are within all of us certain fears that cannot be dispelled by reason, nor by the persuasion of others; such fear can be robbed of its power only when we have finally faced it and emerged victorious, as Fanny did that day.

I prayed to the Lord to send me a child, she thought. *He has answered my prayer.*

Heavily dosed with laudanum as he was, Jonathan Darcy regained consciousness only late in the afternoon. His wound throbbed terribly and he felt surpassingly weak, but the bandages and stitches held. As yet he felt no sign of feverishness or delirium. He had dueled, and he had survived. From such survival, many men would have drawn the wrong conclusions about their own invulnerability; Jonathan, however, gave thanks for his escape and resolved never to act so rashly again.

Different maids and various ladies of the house came in to see to Jonathan's needs. He was propped up on pillows and, after much discussion, it was agreed that he could take a light supper upon a tray. This was delivered by Juliet Tilney herself, albeit with a maidservant present to freshly stoke the fire. Jonathan, ever honest to a fault, said, "Miss Tilney, you look terrible."

Crookedly, she smiled. "I do not doubt it, sir, as I slept not a wink for worry. Tonight, I imagine, I shall fare better."

Jonathan had eaten nothing that day and very little the day before, which meant that even the laudanum could not entirely dim his hunger. He began upon his meal, motioning for Miss Tilney to stay with him. This she consented to do, and furthermore told him of the revelation regarding Mr. Crawford's alibi for the morning of Maria Rushworth's death. When next he paused eating long enough to speak, he said, "I agree with you entirely. Miss Crawford would not have needlessly supplanted one lie with another lie. It was wrong of her to speak untruthfully amid a murder investigation, but I do not believe she did so with any wicked intent. What she told you of Henry Crawford's visit to Miss Haller seems likely to be true."

"Yet so many questions remain."

At that moment, they were interrupted by the entrance of Mrs. Norris, who proudly bore an entire cake and full serving ware upon another tray. "I do not think plum cake shall go amiss, it is very nicely iced, though mind you, this plum cake is as nothing compared to what was once served at Mansfield Park. When I aided my sister in governing the staff at Mansfield, nothing was ever done that was not done to the highest quality. How I missed that plum cake! Poor Maria's efforts at baking never amounted to much, I fear, and we took on a cook from time to time, though it is hard to find good help in this day and age." Mrs. Norris caught herself then, no doubt recalling that all now knew precisely what means she had employed to afford paying a cook's wages. "Well, well, I see they have crowded you with tea and pork and all manner of things, like as not to go to waste, profligate as they are. Yet room can be made for your cake, never fear!"

She set the tray down. Only after a long pause did Jonathan remember to say, "Thank you, Mrs. Norris."

For once, however, Mrs. Norris was not avidly seeking gratitude. The sharpness of her gaze was reserved for Miss Tilney, who had taken a step back. At first, Jonathan thought that perhaps Mrs. Norris had also observed how weary and pale Miss Tilney was, but why should she do so with such evident contempt rather than compassion? Only then did he recall the reason for the wound in his side: that despicable painting of Follett's. The distaste Mrs. Norris showed for Miss Tilney—despite knowing the image to be a false one, despite Jonathan's near sacrifice for the sake of her honor, despite Mrs. Norris not even having seen the painting herself—this, he feared, was a hint of the reception Miss Tilney could expect for a long time to come.

With as much force as he could muster, Jonathan said, "That will be all, Mrs. Norris."

Mrs. Norris had no great enjoyment in being dismissed like a servant, as was plain, but she huffed out to find some other person who could be made to listen to her complain of it.

Neither Jonathan nor Miss Tilney said a word until Mrs. Norris was well down the hallway. He spoke first. "I believe I know what became of Maria Rushworth."

"Good," Miss Tilney replied, "for I have realized what became of Mr. Rushworth."

Briefly they compared their thoughts. Jonathan was gratified not only by Miss Tilney's support for his theory but by her respect for his deduction. Any satisfaction in his own insight was swiftly eclipsed, however, by Miss Tilney's own breakthrough, which he thought he should never have guessed on his own, not even if given a year. Once they were fully in accord, Jonathan requested that the maid (who had been crouching at the fire, trying very hard to look as though she

were not eavesdropping) bring them two articles to examine.
The maid retrieved the requested items with stunning speed,
and did not leave upon their delivery.

"Do you see?" said Miss Tilney.

"I do." Jonathan opened the small box. "And you?"

"Oh, yes, Mr. Darcy. I believe all is now quite clear."

Weary as Jonathan was, as much as he longed to drift back
into the heavy sleep of laudanum, he knew that this resolution was best achieved quickly. He told the waiting maid,
"Send word to Mr. Frost of the police. Summon him here,
for there is a murderer in this house who must be arrested
immediately."

"Yes, sir," breathed the maid, who had not had so exciting a
day in all her life before.

Chapter Twenty-Four

Juliet Tilney was grateful that it took half an hour to summon Mr. Frost to the Bertrams' residence, for it gave her an opportunity to drink some tea and put herself in better order. The mirror affirmed that lack of sleep had darkened her eyes and blanched her skin, but she did what she could in smoothing her hair, pinching her cheeks, and straightening her garments into better order. She knew that at least some persons present would be at pains to deny what she had to say, and thus she wished to look her best. As little as appearances have to do with trustworthiness, we are each of us compelled to some degree by their illusions. Juliet, instinctively comprehending this, endeavored to make herself appear as rational a creature as possible.

Still, Mrs. Norris's glare stung. Still, the mockery of those at the art show rang in her ears. Humiliation still hung heavily upon her. In this matter, however—the murders of the Rushworths—Juliet had regained some measure of pride.

When Mr. Frost arrived, he was seen into the study by Sir Thomas, who seemed to be in no hurry to quit the room again. Then Mrs. Norris bustled in, choosing this precise moment to retrieve the plum cake, a task that apparently could not be accomplished without much dithering and ado. Juliet also spied her mother hovering near the doorway.

She leaned down so that she might whisper to Mr. Darcy—wan and still very weak upon the divan, swaddled in blankets and bandages—"I believe we should consider informing the whole household at once. It will save us many explanations later, and otherwise we shall have to contend with all of them attempting to enter the room every few moments."

"By all means," Mr. Darcy said. His voice had not regained its usual deep timbre, but nonetheless, he seemed to be fully in command of his faculties. Neither the wound nor the laudanum had stolen his sense. If he could but be spared infection, as Juliet prayed, she believed his recovery would be swift and complete. At least her shame had not cost Mr. Darcy his life.

She stood and called out, loudly enough for all eavesdroppers to hear, "Will the family please join us in the study? We have much to discuss that is significant to many persons here."

It did not take long for the company to assemble. Mrs. Tilney and Susan Price, who had been too wild with curiosity to stray far, came almost instantly through the door; Lady Bertram again held Pug in her arms as she sank into the best chair. Mr. and Mrs. Yates came next, followed at last by Edmund and Fanny Bertram. Juliet was struck by the change in Fanny, who appeared rosier and in better cheer than in previous days. Why this should be so, Juliet could not guess; she only hoped that the information they had to share would not devastate her friend anew.

Mr. Frost, a man with much business to conduct throughout the city of London, was less patient with their arrangements. "Your note claimed that you knew the identity of the murderer we seek. Do you or do you not?"

"We do know," said Mr. Darcy, "and we have also learned that you seek two murderers, not one. However, one of them is beyond your reach forever."

"Whatever do you mean?" Mr. Frost demanded.

As the first deduction had been Juliet's, she felt emboldened to begin. "I regret to inform the company that the killer of Mr. Rushworth was the late Maria Rushworth, your sister and cousin." Mrs. Yates gasped, Mr. Bertram went quite pale, and Sir Thomas reddened as if with anger. Juliet remained undaunted. "When we asked her whereabouts on the morning of Mr. Rushworth's death, Mrs. Rushworth assured us that she had been at the art exhibition at that very time, and that she had seen the . . . the scandalous painting on display there. However, as we all have been made very aware, that painting . . . its *face* is unmistakably my own. I met Mrs. Rushworth before she went to the show, then spoke with her again afterward. Unfortunately, it is unlikely that she would not have recognized my face in that image, nor that she would have neglected to tell me of it—or, at least, to betray in some way her knowledge of the foul thing's existence. But she did not. Mrs. Rushworth never went to the exhibition, and thus she lied about her whereabouts that morning, merely repeating what she had heard others say about the paintings on display there."

Most present saw the sense of this, though Mrs. Norris looked as if she would wish to argue. However, it was Mr. Bertram who spoke first, his voice as broken as his heart must no doubt be: "Are you very sure? Behind any doubt?"

"I fear so, sir," Juliet replied. "From the very beginning, we knew your elder sister to have the strongest motive for the murder. Mr. Rushworth had begun to doubt the arrangements he had made for Mrs. Rushworth's child, and the validity of the supposed reason for him to do so. Had he ceased any gifts to Mrs. Rushworth and changed his will, her finances would have become inadequate for her support—Mrs. Norris's 'borrowings' from Lady Bertram could not have wholly sustained their household for long. She might well have been plunged into poverty. Thus she needed Mr. Rushworth to die soon, before his solicitor could change the will."

"How did she do it?" asked Mrs. Tilney, so caught up in the moment that she seemed to have forgotten how thoroughly unconnected she was to those most intimately involved. "How did an ordinary woman overpower a man of Mr. Rushworth's size?"

Juliet, anticipating this question, had already moved one of the study chairs near the wall. "Mr. Frost, would you grant me the honor of your assistance?" He took the seat she indicated, as she walked to the hamper of items the staff had brought them. "Mr. Rushworth was strangled with an item that was firm, smooth, and probably curved. Any garrote of fabric or leather would, we believe, have left a more pronounced mark—is not that so, Mr. Frost?"

The policeman nodded. "What, then, was used?"

Juliet reached into the hamper and drew out a cake hoop, one carved of a single ring of thick wood. "I would wager that not one person in this room has ever baked a cake herself. Yet I have watched my grandfather's cook do so, and some of you may have witnessed it as well. A hoop such as this is placed on a sheet or tray; the batter is poured in; and then all is set in the oven. After the cake has baked and cooled, the hoop is lifted"—she raised the wooden hoop, by way of illustration—"and then the perfectly round cake is completed. There are many sorts of cake hoops, but the best are those like this, as solid as the tree they were taken from. They are sanded smooth and become only more so as they acquire wear and use. And some are wide enough for *this*."

She stepped behind Mr. Frost and lowered the hoop over his head easily, with far less minute attention than she had felt when attempting something similar upon Mr. Darcy while using the embroidery hoop. Finally, Juliet hooked her arm through the back of the cake hoop, which was more than wide enough to accommodate both her arm and Mr. Frost's neck. "If I pull backward—" She did so, but gently, only enough so that all involved could see. "As you see, Mr. Frost cannot reach me. He cannot rise from the chair. He is unable to get his balance or his bearings."

Mr. Frost said, "But how had she the strength?"

"Strength was not necessary. She could have used the weight of her own person. May I demonstrate—just for one moment?" When he nodded, Juliet shifted her position so that some of her weight was supported by the hoop; even this was enough to make Mr. Frost startle in alarm. Instantly she rose anew. "Had I used all my person, sir, you would not have been able to breathe, nor to escape. The mark left upon the throat would be smooth, wide, and regular. I believe no other household item would leave so similar a trace."

"But a cake hoop?" blustered Sir Thomas. "Why on earth should she use such a thing? However would she have conceived of it?"

Mr. Darcy answered him. "We knew, from both Mrs. Rushworth and Mrs. Norris, that Mrs. Rushworth had taken up baking with limited success. She had thus become familiar with these hoops and their use."

"Furthermore," Juliet added, "Mrs. Rushworth appeared resentful of the many tasks she had been obliged to perform herself, without a servant's help, since she abandoned her marriage. She would have been ill-tempered, even angry while doing such work in the kitchen, where the hoop would be close at hand. That, no doubt, is where the evil idea entered her mind."

It occurred to her that she should lift the hoop once more and free Mr. Frost. He rose, rubbing at his throat. "I shall make some trials of the hoop for official purposes, but you have convinced me. Mrs. Rushworth was always the likeliest suspect, and you have provided both proof of her opportunity and the only rational explanation of her weapon. What you have not explained is how Mrs. Rushworth came to be murdered herself."

Jonathan had been so very much impressed by Miss Tilney's clear explanation, not to mention the physical demonstration, that he had thought she would continue her speech to encompass the second murder. However, she instead looked toward him, expectant and eager; this had been his own deduction, and she evidently did not wish to deny him the honor of explanation.

His side ached terribly—the effects of the laudanum were beginning to wear off, and he longed for another dose and the sweet release of sleep. Yet he did not wish to reveal the full extent of his pain to Miss Tilney; she would blame herself, no doubt, and this he could not bear.

So he began. "At first we had no sure motive for Mrs. Rushworth's murder, which was always confounding. The only person who seemed to wish her any ill was Mr. Crawford, but he was demonstrated to be elsewhere at the time of the murder. Furthermore, he had for years maintained this connection to Mrs. Rushworth—one that was ever fraught, yet never broken—and while it might be expected that Mr. Rushworth's death would alter matters between them, that was not yet so evident nor so longstanding that it would necessarily have pushed Mr. Crawford to murder.

"Also, Mrs. Rushworth was killed in her kitchen. Had Mr. Crawford come to call on her, she would have received him in the sitting room. *Never* would she have set a foot in the kitchen with a visitor present, much less one whom she was at such pains to attract and impress." Jonathan had no need to explain this point further; all persons present knew that people of gentility either never spent time in their kitchens—or at least made great effort to pretend they did not. Even his own mother, who stood on no ceremony and laughed at pretension, had never once in his recollection entered the kitchen at Pemberley. "In fact, I would declare it highly unlikely that Mrs. Rushworth would have allowed any visitor to see her in the kitchen in any circumstance save an emergency. Therefore, when she entered that room upon the morning of her death, she could only have been accompanied by a person who was not a visitor. A person who lived there with her."

Every person in the room then turned toward Mrs. Norris, who had become very still. It took one moment too long for her countenance to change toward anger. "Never have I heard such foolishness in my life. I who did everything for Maria! I, an old woman hardly able to hold a cup in my hand, for my rheumatism is very bad, worse than anyone imagines, for if they knew—"

Miss Tilney interrupted her, her tone unexpectedly sad. "You did do everything for Mrs. Rushworth. You gave up a great deal to accompany her into near exile. From all reports, you were devoted to her throughout her girlhood and youth. I can only imagine how galling her elopement must have been for you. Then Ellen's birth—that, too, would have been a blow."

Having taken advantage of that moment to catch his breath, Jonathan continued. "Finally, Mr. Rushworth was murdered. We believe that you came to realize that Mrs. Rushworth was to blame. You told us that she had spoken of Mr. Rushworth to you in your final conversation—which, I believe, was either her confession or a statement that revealed to you the truth. You knew then that you had surrendered everything for a person unworthy of your sacrifice."

Mrs. Norris had begun to back away from them, though this got her no nearer a door; the escape she sought was a matter of the mind, the one thing that can never be escaped. "I tell you, I was not there. I was doing the marketing—the maid saw me leave!"

"Yes, you had gone out to do the marketing, but you must

have returned," Jonathan said. "We know not why. Perhaps you forgot an item you wanted to bring."

Miss Tilney added, "However, it is certain that you did not spend more than an hour at the market, for you returned home with but three radishes. That is not the result of an hour's shopping for food."

For the first time, Mrs. Norris's expression shifted from defiance to uncertainty. She knew now, he realized, that she was trapped.

Jonathan continued. "Precisely what passed between you and Mrs. Rushworth at that time, we cannot know . . . Regardless, it angered you greatly. You were both in the kitchen when your temper overcame you, and you took up the only weapon at hand."

Mr. Frost, wishing to remind those present of his authority in the matter, seized the chance to ask, "What weapon was that? We have been unable to find any similar knife."

"That is because it was not a knife." Jonathan reached for the tray with the plum cake, which still sat beside his divan sickbed, and lifted up the cake server. "Narrow and sharp at the tip, wide at the base. When you examine the serving piece from that household, Mr. Frost, I believe you will find that it matches the wound exactly."

As Jonathan reached for the hamper of items brought to them by the servants, which included a box of silverware that had made the trip with Mrs. Norris from Maria Rushworth's house to this one, Miss Tilney explained how they had formed the connection. "When I found Mrs. Rushworth on the day of her death—forgive my bluntness in describing this, but for clarity I must—I found small white flakes of some unknown substance on her person, surrounding the wound."

"Our man saw that, too," Mr. Frost confirmed. "You do not mean to say . . . it was *icing*?"

"It was indeed, for I also spied ants crawling upon the floor at that time. I was much struck by their number and how swiftly they had been attracted to the blood. However, it was not the blood they sought; it was the sugar in the icing. Sugar always draws ants, and quickly, too."

Mrs. Norris had by now inched herself almost into the corner. "How could I ever have done such a thing? With my rheumatism, it was not likely that I should pick up any weapon and wield it at any person."

Jonathan said, "You do indeed suffer from this ailment, and we have noted that you make a practice of leaving kerchiefs tied around the handles of any implement you must use, so that they are not so difficult to grip." With this he opened the silverware box, which held only serving items. The ladle, the tongs, all had soft cloth knotted around the handles. Only the cake server was bare of such ornament. "This kerchief would have been stained with blood. I imagine you had to throw it in the fireplace, Mrs. Norris, perhaps along with your apron."

"Note also that the other pieces of silver are slightly tarnished," Miss Tilney added. "Only very slightly, but they have not been cleaned in the past months. The cake server, however, shines like new. It had to be cleaned recently, did it not, Mrs. Norris? For you had to wipe it clean of blood."

Fanny Bertram had begun to weep, slumping onto her sister's shoulder. How terrible was the look of betrayal in Mr. Bertram's eyes! "Aunt Norris—how could you have done such a wicked thing?"

All hope of denial had fled Mrs. Norris then, leaving only the determination to have her say. "It was an accident, or—or it was a mere gesture, a moment of anger—I should never have done such a thing, should she not have outraged me so. No person alive, I daresay, could have been more upset than I on that day. For Maria felt no shame for her crime. How I sacrificed for her, how I helped her, and never did she value it! She rejected the fine husband I found for her; she compounded her sin of elopement with the sin that brought about the child; then at last she turned a murderess—it was not to be borne." She seemed to catch herself then, hastily adding, "Though even so provoked, I did not lash out in deliberate malice, this I swear. In but a moment's anger, the thing was in hand, and the task done."

Though until this point Lady Bertram had sat utterly silent, comprehension began to show itself upon her features, slow as the dawn. "Oh, Sister," she said. "It was you who did this. You who hurt my Maria. You killed her, and it was so unkind. It was so very unkind."

"Hypocrites, one and all!" Mrs. Norris shouted. "Quick enough you were, to throw her out when she first erred. Now you pretend to mourn her, though before her death you would have been glad to hear that you would never see her again!"

"No," said Edmund Bertram, rising to his feet. The gesture, simple as it was, silenced Mrs. Norris into cowering against the wall. "You cannot equate that with murder. The ultimate sin is yours, and I fear you shall have to pay the price."

Was that the first instant that Mrs. Norris realized she would be arrested? For she stared in shock as Mr. Frost came toward her, to take her away.

In the resulting hubbub, as the members of the Bertram family embraced and Mrs. Norris was led out the door—for once, completely silent—both of the Tilneys came to Jonathan's side. Mrs. Tilney's color was heightened as she said, "Had the circumstances been any less grave, I believe I should have enjoyed that. My dear girl—Mr. Darcy—you are most remarkable!"

Yet Miss Tilney had no attention for her mother's praise. "You are grown very pale again, Mr. Darcy. We have overtaxed you."

Jonathan admitted, "I should very much like to rest for a time."

Rather than wait for a servant, Miss Tilney poured his next dose of laudanum herself. Though much tumult remained in the household, and the drug could not yet have had time to fully work its powers upon him, Jonathan closed his eyes almost before the spoon had left his lips and surrendered to slumber.

Of the state of the Bertram family, what can be said? Their sincere grief for Maria could not but be worsened by the revelation of her guilt, for now they had to mourn not only the loss of the living person but also her immortal soul. As for Mrs. Norris, all but Susan had known her throughout their lives, and if they had little cared for her company, they had nonetheless trusted her. Their aunt had been irritating and loud, yet ever present, like a squeaky stair that has long since ceased to be remarked upon and is simply another part of the home.

Mrs. Tilney fussed about Juliet, taking the housekeeper's offer of biscuits as an opportunity to see that her daughter finally ate something. Indeed, Juliet felt better than she had since the art exhibition. Its horror had, at least for a brief time, receded into the background, supplanted by justified pride. *What a pity women cannot join the police,* she thought. *I believe I should enjoy doing this more often.*

To stay in London is to hear carriages rushing back and forth at nearly every hour of the day, so the sounds of wheels and horses draw no attention unless that sound slows and stops at one's door—as indeed happened then in front of the Bertram residence. Commotion with the butler and bell confirmed that visitors had arrived. Sir Thomas swore under his breath. "What a time for callers! Whoever can that be?"

In the next moment, the butler announced, "Mr. and Mrs. Fitzwilliam Darcy of Pemberley."

Juliet felt as though she had been bodily pushed back, removed from her fragile happiness to be thrust once more into shame. Jonathan's parents entered the room in such a state of disarray that all could instantly tell they had left their home in the dead of night, taking every express coach possible to reach their son at the soonest possible opportunity. Mrs. Elizabeth Darcy, visibly shaken, did not engage in even the simplest civilities, saying only, "Jonathan—where is Jonathan?"

"He is resting in the room we have made for him," said Mr. Bertram, coming to her side and swiftly leading her to her son. "I will take you there. His wound is not serious, and thus far he is healing well."

Mr. Darcy might have been expected to evince relief at what he had heard. No doubt, to some degree, he felt it. Yet his attention was then turned upon Juliet, and in his gaze she found all shame, all contempt, all blame for an incident that could have cost Jonathan Darcy his life.

"I will thank you," he said, "to quit this place immediately."

Mrs. Tilney would have defended her daughter, and had indeed stepped forward to do so, when Juliet clutched her hand.

"We will go," she promised Mr. Darcy. "You may pretend we are already gone."

Chapter Twenty-Five

How hopeful Juliet Tilney had been when she and her mother arrived in London, and how desolate she felt as they quitted it! Mrs. Tilney had not required much time before she realized that Juliet's cleverness in the matter of the Rushworth murders did not in any way negate the need to immediately leave the city and return home. Therefore, no sooner did they return to the rooms that they had taken than Mrs. Tilney instructed the servants to pack their things into the carriage posthaste.

Juliet knew how very close she had come to a brilliant future with Mr. Darcy—a match with enough material gain to please her demanding grandfather, but far more important, one that would have been built on mutual understanding, respect, and . . . at least on her part, and she fancied on his as well . . . sincere love. That closeness taunted her now. Mr. Darcy had, through his duel, won back some measure of her honor; Mr. Follett, if he held true to his word, would clear her name of the worst calumnies. But the look on the elder Mr. Darcy's face when he saw Juliet again had told her that she would never be forgiven. His family would never consent to a marriage. Thus all had ended.

Nor could she be certain that other men would not shun a woman so tainted by association to scandal. Yet Juliet was not ready to mourn any other lost chances; it was for Jonathan Darcy alone that she suffered. Nothing was to be done save to return home, to the consolation of her father and her siblings, and to endure the wrath of her grandfather. After that, she intended to shut herself away in her room for a very long time, until she could determine what purpose her life could serve.

As she did not foresee ever being reunited with Jonathan Darcy, she also did not imagine that she might someday again be asked to assist in matters of murder. How much more hopeful she might have been, had she reckoned with the true evil of man.

That evening, the various Bertrams took their dinners on trays. Their new houseguests, the Darcy parents, did likewise as they remained with their son. Tomorrow they would attempt to behave as normal; tomorrow they would hold appropriate meals, make proper conversation, and begin to determine how much their aunt's criminality would besmirch the family honor. This night, however, the household needed time to reckon with all they had learned.

Edmund and Fanny had actually got into bed before sundown, and they dined with their trays poised above their laps. This they had done in deference to Fanny's frailty, but truth be told, both felt like invalids in need of soup and kindness. The soup had been provided by the servants; the kindness, they must give to each other.

"You said that I was too quick to excuse those I cared about," Edmund said to his wife, "that where I loved, I saw only the best. Indeed, all our lives, you have been wary of Aunt Norris—you have been conscious of her pettiness and ill temper—and I have always argued her case, believed her no more than an old woman without enough to do. I ought to have looked upon her with more rational eyes. Then, perhaps, I would have seen the evil of which she was capable."

"You had known her since your infancy," Fanny said. Where Edmund excused many, she only excused him, and this almost invariably. "Aunt Norris was almost a second mother to you. It is not natural that you should imagine her so wicked. Even fearing her as I have, never did I imagine her capable of *this*."

Edmund sighed. "Poor Maria—so I wish to say—and yet in the end, Maria proved herself even worse. Never did she see Rushworth as anything but a means to her own ends. She cared only for herself, and, I suppose, for Henry Crawford."

"I do not know if she loved even him," Fanny said. "Winning him once more, wedding him . . . that would have vindicated Maria in her own eyes, at least. She could then tell herself that she had not abandoned Mr. Rushworth for nothing. That alone would have been reason enough for her to wish Mr. Crawford back again."

"I hope you are incorrect, Fanny, but you so rarely are."

Edmund's mild witticism was met, to his surprise, with a confession. "I have been grievously wrong these past many days, however, and I wish to make amends."

"Whatever do you mean, Fanny?"

She took his hand, hardly daring to grasp it. "I said that I would not have Ellen. I was afraid that, resenting my barrenness as I have, I should treat the little girl much like Aunt Norris treated me, which no child should have to endure. But now that I have spent time with her, I see what a dear girl she is, and I find that I can look upon her with no resentment in my heart. Indeed, I believe that heart will be hers soon, as much as it is yours."

Edmund had believed, only moments before, that he might not ever feel true joy again. How wonderfully he had been proved wrong! "This is the one great good to come out of all that has been revealed in these past dreadful days. Whenever we remember this time, we will not only think of our fear, upset, and sorrow. We will also remember that this was when our little Ellen came to us."

"*Our* Ellen," whispered Fanny, and so their family was born.

Another member of the Bertram clan wished to found a family at that time, and he determined that he must act swiftly if he was to preserve his intentions.

"You can imagine how difficult this has all been," Sir Thomas said the next day, as he sat in the Allerdyces' parlor. Miss Frederica Allerdyce had her place opposite him, all attentiveness; her mother had contrived an errand for herself and Priscilla, so that the two were alone. "How greatly stricken our family has been—it will not do to speak of it. Though we are spared the worst of the disgrace, as Maria was estranged from us, and Mrs. Norris but our aunt, I am of course conscious that your feelings, your innate delicacy, might quail from any future connection. Is that so? Or may I hope?"

This was all but a proposal, and Frederica, smiling, gave him all but an acceptance. "It would be a strange sort of delicacy, Sir Thomas, that blamed a whole family for the actions of one. Or two, I suppose. I mean—I would not dream of holding such a matter against you, nor would my family."

How Sir Thomas smiled then! How triumphant he felt! Yet still he wished to reassure her. "We shall distance ourselves from the event. We would come to London but rarely, and not for some time, if you wish. And if you are bored by the country, Mansfield Park will not be our only home! I am purchasing a plantation in Barbados, you know, and I am assured the house there is very fine. You may adventure to the West Indies if you like! Will not that be fine?"

Frederica's shy smile had faded. "Yet—I had thought—were you not selling your plantation? Was it not in Antigua?"

"That one I have sold, but I decided I did not wish to abandon all the family interests in sugar," Sir Thomas said. "How funny to be discussing business with a young lady! But this is the time for such matters, I know." Summoning his courage—not much was required, confident as he was—he said, "Will you share all my earthly possessions and become the companion of my life?"

Half an hour later, Caroline Allerdyce cried, "You *refused* him?"

"I did," Frederica said firmly. Her parents and her sister had gathered with her in her room, where she hugged a pillow for consolation. "I only ever considered a man who had once owned slaves because I believed he had determined to sin no more. Repugnant though his past actions had been, I convinced myself that he wished to do better, that he had found some measure of redemption. Instead, I learned he was only moving his interests from one island to another."

"Could you not have persuaded him otherwise?" Caroline could have shaken the ungrateful girl. "There would have been time for that after your marriage! He is a baronet, a man with a title, the most brilliant possible match for you—and this you have wasted."

Frederica, who had anticipated no better than this from her mother, addressed her father instead. "Papa, even if I could have convinced Sir Thomas to sell that plantation—he would still be the sort of man who did not see that he was doing wrong. The sort who believes that all is acceptable, so long as he profits by it. I could not love a man capable of such corruption. And what if I were not able to convince him? Then I, too, should in effect be a slave owner, and in so doing I would imperil my immortal soul."

Mr. Allerdyce gently patted his daughter's cheek. "You have done what you ought, Frederica. You obeyed your conscience. I am proud to see that you are so firm in your principles, and fine principles they are."

In a rare display of sisterly loyalty, Priscilla added, "I thought he was a dreadful bore."

Caroline, however, could not be consoled. Once she had retreated to her own room with her husband, she complained, "All the money we have spent on this season! All the parties, all the assemblies—all this we have done in the interests of making her a good match. This we achieved! A nobleman asked for her hand, and this she throws away."

"A good match is not merely a material one," said Mr. Allerdyce. "I grant you, there must be income enough to live upon, and not to subject either partner to degradation—but where there can be no respect, no love, there can be no marriage worth the having. I rather wonder, my dear, that you do not know that."

Caroline required a few moments to realize the peril and pain in those last words, and by the time she did, Mr. Allerdyce had quitted the room.

He had consoled her not at all. Even if her husband could forget that Frederica was *twenty-two* years old, Caroline could not. Matches to equal Sir Thomas were few in number under any circumstances, and for Frederica—nearing the end of her most eligible years, too tall, too bookish—weak indeed were any hopes of attracting another bridegroom similarly titled and wealthy.

Yet Caroline did not despair. Still she had Priscilla, who possessed all the ready charm her sister did not. When Priscilla wed Jonathan Darcy, the heir to Pemberley, Frederica would be lifted by association. And now, after the disgrace that had befallen that Tilney girl, the greatest obstacle in Priscilla's path had been removed.

Of course, the young Mr. Darcy would now have to recover from his wound; thinking upon the danger and suffering he had faced prompted the only guilt Caroline felt in the matter. Yet the word was that he was healing well, that his parents would soon take him home to Pemberley to recuperate. As he had survived, she saw no reason to further trouble herself with the uncomfortable particulars of how that duel had come to pass. All that mattered was that Jonathan Darcy remained free, and that his path and Priscilla's should cross again.

Though she never knew it, Frederica Allerdyce's refusal to marry Sir Thomas achieved the very goal she would most have wished: He did not, in the end, purchase the plantation in Barbados. His full moral awakening remained years distant, but his disappointment in love did at least serve to convince him that qualms about slavery were not merely a nicety worried about by overly pious sorts such as Edmund and Fanny. Furthermore, in the absence of the wife he had imminently anticipated, he wished to cling tighter to the rest of his family, and Tom did not doubt that Edmund's promise to disown him was sincere.

The time that Tom might have spent preparing for a wedding and honeymoon instead was devoted to the case of Aunt Norris. There was no question of her guilt, for she had admitted all, but the usual remedy of the law in such matters was the gallows. To have a member of the family publicly hanged—this, Tom could not countenance, from equal parts mercy and pride. He visited many judges, many MPs, to discuss the matter, to point out that Aunt Norris was an elderly woman unlikely to do further harm—that she had acted on impulse, not with malice aforethought—and that she had done so upon learning of a murder committed by the victim, which surely must be considered an extraordinary provocation.

Ultimately, all the influence Tom could bring to bear proved insufficient to free Mrs. Norris, but she was spared the penalty of hanging. Instead, she was sentenced to the other remedy the law prescribed: transportation to Australia. It is tempting to follow her from this point—to behold Mrs. Norris's first encounters with the kookaburra, the cassowary, and the kangaroo—but such are beyond the reach of this narrative, and thus it will be the reader's task to imagine her antipodean adventures. Suffice it to say that she troubled the family no further.

Her absence from Mansfield Park and its environs meant that she was nowhere near the parsonage to which Edmund and Fanny brought little Ellen, welcoming her to her new home. Though in the early days she greatly missed her mother, and even occasionally wondered where Mrs. Norris might be, the child quickly gained affection for the kindly parents who from the first cherished her as though she had been born to them. Though Fanny would ever mourn her inability to bear children of her own, that sorrow lost much of its power once she inherited all the other joys of motherhood. Their lives were the richer for Ellen's presence: Where once the parsonage, though peaceful, had been rather quiet, laughter now rang through the halls. Fanny was among the most patient and attentive of mothers, and very unusually for a woman of her class and time, would even play with Ellen almost as though she had become a child again herself.

In a sense, she had. There are few more profound remedies for an unhappy childhood than the chance to provide a happy childhood for another, and this, Fanny found in Ellen. The games she played, the lullabies she sang, were in a sense for the benefit of not only her adopted daughter, but also her former self, the frightened little girl who had hidden on the stairs in Mansfield Park. As for Ellen, she would barely remember Maria Rushworth—though she ever honored her, and the rest of the family did not burden her with the full knowledge of Maria's misdeeds. For Ellen, Edmund and Fanny were her only papa and mamma, and their family was no less the blessed for the unusual circumstances of its beginning.

The lives of Edmund and Fanny gained even more purpose through their stronger commitment to the antislavery cause. Having become aware of how much they had benefited from the sin of the plantation in Antigua, they could not rest until they had, in some small measure, attempted to pay a fraction of that incalculable debt. Though they were of modest means—and never would touch young Ellen's capital, as that was to form the security of her future life—they helped to sponsor speakers and to give to funds that supported former slaves endeavoring to establish a life in freedom. Nothing would ever cleanse the stain of the plantation in Antigua, but this did not prevent Fanny and Edmund from doing as much as they could, whenever they could. They understood that, even when it is impossible to do enough, it is always possible to do right.

The Darcy family lingered a week in London, until the physician permitted Jonathan to leave. This might have been postponed further, for Jonathan's wound took a long time to heal, and he suffered from a few days of mild fevers—but once it appeared certain that his condition would not worsen, both he and his parents were eager for him to return to Pemberley once more.

They prepared the carriage so that he might lie across one side of the seats in a sort of makeshift bed. Though the wheels jolted and stuttered on rough road from time to time, uncomfortably jostling Jonathan, he was given medicines to soothe his pain and rest his mind.

When they believed Jonathan to be asleep, his parents spoke among themselves. "We must not send him off by himself again soon," Elizabeth said. "He has come to peril twice now in our absence. No, it cannot be countenanced."

(It may be observed that her objection was not fully founded in logic, for Jonathan had also come into peril while in their company, as the fire at Rosings Park had proved the year prior, and if she believed that persuasion could have prevented the challenge and duel, she overestimated parental power over the mind of a young man in love. Yet it is not to be anticipated that anyone, having seen a son wounded, would respond solely in a rational manner.)

"One good has come from all this," said Mr. Darcy, "one good alone, and that is that his connection to Miss Tilney is of course severed."

Elizabeth was not so certain on this point. "We cannot blame the girl for the painting."

"Perhaps not. That was a pernicious trick, to be sure. But the scandal of this duel will resonate for many years to come, and it blights not only Miss Tilney but our son as well. What will become of her, we cannot say. However, we can be certain that Jonathan's reputation will only be darkened if he continues to associate with a young woman so touched by shame. The memory of the duel would be kept alive, whereas for Jonathan's sake, we must wish it forgotten as quickly and completely as possible."

"He will stay at home," Elizabeth said. "When we travel as a family, we will travel only to the houses of our relations, places that Jonathan already knows. Long has he requested this of us, that we allow him to keep to what is familiar. Now, we will obey."

Jonathan, however, was closer to wakefulness than they imagined, for he stirred and muttered something.

"What is it?" his father asked, leaning forward to touch his son's hand. "Are you well?"

Opening his eyes just a crack, Jonathan said, "I am no Claudio."

Darcy and Elizabeth exchanged chagrined glances, believing that their son spoke from feverish delirium, that there was no meaning in his words. Yet Jonathan had heard them and understood perfectly; he wished to inform them that they might devise what plans they liked without making any difference, for he had plans of his own. He intended to find Miss Tilney again. He would not let scandal destroy the potential future he now believed they both ardently desired.

But he was weary, and the medical elixir had stupefied him, so he could make no thorough argument. Jonathan had but three words to say—as much to himself as to his parents—three words that seemed to him to embrace all that he felt, all he intended.

He whispered, "I am Ivanhoe."

Acknowledgments

As ever, my first thanks go out to Team J&J for all their help and support throughout: my agent, Laura Rennert; my assistant, Sarah Simpson Weiss; and the whole gang at Vintage, led by my editor, Anna Kaufman, along with Maria Massey, Natalia Berry, Martha Schwartz, Nancy Inglis, Evan Stone, Perry De La Vega, Nick Alguire, Kelsey Curtis, and Maylin Lehmann Hobaica.

Thanks also go out to the authenticity/sensitivity readers Rebecca Blevins and Mireille Harper for their guidance regarding Jonathan's neurodivergence and the issue of slavery. Their guidance has been invaluable; any lingering errors are wholly my own. I should note that current usage justly and appropriately leans toward referring to "enslaved persons" rather than "slaves," and to "enslavers" rather than "slave owners." However, the period language of this book reflects the older terms that the characters themselves would have used, which is more accurate to the limited, though evolving, perspective of the era. My hope is that, in context, this language does not cause distress.

Additionally, I am grateful to the friends who have provided encouragement and support, including but not limited to: Alys Arden, Chuck and Jolie Breaux, Alex and Anne-Elise Brian, Amanda Collums, Rodney Crouther, Stephanie Davis, Mark and Susan Davis, Marti Dumas, Jennifer Heddle, Jesse Holland, Lydia Kang, Lisa Keleher, Stephanie Knapp, Elliot Lastrape, Marcus and Karen Leblanc, Guillaume and Courtney Louche, Dave Massey, Jo Massey,

Ruth Morrison, Maddie Nelson, Zak Nelson, Daniel Jose Older, Whitney Swindoll Raju, Michael Siglain, Sarah Tolcser, and Brittany Williams. My family—Mom, Dad, Matthew, Melissa, Eli, Ari, and Aunts Susan and Karen—helped me through the hair-raising process of editing while moving, for which I can never thank them enough.

Above all, my thanks and my love to my husband, Paul, who makes everything possible.

THE MURDER OF MR. WICKHAM

The happily married Mr. Knightley and Emma are throwing a party at their country estate, bringing together distant relatives and new acquaintances. Definitely not invited is Mr. Wickham, whose latest financial scheme has netted him an even broader array of enemies. As tempers flare and secrets are revealed, it's clear that everyone would be happier if Mr. Wickham got his comeuppance—yet they're all shocked when Wickham turns up murdered. Nearly everyone at the house party is a suspect, so it falls to the party's two youngest guests to solve the mystery: Juliet Tilney, the smart and resourceful daughter of Catherine and Henry of Northanger Abbey; and Jonathan Darcy, the Darcys' eldest son. In this tantalizing fusion of Austen and Christie, the unlikely pair must put aside their own poor first impressions and uncover the guilty party—before an innocent person is sentenced to hang.

Fiction

THE LATE MRS. WILLOUGHBY

Catherine and Henry Tilney are not entirely pleased that their daughter Juliet intends to visit her friend, Marianne Brandon—whose former suitor, Mr. Willoughby, is taking up residence nearby with his new bride. Meanwhile, Elizabeth and Fitzwilliam Darcy are thrilled that Jonathan has been invited to stay with his former schoolmate, John Willoughby. Jonathan himself is less taken with the notion of having to spend extended time under the roof of his old bully. Then, Willoughby's new wife dies horribly. With rumors flying, Jonathan and Juliet must team up to uncover the murderer. But as they collect clues and close in on suspects, eerie incidents suggest that the pair are in far graver danger than they or their families could imagine.

Fiction

THE PERILS OF LADY CATHERINE DE BOURGH

Someone is trying to kill Lady Catherine de Bourgh. Esteemed aunt of Mr. Fitzwilliam Darcy, generous patroness of Mr. William Collins, a woman of rank who rules over the estate of Rosings Park with an unimpeachable sense of propriety—who would dare? Lady Catherine summons her grand-nephew, Mr. Jonathan Darcy, and his investigative companion, Miss Juliet Tilney, to find out. After a year apart, Jonathan and Juliet are thrilled to be reunited, even if the circumstances—finding whoever has thus far sabotaged Lady Catherine's carriage, shot at her, and nearly pushed her down the stairs—are less than ideal. Also less than ideal: their respective fathers, Mr. Fitzwilliam Darcy and Mr. Henry Tilney, have accompanied the young detectives to Rosings, and the two men do not interact with the same felicity enjoyed by their children. With attempts against Lady Catherine escalating, and no one among the list of prime suspects seemingly capable of committing all of the attacks, the pressure on Jonathan and Juliet mounts—even as more gentle feelings between the two of them begin to bloom. The race is now on to provoke two confessions: one from the attempted murderer before it is too late—and one, perhaps, of love.

Fiction

VINTAGE BOOKS
Available wherever books are sold.
vintagebooks.com